B[r]ighten y[ou]r world
bestseller Li[l]

'A testament to kind[ness]
Sarah W

'Tender, thought-prov[oking]
Daily [Mirror]

'A heart that shines from every page'
AJ Pearce

'Heartwarming and uplifting'
Sun on Sunday

'Moving and beautifully crafted'
Mike Gayle

'It will give you a warm glow'
Daily Mirror

'Full of heart'
Lucy Diamond

'A lovely read'
Bella

'Brimming with charm and compassion . . .
a feel-good celebration of community'
Daily Express

'Beautifully written'
Daily Mail

'A joyful celebration of community'
Observer

'Heartwarming'
Good Housekeeping

'Like a warm hug'
The Sun

'Heartwarming and stirring'
Heat

'Feel-good fiction at its best'
Daily Mirror

3303891753

Also by Libby Page

The Lido

The 24-Hour Café

The Island Home

The Vintage Shop

THE LIFELINE
LIBBY PAGE

ORION

An Orion Paperback
First published in Great Britain in 2024 by Orion Fiction
This paperback edition published in 2024 by Orion Fiction,
an imprint of The Orion Publishing Group Ltd
Carmelite House, 50 Victoria Embankment
London EC4Y 0DZ

An Hachette UK Company

1 3 5 7 9 10 8 6 4 2

A CIP catalogue record for this book
is available from the British Library.

ISBN (Paperback) 978 1 3987 0 8471
ISBN (eBook) 978 1 3987 0 8488

Typeset by Deltatype Ltd, Birkenhead, Merseyside

Printed in Great Britain by Clays Ltd,
Elcograf, S.p.A.

MIX
Paper | Supporting
responsible forestry
FSC® C104740

www.orionbooks.co.uk

For Robin

CHAPTER 1

Down by the river, Kate can finally breathe. The sun is not quite up as she sits on the end of the pontoon dangling her bare toes in the murky green water, feeling suspended between night and day. Everything around her is dim and quiet, a light mist resting on the surface of the river, broken by the slender arms of the willow trees that dip down into the water.

As her light brown hair tickles her face in the breeze, she scoops it up into a messy bun using the hairband that lives permanently on her right wrist, trying to remember as she does when she last showered. But the trees and the birds don't care about the state of her hair or her thrown-together outfit of tracksuit bottoms and hoody. There's no judgement here by the river in the early hours of this late spring morning.

Leaning back on her hands, she practises the breathing exercises she has mastered over the years. *In, one, two, three, out, one, two, three* ... After each deep inhale, she pauses, noticing the quiet gurgles of the water and the smell of wild garlic in the air.

Her shoulders sink down as she exhales. For once, she is able to hear the thoughts in her own head. Not that she wants to listen to them. Instead, she tunes in to the swishing of the long grass in the meadow behind her. The freedom she feels down here by the water feels stolen, but she grabs hold of it anyway.

The truth is, she shouldn't be here. Not this early in the morning and when nobody in the entire world knows where she is. It's not the kind of thing that someone like her should do, someone who, despite how she might sometimes feel, is undeniably a grown-up with grown-up responsibilities. She is thirty-two and has a mortgage and *life insurance*, for goodness' sake. But oh, the water feels so delicious against her toes.

A sound draws her attention to the riverboat moored a little way upstream, its roof covered in raucous flowerpots and a couple of beehives. It seems as though its inhabitant must be getting up, confirmed a few moments later by a curl of smoke escaping from the chimney. Kate takes the smell of the wood-smoke as her cue to reluctantly leave, glancing down at her watch and realising she's already stayed here far too long.

It's not just the activity on the riverboat that hints at a place that is poised to spring into life. For now, the doors on the brightly painted beach huts on the bank are closed, but the stacks of kayaks and paddleboards leant against them are waiting to be pulled down onto the water. A little way down the meadow, people sleep beneath canvas in a collection of old-fashioned yurts strewn with bunting, but before long the doorways will be peeled back and the smell of sizzling bacon will rise on the air, along with the sound of giggling children running about in pyjamas and wellies.

There's a big part of Kate that wishes she could stay here. Stretch out on the pontoon beneath the rising sun and pretend she is somebody with nowhere to be and nothing to do. Or maybe finally find the courage to slip her whole body down into the cool water. She has thought about swimming, but the water always looks so dark and deep here that the furthest she has made it has been dipping her toes. The water still calls to her, though, with its cool promise.

But Kate's time is up. There's only so long you can press pause on your life. It's time to get back to the reality of everything that is waiting for her. As she pulls on her socks and shoes, she tries to push down the rising sense of dread that bubbles up at the thought of returning home. And to not think too hard about what it means that for the past few weeks she has woken in the early hours and tiptoed out of the house to come down to the river alone. So far, she has always made it back in time before anyone has noticed she has gone. She never mentions where she's been. Instead, she slips back into bed, catches a bit more sleep if she can and then cracks on with the day as if everything's fine, all the time itching to get back to the river tomorrow morning so that she can breathe again.

Everything *is* fine, isn't it? So what if she goes off on secret morning jaunts and sometimes fantasises about hopping in a canoe and paddling off into the distance? That doesn't mean there's anything out of the ordinary, she tells herself as she

3

sets off through the fields towards home. Who doesn't want to escape their life sometimes?

Kate lets out a sigh as she climbs over the stile and joins the lane that heads back into the village. However much she tries to justify things to herself, deep down she knows that what she's doing is wrong. It's why she's been keeping these visits and the sense of release she gets as soon as she closes the front door behind her each morning a secret. Because you shouldn't want to escape your life when you have everything you've ever wanted waiting for you back at home.

CHAPTER 2

The motorbike rumbles beneath Phoebe's leather-clad legs as she zips down the country lane, cherry-red hair trailing behind her in a blaze as it escapes from beneath her helmet. She had left the village quietly, aware of her neighbours still asleep in their beds, but now she has reached open countryside, she revs the engine, relishing the tiger's purr that reverberates around her, sending a pheasant squawking up and into the air in the field beside her. She slows as she approaches a bend obscured by bushy hedgerows teeming with cow parsley and nettles, leaning her body with the bike. But then she turns onto a straight, wide road that cuts its way like an arrow across the green expanse of Somerset countryside. God love the Romans. She twists the throttle, really giving the crows on the telephone line above her something to flap about and making her heart race with the thrill of it.

The motorbike was a gift to herself on her thirtieth birthday five years ago. She'd always dreamt of owning one and it's every bit as fantastic as she'd hoped. But Max has been on at her ever since they started dating three years ago to sell the bike and pool their resources on a new Land Rover. He says it would be more practical and that having the bike is irresponsible. But there's no way in hell she'd ever let go of this. God knows she's got enough responsibility in the rest of her life. When she's out on the bike, she forgets everything else except the feeling of the wind on her face, the hyperfocus of following the curves of the road and feeling at one with the machine beneath her. Fat chance she'd feel like that behind the wheel of a bulky Land Rover. She keeps telling Max she'll think about it, though.

She makes it to the supermarket as they are opening the doors, smiling at the sleepy staff and nipping inside for a pint of milk. Really, the milk is just an excuse. Mostly, Phoebe just needed to get out and clear her head. It's been a long week. And it's only Tuesday morning.

She lets herself back into the flat quietly, the silence telling her that Max is still asleep. Their apartment is above a shop, although the premises has been empty for a couple of months. Phoebe still misses the little newsagent that used to be there. The owner, Amit, was an ancient man who had the expression of someone who had seen some serious shit in his time, which Phoebe always appreciated because, despite being less than half his age, so has she. He never raised an eyebrow at a woman in her pyjamas clutching two bottles of wine and several packets of biscuits. He closed the shop when he retired and a new business is yet to move in. Phoebe thought she saw someone going inside yesterday but was running late for work so didn't have time to investigate.

She unclips her bulky boots and unzips her leather jacket,

hanging it on the peg. Underneath, she is already dressed for work, today opting for a denim shirt decorated with daisies that hugs her curves, the sleeves rolled up to reveal the tattoos that wind their way up her forearms. She tries to use her outfits to show when she turns up on someone's doorstep that she's a human being just like them, not just Community Mental Health Nurse Phoebe Harrison. It still doesn't stop people shutting the door in her face sometimes. Not that she ever blames them. It's a huge thing having a stranger come into your home wanting to give you meds and talk about the dark thoughts that have sent you down a spiral. She has to earn their trust before she can make any progress and, God, life hasn't always given her patients many reasons to be trustful.

The open country roads she zoomed along earlier couldn't feel further away as she grabs her laptop and immerses herself in prep for the day ahead. Even after all these years working as a mental health nurse, reading some of the new histories that have been added to her caseload still brings a lump to her throat. Not that she'd ever let anyone see it when she's on the clock. At work, she's as upbeat and chipper as her bright hair and fun outfits.

After an hour of work, she needs a break so grabs her phone to scroll through Instagram, craving the eye bleach of cute videos of pets being reunited with their owners or pictures of beautiful clothes she will never be able to afford to buy. As her finger drags its way across the screen, her attention snags on the holiday snaps of someone she went to school with but has fallen out of touch with, along with most of her friends,

7

each lost one by one to her long hours and, later, their marriages and children. She never meant for it to happen and yet, as she's got older, holding onto friends has felt like trying to clutch rainwater between her hands.

She flicks through glossy snapshots of sea, sunshine and heaped piles of pasta. A holiday. God, just the thought of it makes something inside her relax. When did she and Max last go on holiday? They had been planning a trip for the new year, but then a few of her patients had got really unwell – Christmas is always a hard time of year – so they'd had to cancel. And now it's May and they've hardly spent any proper time together recently. She hasn't been to visit her family in Cornwall for a long time either, she thinks guiltily, picturing her nan, who broke her hip a month ago, the final straw that led her to reluctantly leave her flat and move in with Phoebe's parents.

She starts browsing a few holiday sites on her laptop, images of villas and beaches transporting her to a happier, sunnier place than her case notes and email inbox. As she scrolls, she can almost feel the sea breeze on her face, taste the pina coladas she and Max could drink in a little beach bar where she could feel the sand between her toes and watch the waves. Or maybe they could go for something more remote. A little log cabin in the woods somewhere, a place with no Wi-Fi or phone signal where no one could contact her, needing her. Where she could read a book and take a bath and actually find the energy to have sex with her boyfriend. They could even tag on a trip to Cornwall too on the way back, to see her family.

After extensive scrolling, she finds herself coming back to the first photos she saw on Instagram of her old friend's Italian

8

break. You can't go wrong with Italy. Pizza, pasta, sunshine, wine. Perfection. Just the thought of it makes Phoebe smile.

But her patients ... How would they cope if she went away for a week? It's hard enough as it is to keep in touch with them when she's working five days a week with more overtime than she'd ever admit. But she hasn't used any of her holiday allowance for the year and still has some left over from last year too. Provided there are no emergencies and she finds cover for while she's gone ... Maybe she *could*?

A loud banging rises up through the floorboards.

'Fuck!' she lets out with a jump.

The building below has been empty long enough that Phoebe has got used to the quiet. But now she can make out muffled voices, followed by the sound of the radio. Glancing out the window, she spots a van parked up on the street below and a couple of guys heading to and fro, carrying boxes. She tries to make out any branding that might give her a hint about who her new neighbours might be, but there's nothing discernible.

The sound of footsteps closer to hand makes her look up towards the doorway. 'Oh hey, you're up.'

Max is standing in the hallway, dressed but rubbing his eyes, a strand of his blond hair sticking up and making her heart skip a little.

'How was last night?' she asks him. 'Sorry I couldn't make it in the end. I'd hoped to get there in time to meet you all, but something came up ...'

She tries not to talk too much about the specifics with Max, or anyone else for that matter. It doesn't feel fair to offload this kind of stuff on others when she's a trained professional and still finds it bloody hard sometimes. Plus, there's the privacy of her patients to think about. Last night when she should have been at the pub with Max and a group of his mates there had been an emergency with one of her patients, Frank. He had started having serious suicidal thoughts, so Phoebe and the rest of the team had to arrange an emergency bed in the local hospital's psychiatric ward where Phoebe used to work. As usual, they were pressed for beds, so it took hours. Phoebe waited with Frank all the same though, right past the end of her shift and all the way to the hospital, holding his hand in the back of the ambulance.

'I do know,' Max says, his tone making her recoil slightly. He probably just needs coffee.

She gets up to make him a cup, slipping in a dash of vanilla syrup when he isn't looking. She knows he likes his coffee milky and sweet, but he would never in a million years order a vanilla latte in a coffee shop, thinking it emasculating. He'd rather wince his way through an espresso than ask for what he actually wants, the silly bastard. Hopefully the dash of vanilla will help sweeten his mood, and maybe her guilt too at being the cause of it. But what was she supposed to do? She was hardly going to leave Frank on his own last night or even with one of the other nurses who offered to take over when her shift was up. Frank didn't know them, he knows *her*.

Once the coffee is ready, they sit down opposite one another at the table.

'Thanks,' Max says, wrapping his hands around the mug. 'What's all this, then?' He points at Phoebe's phone, where one of the holiday sites is still displayed on the screen.

The excitement returns to Phoebe's voice as she replies. 'Oh, yeah. So, I know we haven't spent much proper time together recently. Things for me have been kind of hectic ...'

'You could say that again,' remarks Max. 'It wasn't just last night. Remember my birthday?' He takes a sip of his coffee and his face relaxes slightly with the pleasure of it, making Phoebe have to hide a smile.

'I know. And I'm sorry, you know I felt awful about that.'

His birthday had been a tough one. She'd organised the whole thing – a dinner at his favourite local pub with his family and his closest friends. She'd even made a cake, staying up late to get it ready because the time she'd put aside for it had got eaten up by catching up on important paperwork. OK, so it maybe wasn't the world's best cake – it looked absolutely nothing like the picture she'd found online and suspiciously like it might topple over at any moment – but it was a cake and she was proud of it.

But just as she was preparing to leave work and get ready for their evening, she had got a call from a patient who was in crisis. The voices had been getting louder and louder and had now started giving him instructions. They wanted him to hurt himself and he didn't know what to do.

By the time Phoebe eventually arrived at the pub hours later, the meal was finished and Max was paying the bill. She'd tried to explain the situation, but the idea of voices had always perplexed Max.

'Can't he just ignore them?'

Phoebe tried her best to explain how real the voices were to her patients who experienced them, trying to get Max to imagine how *he* would feel if the same thing happened to him. She's thought about it a lot over her career and has always believed it would be absolutely bloody terrifying. But he didn't seem to understand and she was too exhausted to try to explain any further. Even the cake she presented him with at home hadn't helped to lift the mood.

'I know you're fed up with how much I work, but I really want to make it up to you. I think we should go on holiday. It could be just what we need. A proper break. A chance to spend some time together.'

She reaches across the table for his hand, but he lifts it up to his coffee mug at the last minute.

'You really want to go on holiday?' he asked, meeting her eye. 'But you always say you're too busy. Remember New Year?'

God, she had hoped it would be easier than this. But he's probably right to not let her off the hook so easily. She probably has been a pretty shit girlfriend.

'I know. But I really want to make it work this time. How about Italy? Sunshine, enormous pizzas … It'll be great.'

Max downs the last of his coffee and places the empty mug carefully on the table.

'I don't think we should go to Italy.'

'OK, well somewhere else then. France? Spain? There's wine and good food there too.'

But he shakes his head. 'I don't think we should go on holiday at all.'

'Is it the cost? Because I was worried about that too, but I know you're hoping for that promotion soon and I have a little bit saved …'

She'd always hoped that by thirty-five she might own her own place rather than still be renting and have more than the most meagre savings in the bank. It doesn't help that her brother is a high-flying lawyer who goes on both a beach and ski holiday each year with his family. But she didn't go into this career for the money – she would have been pretty disappointed if she did – although she's been right there on all the various marches and picket lines over the years, trying to fight for better rights for nurses.

Since moving in together, Max has covered more of the household expenses than her because he earns far more in his job at a start-up tech company. He never seems to mind, but it weighs on her. She does what she can.

'It's not the cost,' he replies.

'OK …' She really doesn't want to have to do this right now but finds herself sneaking a quick glance at the time on her phone. Shit, she needs to leave soon. Her first patient of the day, Maude, lives a twenty-minute ride away. Her patients are spread out all over the local area. 'Do you not think you could get time off work?' she asks Max, trying her best not to show that she's itching to grab her leathers and go. 'We could go in a couple of months if that would work better for you?'

'It's not that.' Max rakes his fingers through his hair again. 'God, I didn't want to do it like this.'

He looks up at her and as his eyes meet hers again, she realises how wrong she's got this conversation. How wrong she's been getting it all.

'Phoebe, I have to tell you something.'

CHAPTER 3

The walk back home takes Kate across fields and up a sloping valley, the sun just beginning to rise and washing the hills in shades of apricot and candyfloss. She walks alone, except for the birds flying above her. If she were back in London, there would likely be *someone* about. Cleaners and construction workers heading off to work, a doctor finishing a night shift, a group of friends stumbling back from a night out that might have once been Kate and her mates, heels swapped for flats that had been stashed in their bags all night. Not that she has been *out* out in a very long time. She's not even sure that people wear heels on a night out anymore.

At the very least if she were in London and not this village in rural Somerset, she would encounter a ballsy fox blocking her path and engaging her in a staring contest. But she hasn't seen a fox once since moving back to the countryside where she grew up, unless you counted roadkill.

By the time she reaches the edge of the village, there are a couple of dog walkers and early-morning joggers out and about, but the windows of the few shops and the one café are still dark. She passes over the bridge decorated with hanging baskets overflowing with flowers, alongside the riverside pub, the doors currently shut, and by the old red telephone box which has been repurposed as a lending library, the tiny space absolutely stuffed full of books.

As she approaches the Old Post Office, her trainers crunching on the gravel driveway, her chest tightens. She still can't quite believe that the little Bath stone cottage with the red front door and the rose clinging to the porch is hers. It couldn't be further from the South London flat she lived in up until a few months ago. Sometimes when she steps inside, she still feels as though she is walking into someone else's life.

The sound of screaming hits her as soon as she opens the front door, nearly tripping over a basket of dirty washing that is overspilling in the hallway. There are a couple of bin bags waiting to be taken out too that she has to push to one side with her foot, her head vibrating with the noise that fills the small cottage. The relaxation of earlier is quickly replaced by tension that spreads through her whole body.

'Kate? Is that you?' comes a frantic voice from the living room, accompanied by an even louder wail.

Kate steadies herself for a second before following the noise into the room, where she finds her husband pacing back and forth, their three-month-old daughter clutched to his shoulder, her face flushed red with rage.

'Oh, thank God!' Jay says, his broad shoulders visibly relaxing as he looks up at her with dark-rimmed eyes.

Without saying anything, Kate reaches for their daughter and sits down on the sofa, pushing a pile of muslins and toys out of the way. The living room is painted a pale sage green, chosen from searching 'Farrow and Ball but cheaper' when they first moved. She had such a vision for the decoration of this cottage, relishing having a whole house to decorate rather than a tiny basement apartment. The browning banana skin on the windowsill and piles of nappies weren't exactly part of her imaginings, and yet she's very quickly become so used to the mess that she hardly notices it.

'Where have you been? I was so worried about you.'

Kate lifts her top and unclips her bra in a practised motion. The cries have grown even louder, her daughter's face scrunched up in fury.

'I just needed a bit of fresh air, I went for a quick walk.'

For a moment, she focuses her entire attention on getting her daughter to latch, her breasts throbbing as she manoeuvres her into position. Her heart rate rises as her daughter opens and closes her mouth like a goldfish, face a shade of beetroot. But eventually they both find the right spot and the cries stop, replaced instead with soft snuffles. Kate sinks deeper into the sofa, her whole body rushed with emotion as it is every time she nurses.

'I tried calling you, but you hadn't even taken your phone with you.'

Kate's mind flashes back to the moment earlier when she swung her legs out of bed and leant down for her clothes, Jay

CHAPTER 4

Phoebe tries her best to focus on what Maude is saying. Something about the resurrection. She gesticulates enthusiastically, as though she is standing at a lectern in front of a large crowd, even though it's just the two of them in Maude's tiny kitchen.

'I am the resurrection and the life and ...'

It's not like Phoebe to zone out like this, but ever since leaving the flat, her thoughts have been all over the place. As she set off on her motorbike, she told herself that she needed to get it together. She would deal with everything when she got back later. She had to get into work mode. But sometimes it's not as easy as flicking a switch. Now she's finding it hard to concentrate. And conversations with Maude are difficult to follow at the best of times.

'Everyone who lives in me and believes in me will never fucking die!'

Phoebe's thoughts are jolted back into the room. For someone who believes herself to be Jesus, Maude has always had the filthiest mouth. It's one of the things Phoebe's always secretly loved about her. But if you take out the swearing, most of Maude's speeches are direct quotes from the Bible, something Phoebe isn't sure the average person would guess if they heard Maude ranting out loud in the supermarket or on the bus. It's always struck Phoebe that religious leaders of the past would almost certainly be considered mentally unwell if they walked the streets today. They'd probably be arrested.

'He who loves his life will lose it, and he who hates his life in this world will keep it for eternal life.' Maude stretches her arms out wide and then sits down heavily in her chair as though the sermon has exhausted her. She blinks rapidly and Phoebe allows her a moment's pause in case there's anything else she wants to say. It's a trick she's picked up over the years. Often, it's when you think someone's finished that the real truth comes out. But most people don't bother waiting. Or listening in the first place, for that matter.

'And how do you feel, about your life, Maude?' Phoebe asks once she's certain she's finished, pouring them both another cup of tea from the pot.

'My life?' Maude replies, her voice quieter now. 'I don't have a life.'

Phoebe swallows hard at that. It doesn't seem fair to get upset when her patients are the ones who have so much to deal with. But it's not always easy to shove her emotions down inside her. Especially not today. She tucks her bright red hair behind her ears and leans forward slightly to show that she is listening, that Maude has her full attention despite the thoughts whizzing about in her brain.

'I'm sorry to hear you're feeling that way, Maude. That's really tough. Can you tell me a bit more about that?'

The Maude who had stood up and delivered perfect lines from the Bible (well, with some minor alterations) just moments ago has morphed into a very different Maude. She seems shrunken, her shoulders rounded. When she says nothing, Phoebe tries a different tack.

'How about we talk about some of the things you might like to see change in your life? What would make you happier, do you think?'

Maude looks over her shoulder and nods slightly, as if conferring with someone.

'Well, if Judas hadn't been such a bastard, for one.' Despite everything, a smile tugs at Phoebe's lips. But then Maude adds, 'And I'd like to look after bees again.'

Of all the things Maude might have said, this is not what Phoebe was expecting.

'Bees?'

Maybe it's one of her visions again. Sometimes it's hard to tell with Maude.

'Yes. I used to look after the bees at the convent. None of the others wanted to do it, but I loved it.'

Another thing a stranger might not imagine if they were to encounter Maude in the street is that as a young woman, she used to be a nun. It's something Phoebe had been surprised to find out too when she read through her notes, although she should have learnt, after years of working with people, that humans always have the capacity to surprise you. Maude had lived in a convent until her increasingly erratic behaviour and disregard for the rules got her kicked out. From her notes, it seems she never really found her feet after that, her health deteriorating and making it harder – impossible, really – for her to slot back into society.

'I know nothing about looking after bees. Is there a word for someone who does that?'

'An apiarist,' Maude says with a confident nod.

'Well, I know nothing about what's involved in being an apiarist. I'd love to hear more about it.'

This seems to ignite something inside Maude and she springs to life, telling Phoebe in detail about queen bees and the honey she used to steal from the convent, breaking her train of conversation only once to quote scripture, which she does standing up again.

'My son, eat honey, for it is good, and the drippings of the honeycomb are sweet to your taste.'

She sits down heavily once more, seemingly worn out from the mini sermon. It must be pretty exhausting, being Maude.

'Are you OK if I give you your medication now, Maude?' Phoebe asks softly.

Luckily, she doesn't make any fuss this time and Phoebe silently thanks her as she administers the injection as swiftly and smoothly as possible.

As Phoebe climbs back onto her motorbike outside Maude's house after making sure there's food in the fridge and electricity in the meter, she thinks about how the hell she might secure regular access to a beehive. There used to be a community mental health gardening group that had a beehive. but it closed down a year ago after another round of cuts. But this is the first time that Maude has expressed a real interest in anything in a long time. Phoebe can't let her down.

Her next appointment takes Phoebe to a row of two-up two down council houses on the outskirts of a neighbouring town. Pulling up outside the neat little houses, a smile spreads across her face. She's looking forward to this appointment.

Nineteen-year-old Ben has been doing so much better recently. Last time Phoebe saw him, he was bubbly and chatty, telling her all about the latest session of the football club she'd encouraged him to sign up to and even talking about applying for some jobs. She's been in touch with his social worker since, the two of them agreeing that his future is looking so much brighter than when they first met him.

When Phoebe came to this street for the first time, Ben refused to let her in.

'I'm just here for a chat and to help you,' she had said through the letter box.

'No one can help me,' came his muffled reply.

'Well, why don't we talk about that a bit? I'm here to listen.'

There was a pause for a short moment.

'No one ever wants to listen to me.'

'Well, I do.'

Eventually, he opened the door. The first thing she noticed was how young he looked. She knew he was nineteen, but he could have been much younger. He was dressed in shorts and a stained dressing gown and his skin had the pallor of someone who hadn't seen sunlight or had a good hug in a long time. The second thing she noticed was the scar on his left wrist and the fact that it seemed to have healed nicely, which was good. It would never go away, it was too deep for that, but he was lucky to be alive. Although, from looking at him, she wasn't certain that's how he saw it.

She'd simply smiled at him and introduced herself. When he eventually let her in, she did a quick scan of the flat, taking in the warning signs, like the mail piled in the hallways, the overflowing bins and the closed curtains.

On that first meeting, he barely spoke. He let her administer his meds at least and check his blood sugar levels – on top of everything, he'd developed type 2 diabetes from his chaotic lifestyle and poor diet as a child. She talked through the care plan they'd work on together now that he was out of hospital. But he said nothing in reply. She left that first appointment feeling deflated.

But, slowly, things started to get better. When she noticed him wearing an Arsenal shirt on her next visit, she asked him how long he'd been a supporter.

'Forever.'

'Ever been to any matches?'

'When I was little. With me dad.'

'I've never been to a game myself. Tell me about it?'

He talked in detail about the crowds and the pretzel they'd got at half-time and it was the first occasion she'd heard him speak with any enthusiasm about anything. She knew from his notes that his dad wasn't around anymore.

The next time she visited, she brought a large, warm, salted pretzel with her. She'd baked it herself because she couldn't find anywhere in a twenty-mile radius that sold them, not that

24

she ever told him that. After that, things were easier between them.

Sometimes they'd watch *Match of the Day* reruns together. Sitting side by side with the screen in front of them made it easier for him to talk and, little by little, he did, opening up about his life and how he'd ended up in this tiny flat by himself, feeling as if his life had fallen apart. She started following where Arsenal was ranking in the league so she could discuss it with him when she next saw him. Eventually, she managed to persuade him to join a local football club run specifically for other young people struggling with their mental health. Even she had been surprised by the difference it had made. The last few visits he'd seemed like a different person, full of stories of his new mates and the matches they'd played.

He opens the door shortly after her knock. As usual, he's dressed in football kit. He also has the most enormous smile on his face.

'I got an interview!'

'That's amazing, Ben!' she says, following him inside the flat. They both sit down on the small sofa.

'It's at a sports shop in town. My footie mates couldn't believe it when I told them. I could work in a sports shop, how sweet is that?'

He's practically bouncing and Phoebe grins too. These are the moments she lives for.

'That sounds fantastic. And how was your latest match?'

She hadn't thought it possible, but his smile grows even wider. 'It was sick! I scored four goals. And Coach says my footwork has really improved.'

25

'Wow, that's great. And are you still taking your meds?'

His smile slips a tiny bit. 'Well, I didn't take my pills the last few days. I haven't needed them, I feel so good.'

'You've got to keep taking them, Ben. You know that. You might not stay well if you don't keep taking them.'

'OK, OK, I will, Boss, I promise. Can we watch *Match of the Day*? There's this absolutely sick goal I want you to see. You're gonna love it. If you've got time?'

Phoebe isn't quite sure how she's managed to convince Ben that she is interested in football when, actually, she can't stand it. Guys kicking a ball back and forth between one another? What's the point? But it seems she's also managed to convince him to start living again. And that's worth sitting through about a million episodes of *Match-of-the-*bloody*-Day*.

'Sure, I've got time.'

CHAPTER 5

'Hello, Mum!' comes the greeting of the smiling woman on the doorstep as Kate opens the front door, her baby in her arms and her top still hitched up after yet another feed.

'Oh, hi there,' Kate replies, taken aback. The first time someone said that to her – a nurse in the hospital in the hours after her daughter was born – Kate had looked over her shoulder, looking for her own mother. The realisation that the nurse was talking to *her* had felt how Kate imagined a medical student might feel if the air steward on a plane yelled, 'Is there a doctor on board?' and the terrifying silence that followed made them realise they might just be the closest thing.

'I'm Lydia, the new health visitor. Had you forgotten about today's appointment? The three-month check-up?'

'Um, I ...' Kate shifts her daughter in her arms, trying to tug down her top without disturbing her. Before she can answer, Jay is at her side, smiling brightly.

'Sorry about that, I was just working. Come on in. Can I get you anything? Tea, coffee? I'm not sure we have any milk though …'

'That's fine, thanks,' Lydia replies, reaching to take off her shoes as she steps inside.

Kate wants to tell her not to bother – the cottage is hardly a no-shoes household, or even a 'we sometimes hoover' household – but she's already following Jay through to the living room in her socked feet, Kate closing the door and heading on after them with the baby.

Lydia sets some equipment out on the floor and then stands up, beaming, her arms outstretched towards Kate.

'Let's have a look at this little one then. Hello, Rosie!'

Kate hands her over somewhat hesitantly, Lydia taking the baby with the same casual confidence with which Kate would handle a loaf of bread.

'So, how is she doing?'

Lydia starts to take the measurements she needs, Rosie wide-eyed but thankfully compliant.

'She's doing great, isn't she, Kate?' says Jay with a proud smile.

'Yeah, she seems OK. She's still not sleeping for more than two hours at a time, though, often less than that.'

'That's totally normal,' Lydia replies brightly as she expertly undresses Rosie before placing her on the scales. 'Don't worry!'

Kate bites her tongue, not wanting to say that she hadn't actually been worried about Rosie at all.

'OK, that's good to know. I was also wondering if there are any books you could recommend about looking after a newborn?'

During her pregnancy, Kate made endless notes, as though having a baby was a test she could ace if only she revised hard enough. But now that Rosie is actually here … Well, the truth is, it isn't anything like what she read in the books. But perhaps it isn't that the books she read weren't helpful, but just that she hadn't read the *right* ones.

It still stuns her that she and Jay were allowed to leave the hospital with the baby unsupervised. That she went in as just Kate and came out as a mother and was left to figure out everything that came next by herself. That day, she kept expecting doctors to come racing after her, telling her there'd been some mistake and she had to hand her baby back to them for safekeeping. Occasionally, she still wishes they would.

'You can't learn everything from books, Kate,' Lydia laughs. 'Your baby hasn't read the book, after all! It's not a bad thing to want to seek out information, but you have to trust your intuition. That's the most important thing.'

'That's what I've been telling her,' Jay chips in. 'Didn't I say not to worry, Kate? You're Rosie's mum, you'll always know what's best for her.'

Rosie lets out a little gurgle that sounds suspiciously to Kate like, *yeah, right.*

'OK, thanks!' she says, trying to make her voice sound normal. Like the voice of a calm and capable parent. She forces a smile on her face that she hopes does not at all say, *But I've never done this before! I don't* have *any intuition!* If only they could see her phone browser history. All the questions typed in a panic in the middle of the night. *Is it normal for my baby to make weird noises when they sleep? White-noise machines – do they actually work? Can you die from sleep deprivation?*

After a few more checks, Lydia hands Rosie over to Kate. As soon as Rosie is in her arms, she starts to wriggle, twisting her head away from Kate's body, her face scrunched in dissatisfaction.

'Well, she's a perfectly healthy baby,' says Lydia. 'I'm really pleased with how she's doing.'

'That's brilliant,' says Jay enthusiastically. 'I knew she'd be an overachiever, just like her mum.'

Rosie lets out a wail and Kate does her best to comfort her by bouncing her up and down on her shoulder.

'Thanks,' she adds herself. 'That's certainly a relief.'

'And how are you settling into motherhood, Kate?' asks Lydia as she starts to pack up her things. 'Have you managed to see friends and family much?'

'Well, we only recently moved here from London.'

There was a time when Kate thought she would stay in the city forever. Although it took her a while to settle in when she first moved there after university, she found her place as soon as she realised the trick about London: that, really, it's not one city at all but a patchwork of neighbourhoods stitched together by bus routes and Underground lines. Once she realised that she didn't need to feel at home in the whole city, just her little bit of it, things became much easier. And she loved it. The vibrant colours and smells on Electric Avenue where she did her shopping, her favourite cocktail bar in Brixton Village, the undercover market filled with places to eat, Brockwell Park that felt like a green oasis but with the jagged London skyline giving her a feeling of excitement and possibility. And her local lido, the place she went whenever she needed to switch off.

But things changed when she and Jay started talking about a baby. It had come on quite suddenly, a feeling that she could only describe as broodiness but that felt like an aching hunger, akin to homesickness, except for a home that didn't exist yet. A sense that her life that had felt so full up until that moment was suddenly missing something. Everywhere she went, she began noticing babies. It was as though they were following her, with their cute chubby cheeks and wide eyes, and the way they stared up at their parents with such adoration and the parents looked down at them as though they were the only people in the world, even if they were packed in a busy Tube during rush hour. Kate's heart tightened every time she spotted a family, which, in a city home to close to nine million people, meant that her heart received quite the workout.

It wasn't just the babies that she started to spot, though. She began to notice dangers everywhere that she had previously overlooked. The pleasant buzz of traffic became an incessant symbol of pollution and danger. She started googling local crime statistics.

And deep in her gut, she felt a tug back to the Somerset countryside where she'd grown up, recalling memories of a slower pace of life that had seemed so boring when she was a teenager but took on a new appeal once she reached her thirties. It would be nice to live somewhere they wouldn't have to carry a pram down a steep flight of steps every day, where she could hang her washing out to dry instead of having it fill their tiny flat, getting everything damp, where it didn't take an hour to get anywhere on the Tube. Where she didn't have to get on the Tube at all.

It makes her feel old to realise how much her priorities have changed over the last few years. But her priorities *have* changed. And she has changed too. More than she can get her head around recently.

'I haven't really had a chance to meet anyone local yet,' she explains to Lydia. 'But my mum and sister have both been over a lot. They're coming over later, actually. They live nearby.'

Because that was the biggest thing that pulled Kate and Jay away from London in the end. Even though Jay's parents lived near their place in Brixton, Kate just knew that as soon as the baby arrived she would need her own mum nearby. Thankfully, Jay had been understanding, especially once he realised how much more they could get for their money outside of London. They fell in love with the Old Post Office as soon as they saw it, the little cottage with the postbox in the front wall. When Jay saw the outbuilding that could become the photography studio that he wanted to set up to supplement his job as a freelance photographer, the deal was done.

Lydia's face lights up. 'I used to live in London. Tulse Hill. Where were you?'

'That's so funny, isn't it, Kate?' chips in Jay. 'We were practically neighbours; we were down in Brixton, not far from Brockwell Park.'

The memories come back in a visceral rush. The cosy, ramshackle second-hand bookshop run by her friends Frank and Jermaine, their dog Sprout presiding over things from her basket in the window. Kate's favourite bench at the top of the hill in the park where she went whenever she needed to think.

'Oh, Brockwell Park is so nice. Did you ever go to the lido there?' Lydia asks. 'I'd left before it all happened, but I hear it nearly closed down a few years ago. It would have been a massive shame if it had gone – I loved going there in the summer. It was like going to the beach, but without the travel.'

Kate closes her eyes briefly and can see glittering turquoise water and a smiling woman swimming beside her with white hair and eyes as blue as the lido itself, the smell of chlorine like perfume on her own skin, the feeling of ease spreading across her body as she slipped from the steps into the cool water.

When she opens her eyes, Jay and Lydia are looking at her expectantly and Rosie is still twisting in her arms. It feels like just yesterday that she was swimming at the lido every morning. And yet, despite how easily she can picture it all, there's a disconnect, as though she has fallen into another person's dream.

When Kate fails to say anything, Jay answers for her, flashing her a warm smile. 'Kate was one of the people who campaigned to keep the lido open. It's how we met, actually. Kate and I both covered the story at the newspaper we used to work at. She wrote the story and I took the photos. But it became more than a story for you, didn't it, Kate? In the end, she was basically spearheading the whole thing.'

Is it just Kate's imagination or does Lydia look at her a little differently? Assessing whether this woman with the unwashed hair and faint aroma of stale milk could really have once been a headstrong campaigner.

Kate doesn't blame her. She hardly believes it either.

'Well, it wasn't just me.' The face of that same woman with the sparkling blue eyes surrounded by smile lines pops into her head again, although this time she is holding a placard and raising her voice in a rallying cry. *Rosemary*. Even after all these years, Kate still misses her. To many outsiders, their friendship might have seemed an unconventional one, with forty years between them. But somehow that didn't seem to matter. Their friendship had changed Kate. She liked to think it changed them both.

Her attention darts to a framed photo on the mantlepiece of her and Rosemary standing on the poolside on the day that they found out the lido would remain open. They are beaming at one another, arms around each other's shoulders, and their joyful expressions sum up the happiness of that entire summer. The whole of Brixton seemed to turn up after that, as if everyone had needed the nudge of potential loss to remind them of what they had on their doorstep. Kate and Rosemary kept to their morning swims, going early before the crowds descended and before Kate headed to work. Until, suddenly, Kate was left swimming alone.

'Still, what a great thing to have been involved with,' says Lydia, and Kate blinks quickly, tilting her face down towards Rosie and quietly using the same breathing technique she used down by the river this morning.

It's because of the lido that she's been so drawn to the river. She swam at the lido through her pregnancy, right up until their move from London to Somerset the month before Kate's due date. There was no time for swimming after that, what with

34

desperately trying to get the cottage ready for the baby's arrival. And since then … Well, there hasn't been time for anything.

She'd seen photos online of the popular local river swimming spot before they moved – it's one of the things that drew her to this village in the first place. If moving to a village with a lido wasn't an option (and goodness, she had tried), then at the very least she needed to have water nearby. She loved the look of the buzzing atmosphere on that particular stretch of river.

As yet, she hasn't had a chance to visit in normal daylight hours, or found the confidence to actually go swimming on any of her secret early-morning visits. The river seems a very different beast to her beloved lido with its regimented lanes and clear blue water. And she'd even been nervous the first time she swam *there*. Although, back then, she wasn't swimming alone. She had Rosemary as her guide.

'Anyway, I'll leave you three to it now,' says Lydia, picking up her bag. 'But do make sure you keep in touch with your friends, Kate, and maybe you could try to make some here too? There are lots of mum and baby groups in the area that you might like to try. It can be overwhelming being a new mother and it's important to stay connected.'

Jay nods eagerly.

'Thanks, I'll think about it,' says Kate.

Rosie has started to cry again, but Kate does her best to smile, shifting her arms to try to find a position that feels more natural. It's only when Jay shows Lydia out that Kate lets the frozen smile melt away from her face. She only realises the effort it had been taking when she doesn't have to do it anymore.

CHAPTER 6

Just one more appointment. One more appointment of being Nurse Harrison before she can collapse into being just Phoebe again. For now, she is parked at the top of a hill, taking a quick break before heading to her last appointment. She knows the roads around here intimately and has her own mental map of the places that make good spots for a quiet moment, just like when she worked on the psychiatry ward and she knew all the nearby supply closets and toilets where she could rush to for five minutes during particularly difficult shifts.

The motorbike is parked in the lay-by and she is perched on the top of a gate that looks down over the valley, the river just visible at the bottom, winding its way across the countryside. It's a bright afternoon and she closes her eyes for a second, gripping the gate beneath her and feeling the sun warm her face.

Her phone rings in her pocket, breaking the silence. A flash of guilt jabs her as she spots her mum's name.

'Hi, Mum.'

'Hi, love, I thought I'd just try you on the off chance you'd finished work.'

'Just one appointment left,' she says, running a hand through her long red hair. 'Sorry I missed your last few calls, it's been a busy week.'

'Oh, that's OK, I know how busy you are. You work so hard.'

'Too hard!' comes her dad's voice in the background.

'Don't mind your dad,' her mum says softly. 'We both think it's amazing what you do. You're so strong, love. We're both very proud of you.'

They always have been, cheering embarrassingly loudly at her graduation ceremony and helping her out with the cost of extra training even though, looking back, it probably meant they missed out on holidays and nice extras they might have otherwise had. She owes them so much.

'I know you are. It means a lot. How's Nan doing?'

'She's doing all right. I think she's missing the old flat, but we all seem to be bumbling along OK together. Shall I go get her? I know she'd love a chat.'

Phoebe glances at her watch. 'I'd love to, but I've got to go to my next appointment. I'll ring back later, though.'

'All right, love. You take care, speak soon.'

'Bye, Phoebs!' she can hear her dad shouting in the background.

'Oh, and send our love to Max,' her mum says as they're saying their final goodbyes.

Phoebe swallows hard. 'I will do.'

*

It's been a while since Phoebe last saw Tara, her final patient of the day. It always makes her uneasy when there's been a long gap between visits. So much can change in a short space of time. She wishes she was able to check in more regularly, but there simply isn't time. Yet another thing that can often make her feel as though, however hard she tries to do her job well, it isn't enough.

Tara wasn't doing so great the last time they spoke. The voices had been getting louder and more insistent, so together with the team of doctors, they'd agreed to up the dose of her medication.

When Tara opens the door, it's a relief to see that she is wearing clothes. There was a spell when she was convinced that her entire wardrobe had been bugged with recording devices.

'Hello, Tara! It's nice to see you. Can I come in?'

Normally at this point, Tara would peer her head out the door to suspiciously check that no one was following Phoebe before maybe, or maybe not, letting her in. But this time she simply nods and disappears into the living room, leaving Phoebe to follow her.

From an initial inspection, the living room shows some promising signs that things have improved for Tara. The curtains are open and it makes Phoebe realise she's never seen Tara's front room bathed in daylight before. The television is facing into the room, too, instead of turned towards the wall as it was before so that the government couldn't watch her every move.

After Phoebe's long and exhausting day, she feels suddenly filled with optimism. These are some of the best bits about her job – those moments when you can see someone turning a corner, their life becoming brighter.

'Your place is looking great, Tara,' Phoebe says as she sits down in the armchair, Tara positioning herself on the edge of the sofa. The surfaces look surprisingly clean and there's even a sweet, fresh scent in the room. Maybe it's just fresh air, Phoebe thinks as she notices the ajar window. It certainly makes a change from some of the places she's visited today. She looks around again appreciatively. 'It seems like you've been doing really well since we last saw each other.'

But as Phoebe turns back towards Tara, she notices the expression on her face.

'And how are you feeling, Tara?' she asks gently, immediately adjusting her tone.

Tara bites her lip, and despite the cleanliness of the flat, Phoebe notices that her face looks gaunt, her eyes tired.

'They've gone.'

'Who has gone?'

'The voices. They've gone away.'

'Well, it sounds like the medication is working then.'

But Tara's eyes fill with tears.

'I ... I miss them. Now I'm on my own.'

Phoebe takes in the room again, readjusting her thinking. There have never been any photos on display in here, no signs that anyone else has been in the place since Phoebe's last visit. Yes, Tara has tidied up a bit and her medication is having its intended effect, but what else does she have?

Phoebe needs to get back to the clinic to type up her notes and crack on with some paperwork. She's behind on her admin and it will take hours to properly catch up. Not to mention everything that's waiting for her back at home. But all of that can wait.

'I'm going to make you a cup of tea,' she says, standing up and placing a hand very gently on Tara's arm. 'And then let's have a good chat.'

It's late by the time Phoebe's motorbike pulls back into the village. It didn't feel right to leave when Tara was feeling so low, so they talked for a long time, Phoebe trying to encourage Tara to draw on some of the CBT methods she has taught her for when things are feeling overwhelming, like challenging and interrogating her negative thoughts and using breathing techniques to help relax her. It did seem by the time she left that Tara was feeling a little brighter. Phoebe had fished a ready meal out of the freezer and chucked it in the oven for her.

'You take care of yourself, OK? And I'll see you again soon.'

Not as soon as Phoebe would like. As she left, it struck her that, aside from the medication and support she's able to offer, what Tara really needs is friends. But she's not so unusual for being so isolated. Lots of her patients are in the same position, even the most loyal friends and family dropping away over the years when faced with the challenges of what a mental health condition can do to a person. If they even had that support network in the first place.

The van from this morning is still parked up outside the empty shop premises below her flat as Phoebe parks her motorbike on the street. She pauses for a moment to try to see inside the building, but the windows are covered with newspaper and there doesn't seem to be anyone about. Eager to find out who was making all that noise this morning and who her new neighbours will be, she takes a step closer and presses her face up to the glass. Through a small tear in the paper, she is able to glimpse into the shop beyond.

The place is unrecognisable from Amit's newsagent. All the old shelves have been cleared and in their place is a long counter. It looks as though there are some new shelves being constructed against the opposite wall, which would explain the banging she'd heard this morning. But it's still hard to tell exactly what type of business is moving in.

Her shopping bags feel heavy in her hands, so she heads up to the flat, the bottles clinking together as she climbs the stairs.

When she opens the door, she immediately senses the shift in atmosphere just since this morning.

She dumps the bags on the floor and heads straight into the bedroom, opening the wardrobe. Rows of empty coat hangers stare back at her from one half of the rail and a lump that she's been pushing down all day rises in her throat, her vision growing blurry.

So, he's really gone then.

CHAPTER 7

The walls in the nursery are a bright lido blue, matching the paint of the beach-house-shaped bookcase in the corner. On a hanger on the back of the door is the tiniest pink swimsuit – a gift from Kate's lido friends that is as yet unused. This is one of Kate's favourite rooms in the cottage. She decorated it the day after moving in, before even unpacking the kitchen crockery. Jay kept telling her that it didn't matter, the baby wasn't going to care about the colour of the walls, but she was determined to make everything perfect.

She takes a photo of the room now, careful to cut out the nappies and piles of washing she is busy folding, Rosie asleep in a sling on her chest, and instead capturing the bright corner where sunlight streams onto a rocking chair covered in the rainbow blanket given to her by her friends Emma and Leonie when Rosie was born.

Opening her Work Wives WhatsApp group, she sends the picture to them.

In pride of place. It looks so lovely in here and always makes me think of you both xx

The replies come in quickly.

Emma: It looks great! Good choice, Rosie's godmothers!

Leonie: Yeah, well done us. That kiddo's lucky to have such style icons as aunties.

Kate sets down the laundry so she can focus on her phone, checking first that Rosie is still sleeping soundly in the sling. She selects a couple of the most recent photos of Rosie and sends them to the group.

Emma: Ah, isn't she perfect!!

Leonie: She looks sooo much like Jay.

It's what absolutely everyone has been saying to her since her daughter was born. It was the very first thing that her mum said when she met her new granddaughter. Kate never says anything. Because Rosie *does* look exactly like her father.

Kate types quickly with one hand.

Tell me what's going on at work, I'm bored …

Emma is the first to reply again. You're not missing out on much, don't worry. Just a normal day in the newsroom.

But Kate knows there is no such thing as a normal day in the newsroom. No two days are the same, which is one of the things she loves about working at the *Herald*. Compiling the next day's stories, you feel as though you're at the heart of things, in the place where everything is happening. There's always this buzz and sense of energy, partly from all the journalists like her and her friends busily doing interviews and typing away in the same open-plan office and partly from the sense that in the newsroom, nothing is ever certain. Things can change at the last minute if a story suddenly breaks or the editor changes her mind about what stories they'll be leading with. It keeps you constantly on your toes. OK, it can be exhausting sometimes and when Kate said goodbye to her colleagues on her last day before her maternity leave, she'd been happy to leave, looking forward to a break from the relentlessness of it all after years of working hard to climb her way up the rickety journalism career ladder. But now ...

You have to give me more than that. I just watched three hours of *Gilmore Girls* and am now folding laundry.

After Lydia left, Jay headed back out to the studio to carry on working, leaving Kate and Rosie in front of the TV.

Not gonna lie, types Leonie, that sounds kind of dreamy

Emma: Yeah, take me to Stars Hollow NOW please. Although maybe pass on the laundry ...

Leonie: I'd even take the laundry. You know I find it soothing. P.S. Lorelai forever!

Kate: I used to think there was no such thing as too much *Gilmore Girls*, but I think my brain might be turning to pumpkin-spiced mush. Is it just me or is it somehow always autumn in Stars Hollow? What are you both working on today?

There's a pause and Kate stares at her phone, waiting for the replies to come in and give her just a glimpse of the life that was hers up until recently. Is this how smokers feel before their next cigarette? Please, just one drag, one hit of the sounds and atmosphere of the bustling newspaper office.

Lately, most of her conversations have been with Jay, and although maybe they used to talk about politics and social issues, now they mostly discuss their daughter's bowel movements and sleep patterns. The person she spends most of her time with is Rosie and she might be cute, but she's an absolutely terrible conversationalist.

The notifications ping and Kate's heart leaps.

Emma: So sorry, Kate, but Big Boss has just called an all-hands meeting, looks like there's a story breaking. Gotta go!

Leonie: Give that sweet girl a kiss from us! Xx

Kate abandons the laundry for good and sinks down into the rocking chair in the corner, pushing herself back and forth in order to keep Rosie asleep. If her friends are going to give her nothing, then she'll just have to turn to Instagram instead.

The first image she sees is of her friend Jermaine on the side of Brockwell Lido, that post-swim smile on his face that Kate recognises because it used to fill her own face every morning. It's almost as if she can smell the chlorine and feel the sunshine reflecting on the turquoise water.

Below the image from Jermaine's personal account is one from the bookshop account he runs with his husband Frank. There's a photo of Sprout sitting in the window, her golden fur practically glowing in the morning sunshine, and a pile of new hardbacks stacked around her to advertise an upcoming event. As well as the second-hand books they specialise in, recently they've also started running author events. Kate and Jay went to as many as they could back when they were living in Brixton. Kate even helped hook them up with some of their speakers, recommending experts she'd interviewed for the paper who had new books coming out. She posts a comment, wishing them luck for the event, then continues scrolling.

Her favourite restaurant in Brixton Village has uploaded a new menu and she reads it thoroughly, spending a long time deciding exactly what she would order. There's a photo in Emma's Stories of her and Leonie and a few other colleagues at after-work drinks. Kate instantly recognises the décor of the pub just around the corner from the office. She's been there countless times and can almost smell the craft beer and hear the buzz of the London pub that is busy every night of the week.

Her phone feels like an anchor tethering her to her old life and she grips it tightly, scrolling her way through reminders of the choices she has made.

Until Rosie begins suddenly to cry. Kate puts her phone away and wraps her arms around her daughter, rocking back and forth a little more vigorously.

'I didn't mean it,' she says quietly as she kisses Rosie's head. 'I don't really want to be back there. I'm happy right where I am.'

But Rosie continues to cry, as if she doesn't really believe her mother's words.

'Mum, you do know you don't have to clean every time you come over, right?'

Within five minutes of Kate's mother arriving in the cottage that afternoon, she has got the hoover out. Her electric-blue earrings that match the exact blue of her boxy shirt jangle as she leans to unwind the wire and plug it in. Kate watches from the kitchen table, wanting to help but currently tied to her chair as she feeds Rosie. Again.

'I know that, but I like to be helpful.'

Her mum plugs the hoover in and then stands up, tucking a strand of her sharp grey bob behind one ear. She only recently decided to give up her honey-blonde highlights and let her hair go its natural grey. It suits her. She looks great generally, in tight indigo jeans and colourful trainers, a leopard-print skinny belt giving the outfit a little edge. Kate can't help but think how much cooler her sixty-three-year-old mother looks than she does. Earlier, she caught a glimpse of herself in the reflection of the microwave and really wished she hadn't.

'And you *have* been helpful. You've already made me a cup of tea.' Kate lifts it up, leaning to one side to take a sip without risking spilling any on Rosie's head. 'You've done so much for me, Mum.' Her voice wavers slightly as she says it, going through the endless list of kindnesses in her mind. The day they moved in to the cottage, Kate eight months pregnant, her mum and stepdad Brian had come over to help them unpack, insisting that Kate sit down while they helped Jay with the boxes. When Kate was in labour in the hospital, her mum had used her spare key to the cottage to let herself in and cleaned the house from top to bottom. She'd left a fish pie and a bottle of champagne in the fridge. And the last time she visited, she'd pretty much forced Kate to go and have a lie-down while she watched Rosie. When Kate re-emerged, blurry-eyed, having been pulled suddenly from sleep by a phantom cry that turned out to be just in her imagination, there was a wash in the machine, the bins had been taken out and Rosie was still sleeping soundly.

'If she wants to do it, why don't we just let her?' Jay had said when Kate later talked to him about how she was worried they were taking advantage of her mum's help. 'The place *does* look like a tip and I know the last thing either of us wants to do when we have five minutes is clean it.' There are so many things Kate could do in those brief pockets of time that occasionally come when Rosie is settled in her basket or with Jay. Wash herself, catch up with the *Herald*, read a book. Mostly, she just lies down on the carpet and closes her eyes.

'I don't know how I'd have got through these past months without you, Mum,' she says now, her voice properly wobbling.

Her mum abandons the hoover and sits down beside her, reaching for her hand.

'Oh, sweetheart! You know I'm happy to do it.'

Kate sniffs, wiping her face with her sleeve.

'Is everything OK?' Her mother's forehead furrows into a frown and she places a hand on Kate's shoulder and gives a little squeeze.

Kate takes a steadying breath, lightly patting Rosie's back. 'I'm fine, just a bit hormonal, I think. And tired.'

'Of course you are. It's exhausting being a mother. And wonderful, of course,' she adds hurriedly.

Kate opens her mouth to speak, but the doorbell rings. She goes to stand, but her mum is already leaping up.

'I'll get it!'

By the time Miriam returns with Kate's sister, Erin, in tow, Rosie has finished feeding and fallen asleep in her arms and Kate has readjusted her top. And all the things Kate had for

48

a second considered telling her mum have been neatly folded and pushed to the back of her mind.

'Look at her!' Erin says, placing the enormous casserole dish she'd been holding down on the table and heading straight for Rosie.

Kate has become used to this new order of things and waits patiently while her sister gently strokes Rosie's hair and plants a kiss on her cheek before standing straight again and giving Kate a sideways hug.

'Hey, sis.' Kate catches an inhale of her sister's familiar perfume – a gift every birthday from her sister's husband, Mark – and feels a rush of comfort. Erin is nine years older than her so has always felt like more than just a big sister to her. The smell of her perfume smells like safety.

Erin opens the fridge and jostles things about to fit the casserole dish inside. 'Just something to keep you both going. I thought you could do with something hearty. And there's a bag of 3–6 months clothes in the hallway for Rosie. I figured she'd probably be moving up a size now.'

'Thank you. You're the best.'

'It's nothing, I needed to go up to the attic to get down some stuff to make a fancy-dress costume for Arlo and the casserole's just something I threw together with what we had in the fridge.'

Erin is always like this, making out that she's gone to no effort, like the other day when she dropped by with lanolin nipple cream and wine because she 'happened to be passing by' even though their cottage is in the opposite direction to Erin's work. Or the day a couple of weeks ago when a Sainsbury's delivery Kate didn't remember ordering arrived on her doorstep and, after a lengthy discussion with the confused delivery driver, they managed to ascertain that the delivery had been placed by Erin.

Kate has no idea how Erin manages to find the time to look after her little sister alongside running her own business and taking care of two small boys – and somehow manages to look like an off-duty social media influencer in the process. Today, she is dressed in cropped white trousers and a crisp Breton top, a silk scarf tied around her sleek ponytail. Kate only has one child and is pretty certain she forgot to put on deodorant this morning.

She knows that Erin's life isn't without its problems. There have been many long phone conversations over the last few years about silly arguments between Erin and Mark where Kate has had to talk her sister down from ringing a divorce lawyer, patiently reminding her of all the great things about her brother-in-law that *maybe* might outweigh his snoring and his mother.

As a child, Kate idolised her big sister, always thinking of her as glamorous and pretty much perfect. As they've both got older, they've grown much closer, more like friends than doting little sister and perfect older sister. But Kate knows that since having Rosie, she may have slipped back into putting her sister on a pedestal. But how can she not? Erin has always done it all without complaining, without asking for too much help, without falling apart.

'I'll make some more tea,' Miriam announces. Her mother is of the generation that believes that most of life's problems can be if not solved, then drastically improved, by a cup of tea. Erin silently gives her arm a tight squeeze and then fetches mugs from the cupboards. 'Maybe we can have it in the garden? It's lovely out there.' Fresh air is the other thing that Miriam believes is a cure-all, and Kate is inclined to agree with her.

She still can't believe that she is someone who owns a garden, and a proper garden with grass, flower beds, a tree and a view, not the small patch of paving just about big enough to squeeze in a barbecue that constituted the outdoor space of their basement flat in London.

'Oh, by the way, Kate,' her mum says as she pours the tea, Erin pulling a packet of biscuits out of her plum leather Mulberry handbag, 'I just remembered. Last time I came to visit, I popped into that nice café in the village on my way home. You know, the one with all the comfy sofas and that amazing display of cakes. Has a cutesy name …'

'I know the one,' she replies, readjusting Rosie in her arms as a pang of pain shoots up her wrist. After a lot of trial and error, she has found a position that seems to keep Rosie slumbering for a decent chunk of time when she falls asleep like this in her arms. It just happens to be a position that's started to give Kate RSI in her wrists. 'The Cosy Corner.' When she first moved to the village, she imagined writing in the café while Rosie napped in the pram. 'I haven't had a chance to visit it yet.'

'Well, when I was there, I saw a group of young mums with their babies. They looked like a really friendly bunch, so I went over to say hello …'

'You did *not*, Mum,' says Erin, rolling her eyes and nibbling a biscuit.

51

'What?' Miriam lifts her eyebrows, looking at her daughters as though she's completely innocent. 'I only wanted to say hello and that I had a daughter who had just moved to the area who had a new baby.'

'Mum! I love you, but did you have to? I'm thirty-two, I don't need you arranging me playdates!'

'I just thought it might be good for you to make some friends,' shrugs Miriam. 'The women were lovely and say they meet at the same time every week and that everyone's welcome. They call themselves the Tired Mums Club. They've got a flyer up in the café and everything. I know it's hard work having a newborn, darling, but it might make you feel better to put some real clothes on and get out of the house, you know?'

Kate looks down at what has become her standard outfit of maternity leggings and one of Jay's old shirts.

'These *are* real clothes. And I do get out.'

Her mum and sister look at her and their expressions say it all.

'I love you, sis, but I'm not certain I've seen you in anything other than that shirt of Jay's since Rosie was born. And the supermarket doesn't count as "out". Maybe Mum has a point.'

'But I *have* friends.'

Her heart squeezes as she pictures her last night in London. Jay ordered pizzas and they invited everyone over to join them, squeezed into their tiny flat amongst all the packed boxes. Emma and Leonie caught her up on everything that had happened in the office on her first day of maternity leave. Frank and Jermaine from the bookshop were there too, along with Kate's friend Jamila and her mother, Hope, a seventy-three-year-old

Caribbean woman who Kate counts just as much as a friend as Jamila, both brought into her life by the local lido. She'd had her last swim there earlier that day too and as she said goodbye to the staff, it felt as though she was saying goodbye to far more than just a swimming pool.

Her friends have all been messaging her since she left – even Hope, whose texts are always full of amusing typos because she hasn't got to grips with the smartphone Jamila bought her yet. Emma and Leonie came for a visit not long after Rosie was born but the others haven't managed it yet. Frank and Jermaine have the shop, Hope's hip has been playing up so travelling is difficult for her and Jamila is a central London GP with a school-age daughter. Hopefully, Kate will be able to get to London before long to visit, but right now the thought feels about as realistic as her travelling to the moon.

'I know you do,' her mum says gently. 'But they're back in London. You need friends *here*, mum friends. I think it might help.'

'But I'm doing fine.'

'I know you are, you're doing great. But becoming a mother is a huge thing for anyone. You know we will always be here for you, and you have lovely Jay, of course, but you need all the support you can get.'

Kate is reminded of what Lydia said earlier about needing to build a network.

'Some of the women I met when the boys were Rosie's age are still some of my closest friends,' chips in Erin. 'You know I'm always here to answer any baby-related questions, but my

53

boys are a bit older now. It's great to have other people going through the same thing as you at the same time.'

Kate wraps her arms around her sleeping daughter.

All the things she hasn't told them about how she's really feeling swirl around in her head. The thought of sharing those worries with other women also grappling with similar things makes the tension in her body that's been building day by day ease slightly.

Maybe they have a point.

'I'll think about it. Oh, by the way, Jay has a shoot in Bristol tomorrow. Which means Rosie and I are going to be flying solo. Do you think you'd be able to pop over, Mum?'

Up until now, Jay has been working from home, doing up the studio and taking on some freelance editing work. Kate knew he would have to get back to shoots away eventually and at least this one is just in Bristol, so not too far away, but it still feels daunting. Jay is so good with Rosie, always able to calm her down. And to calm Kate down too.

'Sorry, sweetheart, but I'm busy tomorrow.'

'Oh, right. No worries.'

'I'd offer to help,' says Erin, 'but I've got a busy day in the office. We're pitching for a new client.'

It strikes Kate how much she's come to rely on her family over the past few months. Especially her mum, who has been coming over to visit every couple of days. But of course they wouldn't be able to carry on like that forever. They can't always drop everything for her, they have their own lives. She eyes the hoover in the corner, guilt bubbling inside her at how much they've both done for her. Has she been taking advantage?

54

'Will you be all right?' her mum asks anxiously.

Kate gives Rosie a little squeeze.

'We'll be absolutely fine. It will be nice actually, to have some time, just the two of us.'

She's been so lucky to have so much help up until now – far more than a lot of people get. It's time to start learning to cope on her own.

CHAPTER 8

Phoebe grabs a bottle of wine from the rack and twists open the cap, taking a quick swig before pouring herself a large glass. Then she looks around the living room, noticing the gap beneath the TV where Max's Xbox used to sit.

When Max told her that he was leaving, she didn't believe him at first. But then she'd seen how serious he looked and a sick feeling rose in her stomach so it had been hard to focus on what he was saying, her whole body in shock.

'Things haven't been good for a long time – surely you must know that. You're always working. You've never really prioritised this relationship.'

His words had stung mostly because she knew deep down that they were true. But there was only so much of her to go around. Yes, she felt awful every time she had to postpone a date or turn up late. But what was she supposed to do? She didn't want to let her patients down either. How do people do it? When she was younger, she had thought that juggling friendships, relationships and a career would be easy, or at least not this bloody impossible. But now it all feels so overwhelming, as if she's holding the leads of a pack of energetic dogs and they're all determined to head off in different directions.

'I know things have been difficult, but that's why I thought this holiday could be what we need. It could be a chance for us to reconnect.'

As she said it, all the images she'd browsed that morning came flashing back into her mind. Pasta, beaches, a villa with a pool. She'd coped for ages without a holiday, but now that the thought had come into her mind, it felt like a mirage in a desert. And maybe it could be the answer to their problems. Maybe things would look different in the golden light of a Tuscan vineyard. Maybe, it would make him love her again.

But it seemed it was too late for that.

'Look, the thing is, I've met someone else.'

Phoebe couldn't decide whether to punch him or burst into tears. But it probably wasn't a great look for a nurse to get done for assault, and if she started crying, she might not stop and she had to get to work. So, instead, she took an incredibly deep breath – the kind of breath she often coached her patients in but very rarely took herself.

'I've got to go. Let's talk about this when I get back.'

But now he's not here.

'Bloody coward!' she shouts aloud, kicking the corner of the coffee table and instantly regretting it, hopping on the spot and sloshing her wine. 'Bloody coffee table. Bloody toe! Bloody Max!'

She starts to cry as she swears, hot, angry tears sliding down her face, making her feel even angrier. She doesn't cry. She's *strong*.

Her phone buzzes in her pocket and she pulls it out of her pocket, seeing Max's name glowing on the screen.

I'll come back for the rest of my things tomorrow. I've covered this month's rent, but if you want to stay in the flat, you'll need to start covering everything yourself. I'm sorry it ended like this x

Her hand finds the bottle of wine and she fills her glass again. She takes a long sip, the slight numbing sensation that follows a welcome relief.

If you want to stay in the flat, you'll need to start covering everything yourself.

Shit. The flat is hardly pristine – neither of them had the time to keep it particularly tidy – and she has never got around to painting, despite their landlord's insistence that they could make the place their own. But it's still home. She loves the view out over the high street to the valley and river beyond. And there's a squishy sofa and a comfy bed to flop onto at the end of a long day. The flat has always felt like her safe place and she doesn't want to leave. But how is she going to manage to cover everything by herself? So much for a bloody holiday!

As she slumps onto the sofa, her phone rings. As she sees her mum's name, she suddenly remembers she promised she would ring back to speak to her nan. But she's in no fit state to speak to anyone right now. Her face is covered in eyeliner and snot and there's a high chance her tongue is already purple from the red wine. She cancels the call, turning her phone on to silent and placing it face down on the coffee table.

Briefly, she considers the techniques she would advise to her patients if they were in a state like this. She could do a body scan, checking in with how she's feeling in an attempt to get out of her head and into the sensations of her body. But all she can focus on is the throbbing of her toe. She could try box breathing or a visualisation exercise, or, shit, even some *actual* exercise.

But she doesn't do any of that. Instead, she takes another big swig of wine. Who needs mindfulness when you have Cabernet Sauvignon?

The sound of banging suddenly rises up from the shop below, making her jump.

'Not again!'

The noise continues, the bangs followed by whirring and the beat of the radio.

'It's the middle of the night! Who does building work at night?'

She considers striding downstairs to confront whoever it is who has moved into the premises and clearly has no respect for others, but she can't be bothered, so stamps her foot on the floorboards instead. It doesn't make a bit of difference. Wine. Wine will help.

By the end of the fourth glass, everything feels softened, even the sound of the building work below no longer bothering her. A lovely warmth flows through her body. By the end of the bottle, she is fast asleep.

CHAPTER 9

The smell of apple blossom tickles Kate's nose as she stands beneath the tree in her garden, watching the sun set over the valley beyond. There are bees and butterflies circling lazily around the messy flower beds, landing on the petals of fox-gloves, delphiniums and wild, rangy roses. It's in moments like this that she remembers why they moved. The sight of fields and trees in the distance calms her, quietening the questions that have been swirling around her mind ever since her mum and sister left.

'Kate, where's Rosie?'

Jay's voice snaps her out of her thoughts. She looks up as he crosses the garden towards her, coming from the direction of the studio where he has been working all day. His anxious expression jolts her.

Rosie. She realises that standing under the apple tree feeling the evening sun on her face, she hadn't been thinking about her at all.

'She's in her Moses basket inside, I just stepped outside for a second to …'

Why did she come out here? And was it really only a second ago? She suddenly realises she has absolutely no idea how much time has passed since Erin and Miriam said goodbye. After they'd left she had pinged a quick message to her Work Wives group: How's it going there?

But there'd been no reply. They were probably busily making calls and typing at their desks, or heading out if the breaking story required field research. With no response from her friends, she had left her phone on the kitchen table next to the Moses basket where Rosie lay fast asleep. She had only stepped outside to catch her breath. But guilt rips through her now. How did she let herself get so lost in thought that she completely forgot about Rosie?

Jay is already heading in through the kitchen door and Kate follows anxiously. But Rosie is fast asleep in her Moses basket on the kitchen table, just where Kate left her. As they step inside, she stirs, though, and Jay reaches swiftly to lift her up to his chest, cupping her bottom in his hand and nestling her in against his shoulder. Kate watches, thinking how it looks as though Jay's shoulder was made for this. How the two of them fit together perfectly.

'How were your mum and sister? Sorry I didn't come and say hi, I got totally caught up sanding the floorboards.'

'They're OK, thanks. Erin left us food and Mum hoovered.'

Jay smiles above the top of Rosie's fluffy head. 'Of course they did.'

'Mum mentioned a mum and baby group she's seen

advertised in the village. I might take Rosie tomorrow morning while you're on your shoot.'

The way Jay's face lights up makes something inside Kate ache.

'I think that sounds a brilliant idea! You haven't really seemed … yourself. I'm sure it will help to meet some other mums.'

Kate wants to tell him that she doesn't even know who 'herself' is anymore.

But then she pictures her sister's face. In a rush of memories she recalls the day she told Erin that she was pregnant.

Her sister was the second person she told, after Jay. She hadn't planned on telling her the news in the middle of a soft-play centre on a Saturday morning, but it was hard to pin Erin down since she had her boys. It was 10.30 a.m. and Erin was eating a full lunch in the café as they watched Ted and Arlo thrashing about in the luridly coloured ball pit. Kate felt nauseous and couldn't believe that her sister was about to tuck into a tuna sandwich. As Erin lifted the bread to her mouth, she caught her eye across the table as Kate sipped her tea and raised an eyebrow.

'I've been up since five,' Erin explained, wiping mayonnaise from her chin.

Kate had lifted a hand subconsciously to her stomach, thinking about how she would soon become part of the sleep-less-night brigade and feeling strangely excited by the fact that she would finally be joining her sister's club. Kate had spent most of her life trying – and failing – to catch up with her sister. Now they would be on the same page at last.

But telling her sister hadn't gone at all how she'd intended. When Kate made her announcement, Erin's face had dropped.

'I didn't even know you were trying.'

'Well, we weren't really *trying* trying. But I stopped taking the pill a couple of months ago.'

It happened when she and Jay were on holiday in Slovenia. One morning, they woke early in their little cabin and headed down to the lakeside beach. They were the only people there, except for a couple and their young baby. She had tiny pigtails and chubby cheeks and kept lifting handfuls of sand and attempting to eat it, much to the despair of her parents and the amusement of Kate and Jay.

'I think we'd make cute babies,' Jay had said teasingly and Kate had smiled. But then his face grew more serious. 'Honestly, though, what do you think? I know we've talked about it before, but it feels like now could be a good time? I love being a team with you, but maybe it's time to allow an extra member? A really tiny and cute one?'

Later, when they got back to the cabin, they reached for each other with an added fervour, as though making a decision without even saying the words out loud, and Kate knew that the next day she'd throw her pills in the bin.

'You'll make an amazing mum,' Jay had whispered into her ear. And, back then, she hadn't even thought to disagree. She'd felt ready. She loved this baby that didn't even exist yet …

'Just a couple of months?'

Erin's eyes had filled with tears and, in a horrifying rush, Kate's memories from back when Erin was trying for a baby had flashed through her mind. Her sister crying on the phone to her because her period had come yet again. About the pain of having to buy another gift for another friend's baby shower. The scrimping and saving to afford IVF treatment and then all the terrified waiting that came after.

'We've been really lucky,' Kate replied quietly, her earlier excitement replaced with guilt. How could she have been so insensitive? She should have found a better way to tell her sister the news, but then, was there ever an easy way to tell your sister that while you might share fifty per cent of the same DNA, when it came to the fertility lottery, you'd been the one to win the jackpot?

'Yes,' Erin had replied. 'You're really, really lucky.'

Over the past few months, whenever Kate has considered telling someone, anyone, some of the dark thoughts that have been circling her mind, she pictures her sister's face and hears those words repeating over and over in her head. *You're really, really lucky.* And she shuts her mouth again, because she knows that her sister was right. She is *so* lucky. She has the very thing she desperately wanted.

'I'm looking forward to trying the group,' Kate says now, as much to herself as to Jay.

Because, instead of sneaking out to the river every morning, maybe she should take the advice of her family and the health visitor. Instantly, she decides that she won't be going to the river tomorrow. Or the next day. She can't keep running away from her life like that. Going to a mum and baby group will be good. It's the kind of thing other mothers do, isn't it?

She glances at her phone on the counter. Still no reply from Emma and Leonie. She gets it. They're busy. They have their own lives. But maybe Erin was right about needing to make friends here, too. It might still feel strange, but this is her life now and it's time she started treating it that way, rather than feeling as though she's on some weird holiday that she will surely come home from eventually.

CHAPTER 10

The sound of banging jolts Phoebe awake. For a second, everything looks red and then she realises it's because her hair is tangled in front of her face. She tucks it behind her ears and pushes herself up from the sofa, groaning.

'Oh God!' Her mouth feels painfully dry and her head throbs. She takes in the empty wine bottle and the discarded piece of toast she must have made herself at some point last night but forgotten to eat.

The banging intensifies, coming from the floor below. There's a whirring noise and then the radio kicks in too.

'It is too fucking early for this,' she says to herself as she struggles to standing.

She scans the room, taking in how much it has changed just since yesterday.

Max's rucksack usually sits on one of the dining chairs, ready for him to take into work, but today it's not there. Neither are his running shoes, which are always piled by the flat door. But his books are still there on the bookshelves, his biographies and historical novels leant against her medical textbooks and the odd escapist romance bought with the intention of being read on a weekend to unwind, but pretty much all have never been opened.

She isn't sure which is worse – the empty spaces that Max has left behind, or seeing his other things still there, a reminder of the shared life that was shattered by his announcement yesterday. Part of her wants to throw all his things out the window. Another part wants to use them to build a fortress around herself. But ... there's a third part that feels quietly resigned to what has happened. When he told her that he was leaving, it had been painful, but deep down she hadn't been completely surprised. It reinforced something she has always feared about herself – that she is terrible at relationships and is ultimately destined to end up alone.

Her longest relationship before Max was with a dietician called Luke who she dated for six months, meeting him in the hospital where she used to work. But he broke up with her after yet another evening when she'd returned home late after an emergency at work.

'I feel like you care more about your patients than you care about me,' Luke had said to her.

Phoebe ended things with him that evening. It hurt that she had hurt him, but she realised he was right. She *did* care about her patients more than him.

For a long time, Phoebe stopped dating altogether. It was too complicated and she knew she made a terrible girlfriend. She'd been told it enough times over the years.

But she met Max on a very rare night out with her colleagues. He was sweet and funny and managed to break down her barriers, making her imagine that maybe she didn't have to live life on her own. Maybe she could be part of a relationship and have a life outside her work.

Phoebe reaches decisively for a handful of Max's books on the shelf, scooping them into her arms and then fetching a bin bag. She's not making that mistake again.

What time are you coming to get your things? she types quickly to Max, adding a few kisses on autopilot before rapidly deleting them. *No.* Absolutely not.

His reply comes in just seconds later.

I was thinking of coming by this morning before work for a few things – I left my laptop charger behind. Is that OK? Will you be in?

Phoebe shudders.

No, I'll be out. You've still got a key, I take it, but put it through the door when you're done.

It's still an hour until her first appointment, but she quickly pulls on her leathers and grabs her helmet and bag.

Out on the street, the sound of work going on in the empty shop is even louder. The same van as before is parked outside but the shop door is still firmly closed, the sheets of newspaper obscuring the view inside. Who *are* these neighbours and is early-morning building work going to become a regular thing? Jesus, she hopes not. At least it might be a bit more bearable if the business turns out to be a wine shop.

She packs her panniers with the things she needs for the day and climbs onto her motorbike, revving the engine louder than normal as she sets off, the fresh morning air rushing against her face and tugging on her hair. On the bike, she doesn't feel like a hungover mess who has just been dumped and is at high risk of becoming destitute or, at the very least, having to live off porridge and tinned goods for the foreseeable future. She feels powerful.

As she has time to kill, she heads for one of her favourite thinking spots at the top of the hill looking down over the valley, parking and stepping off the bike. Up here, there's a bit of a breeze and with the wide-open view, she feels that she can breathe properly again. Her gaze follows the valley down to the river and it strikes her that she hasn't been down there in ages. When they first moved, she and Max talked about trying paddleboarding or kayaking down there some weekend. But some weekend became never.

Another message comes in from Max.

OK. I'm sorry again how things ended. But I hope one day you'll be able to be happy for me that I found someone who actually wants to be with me and have a life outside of work.

'Fuck!' she shouts to the countryside, startling a cluster of crows, who leap suddenly off the telephone line above her head.

There are many things she wants to type back in reply. But instead she stuffs her phone into her pocket and grabs her helmet and bag, leaving the motorbike tucked behind a tree out of sight of the road. She strides off through the field with purpose, in the direction of the river.

CHAPTER 11

Phoebe is clearly not the only one who has come down to the river in search of something today. She has found a quiet spot in the meadow a little way away from the groups sitting on blankets either warming up after a dip or getting changed into their swimwear.

A couple of customers are gathered outside the royal-blue canal boat which has the words *The Kingfisher Café and Book Barge* written in swirling letters. A man dressed in corduroy trousers and a tweed waistcoat serves what look like home-made cakes through the hatch. Phoebe spies a glimpse inside the boat, where a small leather armchair sits in front of walls of bookshelves. On the riverbank nearby are several wooden crates filled with books and a few people browse contentedly, picking up copies here and there.

'Do you fancy joining us?' The voice makes Phoebe jump, turning in the direction of a woman in her fifties who is standing nearby, dressed in a navy swimming costume with a pink swimming hat on her head. At her side are a couple of younger women, one blonde and curly-haired and looking to be in her mid-twenties, and a red-headed teenager who wraps her arms around her chest as if she wants to fold in on herself and disappear.

'Sorry, I didn't mean to startle you,' says the older woman. 'You were just looking at the water so intently. You look like you could do with a swim, if you don't mind me saying.'

'Is it that obvious?'

'Well, I don't mean to be rude, but I've attended funerals that are cheerier than your expression.'

Despite everything, Phoebe snorts with laughter.

'I guess you might be right.'

'Not been your week?' the older woman asks.

Not been my year, Phoebe feels like replying, but she stops herself at the last minute. Her problems are nothing compared to what most of her patients have to deal with every day.

'Ah, it's all right really. Pretty gorgeous here, isn't it?' She looks around, taking it all in.

'It's my favourite place in the world,' says the older woman in reply.

'A swim in the river always makes everything better,' chips in the younger woman with the curly blonde hair.

Phoebe isn't sure that submerging herself in water is going to solve her problems, but the water does look pretty inviting as it glitters in the morning sun.

'It sounds tempting, but I don't have any swimming things with me.'

71

'That's OK,' replies the older woman, unfazed. 'There's a lost-property box you can borrow from. There's always plenty in there. I'm Sandra, by the way. And this is Jazz, and Hester.' Hester nods in reply and Jazz waves enthusiastically.

'Hey! I love your tattoos. What does that one say?' Jazz asks. She points at the words that wind their way around Phoebe's wrist, just below the delicate string of daisies and sunflowers that wrap up her forearm.

'*This too shall pass*,' Phoebe replies, touching a finger sub-consciously to the words. Her dad's favourite saying. As she thinks of him, she experiences a stab of guilt. Her mum and nan. She was supposed to call them back yesterday. She'll ring them later, but calling them means having to tell them about Max and she isn't sure she feels ready for that yet. 'My name's Phoebe, by the way. Thanks for taking me under your wing.'

'That's all right. We've all been where you've been, standing on the edge, not sure about getting in. But it's worth it – you'll see. Here, this one looks like it will fit you.' Sandra flings a costume in Phoebe's direction. Next, a towel lands at her feet in the grass. Without letting herself overthink it, she starts wriggling out of her clothes.

It's been a long time since she last wore a swimming cos-tume and for a moment she grips the towel around herself, self-conscious about the way the borrowed costume hugs her curves. But fuck it. It's just a body. She drops the towel and forces herself to push her shoulders back, twisting her hair up into a bun on the top of her head.

'What do you think? I think it may be a little ... small?'

The suit fits OK around the hips, but it has a plunging

neckline that feels more fitting for sunning yourself in St Tropez than splashing about in the river. *Jesus*, Phoebe thinks as she glances down, *there's cleavage and then there's just plain and simple indecency.*

'If you've got it, and all that ...' says Jazz.

Sandra is more blunt. 'You look absolutely fabulous, dear. I wish I had a rack like that. Mine have been like raisins ever since I had my darling children.'

Hester's face has turned scarlet and she shakes her head in mortification as the other women laugh.

'Thanks, Sandra. I haven't swum in ages, but at least if I get stuck, I've got my own flotation devices.'

Once they've all stopped giggling, they make their way down towards the water, which, on closer inspection, looks decidedly murky. There are twigs and leaves on the surface and ...

'Is that a fish?' she squeaks.

'Well, I doubt it's a shark,' says Sandra.

'Are river sharks not a thing?'

'Well, if they are, we'll be the ones to discover a whole new species, and wouldn't that be exciting? They might even name it after us!'

'Stop teasing, Sandra,' says Jazz as she eases herself into the water, letting out loud puffs of air as she launches herself into the cold.

Hester is already in, having slipped in gracefully. Sandra runs in with her arms stretched wide, water splashing every-where.

'Are you coming in?' she calls from the middle of the river, where she is now treading water, a wide smile on her face.

'Come on, you don't want to miss out, I promise,' calls Jazz.

Phoebe thinks about all the things she has missed out on because of her dedication to her work, her inability to find a balance, all the missed dinners and holidays and now her relationship too. She thinks back to the message she received earlier from Max. *I hope one day you'll be able to be happy for me that I found someone who actually wants to be with me and have a life outside of work.*

Well, maybe Max was wrong about her. She's not at work now, is she? She's going swimming in a river with a bunch of strangers. She *does* have a life.

'I'm coming!' she yells as she throws herself into the water with a roar.

CHAPTER 12

It has only just turned 8 a.m. but the Cosy Corner is already busy. Kate pauses outside, Rosie snuggled up in a sling on her chest. Looking through the windows, she's suddenly glad about her decision not to bring the pram. It would have been a nightmare having to manoeuvre her way through all the tables and chairs inside the little café, which, as the name suggests, is rather cosy. She still hasn't got quite used to pushing it and often bumps it into things.

Before opening the door, she types a quick message in her group chat with her mum and sister. The group is still called the Mathews Girls, even though Erin took Mark's surname when they married and Kate decided to double-barrel hers. She still thinks of the three of them as the Mathews Girls, though.

Look! I took your advice! I feel like a kid turning up on the first day of school. But I'm sure it will be fun. Thanks for giving me the push I needed xx

She sends a photo looking in through the window at the comfy chairs, bookshelves and display heaving with cakes.

Erin replies immediately. **Hurrah! Good luck, sis, I'm sure it will be great xx**

Kate pauses in case her mum is going to reply too – she's usually pretty quick – but when nothing comes through, she returns her phone to her pocket and pushes open the café door. The group she is looking for are immediately recognisable by the platoon of prams.

Once she's ordered at the counter, the women in the group look up and smile warmly, beckoning her over without her needing to say she is here for their group.

'Is this the Tired Mums Club?'

'Do you need to ask?' laughs one woman, gesturing to her large coffee cup. 'This coffee has three shots in it.'

The women are dressed in an array of tracksuits, leggings and jeans that Kate suspects hold secret elastic waistbands just like hers. There are messy buns and tired smiles, white patches on shoulders, large cups of coffee and plates piled with baked goods.

Even if it took the well-meaning interference of her mother to get her here, Kate is suddenly glad that she came.

'Welcome,' the woman adds. 'It's always nice to see a new face. I hope you don't mind that we meet pretty early, but we've all been up for hours already, right?'

Kate can hear the exhaustion behind the woman's laugh and immediately feels at ease. After months of feeling as if she's existing in a different time zone to her friends who don't have children, here are women who also know what it's like to begin

76

their day in the early hours. For the day never to really end, in fact.

'So, what's your name?'

'Kate,' she replies as she lowers herself into a chair. It's Rosie's first time in a café and she looks a little startled as she gazes about, taking it all in. After three months spent mostly on the sofa, Kate feels the same way.

The woman next to her holds her own baby up in front of her chest, lifting up one of his hands as though he's waving. 'Hello, Kate,' she says in an icing-sugar-sweet voice directed at Rosie. 'I'm Theo.'

'This is Jacob,' says the woman to her right, smiling and placing her hand protectively on the head of her baby, who is dressed in blue dungarees and a yellow T-shirt.

Before Kate can chip in, the other mothers introduce their babies; there's Mabel (big blue eyes, snotty nose), Jackson (mop of black hair, sticky-out ears) and Charlie and Ivy (twins). The babies are all bigger and older than Rosie, but Kate has no idea how old exactly. Surely she should *know* these things now she's a mother?

'Um, sorry. My baby's actually called Rosie. I'm Kate. I didn't realise we were doing baby introductions first.'

'Oh, that's OK!' says Theo's mum brightly. 'It's nice to meet you, Kate, welcome to our group. I'm Lexi. Most of us met through our NCT class, but we decided to open it up to who-ever wants to come along. How old is little Rosie?'

'Three months.'

Kate wonders if the other women are going to introduce

themselves, but it seems that the moment for name-sharing has passed.

'Oh!' lets out Mabel's mum further down the table and Kate watches her go gooey, holding her own older baby a little tighter to her. 'So, you're still in the lovely newborn bubble. I'd give anything to have that time again.'

'I miss it too,' says Jackson's mum. 'Although I don't miss the lack of sleep. How is Theo sleeping now, by the way, Lexi? Has the sleep training worked?'

Lexi sighs and begins to talk in detail about the sleep training plan, before the conversation moves seamlessly onto an update about the babies' bowel movements. Kate wonders how their children would feel if they knew the way their mothers are sharing the most intimate details of their lives like this. And yet she understands it too. That need to talk about the things that so consume every waking (and half-waking) moment but that feel too dull or too desperate to share with anyone else. A desire to look around and anxiously check, *Am I doing this right*?

Kate sways more vigorously as Rosie starts to grizzle. With one hand, she devours a millionaire shortbread, crumbs raining down on Rosie's hair, which Kate brushes away surreptitiously. As she listens to the other women's stories about teething and nappy rash, a pressure builds inside her until she feels as though she's going to burst.

'Do you ever feel like you might have made a huge mistake?'

Frowns dart across faces and Kate's cheeks grow hot with embarrassment. Oh. She must have said the words out loud. She knows immediately that what she's just said is awful, the one thing you're never supposed to think, let alone actually *say*, once you become a mother.

Lexi frowns, tilting her head slightly. 'What do you mean? Like when you realise you've bought the wrong size nappies or have done the poppers on the Babygro up wrong? I accidentally poured orange juice on my Weetabix the other day, I was so exhausted!'

The other mothers look on expectantly, waiting for Kate's reply. She thought that coming here would help her feel less alone, but these women clearly don't know what she's talking about. And she immediately knows why. *Because they are good mothers,* says the voice in her head, the voice that has been talking to her incessantly over these past few months.

'Yeah, just like that.'

'Don't worry,' says Mabel's mother kindly, resting a hand on the table close to Kate's. 'We're only human. We're bound to make tons of little mistakes.'

'I am loving being a mum, though,' adds Charlie and Ivy's mum, expertly balancing Ivy on her chest as she rocks Charlie in the pram. 'I know it's hard work, especially with twins, but I could just sit and stare at them both for hours.'

The expressions of the other women instantly change. Tired faces grow soft and smiley, eyes glisten and turn to look down at their squishy babies.

'Oh, I'm the same with Mabel. I spend so long trying to get her to go to sleep, but then as soon as she's down, I miss her. I end each day by scrolling through photos of her, I just can't help it.'

'Yes!' chips in Lexi. 'It's like *please can I have a break* but

79

also *I can't bear to be apart from you for a second because I love you so much.'*

'Although,' says Jackson's mum with a wry smile, 'I do miss my old body. I'd love to get back to running one day, but right now I can't imagine it. Even standing up too quickly makes me need a wee.'

'Oh God, yes. I wince every time I see a trampoline,' adds Lexi.

'Lexi, I don't think we've ever heard your birth story?' asks Mabel's mother and the others tilt their heads in interest.

'Mine wasn't too bad,' she replies cheerily. 'Twenty-hour labour and she was born in the pool. I did tear, though.'

'Who didn't?'

The others laugh.

'I wish I could have given birth in the pool,' says Mabel's mum wistfully.

'Yours was a C-section, wasn't it?' asks Lexi.

'Yep. Emergency. Pretty awful, to be honest, but we're all safe now, so that's all that matters, isn't it?'

Kate stands up so suddenly that her mug spills half its contents into its saucer on the table and Rosie begins to cry. The others look up in surprise.

'Are you OK, Kate?'

'Sorry, dirty nappy,' she says, making a show of sniffing Rosie. 'I better go.'

'There are changing facilities here,' says Lexi, pointing towards the corner. 'Pretty good ones too, it's why we meet here. I can help if you like?'

'It's OK, thanks, I've got to go anyway,' she says as she grabs her bag. She is beginning to sweat, her heart rate rising. Rosie's cries grow louder and she notices a few of the other groups in the café turning in her direction. She does her best to keep her head down.

'Oh, OK, well, thanks for coming and see you again soon, I hope!' Lexi calls after her.

Kate waves distractedly as she heads rapidly for the door. But she already knows she won't be coming back.

Outside, she takes deep inhales, counting to ten in her head like her former therapist taught her. She has worked so hard on learning to control the panic that used to control *her*. But now she can feel it wrapping its tentacles around her and tightening its grip.

With her arms wrapped around Rosie's back in the sling, she sets off quickly through the village. She isn't quite sure where she is headed, just that she needs to get away from the café as quickly as possible.

It's only when Kate reaches the familiar gate that she realises where her feet have taken her. The river might have seemed magical in the misty early mornings, but now the water glitters in the sunshine. Everything appears in high contrast; the long grass in the meadow a vibrant green shot with pops of colourful buttercups, poppies and pink and white clover.

Kate makes her way over to the bank. An older woman lies on her back in the river, arms and legs spread in a starfish shape as she floats, grey hair spreading out around her. Another woman swims a head-up breaststroke in the opposite direction and, as she passes by, a dragonfly flits above her head, its wings flapping an iridescent green.

The desire to jump in is suddenly like a physical ache that spreads through Kate's whole body. The water is tantalisingly close now. She can see it lapping against the reeds. If she could just get in the water, she knows she would feel better.

But a little noise from inside the sling reminds her that while the water might be right there, she can't dive in.

Tears of frustration prick at her eyes. *If Rosie weren't here ...* But even as she thinks it, she hates herself for it. It's the kind of thought she feels certain the other women at the Tired Mums Club never have, those mothers who clutched their babies so tightly.

Kate turns away from the water, blinking back tears of frustration and shame. But just as she is about to leave, her eyes fall on a noticeboard that she hadn't spotted before. It is dotted with flyers and posters, some printed but most handwritten. Notices about lost swimwear, the number of someone offering kayaking lessons and, in the centre, an official-looking laminated poster that catches Kate's attention with its bold, typed font.

The Farleigh-on-Avon River Swimming, Bathing and Recreational Water-Based Activities Club (FoARSBRWAC) invite you to join us every day at 8.00 a.m.

Kate reads the notice twice. Even after a second reading, she isn't entirely sure what the group is exactly for. River swimming she understands, but what exactly constitutes a 'water-based activity'? There isn't any information to help her, other than the time that they meet.

There's something about it that intrigues her, though. When she set out this morning to join the Tired Mums Club she had hoped to find a sense of community, but she left the café feeling more alone than ever. She misses Emma and Leonie and the buzz of her job at the newspaper. They'd replied late last night, apologising for being out of touch, but hadn't told her more about the story they must be working on, and Kate had the sense of being on the outside, not right in the middle with them where she used to be.

She misses the people she swam with every morning at the lido too, even if she didn't know all their names. Most of all, Kate misses Rosemary. Her old friend wouldn't expect Kate to explain all the complex feelings that have been crowding her brain recently, jostling about for space. She'd just swim with her, then suggest they share a slice of cake together in the café afterwards.

The Farleigh-on-Avon River Swimming, Bathing and Recreational Water-Based Activities Club sounds intimidatingly official. Nothing like the casual, friendly swims she used to share with Rosemary and her other swimming friends. And besides, the grizzling coming from inside the carrier on her chest is a stark reminder of all her responsibilities. She couldn't join a swimming club when Rosie is so reliant on her.

But she takes a photo of the sign anyway.

As she's about to put her phone away, it buzzes with a new notification in the Mathews Girls group chat.

Erin: How was the Tired Mums Club, Kate? Hope you made some new friends! Xx

There's still no response from her mum. It's not like her to not reply, but she hardly blames her. Kate has definitely become increasingly active in their group recently, sending endless photos of Rosie and baby-related questions, often when she's nap-trapped on the sofa and her friends are busy working so she doesn't have anyone else to talk to. She wouldn't blame her mum if she'd decided to mute the group for a while, just to take a breather. God, are even her own family becoming sick of her? No wonder she didn't fit in with the mum and baby group.

She can sense the eagerness in her sister's message – and maybe, behind it, the hope that in Kate making some new friends she might stop relying so heavily on her family.

Everyone was really nice and welcoming, she types back. **Thanks for persuading me to go! Xx**

It isn't technically a lie. The other mums *were* nice. Kate just didn't feel as though she belonged.

CHAPTER 13

The pounding in Phoebe's head has eased to a background ache and she feels more awake than she has in a long time, as if the water has given her a jolt of caffeine.

'I can see why you come here,' she says to the other women as they drift downstream together, leaves and petals floating on the surface of the water alongside them. 'This is fantastic.' From their position in the water, Phoebe can see the riverbank up close, spotting the violets and wild garlic dotted about in the tangle of brambles. Reeds and puffs of cow parsley wave slightly back and forth in the breeze.

'I think I might be addicted,' says Sandra as she rolls onto her back for a moment and floats, head tilted towards the sky.

'I can think of worse addictions.'

At first, the water had felt bitingly cold, despite the warmth in the morning sun. But after a few vigorous strokes of breast-stroke, she had got used to the temperature, her breathing returning to normal and her body relaxing. It appears to have had the same effect on the other women too. Even Hester, who had been so tense and shy on dry land, seems softer, the frown slipping away from her face.

Phoebe follows Sandra's lead and twists onto her back, the four of them floating and looking up at the trees.

Phoebe can spot patches of blue sky and white clouds through gaps in the leaves.

'Is it just me, or does that cloud look like a penis?' she says suddenly, breaking the silence and making the other women laugh.

'Hey, I was just thinking it looked like a cute rabbit,' says Jazz. 'You've ruined it for me now!'

What would Max think if she could see her now? Not just having skipped her usual morning paperwork but swimming and laughing in a river with strangers. Not that she wants to think about Max right now.

A loud noise from upstream makes the women turn to look behind them. *Thwack. Swoosh. Thwack. Swoosh.* The sound grows louder and, as it does, the stillness of the river is disturbed, ripples spreading in all directions. Birds scatter from the surrounding trees in a flurry of feathers.

'Quick, swim to the side!' shouts Sandra.

A narrow rowing boat appears around the corner, a bent figure facing the other direction, muscled arms firmly pulling the oars. The rower lets out grunts of exertion as the boat zips along the water, heading straight towards them. Panicked, Phoebe does her best to manoeuvre herself out of the way, but it's been years since she last swam and she feels as though her arms are dragging through honey.

'Hey!' cries the lifeguard, standing up from her chair and blowing her whistle. 'Swimmers in the water!'

The rower twists to look over his shoulder, his eyebrows rising in surprise. By now, Sandra and the others have made it over towards the reeds and out of the way, but Phoebe is still directly in the path of the boat. 'Watch out!' the rower shouts back in a deep, slightly accented voice, digging the oars down into the water and sending droplets everywhere.

'Shit!' She is trying to swim but barely getting anywhere, the current that she'd hardly noticed before now pushing her backwards. 'I'm not moving! Why am I not moving?' She kicks harder.

'Here, take my hand,' shouts Sandra, who has grabbed hold of a tree branch to anchor herself and is reaching out her arm. Phoebe grabs her hand and is pulled out of the way just in time.

The boat slows, spray erupting in the air.

'You need to be more careful!' says the lifeguard crossly. 'This is a well-known swimming spot. Rowers and kayakers are welcome, but you must be careful, there could have been a serious accident.'

Now that Phoebe is out of the way of the boat, she catches her breath, readjusting her swimsuit so she's not flashing anyone. People talk about not wanting to be found dead in dirty underwear, but the thought of her body being dragged up onto the riverbank in a swimsuit that makes her look like she's a wannabe auditioning for a remake of *Baywatch* is frankly just as chilling.

The streamlined boat has stopped now, the oars resting

limply in the water. The rower checks his watch, pressing a button that looks like some sort of timer before looking up.

Up close, the man looks younger than Phoebe initially thought, perhaps a little older than her, with just a few flecks of grey scattered about his dark brown hair, which is short at the sides but thick and curly on top, damp with either sweat or river water. He's dressed in skintight Lycra and there's a fine glimmer of sweat glistening on his tanned forehead, which is currently creased into a frown. His shoulders are broad, but the rest of his physique is slim, which is just as well because the boat is incredibly narrow. Phoebe can't imagine she'd fit inside, certainly not without capsizing it.

'Other people use this river too, you know,' snaps Sandra, her hand still wrapped protectively around Phoebe's arm.

The rower looks around as though only just taking in his surroundings. His chest rises and falls rapidly.

'Sorry.' But he doesn't sound at all sorry.

'Well, next time be more careful,' says the lifeguard. 'There's space for all of us here at the river if everyone is considerate.'

The rower glances down at his watch again. Sandra lets go of Phoebe's arm and together they swim around the boat and back towards the bank. Once they are out of the way, the rower picks up his oars, digging them smoothly into the water. In a few strokes, he has disappeared around the river bend and the water is still again.

'Are you OK, Phoebe?' asks Jazz, Hester watching on with a concerned expression.

'Yeah, I'm fine thanks,' she replies, summoning a smile despite her still-racing pulse. 'No limbs lost. Only my dignity, and who needs that, eh? I think I lost that as soon as I wrestled myself into this bloody swimsuit.'

'Right, I think that's enough excitement for one morning,' says Sandra, heading up the bank, Phoebe and the others following behind.

Once they're on dry land, Phoebe rubs herself vigorously with the towel to warm up.

'Oh wow, I hadn't noticed your other tattoos, I thought they were just on your arms,' says Jazz as she pulls a large hooded towel over her head.

'Yeah, I might run out of space soon,' Phoebe laughs, glancing down at her bare legs. They are absolutely covered in tattoos, mostly delicate line drawings of plants and flowers. 'I know they're not to everyone's taste, but I love them.' Getting a new tattoo gives her a similar rush to a ride on her motorbike. When so much of her life feels heavy, there's a lightness to decorating her skin just for the joy and beauty of it. And maybe there's something about the pain of it too. She got one of her tattoos – a rose on her left ankle – when Phoebe first lost a patient to suicide. Roses were Laura's favourite flower. She was twenty-two.

When she applied for her first nursing job, she'd been nervous that having so many visible tattoos might put off an employer but when she'd gently raised it in the interview, the head nurse hadn't flinched. 'Does having tattoos impact your ability to take blood and fit cannulas?'

'Um, no,' Phoebe had replied.

'Then I don't give two hoots about your tattoos.'

It's nice to think that some attitudes have changed. She's

pretty certain that the response might have been different a few years ago.

'I've always wanted to get one,' says Jazz hesitantly. 'But it feels like a big commitment ...'

'If you want one, you should just go for it. Life's too short not to.'

Phoebe's job has taught her that much.

'You'd look great with a tattoo,' she adds and Jazz smiles warmly.

Thinking about work makes Phoebe dig quickly for her phone in her pile of clothes, checking the time. Shit. She's running late.

'God, I better go,' she says, pulling her jeans onto her still-damp legs.

'But you'll miss out on the best part of these swims,' says Sandra as she tugs down her swimming costume, not seeming to care one bit about flashing everyone at the river, and then pulls on her bra.

'And what's that?'

Hester points to the Kingfisher Café and Book Barge. 'They do a great cup of tea.'

'I'd love to, but I've really got to get to work.'

She realises suddenly that she hasn't even found out what these three women do, or told them about her job. Hester looks like she might be still at school, but what about the others? In the water, it felt as though their outside lives didn't matter. As she swam, she wasn't a nurse, she was just Phoebe.

'OK, but we'll see you again soon, I hope?' says Sandra.

Phoebe grabs her helmet and clips her feet back into her

boots, her mind already racing with the day's appointments and her worries for each of her patients. It feels as though the swim in the river was a brief holiday and she has come crashing back to reality. Her first appointment of the day is with a new patient. She absolutely can't be late.

'Sounds great!' she says brightly. 'It was so nice to meet you all and thanks again for getting me in the water!' But even as she says it, she isn't sure if she'll really make it back. As much as she enjoyed the swim, she can't escape the reality of her responsibilities. She might have set them down on the riverbank for a while, but they are back again now, weighing heavily on her shoulders.

She waves a hasty goodbye and then races off across the meadow.

As soon as she climbs onto her motorbike and speeds off in the direction of her first patient, she leaves Just Phoebe behind, ready to become Nurse Harrison again.

CHAPTER 14

'How was the mum and baby group?' Jay asks when Kate arrives home, having taken the long route back to the village along the river path. The walk has sent Rosie to sleep and her arms and legs dangle limply out of the sides of the carrier.

'Not great,' replies Kate, struggling to kick off her shoes without disturbing Rosie. 'It was kind of weird – all the other mums introduced their babies but not themselves.'

'Hmm, that does sound weird.'

'It was as though they'd forgotten they existed too and it made me feel pretty awkward when I went right ahead and said my own name. They were all perfectly nice, but it just didn't feel like my crowd.'

'I'm sorry it wasn't what you were hoping for. I thought it might be a nice chance to make some new friends.'

'Yeah, me too.'

'I'm sure there will be other groups you could try, though.'

Kate knows he means mum and baby groups – maybe a music class or baby sign language or something – but all she can think about is the poster advertising the river swimming club.

'Hmm, maybe ...'

'I know you miss your friends in London, but you will settle in here. You just need to give it time.'

'I know. And I'm sorry, I know it was me who persuaded you to move here with me.'

It's something she thinks about all the time. On days when she misses London so badly it's like a toothache, she sharply reminds herself that she chose this. All of it.

'Hey, I know I was reluctant at first, but we made this decision together. And I'm loving having my studio to work on, I'm really excited about how it's coming together. We haven't been here for long. It will start feeling like home soon.'

'I'm sure you're right.'

It's only once her shoes are off and she's hung her jacket on the coat rack that she notices the pile of Jay's camera bags in the hallway.

'Oh, it's your shoot today. I'd forgotten.'

'Yeah, I wanted to wait until you got back so I could say goodbye, but I should really get going now. I'll be back around seven. Are you sure you're going to be OK on your own?'

'I'll be fine,' Kate replies with a forced smile. 'I had to do this eventually.'

Jay reaches for his bags but stops before picking them up, glancing over at Kate with a serious expression on his face. 'I don't want to go. I don't want to leave you both.' His voice sounds strained and it hits Kate that perhaps Jay has been dreading this day just as much as she has. She can't help but think that if she were in his position, she'd be running out that door.

'Everything's going to be fine, honestly,' she says, as much to herself as to him. 'I'm going to take Rosie to the supermarket – we're nearly out of nappies and bread. And chocolate.'

'Essential items, then.'

'Exactly. Now you really should go, otherwise you'll miss your train.'

'OK. I love you, both of you.'

He lingers for longer in their kiss than Kate was expecting. She tenses as his lips soften open. What is wrong with her? She used to love nothing more than kissing him, but recently her skin has prickled every time he has reached out to touch her. After what feels like a reasonable amount of time, she lets herself pull away. If Jay notices her unease, then he does his best to hide it.

'OK then, sweetie,' he says, leaning to kiss Rosie's cheek. 'You look after your mum. I'll miss you, both of you.'

As soon as the door closes behind Jay, Rosie opens her eyes and begins to cry. Loudly. The walls of the cottage suddenly feel as though they're pressing in on her and Kate finds herself thinking back to the freedom and fresh air of the river.

'Come on, let's get you fed and go out and get the things we need,' she says in a sing-song voice.

One feed and two nappy changes later, Kate is bundling Rosie into the car seat. Once Rosie is settled, a striped hat hand-knitted by Hope on her head, Kate takes a quick photo and sends it to Jay. His reply comes immediately.

Ahh, our girl, look at her! On the train safely. Good luck and have a good day. I love you xx

When Kate arrives at the supermarket car park, she hesitates for a moment before pulling into a parent and child bay, feeling a bit like a fraud as she does so, despite the baby grizzling in the back seat.

'Right. How do we get this car seat out then?'

She tries one of the buttons, but nothing happens. There's another on the other side, but however much pushing and wiggling she tries, the seat doesn't shift. Grabbing the handle on the top does nothing either. Rosie looks up at her with wide, questioning eyes.

'It's OK, sweetie. I just need to figure this out ...'

But the harder she tries, the more determinedly the car seat remains fixed in the back. Her skin begins to prickle. Could she simply carry Rosie in her arms around the store? But then how would she push the trolley?

'I suppose I could leave you in the car for a minute, I won't be long ...' But as soon as she thinks it, she shakes herself. 'No, of course not.'

It's only the start of her first day alone with her daughter and already Kate wishes Jay was here. Why can't she just *do* these things?

'Come on, you bastard!' she shouts, giving the seat another vigorous wiggle.

A passing shopper turns in her direction with a frown, glancing from Kate to Rosie and back again.

'I didn't mean …' she begins, but the woman shakes her head and continues pushing her trolley at a brisk pace.

Finally, a specific push of the button and a wiggle of the handle manages to get the car seat free. 'Right! Let's go get the things we need.'

There are only a few items on Kate's shopping list, but it takes longer than she had expected, because every few minutes, she is stopped by someone wanting to peer and coo into the trolley and ask Kate for a name (the baby's, not hers, of course). They are usually older and always smiling, the good intentions audible in the softness of their voices.

They grow up so fast. Just you wait until they're walking/ talking/a teenager … And the most common of them all, the phrase that is the mantra of well-meaning strangers to new mothers everywhere: *cherish every moment*. It's a message that was also written in so many of the cards that she was sent when Rosie was born. The kindest of words that still manage to stab her right in the heart.

As each new person stops her, Kate smiles and grits her teeth, nodding politely.

By the time she has selected nappies, a few ready meals and an emergency stash of chocolate, she is exhausted. Rosie is clearly tired from the attention too as she has fallen asleep, her eyelids flickering gently. Kate stands in the bread aisle in front of the wall of plastic-packaged loaves, overwhelmed by the selection. When did buying bread become so difficult?

One of the things she grew to love the most about London was the endless choice, all the foods she could eat and places she could go, but right now she doesn't want to have to decide between white and wholemeal or half-and-half, regular or thick-sliced. She just wants someone to tell her what to buy. And perhaps how on earth to be a good mother, too.

'Oh, she's lovely,' comes a voice at her side and Kate braces herself as she looks up to see a woman a little older than her peering at Rosie with a faint smile on her face.

'Thanks.' She just has to pick a loaf and then she can get out of here.

'How old is she?'

'Three months.' Kate doesn't mean to be short, but she really needs to get home. She never thought that a quick food shop could feel so overwhelming.

'Oh wow, so very new still then,' replies the woman with a smile. 'My own daughter is nearly ten. I can't believe how quickly it's gone.'

Kate nods silently, bracing herself for the woman to tell her that she must – she absolutely must – savour every single second of it. It doesn't matter that she hasn't slept for more than a two-hour stretch in three months or that many of the seconds she should be savouring are spent changing nappies or listening to her baby screaming and having no idea what to do about it. None of that matters. If she is not enjoying it, *cherishing* it, then she is doing it all wrong.

But, to her surprise, the woman doesn't say any of that. Instead, she tilts her head slightly. 'Of course, it doesn't feel quick at the time, does it? The days can feel absolutely bloody endless.'

'I …' Kate is so startled that it takes her a moment to think of what to say. She glances at the woman more closely this time.

Her expression is sympathetic and thoughtful and makes her feel she can open up a little. 'They can sometimes,' she admits.

'God, I remember that early bit so well. It's so, so hard, but everyone tells you how much you should be enjoying it, don't they? But what are you actually supposed to enjoy? Having a newborn is like having a tiny dictator ruling your life – a cute one, sure, but still. It's absolutely relentless. You're amazing to be out and about, I don't think I left the house for months. And when I did, I was definitely still in my pyjamas.'

'I mean, I wouldn't exactly call this a chic outfit,' Kate replies, gesturing at her tracksuit bottoms and top with its pale sick stain on one shoulder. The woman laughs slightly, but in a way that doesn't make Kate feel as though she's in any way a joke.

'So, how are you doing?' the woman says more seriously now, looking at Kate intently. As she does, Kate realises that although the woman glanced in at Rosie to begin with, for the rest of the time her eyes have been on her. Kate. For the first time since arriving in the shop, she feels seen. As though she's been a ghost but has finally found someone who can see the woman who used to exist and maybe still does.

'It's hard,' she says carefully. 'It's been really hard.'

A lump expands in her throat as she finally says aloud the words she has been wanting to say to her husband and family ever since Rosie's birth. She has tried several times, buoying herself up to start the conversation but always losing confidence at the last minute, reminded of all the messages from all those well-meaning people telling her how happy she must be. Of her sister's words when Kate told her she was pregnant, reminding her of how lucky she is.

The woman nods in understanding. 'And I bet that's an understatement, right?'

Kate blinks rapidly.

'I didn't think it would be like this,' she says after a moment's pause. She knows that the obvious question is, *what did she think it would be like*? Was she naïve to expect motherhood to be any less overwhelming? But then she thinks back to the stacks of books she read and the swathe of working mothers she followed on Instagram when she found out she was pregnant. Journalists like her who made the juggle of work and family life look chaotic but ultimately rewarding. Over recent months, she's found herself going back to their accounts, obsessively trying to find something of her own experience in the photos, but seeing nothing she can relate to in the tired but smiling faces and tastefully decorated nurseries. She has tried to recall conversations with her own mum and sister too, but they had both talked so glowingly about motherhood. Yes, they warned her, she would be tired. But she would be so happy too.

'I remember that feeling,' replies the woman in the supermarket, nodding knowingly. 'I felt like I had been sold a lie, to begin with. But I promise you, it gets so much better. I know that might not help right now, but it gets so, so much better. Anyway, sorry, I didn't mean to ambush you, especially when you've got enough on your plate. I'll leave you to it.' The woman steps away, but then pauses, reaching out a hand and resting it for a second on Kate's arm. 'Don't forget to look after yourself. It can feel hard, selfish even. But you deserve to do things that are for you, not just for her.' She smiles again and then turns away before Kate has time to say anything in reply. She is left standing alone with her baby in the aisle of the supermarket, holding onto the stranger's words like a lifeline that is keeping her afloat.

It's only when she arrives home later that she realises she forgot to buy any bread.

CHAPTER 15

As Phoebe's motorbike pulls up on the gravel turning circle outside the large Georgian house, she double-checks she has the right address. *1 Magnolia Street.* An elegant number 1 is carved into the stone façade, where wisteria climbs its way around the enormous sash windows. She parks alongside a gleaming white Land Rover, taking in the imposing building in front of her.

When it comes to her patients, there are certain types she has become familiar with over the years. There are the patients whose lives started badly and never really got any better, drifting from care to temporary housing and in and out of hospital and local police stations. There are many who have been dealing with mental ill health since they were teenagers, people who Phoebe has got to know over the years as they bounce back and forth between independence and hospitalisation.

But then there are also the new patients who join her

caseload having had no known mental health problems until the day they turned up in A & E, having tried to kill themselves with their dead husband's razor.

Mrs Ramsgate is one of those patients. Phoebe pulls out her laptop to quickly check her notes, before slipping it back in her bag and heading towards the front door. As she draws closer, she spots a few signs of disrepair that no one would notice if they were just driving along the street, glancing for a moment at the impressive building. The paintwork on the window frames is peeling and there is a row of withered houseplants visible inside. Phoebe has never been one for houseplants herself. It's enough trying to keep herself and her patients alive.

She knocks on the large brass knocker and steps back slightly to wait.

The door is pulled rapidly open by an incredibly slim woman around Phoebe's age, dressed in tight jeans, a crisp white shirt and a navy gilet. Diamonds sparkle at her ears, her golden blonde hair pulled back from her face with a velvet headband. Her eyebrows rise for a second as she takes Phoebe in, before her expression settles into a tight-lipped frown.

'You must be the gardener, we've been waiting for you. I hope you don't think I'll be paying you for the full three hours.'

Phoebe smiles politely. It's not the first time something like this has happened. 'I'm afraid you wouldn't want me anywhere near your garden. I'm much better at looking after humans than plants. I'm Phoebe, a mental health nurse here to see Mrs Ramsgate.'

'Oh.' The woman's nose wrinkles as if Phoebe is emitting an unpleasant odour. To be fair, she didn't have time to go back

102

home and shower after her morning swim, so there is a chance she does have a slight waft of river to her. But she'd brushed her hair and checked her make-up, reapplying her bright red lipstick to make sure she looked put together and neat and not as though she'd spent the morning on a riverbank.

But Phoebe doesn't think that's the problem.

'You don't look like a nurse.' The woman casts her eyes up and down, taking in Phoebe's motorcycle boots, jeans, leather jacket and the helmet under her arm, her bag in the other. Just wait till the jacket comes off and she sees the tattoos.

'Here's my identification,' Phoebe says, tugging a lanyard with her photo and details out from inside her jacket to show it to the woman, who barely glances down. 'Or I could demonstrate if you'd like? I'm extremely quick at finding veins for blood tests if you'd like to give me your arm?'

The woman's eyebrows raise again and Phoebe immediately regrets the joke. Sometimes they can be a way of breaking the ice, but this woman appears to be carved out of an iceberg.

'Why aren't you wearing scrubs?' she asks, her nose wrinkling again.

'We tend not to wear them in my line of work. We find it can help the people we work with if we don't look too formal. Some of our patients are a little wary of health professionals. Can I come in? Is Mrs Ramsgate inside?'

'Of course, sorry,' says the woman, composing herself and holding the door open.

Phoebe follows her through into a large tiled foyer, a sweeping staircase leading upstairs. All the furniture looks antique and there are framed portraits on the walls, but the surfaces are dusty, a stack of mail teetering on a table in the middle of the room. Phoebe catches a glimpse through to what looks like a very masculine study, noting the empty chair and the jacket that still hangs there.

There's an old-fashioned telephone seat next to the door and Phoebe perches there to take off her clunky boots. She puts down her helmet and takes off her leather jacket too, hanging it neatly on the back of the chair.

'Oh, you don't have to do that,' the woman says, glancing down at Phoebe's socked feet. She went for rainbow stripes today. 'It's not exactly tidy in here …' Embarrassment tinges her voice.

'That's OK. It's still your home. Or your … mother's, maybe?'

'Yes, sorry. I'm Arabella.' She reaches a hand up to smooth an invisible stray hair. 'Mum's upstairs. I've been staying ever since …' Her voice catches, cracking slightly. Her welcome might have been less than warm, but Phoebe immediately feels sorry for her. Her face might be smoothed with what looks like incredibly expensive foundation, but Phoebe can still see the dark shadows beneath her eyes. And a glance at her hands shows that her manicured fingernails are bitten, the skin around her cuticles red and sore. She's learnt over the years to look closely for certain signs, not just in her patients, but in their loved ones too. If they're lucky enough to have loved ones to support them.

'Ever since she got back from hospital?' Phoebe finishes gently for her.

Arabella nods silently, her eyes glistening.

'She's very lucky to have you looking out for her,' Phoebe

104

says, placing a hand lightly on Arabella's arm. She flinches at the touch but doesn't move. 'But I'm here to help you now. This all must have been really tough on you.'

All of Arabella's poise and frostiness melts away as she breaks down into tears. Phoebe keeps her hand on her arm, waiting patiently as the emotion spills out. She senses that Arabella doesn't need words right now, just someone to be with her and let her not be OK.

Eventually, Arabella sniffs loudly, wiping her nose with her pristine white sleeve. Phoebe pulls a pack of tissues out of her bag and hands one to Arabella.

'Thanks,' she says with a sniff. 'I know she's been feeling low ever since Daddy died. It's been hard on all of us. But I just never thought she'd do something like this ...' She wraps her arms around herself, her slender frame sinking in on itself.

'It must have been a real shock,' Phoebe says softly. 'But the fact that she has been discharged from hospital is a good thing. It means the doctors there think she isn't feeling like hurting herself anymore.'

Because Phoebe knows that's what Arabella will be thinking. If her mother could attempt something like this once, what's to say she won't do it again? The unfortunate answer is that there are never any guarantees. But Phoebe will do her best to make sure that doesn't happen.

'Why don't you show me through to your mum and then go and have a lie-down? You must be exhausted.'

Arabella nods meekly. 'I haven't really been sleeping. She's upstairs. I've been trying to persuade her to get out into the garden, she and Daddy always used to love spending time there. That's why I called a gardener. I thought if I could spruce things up a bit, maybe I could tempt Mum outside.'

Phoebe follows Arabella up the curving staircase and along the corridor to a large bedroom that faces the garden. Camilla Ramsgate looks tiny beneath the covers of a grand four-poster bed, a patchwork quilt laid across her lap as she leans back against a pile of cushions. The curtains are open, which Phoebe suspects must have been Arabella's doing, but instead of looking out at the trees in the garden, Mrs Ramsgate stares down at her hands, her hair falling slightly in front of her face. There is a threadbare chaise longue beneath the window and Phoebe spots a crumpled sleeping bag there alongside a book.

Arabella catches her looking and says very quietly, 'I haven't wanted to leave her.' Then, more loudly and with a forced jollity to her voice, she says, 'Mummy, Nurse Harrison is here to see you.'

The woman in the bed glances up, her expression vacant.

'Oh,' is all she says. Then she goes back to looking at her hands.

Arabella shoots a look at Phoebe, biting the corner of her thumb.

'It's OK,' Phoebe says quietly to her. 'We'll get to know one another and I'll call you if we need anything, OK?'

Arabella pauses for a moment, watching her mother. Then she nods slightly and slinks off down the corridor, leaving Phoebe and her patient alone.

Despite the size of the room, the atmosphere is oppressive. Phoebe wonders when Mrs Ramsgate last went outside.

'It's nice to meet you, Mrs Ramsgate. Is it all right if I call you Camilla? You can call me Phoebe.' Phoebe takes a small velvet chair from its spot opposite an antique dressing table and drags it over to the bedside.

'Yes, that's fine.' Camilla lets out a sigh as if even saying those few words has taken it out of her.

Phoebe settles herself in the chair, not rushing to say anything else just yet. She has learnt the value of silence over the years.

Camilla glances through the doorway, as if only just noticing that Arabella has left, or was there in the first place.

'I hate how much she worries about me. I know she wants to see me up and about, but I just feel so tired.'

'That might well be a side effect of your medication. And fatigue is a big part of depression.'

'Depression...' Camilla says, as if reading a word in a foreign language aloud for the first time. 'You know my generation doesn't really believe in things like that.'

'It's certainly an attitude I've encountered before,' Phoebe admits.

Camilla twists her pearl earrings between her fingers, the flash of several rings glinting on her hands. As her sleeve slips, Phoebe catches sight of the scars on her left wrist. They have healed nicely, but she knows from past patients that the marks will never disappear completely. They'll always be a part of her.

'I was taught to keep my emotions to myself,' Camilla continues, adjusting the quilt on her lap. 'Strong upper lip and whatnot.'

'Except that doesn't always work, does it?'

'No. Quite.'

Phoebe glances at Camilla's bedside table where a pill bottle and glass of water stand alongside several silver-framed black-and-white photographs of a young couple on their wedding day. Although Camilla might have changed dramatically since then, she is still recognisable in the photographs of her in her white lace wedding dress. Phoebe's attention is drawn particularly to the photograph in the middle, where Camilla's head is turned towards her husband's, looking up at him with a proud smile as he faces the camera, beaming, his face slightly obscured by a blur of confetti.

'Besides,' Phoebe continues, 'I'm not so interested in diagnoses and medical terms like that. For now, I really just want to know how you're feeling. Do you think you could tell me a bit about that?'

Camilla sighs in response, saying nothing.

Phoebe glances at the photos again and decides to try a different approach.

'What was your husband's name?'

For the first time since Phoebe arrived, a smile appears on Camilla's face. She reaches out for the central photograph on the bedside table, lifting it towards the light. 'Edward. My Teddy.'

'You look very in love.'

'We were.' Her eyes grow misty. 'Of course, all couples have their little arguments. And, my goodness, his snoring … But we were in love. Right until the end.'

Phoebe's attention drifts to the table on the other side of the bed. There are a pair of reading glasses folded on top of a copy of a political biography. Propped up beside it is a small, framed photograph, this time of Camilla on her own, perhaps in her twenties, smiling broadly, a rose tucked behind one ear.

It's hard, sometimes, to imagine that there was once laughter and great joy in her patients' lives when she meets them at their rock bottom. Seeing the photographs draws to Phoebe's mind a very different Camilla, a Camilla who perhaps laughed easily and smiled often. Who cheated at Scrabble but whose charm let her always get away with it. Phoebe's hope is that the person in that photograph is still in there somewhere.

'I understand it happened quite suddenly. That must have been a huge shock for you.'

Camilla nods, wiping tears from her sparkling blue eyes. 'Yes. I didn't get the chance to say goodbye. And after that … Well, I just couldn't imagine my life without him. I still can't, really.' She puts the wedding photo down, her hand trembling slightly. Then she takes a deep breath, pushing her hair behind her ears and meeting Phoebe's eye properly for the first time. 'I do *want* to feel better, though. For Arabella more than anything. She's already lost her father …' Her voice trembles again and she stops, unable to continue.

'Well, the fact that you want to feel better is a huge thing. That's the start of things getting better, even if I know it mustn't feel like that right now. What I want to do in our time together is to help you find some things to feel hopeful about again, and to give you some tools to help when those dark feelings descend, as I'm sure they will sometimes. And if those feelings ever get overwhelming, I'm here for you to talk to. I can imagine there's only so much you feel able to tell your daughter about how you're feeling.'

Camilla nods. 'I don't want her to worry about me. But I hate having to be dishonest when she asks if I'm OK.'

'That's understandable. But you can tell me anything, however bad it might seem.'

Another nod.

'One of my first steps is going to be trying to get you out of this room. It's a beautiful room – in fact, it's about the size of my whole flat …' Is Phoebe imagining it or does Camilla smile slightly at that? There's certainly a glimmer of amusement in her eye that gives Phoebe hope. 'But I think it might help to get out and reconnect with some of the things that used to make you happy. What did you love to do before all of this happened?'

The older woman's attention drifts to the window, where the trees sway slightly, bright green leaves dancing against a sky scattered with pale clouds.

'I loved to spend time with my husband.'

Phoebe kicks herself as she sees Camilla closing down again, her lips drawing tightly together. She fell into that one. Perhaps she should have phrased it differently.

'What about things you used to do just for yourself? Can you think of a time you did something for yourself that made you really happy?'

Helping her patients isn't about getting them to live a version of their life that she thinks will make them feel better. It has to come from them. And that can mean all sorts of different things. It might even mean looking after bees, Phoebe thinks to herself, recalling her patient Maude. She still hasn't worked out how to help realise that particular ambition. She files the thought away alongside the many other things on her to-do list.

'I ... I don't know.' Camilla frowns, the question clearly rolling over in her mind. She looks up, meeting Phoebe's eye. 'What would your answer be?'

It takes her by surprise. When *has* she felt truly happy in the past? She expects some memory of her and Max to pop up, bringing with it a stab of pain, but instead, the image that comes to mind is of glittering blue water, warm sun and the feeling of sand between her toes and salt on her lips.

'When I was younger, I used to love swimming in the sea. I grew up in Cornwall, so I basically lived on the beach. Although swimming hasn't been a big part of my life in recent years.'

Or at all. She hasn't had time for swimming. She signed up to a gym with a pool once but ended up never using her membership so cancelled it a few months later. But then there was this morning's impromptu dip. She thinks back to laughing with Sandra, Jazz and Hester and to the soothing feeling of the cool water on her skin. God, it had felt good.

Camilla nods again, a thoughtful expression appearing on her face. 'I started running a few years ago. I wasn't very fast and never went particularly far, but I did enjoy it.'

'There we go,' Phoebe replies enthusiastically. 'That's a great start. Going out for a gentle jog sounds like a brilliant idea.'

'Oh, I don't know. I can't see myself doing that now ...'

Phoebe can sense Camilla retreating inside herself. Shit. She thinks about Arabella and how terrified she clearly is about

111

her mother's well-being, however hard she might have tried to hide it when she first opened the door to the big old house that seems so empty with just the two of them in it.

'It might help you feel more like yourself again,' she tries, tentatively.

But Camilla shakes her head, her eyes filling with tears again. 'I won't ever feel like myself again.'

A silence descends on the grand, sad room. Phoebe runs through all the techniques she could try but for once finds herself struggling to know how to pull Camilla out from her darkness. And then an idea occurs to her.

'How about this. I'll get back to swimming if you get back to running.'

'Really?' Camilla raises an eyebrow, fixing Phoebe with a challenging expression that says she doesn't really believe her. The expression just makes Phoebe feel even more determined. She wants to do something to make Camilla feel that she can trust her. And it strikes her now that maybe she's been something of a hypocrite in the past. How can she expect her patients to follow her advice about exercising, eating well and finding time for the things that help their mental well-being when she doesn't follow her own advice? Is she just a massive fraud?

'Yes, really. Next time I visit, I promise I will have gone for a swim. I'll tell you all about it and you can tell me about your run. Deal?'

Camilla might have lost the love of her life, and, for a while, all hope for the future, but Phoebe wants to show her that there *are* things that could make her feel happy again. And she wants to do whatever she can to stop this woman's daughter

112

from feeling as though she can't leave the room for fear of what her mother might do to herself.

She senses Camilla hesitating as she glances around the room that has been her whole world since returning from hospital.

'I should stress,' Phoebe says, attempting a wry smile, 'me agreeing to go for a swim is a big deal. It's been months since I last sorted out my bikini line.'

A loud noise bursts out of Camilla's mouth. It takes Phoebe a second to realise that it's laughter.

Within moments, Arabella appears at the door, looking flustered.

'Is everything all right?' She rubs her eyes, her hair mussed from sleep. She glances between her mother and Phoebe and back again, her eyebrows shooting up as she sees the smile on her mother's face.

'Everything's fine,' assures Phoebe. 'Your mum has just agreed to go for a jog.'

Phoebe isn't sure if Arabella would look more shocked if she'd said her mum had just agreed to do karaoke on live television. While naked.

'Really?'

Phoebe looks at Camilla questioningly. She wouldn't normally push a patient like this, but over the years, she's got pretty good at getting the measure of people. And she can sense a steeliness beneath Camilla's vulnerability. She just needs a helping hand.

'Yes,' nods Camilla determinedly. 'You heard correctly.'

Arabella's shoulders sink and she rushes to her mother's side, reaching for her hand.

'That's wonderful, Mum!'

Mother and daughter lock eyes, a look of great meaning passing between them. Phoebe can see how tightly they hold each other's hand. She casts her eyes up quickly at the ceiling, a trusty technique of hers. She will not let herself cry.

Arabella remains in the room, perched on the side of the bed, holding her mum's hand, while Phoebe does the medical checks she needs to do. When it's time for her to leave, they are still sitting like that, quietly holding on to one another.

'I'll leave you to it. It was lovely to meet you both. I can see myself out.'

Both women seem so caught up in one another that she isn't sure they heard her at first. But just as she is about to leave, a voice reaches her from the bed. 'And don't forget your side of the bargain too, Phoebe.'

Phoebe nods, lifting her hand to wave goodbye.

'A promise is a promise.' And when Phoebe makes a promise to her patients, she doesn't let them down. It's a principle that might have cost her love life, but it's what makes her so good at her job.

She'd better buy a swimsuit. And one that actually fits.

CHAPTER 16

If the cottage was messy before Jay left for his shoot, after Kate's first day alone with Rosie, it now looks like a scene from one of those television programmes where people seek professional help to sort out the state of their homes. The kind of programme she used to watch from behind a pillow, cringing at how anyone could live like that. There are books and muslins and toys strewn everywhere, plates of half-eaten food from where Kate made several attempts to eat before being interrupted by her daughter's cries, and a pile of nappy bags in one corner because she hasn't found the energy to take them to the outside bin.

Kate reaches for her phone, wondering if it's too early to call Jay to ask when he'll be back. He was due home at seven. It is now 7.01.

How is it possible for one single day to feel about three weeks long?

Rosie has been crying non-stop for fifty-seven minutes. Kate has tried everything. Feeding, burping, rocking, holding her in her arms and laying her in her Moses basket. The sound of her crying fills the entire cottage and every space inside Kate's mind.

She checks the phone again: 7.02. Where is Jay?

'How about I sing to you?' she tries. 'Now, what could I sing ...?' She racks her mind, attempting to recall nursery rhymes from her childhood but coming up with nothing. 'What kind of mother doesn't know a single nursery rhyme? I'll just have to think of something else ...'

Which is how she comes to sing 'Wonderwall' to her daughter, each chorus getting wobblier and wobblier as her face grows snottier. When she finishes and Rosie is still crying, Kate continues through the very limited repertoire of the songs she knows by heart. Adele's 'Someone Like You'. 7.04. The soundtrack to *The Fresh Prince of Bel-Air*. By midway through a Christmas carol pulled from the very recesses of Kate's mind and her Church of England education, Rosie has finally fallen asleep in her arms and Kate's face is wet with tears.

At 7.07, the front door opens and Kate rapidly wipes her face, blowing her nose on her sleeve. She leaps up, Rosie thankfully conked out after the exhaustion of her crying session.

'Hi, honey,' says Jay as he kicks off his shoes and sets down his camera bags in the hallway. 'I've missed you both, how are you—'

But before he can finish, Kate hands Rosie across to him. 'Can you take her? I really need the loo.' She pecks him quickly on the cheek and he nods, somewhat bemused, as Kate dashes upstairs.

Inside the bathroom, she locks the door and sits down heavily on top of the loo seat, pulling out her phone and typing a message in her Work Wives group.

Free for a video call?

She hasn't spoken to an adult human since her trip to the supermarket that morning. She could, of course, talk to her husband, but he will likely want to hear in detail about Rosie's every burp and bowel movement and Kate really wants to talk about something else, *anything* else.

Thankfully, Emma and Leonie reply quickly.

Leonie: **Sounds good, just back from work, so perfect timing x**

Emma: **Yes! Would love to see your face xx**

Kate: **You might regret saying that, I'm a state as usual. Give me 5 mins.**

She flushes the toilet and washes her face with cold water, checking that her eyes don't look too puffy before heading back downstairs. Jay and Rosie are curled up together on the sofa, Jay stroking Rosie's hair and looking down at her adoringly.

'How was the shoot?'

Jay doesn't take his eyes away from Rosie as he replies. 'It was OK. The client seemed happy with what we got. I'll need to edit the shots over the next few days. How was your day?'

'It was fine. I'm just going to chat with the girls, are you OK to put her to bed?'

'Of course. I'll cook us both some dinner afterwards – it

looks like you could do with a proper meal.' He glances at the plates of abandoned snacks.

'Yeah, sorry about the mess …'

'Don't apologise. Are you sure it was OK?'

Kate nods but avoids his eye. It strikes her as she turns to leave that she used to tell Jay everything. But there seems so much more at stake now. She isn't just his wife anymore, but the mother to their child. If she let herself be truly honest with him, it might change the way he thinks about her forever. There are certain things that just can't be unsaid.

'It's so good to see you both!'

The sight of two of her best friends smiling back at her from her phone screen gives Kate exactly the boost that she'd hoped it would. She wishes she could reach through the screen to hug them, Emma beaming at her from the bed that Kate has crashed in several times over the years after nights out and Leonie reaching for a mug of tea from the table beside her fuchsia sofa.

'You too,' says Leonie. 'We miss you! Where's Rosie?'

Often when they speak, Kate is only semi-dressed, Rosie clamped to her, feeding, but her friends never seem to mind.

'Jay's just taken her up to bed. It means you have my full attention for once. And look what I can do …'

She jumps up, waving her arms.

'I've got both hands free! I could do anything!'

'Simple pleasures, Kate,' laughs Emma.

With a puff, Kate collapses back onto the sofa.

'Yeah, I don't have energy for much, though.' She reaches

for one of the biscuits that she grabbed before the call. Leonie sips her tea and Emma reaches for a glass of wine. For a second, it's almost as if they are all in the same room together. 'So, you never told me about the story you've been working on? That big meeting you mentioned?'

Both Emma and Leonie look shifty.

'We'd love to tell you about it, but it hasn't gone live yet and we were given a pretty severe bollocking by the editor to keep everything confidential. Do you remember that leak we had a couple of months ago?'

'But I'm not anyone! I work there too.'

There's that shifty look again.

'Well, you're technically not working right now …'

Kate does her best to adjust her expression to hide her hurt. 'Right. OK. I get it.'

'You know that we'd love to chat to you about it if we could. Although, honestly, it's not the most exciting story, I'm not sure why the editor's so hyped about it.'

'It's fine.' She takes a breath, trying to make her voice sound more cheerful than she feels. 'So, what else is going on? How's wedding planning going, Em?'

Emma's face brightens at the mention of the wedding. 'Oh, you know, there's still a lot to do. But I'm getting very excited about the weekend. Leonie booked me an appointment at this boutique in Islington where they give you prosecco and everything – the full shebang. We figured we might as well go all out. I'm hopefully only going to wear a wedding dress once!'

Kate frowns. 'Dress shopping?'

'Yeah, the wedding's only six months away now. Apparently,

I've left it pretty late to find a dress. Who knew most brides bought theirs like a year and half in advance? Classic me, trying to organise a wedding in half the usual time, but hey, I like a challenge.'

Emma is still grinning, but Leonie seems to have clocked Kate's expression and is looking flushed.

Kate tries to keep her voice steady. 'I'm a bridesmaid too, shouldn't I come with you?'

Emma's smile drops suddenly from her face. 'Oh. I didn't think ...'

'We assumed you wouldn't be able to make it,' chips in Leonie.

'You could have asked me,' Kate says quietly.

'Oh God, Kate, I'm sorry,' says Emma, her face glowing red now.

Leonie helps her out. 'We didn't want to put any pressure on you. What with Rosie being so little and you not being in London anymore ...'

'But obviously I'd *love* to have you there, if it's not too much for you.'

There's so much that Kate wants to say. Like, *I just had a baby, I didn't move to a different continent.* And, *My best friends are moving on without me.*

Kate was there when Emma and Sanjay first met. He had just joined the IT department at the *Herald* when Emma's computer spontaneously crashed. She was on a deadline and was terrified she'd lost all her copy. Sanjay not only managed to restore her work but, most importantly, managed to keep her calm, which was no mean feat given she'd been close to throwing her computer out the window when he'd arrived on the news floor. Over the next few weeks, Kate had watched on, amused, as her friend mysteriously encountered a whole string of computer-related issues which required calling Sanjay to come up and take a look. She would never have imagined not being there to help Emma choose her wedding dress. And yet hurt stops her from saying, 'I'll be there.'

'No, it's fine, it sounds like everything's organised now. Hey, I think I can hear Rosie crying, I should probably go.'

'Wait, Kate, we didn't mean to ...'

But Kate is already waving and then hanging up. Because if she stayed on the phone any longer, her friends would see her cry and that's the last thing she wants.

She knows she's probably being petty. But the feeling of being left out is like a stomach ache that she can't ignore. It takes her right back to the café that morning when she'd stepped inside hoping to feel a sense of connection with the other mothers but left feeling more isolated than ever.

If her friends don't want her there, then she doesn't want to go.

CHAPTER 17

When Phoebe pulls up outside her building at the end of the day, she has a brief moment where she wonders if she's totally losing it, because the view of the high street looks very different to when she left that morning. It has been a long day, after all, so maybe she's just hallucinating. But as she climbs down off her motorbike, she realises her mind isn't playing tricks on her. The shop below her, which had been closed this morning and for months before, is finally open. The newspaper covering the windows has disappeared, revealing shining glass framed by a dark green awning, *Giuglia's* written across it in swirling gold font.

Eager to discover what business she'll now be living above and who has been waking her up in the early mornings, Phoebe grabs her things from the bike's panniers and then heads straight for the new shop. From the pavement outside, she peers in through the shining window.

The shop couldn't look more different to Amit's old news-agent. The whole place is fresh and sparkling, the grubby but functional linoleum having been ripped up to reveal wooden floorboards and the walls painted a soft duck-egg blue. The counter that Phoebe had spied through a chink in the news-paper is now piled with tarts, cakes and heaped bowls of jewel-coloured salads, a gleaming silver coffee machine set up on another counter right at the back. The shelves that were being constructed, and that likely caused the bulk of the noise, are stacked neatly with boxes of pasta, bottles of olive oil and, Phoebe spots with a twinge of excitement, wine. A brightly lit display houses an array of cheeses and charcuterie meats. Hanging from the ceiling are the pastel-shade boxes of pan-doro and panettone, suspended from ribbons.

As well as the shop area, there is a little café section with a few tables and a counter facing out onto the street. There's already a customer inside, a man in his seventies sipping from an espresso cup and reading a paper which Phoebe notices is in Italian.

Unable to stop herself, she pushes open the shop's door. A bell tinkles, but she is too enchanted to notice the sound. The place smells incredible. Like sun-kissed tomatoes, freshly baked focaccia and smoky, nutty coffee. Everything looks so fresh and delicious, reminding Phoebe that it's been a while since she had a proper meal made with proper ingredients not just something packaged in plastic that can be chucked in the microwave. Her stomach grumbles, imagining the taste of the salty prosciutto laid out in the fridge and the ripe, fuzzy peaches piled in a crate by the window. It feels as though she has stepped from Somerset straight to Italy. She thinks of Max and the holiday she'd pictured for them both, the breakfasts they could have had outside in the sunshine, reading and drinking espresso. Rome! Florence! A fucking *break* from everything. The disappointment of it all comes back in a painful, deliciously scented rush.

'*Ciao!*' comes a deep voice from the doorway leading through to the kitchen and Phoebe looks up, startled.

'Oh,' she says as she meets the dark gaze of the man coming to stand behind the shop's counter, wearing a dark green striped apron covered in flour and wiping his hands on a tea towel slung over his shoulder. His shirtsleeves are rolled up to reveal tanned, muscular forearms and, as Phoebe takes in the dark hair on his arms, she realises she's seen those arms before, those broad shoulders and that dark, curly hair that looks like it may never have been brushed, a particularly wild few strands falling down over his left eyebrow. 'Oh. It's you.'

The man laughs slightly, rubbing his forehead and leaving a trail of flour there, which would be cute if Phoebe wasn't suddenly so indignant.

'Um, yes, I am me.'

His accent is British but with the slightest Italian inflection that Phoebe somehow imagines might be stronger when he's just woken up, immediately kicking herself for the thought because it also brings to mind his thick curls charmingly stuck up with sleep, which is something she absolutely does not want to think about.

A chuckle comes from the older man sitting with his paper. But Phoebe doesn't join in.

'You nearly bloody killed me this morning!' At that, the customer nearly spits out his coffee. 'I was swimming at the river and you came charging along in your boat, not looking where you were going. You could have decapitated us all!'

The man in the apron shoots a look in the direction of his customer. 'Just a misunderstanding!' he says, waving a hand, but the customer shakes his head, picking up his paper and throwing a note down on the table in its place. Once the man has left, the guy in the apron shoots Phoebe a frown.

'Hey, you just lost me a customer! My first, actually.'

'Well, it serves you right!' She recalls Sandra grabbing her arm and pulling her out of the way of the oncoming boat and the way he had glanced down at his watch as though *they* were inconveniencing him by interrupting his session.

'I didn't see you. Obviously,' he grumbles.

'You should have been looking where you were going. *And* you've been keeping me awake.'

'What are you talking about?' His voice is tight and strained and she can hear a sigh just waiting to come out, as though he's talking to an exasperating older relative who is losing their marbles. But she doesn't care. She's had a long day and that surly expression on his annoyingly perfect face is making her blood boil.

'I live just upstairs.' She gestures to the ceiling. 'All the noise has kept me up. Who does drilling at seven in the morning?'

She's aware that her cheeks are likely flushed by now, probably perfectly matching her hair. When she first dyed it, she was thinking Ariel vibes – growing up by the seaside, *The Little*

125

Mermaid was always her favourite – but now she probably looks more like a traffic light.

'There's been a lot to do to get the place ready,' he says with a shrug, crossing his arms. As he does, the muscles on his fore-arms tauten and somehow it only makes her crosser. How dare he have such beautiful arms! He pulls his lips into a tight line. 'I've had to get my guys to do overtime to get it all done. And unfortunately no one has yet mastered the art of silent drilling or sanding. None of the other neighbours have complained.'

'That's because the next-door flat is owned by a ninety-year-old called Marjorie who is completely deaf!'

'Well, there we go then. I haven't been disturbing anyone else.' He even has the audacity to flash her a smile. What's wrong with this guy? He might look like he could be the ambassador of some wholesome outdoors brand or natural but delicious cereal bar, but he's rude, making Phoebe's skin prickle with irritation. She misses Amit. Yes, he may have had alarmingly long grey hairs growing out of his ears, but he was quiet and always mindful of his neighbours sleeping just up-stairs. 'Nice bike,' he says, nodding out the window. She feels thrown by the comment and suddenly conscious of the fact that she is sweating beneath her leather jacket and really needs a shower.

'Thanks, I love her.' Why did she say that?

'I'm not surprised,' he replies simply. 'Look, I'm sorry about this morning at the river, but everyone was fine, weren't they? And the shop's open now. Unless my builders have fleeced me and everything in here falls down by the end of the week, there should be no more drilling or hammering happening down here. Just great food and excellent coffee. Would you like one, by the way? I'll give you a neighbour's discount.'

Phoebe ignores his question and the fact that the smell of the espresso in the air is making her mouth water.

'What about the radio?'

'Ah. That, I can't make any promises about. Who doesn't love a bit of Magic FM?'

She's suddenly exhausted, too exhausted to be here arguing with this man and surrounded by smells that are both appealing and painful all at once.

'I'm going now.' As she spins around, her eyes fall on a basket of freshly baked bread and she thinks of her empty cupboards upstairs and the sensation of chewing down on a crusty, fresh loaf. She remembers the wine she spotted earlier on the shelves in here too, which would go perfectly with the cheese over on the counter. But she storms out empty-handed, on principle.

When Phoebe pushes open her front door, she wonders if she might be hallucinating again. It takes her a second to realise that she's not.

'Fucking Max.' She looks around, taking it all in. '*Fucking Max!*'

Where the dining table, chairs and sofa used to be is one huge patch of bare carpet. Apart from the pictures on the walls and Phoebe's books stacked on the built-in shelves, the living room is completely empty. Max has left one single wooden chair – a chair Phoebe remembers finding on the street when they first moved in and sanding and painting. But everything else is gone. She charges through to the bedroom. The bed frame has gone, the mattress left behind on the floor.

Without thinking, she dials Max's number. It will be the first time they've spoken since he left, but she's too angry to stop herself. He picks up after a few rings, but she doesn't let him say anything before cutting in.

'What – and I mean this deeply – the *actual fuck*, Max?'

'Oh, I take it you're back from work then.' He does at least sound hesitant, but it does nothing to stop Phoebe's anger.

'Where's all our stuff?'

'I only took the things that I bought.' His voice has a righteous tone to it that makes Phoebe's skin crawl. She can hear someone pottering about in the background. It must be her. The woman Max left her for, the woman he is now living with and who is presumably now sleeping on *her* bed and sitting on *her* sofa.

'You took *everything*.'

'Well, yes. I did buy everything, remember.'

'Only because you insisted on "upgrading" all my furniture. I was quite happy with my old IKEA stuff.' If she thinks about it now, mostly he hadn't even asked her, just assumed she wouldn't mind some ratty MDF coffee table being replaced with something modern and expensive, made from glass and brass. And she hadn't minded, not especially. But that was before she came home to an apartment void of any furniture.

'I did leave you the mattress.'

'Oh, well, that's OK, then. *Thank you*, Max. Thank you so bloody much for being so generous!'

'You don't have to be like this, Phoebe. Some couples

128

actually manage harmonious break-ups. I always thought that would be us.'

'You *always* thought? So, you've been thinking about this for a long time, then?' Jesus, had their whole relationship been a sham? How could she have been so stupid? She should have kept her promise to herself to not date after Luke.

Max lets out a sigh that reminds her of her conversation with Luca and makes her even more fuming. 'You know what I mean. I just thought we could handle this in a civilised way.'

'Right. After you cheated on me, left me and took *all of our fucking furniture.*'

From the corner of her eye, Phoebe spies a bottle of gin on the counter. Last night, she had been restrained, sticking only to wine, but now all she wants is to open that bottle. Why is she even bothering to speak to Max? They are over, something that now feels dazzlingly clear.

'Goodbye, Max,' she says decisively, hanging up before he can say anything else. She grabs the gin bottle and twists open the lid, taking a swig. It hits the back of her throat, making her cough. But by the second swig, her hands have stopped shaking, a pleasant warmth spreading through her body. She pours herself a large glass, topping it up with tonic and a slice of a lemon she finds at the back of the fridge, which seems fine enough once she's scraped off the mould. Then she sits down at her single wooden dining chair and drinks it, staring out the window at the street below.

What a fucking day. She takes another long glug of gin. What a fucking week. Her phone buzzes in her pocket. For a second, she wonders if it might be Max, sending some message about how grateful she should be that he didn't take the in-built bookshelves or the oven. But luckily for her phone and her window, it's not Max.

This is Camilla Ramsgate. I just wanted to let you know that I contacted a local running group after our chat. They seem very welcoming and say they have lots of beginners and people getting back into running like me who do a mix of walking and jogging. I'm going to meet up with them tomorrow. Arabella is delighted. Thanks for giving me the push I needed.

A warm glow spreads its way through Phoebe's body, and not just because of the gin. After everything that has happened over the past couple of days, the message lifts her up. For all the difficult parts, this right here is why she loves her job. This feeling, which is unlike any other she's ever experienced. It's why she sticks at it through everything. Because small moments like this are not actually small at all. They're huge.

Thankfully, her phone's autocorrect catches the typos in her own reply before she sends it.

That's brilliant, well done, Camilla. I can't wait to hear all about your run.

Camilla Ramsgate's reply comes in quickly.

Don't think I've forgotten about our deal. I want to hear about your swim too.

Phoebe smiles to herself. She can just picture Camilla's expression, that same challenging look that had sparkled in her eye when Phoebe promised she would go swimming again if only to encourage Camilla out of her comfort zone. It was a

130

look that was so different to the vacant stare that had been on her face when Phoebe had arrived in her stuffy bedroom.

Before she can send another reply, the doorbell rings sharply, making her jump. When she opens it, there is no one there, but there is a large paper bag resting on the doormat.

'Hello?' she calls down the stairs, but the front door has already closed; whoever made the delivery already gone.

She takes the paper bag through to the kitchen and carefully unpacks its contents. Inside is a large box of rigatoni pasta and a jar of home-made arrabbiata sauce, a small bottle of olive oil and a waxed paper package that Phoebe unwraps to reveal several slices of prosciutto and a chunk of Parmesan cheese. Inside a small white tub is a plump ball of juicy burrata. There's a loaf of crusty bread, a beautiful box of biscotti, and nestled among everything is a bottle of red wine. As she lays the items out on the counter, she notices for the first time the curling text on the front of the bag. *Giuglia's.*

CHAPTER 18

It's 4 a.m. and Kate is wide awake again. Why does her body do this to her? Jay is snoring and Rosie is asleep in her Moses basket after a feed, but Kate's mind doesn't want to switch off, no matter how much her body craves sleep.

She reaches for her phone. There are new messages from Emma and Leonie sent last night, individual ones, as well as the messages they put in the group chat apologising for not inviting her to Emma's wedding dress shopping trip.

Sorry again for messing up, Kate, wrote Leonie. If you change your mind, here are the details for the dress shop. We'll be meeting there at 11.30 on Saturday. Would be lovely to see you xx

She doesn't feel ready to reply yet, hurt still sitting like a stone in her stomach at the feeling of having been left out by her closest friends. It reminds her of all the times she felt out of place as a child for being too quiet, too bookish or not *something* enough, the something being too hard to put her finger on. Over recent years, she'd finally found her tribe and come to feel happy in her own skin, so being excluded again like that stings. She reminds herself that she's a grown-up – somebody's actual *mother* – but it doesn't take away the pain.

Kate clicks on the link, though, bringing up the website of an incredibly chic bridal boutique in Angel. The dresses all look to be designer, nothing like the second-hand dress Kate bought for £50 from a vintage shop to wear to her own wedding at Lambeth Town Hall.

Sleep still evading her, she scrolls back through the photos on her phone until she finds her wedding pictures. The morning of her wedding, Kate went for a swim in the lido. As she walked into the town hall to be married, she smelt like chlorine and the rosemary nestled amongst her bouquet of daisies and cornflowers, a nod to the one person who couldn't be there in person. She'd been there, too, in the second-hand wedding rings that Kate and Jay slipped onto each other's fingers, left to Kate by a woman whose marriage lasted more than fifty years.

After the ceremony, they headed to Brockwell Park for a picnic. It had rained, but they didn't care, all huddling under rainbow umbrellas beneath the trees. There's one photo that's a particular favourite, which shows her and Jay standing at the top of the hill in the park under an umbrella. You can just make out the guests in the background, but Kate and Jay are focused only on one another, kissing as the summer rain falls down above them.

We looked so happy, Kate thinks as she turns to take in the sight of her husband sleeping beside her now, his body curled up and facing away from her. It feels as though a distance has grown between them recently and she doesn't know how to fix it. Will she ever be able to get back to that feeling she had as they sheltered under the umbrella together, so in love and so hopeful about their future?

She keeps on scrolling, images of their life together flashing by. Pictures of the lido on sunny days and rainy ones, meals with friends, snaps of the fruit and veg stand on Electric Avenue when the colours just looked too delicious not to capture. Eventually, she comes all the way back to the last photo she took – the sign for the Farleigh-on-Avon River Swimming, Bathing and Recreational Water-Based Activities Club.

Looking at it again, she remembers her conversation with the woman in the supermarket whose words had felt like a hand reaching out to her, pulling her out of a swirling current. *Don't forget to look after yourself.*

For the past five years, looking after herself has meant swimming. She *has* to get back to it. Even if that means having to brave the intimidatingly official-sounding swimming group. Kate thinks for a moment about what Rosemary would say, a smile appearing on her face at the thought. Rosemary would tell her to dig out her swimming costume and get in the water. '*Because you never regret a swim.*'

CHAPTER 19

The first thing Phoebe thinks when she wakes up is, *Coffee*. Normally, she makes herself one as soon as she is up and drinks it in the armchair by the window, enjoying watching the village begin to stir below. But there'll be none of that this morning because her armchair, like the rest of her furniture, save for the single dining chair and the mattress she slept on last night, is gone. The second thing she thinks is, *Bloody Max*.

Once she's dressed and about to start up the coffee machine her eyes land on the Giuglia's paper bag on the counter, its contents mostly consumed last night on the floor, with the parcels spread in front of her and the bottle of gin in one hand. Even though she'd been hungry, part of her had wanted not to like any of it because she was still angry at the shop owner for his arrogance on the river and again when she'd tried to get an apology out of him. But everything was *delicious*. The prosciutto had melted on her tongue and the Parmesan made her entire mouth tingle.

She decisively grabs her things for the day and heads downstairs.

It might still be early, but the 'Open' sign is flipped round in the deli window and the bell tinkles as she pushes the door. The curly-haired owner looks up from behind the counter where he had been setting out a batch of tarts and pastries, his dark eyebrows raising questioningly and a half-smile appearing on his lips. Today, he is in slim-fit black jeans and a green T-shirt that matches his apron. The apron itself is just as flour-dusted as before. His face is shadowed by stubble and his hair looks especially wild. Phoebe wonders whether perhaps he has noisy neighbours too. It would serve him right.

'Hello, neighbour,' he says. 'Did the sound of me dropping a teaspoon just now wake you up?' He smiles wryly, revealing a little gap between his top teeth.

Phoebe considers walking straight back out again, but then gets a hit of the scent of espresso and just the *smell* of it makes her feel more awake. She sits down defiantly at the table right opposite the counter, even though she is the only customer and there are plenty of other free tables. She crosses her legs in front of her, her chunky motorbike boots scuffing slightly against the freshly mopped floor. She fights the urge to reach down and wipe the mark away with a paper napkin.

'Cause total chaos on any local waterways recently?' comes her retort.

He makes a sound that could be a cough or a laugh. But then his expression settles and he rolls his neck, wincing slightly as something clicks. 'No, I didn't manage to get down there this morning. There's still a lot to do here ...'

She notices the dark shadows under his eyes again and as she does, her own tiredness gives her a little nudge.

'Can I get a long black, please? With three shots.'

'Three shots? Are you sure? My coffee's pretty strong.'

'Are you saying I can't handle it?'

She's expecting another sharp reply to bounce back at her, but to her surprise, his expression shifts and he shakes his head.

'More that *I* can't handle it. It's delicious stuff, but it makes me bounce off the walls. I stick to decaf now, otherwise I'm a total mess. Give me a hazelnut decaf latté any day. I know – I'm an embarrassment to my homeland!'

He says it with total ease, laughter in his voice. Phoebe thinks of Max and how he'd rather drink a coffee he hated than admit he preferred his sweet and milky. She'd always found it kind of endearing, but now she wonders whether it was actually kind of ridiculous.

'Three shots is good.'

The shop owner nods and turns towards the coffee machine. 'One cup of rocket fuel coming up.' The muscles on his broad shoulders tense as he reaches for the levers and Phoebe forces herself to look away, focusing on the shelves of pasta instead while he prepares her drink.

'I wanted to say thank you for the food, by the way. I'm assuming that was you.'

His face flushes as he places the coffee down on her table, a biscotti resting on the saucer. He runs a hand through his messy curls, 'messy' becoming 'out of control'.

'I figured I probably owed you an apology. But I've always been better with food than words.'

'Well, it was all delicious.'

The pink spots on his cheeks spread to his forehead and his mouth tightens slightly as though he's trying very hard not to let himself smile.

'I'm Luca, by the way.'

'Not Giuglia, then?' she asks, gesturing to the sign behind the counter that displays the name of the shop in a gold font.

'Ah, no. That's my mum. Did you think I *look* like a Giuglia?'

'Um, no, you look …' She clears her voice. She can't seem to finish the sentence. 'Luca probably suits you better. I'm Phoebe.'

He nods. 'And what's her name?'

'What?'

Phoebe follows the tilt of his head to where he's gesturing towards her motorbike parked up outside the shop.

'Oh. That's Frances.' It's her turn to flush now. Why did she let that slip out? She didn't even admit to Max that she'd named her bike, but of course she had, the second she had spotted her at the showroom. She just looked like a Frances.

She's expecting him to laugh, but instead he just nods. 'Mine's Roberta.'

'You have a bike?'

'Had,' he corrects, swallowing hard. 'A classic Ducati. I had to sell her to help finance all this.' He gestures around him with the tea towel that had been flung over his shoulder.

'Oh my God, that's so sad!' It comes out before she can help herself. But it's got her thinking about her own motorbike. Will she have to sell it now that she's living off a solo income – and a nurse's income at that? Her eyes well up at the thought. Not Frances.

'Well, hopefully it will be worth it,' Luca says, looking around the shop with a faraway expression. When she's certain he isn't looking, she grabs a paper towel and ducks under the table to give the black scuff mark she made with her foot a quick wipe.

When she sits back up again, Luca is watching her with a strange expression on his face. Phoebe coughs and glances up at the clock above the counter. Shit. She downs the last of her coffee, pocketing her biscotti for later.

'Work?' he asks as she grabs her things and tucks the chair under the table.

'In a bit. But first I'm going for a swim.'

'At the river?'

'Yeah. Hopefully there will be no water menaces out today.'

It still feels strange to think about going back for another swim. Two days of exercising in a row … It has to be a personal record, despite how much she bangs on to her patients about the benefits of moving their bodies.

'Apologise to your swimming mates for me, will you?' Luca says, slipping his hands in his apron pockets and shifting on the spot. 'I was having a bad morning.' There's that tired look on his face again, that slightly distant glaze to his deep brown eyes.

She wants to press him to tell her more – she can't help herself, given her profession – but reminds herself he's not a patient. It's none of her business. Plus, she's going to be late if she doesn't leave soon. And she can't be late. She made a promise to Camilla Ramsgate. And, actually, she's looking forward to seeing Sandra, Jazz and Hester again.

'The coffee was great, by the way,' she says as she's leaving.

Luca is behind the counter again, tinkering with the display, his dark eyes focused intently on the baked goods, his teeth biting down on his bottom lip. He looks up at her and something about the look he gives her makes her stand up a little taller.

'Bye, neighbour.'

CHAPTER 20

As Kate crosses the field that leads down to the river, she can't quite believe that she's going to swim. Last night, she spent an hour plugged up to the electric breast pump that Erin had given her but that she hadn't used until now. The droning whir made her feel like a cow at an industrial dairy, but she didn't care. If that's what it took to get back in the water, then it would be worth it.

Jay had rearranged his work schedule so that he could take care of Rosie and it was he who had gently pushed her out the door as she hesitated on the threshold, swim bag under her arm but guilt sitting in her stomach at the thought of leaving them, however desperate she might feel to get back to the water.

'Go! We'll be fine.'

It felt strange to step out without a pram or Rosie in the sling. It struck her that no one walking by would know that she was a new parent, even though the change felt so drastic to her that she feels as though she has 'new mum' tattooed on her forehead.

She hears the river before she sees it. A quiet yet inviting 'shh' as if the water is telling the world to be quiet and listen. But unlike on her secret dawn visits when the only other noises were the birds and the breeze rustling through the reeds, this morning there are voices, too, and the happy sound of splashing. As she pushes through the gate that leads down to the riverbank, she makes out the lilting sound of jazz music coming from the Kingfisher Café and Book Barge. The curtains that were drawn whenever she snuck down here in the semi-dark are now flung open, revealing walls of bookshelves and a tiny stove with a hissing kettle on top, home-made cakes piled in the hatch, where a man in mustard tweed serves a small queue of customers.

It feels strange to see what had felt like Kate's secret place come totally alive. A lifeguard sits on a striped deckchair, and although it's still relatively early, there are a few people already swimming, plus a couple dragging a kayak down from the beach hut boat store. A silver-haired man dives neatly into the river from the diving board and Kate searches around to try to find someone who might belong to the swimming club. She's expecting someone with a clipboard, maybe a megaphone. But the only people she can see who are not already in the water are a group of four women of different ages gathered on a checked picnic blanket. They look friendly, so she heads over.

'Hi, my name's Kate. I wonder if you can help? I'm looking for the Farleigh-on-Avon River Swimming, Bathing and ...' She searches her mind for the rest but can't remember it. Why would anyone give their group a name that long?

'Recreational Water-Based Activities Club?' finishes the oldest of the women, who looks a little older than Kate's mum and is dressed in an enormous red changing robe, her hair hidden beneath a multicoloured flowery swimming hat. 'You've found us! Welcome, I'm Sandra!'

Warmth radiates from her as though she were a walking sunbeam.

'I'm Jazz,' says the woman beside her, who Kate guesses is in her twenties, wild blonde curls bouncing on her shoulders and a broad smile on her face. She's wrapped up in a stripy towel, a pile of clothes at her feet. 'And this is Hester.'

The red-headed teenager nods in Kate's direction before looking back down at her feet, bare in the long grass. She's dressed in a swimsuit but with a hoody over the top, the sleeves of which she pulls down over her hands.

'And you're not our only newbie! This is Phoebe, she swam with us yesterday and thankfully we didn't scare her off,' says Sandra, gesturing towards the fourth woman, who looks around Kate's age and has the most amazing colour hair she has ever seen, somewhere between red and purple. She's wearing a red-and-white striped swimsuit and dotted about here and there on her bare skin are the most beautiful tattoos, delicate plants and flowers that make her fit in perfectly with the wildflower meadow that surrounds them.

Kate suddenly feels very conscious of her own appearance – the messy mum bun on the top of her head, the jeans that feel uncomfortably tight but that she was determined to squeeze into, sick of spending every day in tracksuit bottoms. There may possibly be baby sick somewhere on her person ...

143

'Wow, I love your hair,' says Kate. 'And your tattoos … they're beautiful.' She tries her best to hide the awe from her voice, but as she spots the leather jacket and motorcycle helmet on the grass by Phoebe's feet, she feels as if she's back at school again, the nerdy, mousy girl who spent most of her time in the library and has no chance of befriending someone this cool. But Phoebe smiles warmly back at her.

'Thanks! It's nice to have someone else here who's new too. Makes those "new kid at big school"' vibes less daunting.'

The fact that Phoebe's thoughts so mirror Kate's own makes her nod her head vigorously. 'Yes! Me too!'

The others are busy getting ready, Sandra unzipping her changing robe, Hester pulling off her hoody and Jazz wriggling about beneath her towel, so Kate quickly starts pulling off her own clothing, her swimsuit already on beneath. As she wobbles on one foot while tugging off her jeans, Phoebe reaches out an arm to steady her.

'Thanks.'

'I can't remember the last time I took up a hobby,' says Phoebe once Kate has managed to extract herself from her denim – skinny jeans were a bad idea – and is ready in her swimsuit. 'Maybe never?'

Kate thinks back to her very first swim at the lido and how nervous she'd felt. Before that, she hadn't swum since she was a teenager. Her swims didn't start as a hobby, though, they began as work, although very quickly became so much more than that. Her skin tingles with anticipation at the thought of finally getting back into the water.

'I used to swim regularly at my local lido, but this is my first

144

time wild swimming. I think I'd be too nervous to go in by myself. Not knowing what's beneath me freaks me out a little bit. That's why I thought I'd give this group a go.'

The other women are ready now and all lined up in an array of swimwear. Kate tries to get a sense of their personalities from their choices. Phoebe's is a modern twist on a retro style, while Jazz's frilly pink bikini looks like the kind of thing you might buy for a hen do but then never wear again. Kate kind of loves it. Hester wears a black and purple sporty Speedo with a racer back and Sandra is in a sturdy navy swimsuit almost certainly from M&S that looks like it has a stomach control panel.

Kate wraps her arms self-consciously around her own stomach. She'd been determined to fit into her favourite old yellow swimsuit that she bought as a treat when the lido was saved, but it clings tightly to her stomach. Becoming a regular swimmer changed her relationship with her body, encouraging her to focus on the way she feels in the water rather than the way she looks. And stripping off in front of women of absolutely every shape and size in the changing room quickly dispelled her idea of there being one ideal blueprint for a human body, making her far more comfortable in her own.

But going through pregnancy and birth has been a disorientating experience. Her body feels like a stranger now and it's proving hard to adjust. Beneath her swimming costume, her breasts give a little throb, another reminder that her body doesn't feel like her own anymore. She fed Rosie before she left, but she can already feel that telling ache in her chest. God, she hopes she doesn't leak.

'I must admit, you're all not what I had been expecting,' she says, readjusting her arms to cross in front of her chest.

'Is it because of the name?' asks Jazz. 'Sandra, I told you we should change the name! Or at least make a nicer poster.'

'What's wrong with the one we've got? It's laminated! I bought that laminator specially!'

Hester rolls her eyes.

'The poster was, um, concise,' Kate says practically. 'Apart from maybe the name.'

'Are you saying that the Farleigh-on-Avon River Swimming, Bathing and Recreational Water-Based Activities Club doesn't just roll off your tongue?' says Jazz wryly.

'Bloody hell!' laughs Phoebe. 'That's a bit of a mouthful, isn't it?'

'Well, we started out as the Farleigh-on-Avon River Swimming Club,' Sandra explains. 'But some people who swim with us prefer to just bob about and float, so we added "bathing" to make it more inclusive.'

'I'm more of a dipper than a swimmer,' agrees Jazz.

'Exactly. We want to welcome everyone, whether they want to zip up and down like Hester or drift with the current like Jazz and I.'

'What about the "Recreational Water-Based Activities" bit?' asks Phoebe.

'You'll see later,' replies Sandra. 'But, come on, I think it's time we got in, don't you?'

Together, they head down the riverbank towards the water, mud oozing between Kate's bare toes. It's nothing like the concrete poolside at the lido. A bee buzzes past her nose, the long grass tickles her legs, and the perfectly clear water of the lido flashes into her mind. This is certainly no lido. At the lido there was the smell of chlorine and neatly marked out lanes. Here, there is mud, leaves, mysterious ripples and an earthy smell in the air. A scuffling noise in the undergrowth makes her turn quickly in that direction.

'Probably a water rat, or maybe a vole,' Sandra says, following her gaze.

'A *rat*?'

Is she really about to share her swimming spot with rats?

'I've heard there are otters here, although I've never personally seen one,' says Sandra. 'Pretty magic to think they might be about, though.'

'I like *that* idea,' says Phoebe.

Looking around her, Kate can't deny that there is a certain magic to this spot. The way they're tucked away under the trees with only the meadow and fields surrounding them makes her feel as though everything else in her life is far away.

Hester is the first in, heading for the diving board and diving elegantly. When she bobs back up, the expression on her face has been transformed from somewhat sullen into a huge smile that opens her face, making her blue eyes sparkle. Sandra goes next, taking strides through the shallows before launching herself forward with a big splash and lots of puffing. There's a little shriek as Jazz follows her.

'We better not get left behind,' says Phoebe and she gives Kate a nod and then joins the other women. 'Bloody hell!' Phoebe shouts, kicking her arms and legs in a vigorous breast-stroke. 'I forgot how cold it was!'

The lifeguard on the bank glances in their direction but simply shakes her head, smiling.

'We come here all year round, this is practically *tropical*, dear,' says Sandra, treading water in the middle of the river. 'You wait until the winter. Although, there's something lovely about seeing the frost in the meadow. And walking down the bank in the snow ... Now, that's really something.'

'It sounds bloody awful!' says Phoebe, but there's a big grin on her face. 'Are you coming, Kate?'

Kate tilts her head towards the trees for a moment, enjoying the feeling of a breeze on her face and freedom in her heart. Being here and meeting these women ... She feels like herself again.

'Just you try to stop me!'

Kate doesn't just step into the river. She leaps.

CHAPTER 21

The river stretches ahead of them before curving around a bend. Side by side, the women set off at a leisurely pace, following the river's wiggly route.

'How does it compare to your lido?' asks Phoebe.

Kate looks around, taking it all in. Everything looks different from this level, her nose in line with the reeds and the bluebells growing on the banks. She spots a huddle of lily pads, a bloom swelling but not yet ready to unfurl.

'The water feels different. It's almost ... silky. It's weird not having any lanes. I could swim anywhere I like!' She demonstrates by zigzagging her way across the breadth of the river, making the other women laugh. 'But it's wonderful to be back in the water.'

There are things she misses, of course. The familiar faces of her friends, the thought of warm showers afterwards. But the feeling of being in the water is the same. The way it loosens the knots in her shoulders and makes her take deeper, slower breaths; that pleasant ache in her limbs as she kicks and pulls, making her feel connected with her body again. God, she's missed this.

'I'm glad to be back too,' agrees Phoebe. 'I came here the first time sort of by accident. This lot forced me in.'

'But you didn't regret it, did you?' says Sandra, her colourful swimming hat like a beacon as she leads Kate, Jazz and Phoebe upstream. Hester has raced off around the river bend in a confident front crawl, but every now and then she turns back to swim with the group for a while, that same smile that appeared when she jumped in never leaving her face.

'Well, I'm back again, aren't I?' teases Phoebe.

'You never regret a swim,' says Kate, thinking of her old friend Rosemary as she does.

'Seriously, though, I was really excited this morning thinking about coming back,' continues Phoebe. 'Way more excited than is probably considered normal for the thought of throwing myself into muddy, cold water.'

'If you're not normal, then we're all not normal either,' says Sandra.

'Ahh,' adds Jazz, letting out a long sigh. 'They should prescribe this on the NHS. I'd been about to lose it this morning with my folks. I'm back living with them for a while,' she explains, 'and, God, I love them. But they do my head in sometimes too.'

'Everyone needs their own space,' says Sandra kindly.

'And this feels like mine!' Jazz rolls onto her back for a

moment to float, kicking her toes, the bright flash of pink nail polish contrasting against the dark green of the water.

'I'm so glad I came,' Kate says, following Jazz's lead and floating on her back, keeping her head up so she can still chat. 'I really needed this.'

'Oh yes?' asks Sandra, her tone encouraging Kate to continue. She already feels comfortable with these women, but they know nothing about her. The thought feels freeing. Here, she doesn't have to be the woman in the tracksuit bottoms who is chronically sleep-deprived and spends far too long scrolling social media. She can be anyone. She can be *Kate* rather than *Mummy*.

'Things with … work have been quite stressful recently. But I already feel calmer.'

'I get that,' comes a quiet voice. Kate hadn't even noticed Hester rejoin the group, swapping her efficient front crawl for their more leisurely breaststroke. 'I'm doing my AS levels and I get stressed. But on the days when I swim … I feel better.'

'How could anyone *not* feel better when they're down by the river?' says Sandra. 'We're happy to have you here, Kate. And you too, Phoebe. And if we're lucky, we might see a kingfisher. There's one around here. I've named him Bert.'

'Why Bert?' asks Phoebe.

'Oh, no reason.'

A white feather glides in front of Kate's nose, followed by a sprig of cow parsley. The cottage couldn't feel further away right now. There's something thrilling about knowing that her phone is on the riverbank along with her clothes. No one can reach her here, needing her. Just thinking it opens the door for that all-too familiar feeling of guilt to creep in, though. She remembers the words of the mum at the Tired Mums Club. *I can't bear to be apart from you for a second.*

'Swimming always makes me feel like singing,' declares Sandra suddenly. 'Would anyone mind?'

'You know you don't need to ask,' says Jazz, making Kate think that singing in the river must be a regular occurrence for Sandra.

Luckily, she has a beautiful voice. She sings softly, her words mixing with the sound of the birds and the quiet gurgles of the river. Kate recognises the words to 'Morning Has Broken', a hymn she remembers from primary school. It's been a long time since she last heard it. She has never considered herself religious and yet, hearing Sandra sing the hymn while they swim down the river in the morning sunshine, it feels surprisingly fitting.

Praise for the morning, praise for the singing . . .

Kate lets out a long sigh.

'Look!' exclaims Sandra suddenly. 'It's Bert!'

A flash of brilliant turquoise and orange whips by. Kate watches as the darting shape crosses the river and pauses on a branch for a second before flying away again. Although fleeting, there is something about the vivid colours against the backdrop of browns and greens that takes her breath away.

Only once she's certain it's gone does Kate break the moment's awed silence.

'I can't believe we saw a kingfisher! I've never seen one in real life before.'

Jazz is beaming. 'We love it when we see him. Always makes the swim extra special.'

'I've always wanted to see a kingfisher,' says Phoebe.

Sandra is the only one not to join in with their enthusiasm. Her expression looks lost as she watches the spot where the kingfisher just sat.

'Are you OK, Sandra?' Phoebe asks. A deep frown lines the older woman's face and her eyes glance about as if searching. Kate meets the eye of Phoebe, then Jazz and Hester and they all share a questioning look, silently asking one another, *What happened there?*

But as quickly as it arrived Sandra's frown passes and she turns to face in the other direction, back towards the meadow.

'Come on, I think it's time for the "Recreational Water-Based Activities" part of our swim. Let's head back to the riverbank.'

CHAPTER 22

'So, by "Recreational Water-Based Activities",' says Phoebe, dressed again now but her skin still tingling from the cold water, 'you mean …?'

The women are all dressed, but all look a little less neat than before, hair wet and bedraggled. Without saying anything, Sandra leads them over towards the Kingfisher Café and Book Barge. Phoebe's stomach rumbles at the sight of the piles of baked goods displayed in the hatch, a handwritten chalkboard menu propped outside.

The silver-haired man on the boat looks up from a battered paperback and flashes them a smile, his cheeks ruddy. 'Ahh, good morning, ladies. What will it be today? I've got a freshly baked Victoria sponge, which is pretty excellent, if I do say so myself.'

'Cake,' says Jazz, turning to Phoebe to answer her earlier question. 'Recreational Water-Based Activities means cake.'

Phoebe lets out a laugh, Kate joining in. 'Now, that's something I can get on board with.'

'Well, a swim isn't really a swim unless you have cake afterwards,' says Sandra. 'It's a very important part of our club. In the winter, I'd even say it's *the most* important part. When it's too cold to swim for very long, at the very least we can sit by the river and enjoy a slice of cake and a hot cup of tea. Thanks to you, dear Hamish.'

The man in the tweed beams at Sandra's words, his chest puffing up and his already red cheeks growing crimson. 'Ah, you're my favourite customers.'

'You say that to all your customers, Hamish.'

'It doesn't mean it's not true.'

Phoebe glances at her watch.

'In a rush?' asks Sandra.

'Just for work,' Phoebe replies, surprising herself with her choice of words. When has work ever been *just work* to her? But when she was in the water, she found her mind for once wasn't on her patients and her endless to-do list. It was impossible not to be in the moment when you were somewhere so beautiful. 'But, fuck it, I think I have time for a bit of cake first.'

She chooses the Victoria sponge, on Hamish's recommendation. He passes a huge slab of it across to her on a china plate decorated in a floral pattern. Her tea comes in a matching china cup, but as she and the others head back over to their spot on the grass to eat, it seems that they have all been given a mismatched array of crockery from what appears to be Hamish's personal collection. Sandra's bears the face of

Princess Diana, while Jazz has a more tasteful blue-and-white-striped Cornishware mug.

'What does yours say, Kate?' she asks, trying to read the words.

Kate turns it around to face her and Phoebe almost spits out her tea.

'Jesus! I'm not sure that I want to think about Hamish being the *World's Best Lover*.' She lowers her voice, not wanting to offend the tweed-clad baker. 'Although, who knows, maybe it's actually quite a burden having powers like that.'

'You'd be surprised,' Sandra replies, taking a dainty bite of a cherry Bakewell. 'I'll always remember the night we spent together not long after my divorce. That barge might be cramped, but he's a man who knows how to make the most of what he's got.'

Jazz snorts with laughter, spraying cake crumbs.

'Wow, Sandra,' chuckles Phoebe. Next to her, Kate covers her mouth with her hand, clearly trying not to choke on her cake.

'Oh, sorry, dear,' Sandra says, turning to Hester. 'Cover your ears.'

Hester lets out a sigh. 'I'm seventeen, not seven.' But the smile that had appeared as soon as she entered the water is still there.

'We both decided that we're better off as friends,' continues Sandra. 'And besides, I'm quite happy being single. Two marriages were more than enough for me, thank you very much.'

'So, you come here every day?' Kate asks, tactfully changing the subject. The other women nod.

'Pretty much,' says Jazz. 'Do you think you'll join us again, both of you?'

'I don't know if I can manage every day,' says Kate, biting her bottom lip, a shadow passing across her face. 'But I'd definitely like to come back.'

'Me too,' says Phoebe. 'As much as possible, even if just for the cake.'

The others laugh and a warmth spreads through Phoebe's chest that reminds her of the first sip of a gin and tonic. Except hopefully this won't give her a hangover.

'Let's get a quick picture,' says Jazz, reaching for her phone. They jostle together, smiling.

'I should probably get going now,' Phoebe says once she's finished the Victoria sponge, which really was as good as Hamish promised. 'It was nice to meet you, Kate, and to see you all again.'

'It was lovely to have you with us, Phoebe,' says Sandra.

'Oh, we should add you to our WhatsApp group,' says Jazz as Phoebe collects her things, clipping up her motorcycle boots and tucking her helmet under her arm.

She is part of a family WhatsApp group and that's it. If she scrolled through her phone, she'd find the ghosts of a few WhatsApp groups past, reminders of friendships that she has let fizzle out. A group with a few other nurses, one with her former colleagues on the psychiatric ward and one with some old uni friends. They were all fairly active at one point, but as life and work schedules got more hectic, the messages petered out and eventually stopped completely.

'Thanks, I'd like that.'

Jazz hands her phone over and Phoebe types her number in then passes it to Kate to do the same.

'Right, see you all again soon!'

She leaves them chatting and finishing their cakes and heads back up the meadow, her mind switching into work mode and running through her appointment schedule for the day. She's been worrying about Tara since they last saw each other. The thought of her loneliness has stuck with her, making her heart ache every time she thinks about her. She's gone over and over in her mind whether the medication is the right choice. But then she remembers how terrifying Tara used to find the voices, especially when they were telling her what to do. It feels sometimes like there's no perfect answer in her job. There's no neat solution for the mind, no stitches or cast for the brain.

Then there's Maude and her beehives. Phoebe might not have promised anything, but she still feels a sense of responsibility. If there's something that might help her, then she wants to make it happen. But, unfortunately, all her years of training didn't equip her with the skills to magic beehives out of thin air.

At least she's feeling positive about her meeting with Camilla Ramsgate after the message she received telling her she had been for a run as promised. It will be good to hear how it went and to be able to tell her about her own side of the bargain. She's been swimming, not once but twice! She can't wait to tell Camilla about the kingfisher, and about the other women she met. Hopefully, Camilla has found a running group that's just as supportive.

Once she's back at her motorbike and has pulled on her

helmet, Phoebe feels her phone buzz in her jacket pocket. There's a missed call from her mum and a voice message.

'Hi, love, hope you're doing OK. I was just trying on the off chance. It would be great to get a time in to chat; your nan would love to hear from you. She's doing OK, still adjusting to not having her own space, I think, bless her, but I know she'd love to hear your voice. Anyway, love, give us a call when you can.'

She catches the sound of her father's voice in the background, adding, 'Hope you're not working too hard.'

'Oh, and send our love to Max,' her mum adds before ending the call.

Her phone buzzes again, two notifications coming in one after the other. The first is from WhatsApp, telling her she has just been added to a group called FoARSBARWBAC. It's maybe the longest abbreviation she's ever read, and she's used to dealing with medication. She's not surprised that Kate was expecting a very different kind of group based on the name and yet Phoebe thinks it sort of suits them too. It's quirky and all-encompassing and they are certainly a motley group who have at the same time made Phoebe feel immediately welcome.

A photo pings through quickly after. It's the picture Jazz took and shows the five of them huddled up together, hair dripping and huge smiles on their faces, the river behind them.

Great swim this morning, ladies. See you soon! Xx

She hardly recognises herself compared to the reflection she's grown used to seeing frowning back at her in the bathroom mirror in the mornings. Fuck, she looks *happy*.

Next, she clicks on the email notification from her boss, Mel.

Hi Phoebe,

It's been a while since we last saw each other. Can you meet me at the clinic tomorrow at 5.30 p.m. after your last appointment? It would be great to have a proper catch-up.

Mostly, Phoebe works independently, travelling around to visit her patients, with occasional drop-ins at the clinics. She's supposed to have regular one-to-ones, but Mel is just as busy as her, even more so, so they often get missed in favour of more time with patients. That's their priority, after all.

The meeting has been scheduled for tomorrow. It will be their first catch-up in a while and Phoebe would like to have good news to tell her – especially now that Max has gone and she has to start covering rent and bills by herself and the security of her job is more important than ever. Maybe, if she can show Mel that she is handling her heavy workload well, she might even have a chance of a promotion.

As she climbs onto her motorbike, anxiety creeps its way back into her body at the thought of the future and the empty apartment waiting for her. How is she going to afford new furniture on top of everything else? It's a small village, so if she has to move, it's unlikely she'll find anything in Farleigh-on-Avon itself. And she doesn't want to go, especially not now. Not now she's an official member of the Farleigh-on-Avon River, Swimming, Bathing and Recreational Water-Based Activities Club. Or FoARSBRWAC for short.

CHAPTER 23

Kate knew it would feel good to get back into the water again, she just didn't realise quite how good. Her whole body feels lighter, as though the river water has washed everything she'd been carrying away. There's a pleasant ache in her shoulders and a tingle on her skin. As she walks back to the village after saying goodbye to the other women, she feels alive, euphoric, invincible.

But all of that rapidly disappears as soon as she turns onto the lane that leads to her cottage. She hears it immediately: crying coming from the direction of the Old Post Office. By the time she reaches the cottage, it is so loud that she glances at the neighbouring houses, half expecting to see angry faces peering out the windows. All the peace she felt down at the river shatters, replaced by anxiety and the familiar creeping sense of guilt.

She steadies herself for a second before opening the front

door. As soon as she steps inside, she'll be Mummy again. She just needs one more moment of being just Kate. Tilting her head, she watches a buzzard soar overhead and remembers the feeling of the river water on her skin. And something hits her with the same force as the sound of sobs coming from within the cottage: when she was in the water, she didn't think of Rosie once.

Kate pushes open the door and drops her swimming bag on the floor, Rosie's screams reverberating around her.

'Hello?'

She finds Jay and Rosie in the living room, Jay pacing back and forth with Rosie in his arms, his cheeks almost as flushed as hers. A look of relief appears on his face as soon as he spots Kate.

'Thank God you're back!' His voice sounds exhausted and Kate glances from him to Rosie, whose face is a violent pink, her hands scrunched up into angry fists. Jay holds her against his shoulder, rocking her back and forth, but it doesn't seem to make any difference.

'What's going on?'

'I couldn't get her to take the bottle. I tried everything.'

Kate is already reaching under her T-shirt to unhook her bra.

'Why didn't you call me?'

'I wanted you to have a good time. And I wanted to be able to do it. I read so much stuff online. Stroking her cheek, brushing the bottle against her lips … None of it worked.'

As soon as Rosie is in Kate's arms, she stops crying.

'That's better,' Jay says, 'she just wanted her mummy.'

Kate looks down at her daughter, who blinks up at her with wide eyes. 'But she always seems so much happier with you,' she says.

Kate sometimes thinks that maybe her daughter doesn't like her very much. Whenever she has thoughts like these, she pushes them down, knowing it's probably not something you should think about your own baby. But now, as Rosie looks up adoringly at her, her mouth opening and closing slightly, Kate's stomach flutters.

She focuses on getting Rosie to latch, relief flooding her as Rosie begins to feed. When she turns back to Jay, he is leant over, his elbows on his knees and his head in his hands. His shoulders are shaking, and for a second, she thinks he might be laughing, but then she spots a tear dripping down onto the carpet.

'Hey, what's the matter?' Ever since Rosie was born, tears seem to be constantly just below the surface for her, as though giving birth ripped off a layer of skin, leaving her exposed and vulnerable. But Jay hasn't cried since the hospital.

He sniffs loudly, wiping his face with the back of his hand.

'Sorry. I wanted to be able to manage. I know you needed a break. What good am I to you if I can't help you? And what good am I to her if I can't even feed her?'

Watching the tears slide down his face, something inside Kate cracks wide open. Maybe she should have headed straight back after the swim. But it had felt so good to sit on the bank with her new friends, sharing cake and easy conversation and watching the river.

She looks at her husband more closely now, taking in the

shadows beneath his eyes and the lost look on his face. She knows he's been tired since Rosie was born – they both have – but he'd seemed so happy.

'Jay, she adores you! I see the way she looks up at you. Sometimes I think she only likes me for my breasts,' she admits.

'That's not true!' Jay answers quickly. 'You're her mum. And you're literally keeping her alive! It's just awesome what you're doing for her. I feel useless sometimes. Like I'm not doing enough for her, or for you. Like you don't even need me. And I really want to do a good job. I so want to be a good dad ...'

His voice cracks again, his shoulders slumped. Looking at him, Kate wonders how she missed the pain and worry on his face that seems so obvious now. Maybe she just hasn't looked closely enough. Maybe she hasn't even been able to contemplate that he might be struggling too because she has needed him so much, his steadfast, reassuring OKness. But that's a lot of pressure to put on someone.

She strokes his back gently as she looks down at Rosie's face, her eyelids fluttering as she feeds. She looks so peaceful suddenly, her face slack and soft. In moments like these, Kate feels the enormous privilege of being able to do this for her child. But like everything to do with motherhood, there's another side to it too.

'I'm glad to be able to do this, but it does come with a huge amount of responsibility. The thought that I'm solely responsible for whether she eats or drinks? It's terrifying! And sometimes I wish I could just do cuddles without having to get my boobs out.'

'I can see that,' Jay says, wiping his face again and looking

164

up. 'I guess there are good and bad parts of both our roles.'

'And you *are* a good dad,' she says, her voice cracking. 'When I see the two of you together ... I just *see* it. How much you love her. I always knew you'd be a great dad. It's one of the reasons why I married you.'

For all the ups and downs they've had in their relationship, it's one thing she's never doubted.

'I hope you know how amazingly you're doing, Kate,' Jay says softly. 'I'm so, so proud of you. The health visitor was right – you're a natural.'

And then Kate's heart really cracks open. She tries to hold the tears back at first, not wanting to step on Jay's moment. But they've been bottled up inside her for so long that once the first tear has fallen, the others come pouring out after.

'I'm not, though. You have no idea ...'

He shuffles closer to her, wrapping an arm around her shoulders as she continues to cradle Rosie in her arms. As she lets him hold her, she thinks how much she doesn't deserve it. He shouldn't be comforting her like this, not when she's such a fraud. For so long, she's been trying to keep everything at bay but she can't keep pretending anymore. It's too exhausting.

'What is it, Kate? What's wrong?'

'*I'm* what's wrong,' she says between sobs. 'I'm not a natural at all. I'm an awful mother. And you'll think so too when I tell you the truth ...'

CHAPTER 24

Kate just knew that meeting her baby would be the greatest moment of her life. She had a clear vision of the moment in her head, created by every book she'd ever read that featured childbirth, every film or TV show she'd watched with a woman lying on a hospital bed, yelling and screaming. She'd be sweaty and exhausted. Probably, she would have just sworn at her husband or a medical professional. But as soon as her daughter was finally placed in her arms, she would cry tears of joy. She would recognise her face immediately. She would feel euphoric. Complete.

They told Kate to make a birth plan, so she did. When she was pregnant, the midwife presented her with the options as though offering her a menu at a restaurant. The choice was overwhelming, but together with Jay, they made decisions about every small detail, from where she'd like to give birth (in a birthing pool, of course) to the type of pain relief she'd be happy to accept. They spent hours making several playlists to bring with them to the hospital: a calming one for when she needed to relax and one filled with her favourite upbeat, invigorating tunes for when she needed a boost. Jay packed her hospital bag for her, along with a diagram detailing where everything was located in case they forgot.

When she went into labour a week after her due date, she didn't feel scared. She felt prepared and in control. Jay was with her and her mum and sister weren't far away. And even as the labour progressed and they headed to the hospital, Kate remained calm. As the contractions grew more frequent and intense, she held onto the image she had in her mind of holding her daughter for the first time. Every now and then, she thought of the lido, picturing herself floating in the cool blue water. Once all of this was over, she would be handed her baby and everything would be worth it.

She couldn't pinpoint the exact moment when panic invaded the room, but after hours of exhaustion but general calm, something shifted. As she looked up, she caught a shared glance between the midwife and her assistant and for the first time since her contractions began, Kate started to wonder whether maybe she couldn't actually do this after all.

What happened next took place in a blur, until, before she knew it, she was out of the birthing pool and on a hospital bed and the room suddenly filled with people. Everything after that came in snapshots. The repetitive beep of a monitor. The shuffle and squeak of shoes as the doctors and nurses moved about swiftly. The hot, clammy clasp of Jay's hand in hers as they gripped one another as though they were holding each other afloat.

When Rosie finally, and with much assistance, arrived in the world, there wasn't the startled cry that Kate had been imagining. Kate held her breath for a second, waiting for it to come a beat later. But it didn't. She reached out her arms, but instead of being handed her baby, the doctors whisked her away, their backs shielding her from view on the other side of the room.

Finally, there came a cough, a splutter and a wail. A sigh of relief spread around the room and Jay squeezed Kate's hand even tighter, tears flooding his face. But Kate didn't share the feeling of relief that was in the air. Because where was her baby? They still had her baby.

There's no way Kate could have said how long it was between Rosie being born and being handed to her. It felt like days but was probably no more than minutes. Eventually, she was bundled up in a white blanket, a pink hat atop her head, and brought over by a smiling doctor.

'Everything's fine now, don't worry. She just needed a bit of help getting started. But here she is. Here's your daughter.'

With trembling arms, Kate reached up to receive her child, ready to finally experience the moment of overwhelming joy she had pictured for so long. But as she pulled the swaddled baby into her chest, there were no fireworks exploding in her heart and no warm glow spreading through her body.

When she'd made her birth plan, Kate had known that things might change, that you couldn't predict exactly what would happen during something as momentous as birth. But the one thing she never even stopped to think about was that the moment when she met her baby wouldn't be anything like she had been expecting.

Kate held her daughter in her arms for the first time and felt nothing ...

'At first, I thought I was just too exhausted to feel anything,' Kate explains to Jay, her voice finally close to even again after managing to force out everything that has been eating her up inside for so long. 'I thought it would come with time.'

She glances down at Rosie, who is now asleep in her arms, and fresh tears prick in her eyes, but she forces them back. She remembers returning from the hospital for the first time with her new baby, sinking, exhausted, into her own bed and turning over to stare into the Moses basket beside her, taking in every detail. The pink, wrinkled face, the tufty ginger hair, the clenched fists, the downy hair on her cheeks, her tiny nose.

This person had lived inside her for nine months. Kate had read to her and taken her swimming at the lido, feeling her tiny feet kicking in her ribs in time with her own strokes. She had felt that she knew her unborn child already. But as she looked at the baby asleep beside her, it felt as though she was looking at a complete stranger.

'I did think about saying something. I considered telling the midwife when she came to visit, maybe Mum or Erin.'

'And me?' Jay asks.

Kate winces slightly, knowing how bad it sounds that she didn't immediately turn to him.

'I did want to. But as the days went by, I lost my nerve. You seemed so happy. Every time I looked at you, there was this enormous smile on your face. It was just so obvious that you felt it. All the things that I thought I would feel too. They came naturally to you.'

'I'm so sorry you felt you couldn't tell me.'

'You don't need to apologise. And I don't mean to make you feel bad. I'm just trying to explain …'

Three months might have passed since Rosie's birth, but sometimes it feels as though Kate is still there, stuck in those moments she has tried so hard to forget. Poised with her arms outstretched for her child, waiting to feel everything she had dreamt of and that had kept her going through her labour.

'Do you remember when your parents came to visit shortly after she was born?'

Jay nods.

'They kept telling me how Rosie was the spitting image of you. "She's all Jay," your dad said.'

It's something people have kept saying to her ever since Rosie was born. The first time she heard it, from a nurse on the maternity ward looking from Jay to Rosie and back again, Kate had wanted to say, *But I grew he*r! Then, as time went on, she stopped fighting it. Because Kate can see nothing of herself when she looks at her daughter.

'I remember,' Jay says quietly. 'I didn't even think what that might feel like for you. I'm so sorry.'

'And then there was this moment when your mum had been holding Rosie for a while but suddenly handed her back to me, apologising for hogging her. "I remember when Jay was a baby, I never used to let anyone hold him," she said to me. "I just couldn't stand it if he wasn't with me." And there I'd been, happily letting Rosie go to your mum for as long as she wanted.'

'You know Mum didn't mean anything by it. She didn't mean to make you feel bad.'

'I do know. No one has meant to make me feel bad. The people who stop me in the supermarket and tell me to cherish every second with my baby because it goes so fast. The friends who tell me how perfect she is. My mum and sister for adoring her as much as I always hoped they would. But it has all just made me feel as though there's something wrong with me.'

'But, Kate, there's nothing wrong with you.'

Kate looks him dead in the eye now. 'But of course there is. What kind of mother doesn't love their baby?'

Because the truth is that when she holds Rosie or feeds her or rocks her to sleep, Kate feels as though she is pretending, acting out some part she doesn't know the lines for. Inside, she feels numb. And every day that passes, she hates herself a little bit more for it.

Rosie begins to cry in Kate's arms and she instinctively begins to rock her in the particular rhythm that she has learnt does the best job of soothing her. She strokes the corner of her eyebrow.

'She deserves so much better than me,' she says quietly, looking down at her daughter. 'She deserves the very best.'

'You know what I think?' says Jay. 'I think that love is a verb.'

It's so surprising that Kate glances at him, her attention pulled away from Rosie. 'What do you mean?'

'It's not just a feeling, but something you do. It's all the ways you show up for a person. Like the way you let me sleep through the night, even when you're exhausted, because you don't want me to be tired too. Or how, when I went on that shoot the other day, you sent me photos of Rosie all through-out the day because you knew it's what I needed.'

'I knew you missed her,' she sniffs.

'Exactly. You were thinking about me. You might not feel the warm, gushy feelings towards Rosie that you thought you would. And I'm so sorry that you haven't had those feelings yet. I'm no expert, but I think it's probably normal given everything you went through with the birth. I did get that rush you talk about, but, honestly, I think it was mostly relief. Kate, I wasn't the one lying there on that hospital bed and I can understand that you probably didn't get to feel any relief at all.'

'No,' she says in a tiny voice. 'I felt terrified. I *still* feel terri-fied, even though everyone has assured me she's perfectly healthy. What if they missed something?' She looks down at Rosie's head, stroking her hair. 'Because for all the things I don't feel, I *do* feel this fierce protectiveness towards her. I know it's my job to look after her.'

'Isn't that love?' says Jay, causing Kate to frown, thinking. 'Just because you don't feel certain feelings you thought you would, that doesn't mean you don't love your daughter. You are doing love every time you feed her, *constantly* through the night. Every time you rock her or sing "Wonderwall" to her completely off-key ...'

Despite everything, she laughs, her laughter merging with her tears. Jay squeezes her tighter.

'You're doing love for her right now.'

172

They both gaze down at their daughter, her expression pure contentment as she nestles into Kate's collarbone, her fist wrapped around a lock of Kate's hair. Kate tries to take a deep breath and consider the possibility that maybe she isn't such a terrible mother after all.

'Let me ask you this,' Jay carries on, his body warm and reassuring against hers. 'Did you fall in love with me the moment you saw me?'

'Um …' She glances at him, wondering if it's a trick question. They worked with each other for about six months before Kate even really noticed Jay existed. And when they did connect, they were friends at first before it led to anything else. She was nervous about rushing into anything, cautious, like she's always been in all other areas of her life.

'I *know* the answer is no,' Jay says when Kate doesn't answer. 'With us, it happened quicker for me than it did for you. I was smitten early on, but you needed time to get to know me. We still ended up in the same place – both of us in love, because I *know* you love me, Kate. But what I'm getting at is that people are different and they fall in love differently. Some do it quickly and others, probably quite sensibly, take their time. From everything I know about you, how considered and thoughtful you are about everything you do, it makes sense that you haven't fallen head over heels with Rosie straight away. You're getting to know each other. That's just the way *you* fall in love.'

Thinking about it now, Kate can't put her finger on the exact moment when her feelings for Jay changed from admiration and friendship to love. It just feels as though it has always been there, this huge love that fills up every bit of her even when

173

they are going through a tough patch. But, of course, it wasn't always there. It grew.

'You'll get there, Kate. I know you will. Because I know you and I know that you have a big heart and that once someone finds their way in there, they're in for good.'

'Maybe you're right,' she says, sniffing and wiping her face.

Jay squeezes her shoulder, pulling her close.

'I'm not right about that many things. But I'm confident that I'm right about this. I'm right about you, Kate Mathews-Chapman.'

CHAPTER 25

The sun beams down overhead as Phoebe pulls up outside Number 1 Magnolia Street, the tyres of her motorbike crunching on the gravel. She knocks confidently on the door, turning for a second to enjoy the feeling of the sun on her face. The wisteria that covers the façade of the house is in full bloom and from here she can see the gate that leads through to the garden. Hopefully, Camilla has been spending time out there again, the way she used to with her husband. Perhaps she's out there right now, Phoebe thinks to herself as she steps back from the door, looking around her. When there's still no answer, she knocks again, louder this time.

She's about to reach for her phone to try calling when Arabella answers the door. She is dressed just as neatly as before, today in cropped indigo jeans, ballet pumps and a cream blouse.

'Hello! I was starting to think no one was in,' Phoebe says brightly, but then she sees Arabella's expression. 'Is everything OK?'

Arabella rubs her eyes and Phoebe notices that she looks even more tired than yesterday, regardless of her pristine outfit and make-up.

'Today isn't a good day.'

Phoebe's heart sinks.

'I'm sorry to hear that.' She tries to hide the disappointment from her voice. She takes a steadying breath, finding that inner strength that she knows her patients and their families need from her. 'I'll have a chat with her and see what we can do to improve things for her. Where is she?'

She looks around, hoping to catch a glimpse of Camilla maybe having breakfast downstairs in the kitchen or even through the French doors pottering about outside.

'Upstairs. She hasn't left the room since your last visit.'

The words hit her hard. She thinks back to the message she received from Camilla and how pleased she'd been that she'd made such quick progress, going for a run so soon after their appointment. But maybe she should have seen through it, or at least questioned it. But it had been so nice to receive some positive news for a change.

'I know my way, I can head on up,' Phoebe says, pulling off her boots and leaving her things on the telephone seat like before.

Arabella nods, sighing. But as Phoebe is about to head up the stairs, she speaks again.

'Would you like a cup of tea?'

'I'm OK, but thanks for asking. I'll let you know if we need anything. You go have a rest.'

Arabella nods. 'OK, I think I will. Thank you. I'm glad you're here.'

It's not much, but Phoebe holds on tightly to those words as she heads through the old house towards Camilla's bedroom.

The door is ajar and she taps lightly. When no response comes, she says in a clear voice, 'It's Phoebe here – Nurse Harrison. I'm coming in, OK?'

The room is mostly in darkness, a single beam of sunlight forcing its way in through a gap between the curtains. There's a stale atmosphere, the air musty and heavy. If sadness had a smell, this would be it. Camilla Ramsgate is curled up in the bed, this time on her side facing away from the doorway.

'Hello, Camilla.'

She doesn't reply.

'I'm going to open the curtains, OK?'

Light streams into the room, illuminating flecks of dust. Arabella's sleeping bag is still curled up on the chaise longue and there's a plate of untouched toast on the bedside table, alongside a cup of what Phoebe guesses must be cold tea.

'I'm going to get you a glass of water.'

She takes an empty glass from the bedside table and heads into the en suite. While she's there, she scans the room for telltale signs, spotting bottles of pills lined up by the sink.

'I think it would be good to try to drink something,' she says once she's back at Camilla's bedside. She crouches down beside the older woman, whose eyes have a glassy, empty look to them. It's as though she's somewhere else completely. 'Can you drink some of this for me, please, Camilla?'

Silently, Camilla pulls herself to sitting, so slowly that it's as though even that movement is too much to manage. While she drinks, Phoebe takes her pulse and blood pressure, noting them down.

'I'm sorry I lied to you.'

Camilla's voice comes out as a croak, making Phoebe think it's maybe a while since she last spoke.

'You don't have to apologise to me.'

'I was going to go. I found my old trainers.' Camilla nods in the direction of the dressing table and Phoebe spots a pair of trainers arranged neatly beneath, a folded pair of leggings on the chair. There's something about the sight of them there, so hopeful in a room that feels so tired and sad, that breaks her heart a little bit. But she works hard to keep her expression neutral.

'What stopped you?'

Camilla puts down the glass of water, her eyes flicking to the photographs on the bedside table. She looks even more shrunken than the first time they met and Phoebe makes a note to tell Arabella about some high-calorie shakes she could get if Camilla isn't feeling like eating.

'Our conversation last time reminded me how much I used to enjoy running. The thought of going again ... I was actually looking forward to it.'

'Well, that's a great start,' Phoebe says enthusiastically. When someone is struggling with depression, showing an interest in anything is a big step. But Camilla's eyes shine as she blinks back tears.

'The thought of running again ... It made me happy. I realised I hadn't felt happy once since Teddy died.'

Phoebe listens carefully, trying hard to hear what is really being said between Camilla's words.

'And how did it make you feel, to feel happy again?'

The tears fall faster now, Camilla letting them drip onto the quilt.

'Terrible. How can I possibly feel happy when he's gone? To be happy without him ... That means I'm moving on.'

Phoebe reaches out for Camilla's hand. The older woman lets her take it.

'And you don't feel ready to move on?'

Camilla shakes her head.

'I know what I told you before ... That I want to get better for my daughter. And I do. She deserves that. But ...' She trails off, wiping her face with the sleeve of her silk pyjamas.

'Have you been taking your medication?' Phoebe asks softly, thinking of the pill bottles she saw in the bathroom. They were all full.

Camilla bites her lip.

'You've caught me out.'

A glimmer of life returns to Camilla's eyes and Phoebe holds onto it, letting it give her hope. Something has to.

'You deserve to feel happy, Camilla. Do you really think this is what Teddy would want for you? It sounds as though he loved you very much. I think he would want you to find happiness again. Isn't that what you would want for him if the situation were reversed?'

'Of course!'

'Moving on doesn't mean that you didn't love him. Or that you have to stop loving him.'

179

Camilla doesn't say anything, but Phoebe can tell that she's thinking.

'Would you let me give you your medication? I really think it could help you.'

Camilla nods, allowing Phoebe to do what she needs to do without complaint. It's a first step at least. Phoebe holds her hand the whole time.

By the time Phoebe leaves, Camilla is up and dressed, having a cup of tea in the kitchen with Arabella. She told Phoebe she didn't feel up to going out into the garden, but together they decided that ditching the pyjamas and getting out of that room could be a first step. Arabella seems relieved, flapping about her mother, fetching her a cushion and pouring the tea.

'Thank you,' she says to her as she shows Phoebe to the door.

'You're welcome. I'm just doing my job. I'll see you both again soon, OK?'

She tries her best to feel heartened as she shuts the door to Number 1 Magnolia Street. Maybe the appointment hadn't gone how she had hoped, but at least Camilla had taken a small step. But it's hard not to feel thrown, especially after the brightness of her morning and her hopes for Camilla. It's disappointing and part of her wonders if it's her fault. Did she push Camilla too far by encouraging her to go running? Should she have started with smaller steps first? And will she ever be able to help show Camilla that life is worth living even now that her husband is gone? The weight of responsibility presses down on her. She doesn't want to let Camilla down, or Arabella either.

As she's about to set off, her phone rings in her pocket.

'Hello, is this Nurse Harrison? This is Sergeant Halifax. Do you think you could come down to the station? We have a woman here who is asking after you. I believe she is one of your patients. Oh, and you might want to bring some clothes.'

CHAPTER 26

As the police officer explains the situation when Phoebe eventually arrives at the police station, a bag bundled under her arm, she has to try very hard to maintain a straight face. Not because the situation isn't without its serious, worrying parts, but because sometimes laughter is the only response.

'Someone called to alert us to a woman walking down the middle of the dual carriageway. Said her arms were outstretched as though she were on the front of a ship or something. Didn't have a stitch on her. Not a stitch. We sent a patrol car out to pick her up. She was chatting a lot – sounded like some religious stuff. She was luckily pretty co-operative. Got in the back no problem. I think she was talking about bees at one point? She mentioned your name and we found we had your number saved from last time.'

'Thanks for calling me,' Phoebe replies, making sure she keeps her voice steady and professional. 'Her social worker is on her way too. Can I go and see her?'

'Yeah, of course. She's not in any trouble. We just thought it best to keep her here till you got here. Didn't want her getting cold.'

Phoebe smiles at the police officer behind the desk. She recognises him from a previous visit to the station. Thankfully, they seem pretty understanding here. It isn't always the case, of course, which is why she always likes to get there as quickly as possible when she gets a call like this. Some aren't as compassionate as Sergeant Halifax.

He shows her through the station until they reach what looks like a staff meeting room. The door is open and sitting at a table inside, drinking coffee from matching paper cups, are a young female police officer and Maude, who is dressed in an oversized police uniform.

She looks up as Phoebe enters. 'Oh, give thanks to the Lord!'

The police officer looks over with a smile. 'Hello, there. Maude and I have just been having a chat. I've learnt a lot about beekeeping.'

So, it seems that the interest in beekeeping that Maude expressed at their last appointment was more than a passing comment, making Phoebe feel even worse about not having found a way to reconnect her with her former passion yet.

'Hi, Maude. It's good to see you. Shall we go and get you changed so we can give this uniform back and then I'll drive you home?'

Maude pauses, tilting her head to look over her shoulder as if to confer with someone, as she often does. Phoebe waits, used to this habit of hers. 'Praise be!' she says, taking the last sip of her coffee and placing down her cup.

'Thanks for keeping me company, Maude,' the young police officer says with a kind smile. She can't be long after joining the force, but Phoebe can tell immediately that she's going to make a great police officer.

'Don't forget what I told you about the bees,' says Maude. 'It's a common misconception, but they're very docile really. They only get angry when they feel as though they're under attack.'

Hearing her words, Phoebe recalls another phone call she received like this a few years ago. That time, the police had been called by the staff in a shopping centre when customers had started to grow wary of the woman in her sixties who was shouting Bible quotes at an increasingly loud volume. The officers then had been firm, thinking a direct approach the best course of action. But something about the tone must have frightened Maude because she'd grown frantic. By the time Phoebe had arrived, she'd been so worked up that it had taken a long time to calm her down.

But now, thankfully, she seems at ease.

'I won't forget,' says the young police officer. 'You take care of yourself, all right?'

'Thank you,' Phoebe says with meaning as Maude heads for the door, Phoebe holding it open for her. 'I'm glad it was you and Sergeant Halifax who picked her up.'

'What were you doing out on the road like that, Maude?' Phoebe asks gently as they make their way to a nearby bathroom. 'You could have got yourself killed.'

Maude rolls her eyes. 'Isn't that what resurrections are for?'

Phoebe covers her smile behind her hand.

'What about the other people on the road who aren't immortal, then?' she says more seriously. 'You could have caused one of *them* to have an accident. Where were you going anyway?'

'I was trying to get back to the convent. The bees needed me. No one's been looking after them since I left.'

Maybe if Phoebe had found a way for Maude to get back in touch with her old love of beekeeping, then this might not have happened.

'And your clothes?'

'They were just holding me back.'

'Well, I'm afraid you're going to have to put some on now because we need to give that uniform back, as much as it suits you. I grabbed some of my things from home; I hope that's OK just until we get you home.' She had wanted to get to the station as quickly as possible so grabbed the first things that came to hand in her wardrobe. They are, thankfully, around the same size, even if Maude is thirty years older than her.

'How do I look?' Maude asks as she emerges from the toilet stall a few moments later. Phoebe works very hard to suppress her laughter. In her hurry, she didn't notice that what she thought was a plain white T-shirt is actually a slogan tee she wears when cleaning the flat.

Maude spreads out her arms to better display the words 'Yes, sir, I can boogie,' written across her chest in bold green letters. Paired with high-waisted red jeans and a pair of bright red Converse, it's quite a look for someone who usually dresses in long, loosely fitting dresses in shades of grey and black, reminiscent of the convent.

'You look fantastic, Maude.'

She gives a little twirl and this time Phoebe lets herself laugh because Maude is laughing too.

'Come on, let's get you home. Amanda, your social worker, is meeting us outside to drive you back.'

'That's a shame. I hoped I'd get a ride on the back of your motorbike.'

'Maybe next time,' Phoebe says with a smile.

They head out of the police station, saying goodbye to the officers they pass on the way. A visit to the police station hadn't been on her to-do list for the day. But at least that's one thing she can say for her job: no two days are ever the same.

By the time she arrives back in Farleigh-on-Avon at the end of the day, Phoebe is exhausted. Thanks to the morning's excursion to the police station, the rest of the day has gone by in a frantic rush of constantly feeling she's falling behind. As she met with a few new patients, she tried extremely hard not to look flustered or to glance at her watch. She wanted to show them that she had all the time in the world for them, even if her packed diary said otherwise. As well as the new patients, she'd popped in to see Ben. He seemed less perky than her last visit, but she tried not to worry too much – mental health came with its ups and downs and at least he was on a better track than a lot of her patients, with his beloved football club to go to twice a week and job interviews lined up.

Lunch had consisted of a chocolate bar, a packet of crisps and a soggy sausage roll grabbed from a service station on the way between appointments. While she was there, she grabbed a frozen pizza too, knowing she wouldn't have the energy to cook when she got home.

Her last appointment of the day was with Tara and Phoebe was gutted to see that her mood hadn't improved since her last visit. She was still taking the medication, for now, but the loneliness of the silence that surrounded her now that the voices had gone was becoming hard to bear. Phoebe turned on the radio, hoping that the background chatter might help but knowing it was no substitute for human contact.

'Do you think you'd like to try some of the community groups we talked about before?'

But Tara had shaken her head. 'I couldn't. I can't ... I can't go outside. You know that.'

And Phoebe did. Tara hadn't once left the house in all the time that Phoebe had been visiting her, no matter how hard Phoebe and the other people who cared for her tried to persuade her. At first, the voices had been what kept her a prisoner in her own home, telling her that awful things would happen if she went outside. But even though the voices have gone, it seems the fear hasn't.

Before leaving, Phoebe did a quick check of Tara's kitchen – a common tactic of hers to work out how her patients are *really* doing. On discovering that the fridge was practically empty, she sat with Tara while she placed an online food order, not leaving until she was certain that there would be supplies arriving in the morning.

'And I've put a pizza in the oven for you. I accidentally bought one too many at the shop earlier. It would only go to waste otherwise.'

Now she's finally finished for the day, her motorbike parked up outside the flat, but with nothing for her own dinner and not enough energy to go back out to the shops. She's just thinking about the bottle of gin waiting for her upstairs when she spots someone she thinks she recognises walking towards her along the pavement.

Although the mousy-haired woman is dressed in tracksuit bottoms and a hoody, Phoebe can immediately recall her in a bright yellow swimsuit when they swam together at the river this morning. Jesus, was it really only this morning? Her day has felt about three weeks long.

To her surprise, the woman isn't alone. She is pushing a navy pram, a soft rattle shaped like a star hanging from its canopy.

'Kate?' she asks as the woman draws closer.

The messy bun on the top of Kate's head bounces as she looks up from where she'd been peering inside the pram, her eyebrows rising in surprise.

'Oh, hi Phoebe.' She appears decidedly flustered, her cheeks colouring.

Phoebe catches a glimpse inside the pram of a tiny baby wearing a pink-and-white striped onesie. She is fast asleep, her arms flung out above her head.

'I didn't realise you had a baby.' The morning might already seem a long time ago, but she tries to recall their conversation at the river. She's certain Kate mentioned something about work ... But then, how much did any of them really reveal about their lives beyond the river, however happily they had chatted together?

'Oh, yeah,' Kate says, shifting somewhat uncomfortably on the spot. 'This is my ... daughter, Rosie. Short for Rosemary.'

Is it Phoebe's imagination or does Kate hesitate before the word 'daughter'?

'Nice name.'

A faint smile appears on Kate's face.

'Thanks. She's named after an old friend. Actually, the person who first got me into swimming.'

'How old is she?'

'Three months.'

'She's cute.'

'Thanks.' There's something about Kate's expression that looks conflicted. Phoebe notices the dark bags under her eyes that she hadn't spotted when they were down at the river, where nature seems to put a filter over everything, making it brighter and softer.

She thinks of the gin and tonic waiting for her upstairs. Then she looks at Kate again.

'You don't fancy a coffee, do you?'

Kate looks startled but pleased.

'That would be lovely.'

Phoebe starts leading them towards the Cosy Corner, but Kate gently grabs her arm.

'Um, do you mind if we go somewhere else? This place right here looks promising?' She gestures behind them. 'I've been wanting to go since it opened, but this little one means I basically never get out anymore. Ooh, it looks like they do wine too ...'

Phoebe looks through the window, catching sight of Luca standing on a ladder, reaching for a bottle of olive oil from

189

one of the top shelves. His T-shirt has lifted slightly, revealing a slice of tanned back. She immediately looks away.

'Here, let me help you,' she says, holding the door open as Kate wrestles with the pram.

For the second time that day, Phoebe steps through the door of Giuglia's. Except, unlike this morning when she felt excited about the day ahead, now disappointment and exhaustion weigh down her steps. Thank God they serve wine.

CHAPTER 27

Kate takes a long sip from her large glass of Italian white, savouring the smell and the warmth that fills her throat as she swallows. It's her first taste of alcohol since having Rosie. She's been trying to avoid it because of breastfeeding, but when Phoebe ordered a bottle from the handsome deli owner, she found herself not wanting to say no. She can 'pump and dump' later. She needs this, especially after the emotions of the day.

'I'm sorry I didn't mention Rosie when we chatted this morning,' she says to Phoebe after taking another sip. Catching her eye across the table, she notices how Phoebe's expression seems to have been relaxed by the wine too. It's just the two of them in the deli, but the owner has discreetly disappeared to the kitchen, where Kate can hear sounds of him moving about, preparing the food they've ordered.

'You don't have to apologise. I guess we didn't share that much about ourselves at all. Too busy spotting kingfishers and eating cake.'

'And yet we saw each other semi-naked.'

Phoebe lets out a laugh. 'That's very true. I'll be honest, I nearly didn't recognise you in your clothes.'

They share a giggle.

'I've always thought it's a strange thing about swimming,' Kate says. 'You take all your clothes off in front of total strangers in the changing room – or by the river, in our case this morning – but then you put them back on again and go back to your dry-land life, maybe not seeing those people again until the next time you're wriggling into a swimsuit alongside one another.'

'Or until you bump into them in the street and that stranger forces you to come for coffee with them, which turns into wine,' says Phoebe with a smile, raising her glass.

'You absolutely didn't force me. I was pleased to see a friendly face.' Looking over at Phoebe, Kate senses that maybe she has had a bit of a day too. 'Long day?' she asks.

Phoebe slumps a little lower in her chair, taking another long sip of her wine.

'Something like that.'

'Tell me about it?'

On the other side of the table, Phoebe raises an eyebrow.

'Are you sure you want to hear?'

'Positive. It will be nice to focus on someone else's baggage for a change.'

Phoebe raises an eyebrow but doesn't say anything. Instead, she takes a deep breath and starts to talk. Kate sips her wine and listens as she describes the pressures of her job. Kate can hear the stress in Phoebe's voice and wonders how she missed

192

it earlier when they swam side by side in the river. How didn't she see that this woman who is so different from her in so many ways carries so many of her own fears?

'I get that feeling of letting people down,' she tells Phoebe. 'I feel it all the time with my daughter. It's like, however hard I try, I'm still getting it wrong. And it matters so much. I *can't* get it wrong.'

'Yes!' says Phoebe, slapping a hand on the table. 'That's exactly how it feels.'

'And I bet you feel guilty too because you chose your career? So you feel like you should just be able to suck it up and cope with the hard parts?'

'That's exactly it. My patients need me to be strong.'

They nod at one another in understanding and Kate suddenly feels very glad that they ran into one another. When Phoebe gets onto the subject of her ex-boyfriend, Kate can feel her fists curling in anger on behalf of her new friend.

'He took all your furniture?'

Phoebe nods.

'So, what have you been sleeping on?'

'A mattress on the floor. The benevolent bastard left me the mattress at least.'

The kitchen door swings open and the owner of the deli comes towards them holding a large wooden board piled with slices of cheese, rolls of cured meats, chunks of bread and little pots containing oils and olives.

'Jesus, that looks fucking amazing, Luca,' says Phoebe, smiling up at him.

As Kate looks on, she wonders if there is something going on between him and Phoebe.

'Luca nearly killed us in the river the other day,' says Phoebe. 'He has apologised, although I'm not certain if he means it.'

'And I'm not certain Phoebe has forgiven me.'

'We're neighbours,' Phoebe explains, gesturing above her head. 'I live just upstairs.'

'Oh! That must be pretty great, having somewhere like this right on your doorstep. It's a lovely place, even nicer inside than it looks from the street.'

Luca's cheeks colour and he runs a hand through his dark hair. 'Thank you. I'm not sure I've been the best neighbour so far …'

'Awful,' Phoebe replies and Luca raises an eyebrow.

As Kate watches the way Phoebe and Luca look at one another, she desperately wants to question Phoebe about the clear *something* that's going on between them but decides to hold back. They don't know each other well yet.

'Anyway, I'll leave you both to it. Enjoy.'

Once he's gone, Kate takes another sip of her glass of wine, noticing as she does that Phoebe has already poured herself another large glass.

'It sounds like you've got a lot on your plate,' Kate says gently once they are alone again, Luca back in the kitchen and the rest of the tables in the deli empty. 'I think it's amazing what you do. But it's a lot of responsibility. It must be heavy to carry sometimes.'

Kate's phone buzzes in her pocket.

'Do you mind?' she asks, gesturing to her phone.

'Go ahead,' mumbles Phoebe, her mouth filled with cheese.

As Kate reads, she lets out a sigh, a frown creasing her forehead.

'What is it?'

'It's my work friends ...' Kate explains about Emma's wedding dress shopping trip and how she was left off the invite list. 'I know it sounds silly when I say it all out loud. But I still feel hurt. Leonie just sent me another message with a reminder of the address of the dress shop and time of the appointment. It's on Saturday.'

'And you're still not going?'

'I don't know ...'

'Do you want to be there?'

Kate pictures Emma stepping out of a changing room wearing a white dress and the inhale of breath she just *knows* she would take seeing her friend looking so beautiful but, most importantly, so happy.

'Of course I do. She's one of my best friends.'

'So, I think you have your answer then.'

'It sounds so simple when you say it.'

Kate watches as Phoebe takes another slug of wine and twists her red hair around her finger.

'Maybe it is? They're your mates. They obviously love you and I doubt they meant to hurt you.'

'Maybe you're right ... I miss them.'

'And maybe they miss you too?'

'Hmm, I hadn't thought of it like that. I guess I just keep picturing them going to work together and having drinks and things and I feel like I'm on the outside.' And it's not just now.

When she returns to work after her maternity leave, she will only be in the London office one day a week, working remotely the rest of the time. It feels as if one chapter of their friendship is over forever.

'But you're having this whole new life too,' Phoebe says, gesturing towards the pram. 'I've never been certain if I want kids or not, but I still remember feeling left behind when my brother had his first. Then his second. I love being an aunty but sometimes when I look at my brother and his family, I feel like he's part of this whole different world and belongs to a club I'm not invited to. Your friends might feel that way too.'

It shocks Kate to realise she hadn't even thought of it like that before. How has she got so caught up in her own worries that she hasn't put herself in her friends' shoes? And now, by not responding to their messages, she might have pushed them away for good.

'Thanks, Phoebe. I think I needed to hear that.'

'And I needed to offload. I don't often talk about work stuff. Thanks for listening.'

'It's a pleasure. I imagine you do your fair share of listening in your job. But you need to be able to talk too. And if you ever feel like doing it again, you know where I am. You have my number from the WhatsApp group.'

'Thanks, Kate,' Phoebe says, her eyes growing misty.

'I really mean it too.'

'I know.' Phoebe takes a deep breath and reaches for a slice of prosciutto. 'So, do you think you're going to start swimming regularly with the group?'

'Yes,' Kate says with a smile. She's already talked to Jay

about it and he's agreed to look after Rosie in the mornings so she can go. He was delighted, in fact. 'I don't think I'm really myself when I don't swim. Jazz was onto something when she said outdoor swimming should be prescribed on the NHS.'

'Hmm,' says Phoebe, a light appearing in her eyes. 'That's actually really interesting ...'

At that moment, Rosie begins to cry. Kate rocks the pram back and forth with her foot and checks the time on her phone.

'I should probably get back and get her to bed, if you don't mind?'

'That's fine. I'm ready for bed too.'

'I know that feeling,' Kate says with a laugh. 'I'm always ready for bed at the moment. Anyway, I'm really glad we did this.'

'Me too.'

They hug one another with more warmth than might be expected from two people who were strangers at the start of the day.

'See you soon,' Kate says as she puts down some money for her share of the food and waves goodbye, hoping that it will turn out to be true.

As she pushes Rosie back towards home, she takes long, steady breaths. Everything that she has been worrying about is still there, but she feels a new lightness since speaking the words out loud to Jay. She realises that the reason she took so long to open up to him was because she was terrified of him judging her as a terrible mother. But now she wonders if the only person who has really been judging her is herself. Her conversation with Phoebe has helped too, giving her a new perspective on the situation with her friends.

She adjusts her grip on the pram so that she is manoeuvring it with one hand. In the other, she grabs her phone and starts looking up train tickets to London.

CHAPTER 28

'The food really was fantastic,' Phoebe says once she and Luca are alone in the deli. She's pretty certain she's going to be dreaming about this food for weeks. The wine might also have something to do with her inhibitions dropping in front of her new neighbour.

'Really?' Luca asks, his face lighting up as he turns from the counter, where he'd been vigorously stirring a glass bowl of a creamy-looking liquid that fills the shop with the scent of lemon and vanilla.

All throughout her conversation with Kate, Phoebe had been aware of Luca's presence in the kitchen or pottering about in the shop rearranging things on the shelves, even if she really didn't want to care. Now that his attention is focused entirely on her, she feels her neck growing warm. Wine. It must be the wine.

'Yeah. Really, really good.'

'Did you like the olives?' he asks excitedly. 'I spent ages finding a Sicilian supplier who does the absolute best Nocellara ones out there. In my opinion anyway. I don't understand how anyone could *not* like olives, but some people ... I always think it's because they haven't had very good olives. Saying you don't like olives is like saying you don't like fruit – there are so many different kinds.'

He trips over his words, as though his mouth can't keep up with his enthusiasm. His voice is bright with excitement, making him seem suddenly younger, and his hands gesture wildly. It makes her look a little more closely, noticing that his eyes are closer to caramel than hazelnut – if you were going to be precise about it.

'They were great. What's this?' she asks, pointing to one of the final slices of cured ham that remains on the board to distract herself from analysing the exact shade of his eyes. Jesus, maybe she *has* had one glass too many! 'I've never had anything like it.'

'I love that one. It's a Crudo di Cuneo from the foot of the Alps. It's been cured for ten months, which is what gives it that amazing flavour. Look at that distribution of fat, isn't it beautiful?'

'Um, I guess so ...'

'Sorry. I can get a bit carried away when I talk about food.'

'Don't apologise. It's nice to see someone who's passionate about what they do. What's that you're making?' she asks, gesturing to the bowl.

'Sweet ricotta filling for tomorrow's cannoli. They were my favourites growing up. My mum's ones are the absolute best.

I'm doing a batch of chocolate chip, one of pistachio and a lemon and vanilla. I was up late last night trying a few alterations to Mum's recipe, although I'm not sure I've perfected it quite yet. Hey, could you try some of the filling and let me know what you think?'

As he turns away for a spoon, Phoebe reaches for the bottle of wine, only to find it's empty. Kate has left nearly half a glass on her side of the table. Would it be so bad to finish it off? It would be a shame to let such nice wine go to waste, she tells herself as she quickly pours it into her own glass while Luca's back is still turned.

'Here we go.' He passes over a spoon laden with a scoop of the creamy filling.

'Wow! That's good,' she says as she licks the very last scrape of sauce off the spoon.

'You think so? I'm not sure ...'

'No, seriously, that's the best canno ... callo ... cannoli I've ever tasted.'

He laughs, and Phoebe thinks it might be one of the nicest sounds she's heard in a long time.

'I'm glad you liked it.'

She suddenly becomes aware of how foggy her brain feels. Maybe she should have stopped after a glass or two of wine. But she needed it after the day she's had – after the *week* she's had. It feels good to have everything softened like this. She feels relaxed. So relaxed, in fact, that she finds herself standing up and taking a step towards Luca.

He gives her a questioning look, raising one of his dark eyebrows. As if he's asking a question she isn't entirely sure of the answer to, only that his eyes look like caramel and he smells like vanilla and has a smudge of icing sugar on his nose and she misses the feeling of being held by someone and, well, why shouldn't she just kiss him if she bloody well wants to?

She wobbles a little on the spot and Luca reaches out and takes hold of her hips, steadying her. The heat of his hands through her jeans gives her the confidence to lean forward, tilting her body towards him, mouth reaching for his. His lips are warm and surprisingly soft and it feels so good … until suddenly he is dropping his hands from her hips and stepping backwards. Phoebe stumbles, her arm catching against the table. The empty bottle of wine rolls onto the floor with a loud smash, followed by the wooden board, scattering the last remnants of the delicious food everywhere.

He stares at her and at the mess and she steadies herself against the table edge, her head spinning and embarrassment pooling in the pit of her stomach.

'Oh shit.'

'Don't move, let me clear this up.' Luca darts quickly into the kitchen, but Phoebe feels too mortified to wait until he returns. All she can think about is the feeling of him stepping away from her. She throws some money for the meal on the table and picks her way through the broken glass, letting the door swing shut behind her as she races, stumbling, upstairs to her empty flat.

CHAPTER 29

Phoebe hadn't planned to go swimming again so soon, but when she wakes early the next morning with the taste of wine and regret in her mouth, she grabs her swimming things without thinking, loading them onto her motorbike alongside her work gear. She tries hard not to glance into the window of Giuglia's as she sets off, or to think about the delicious espresso she could be having right now if she hadn't made such a bloody fool of herself last night.

Every time she thinks about what happened, she cringes. Of course Luca had stepped away from her. She had totally misread the situation and now she will have to spend the foreseeable future trying not to run into the person who works directly below where she sleeps. And ordering two separate coffees every morning from the Cosy Corner because the staff there refuse to serve her a triple shot.

She arrives with a headache pounding against her temples,

but as soon as she sees the meadow and the water running through it, something inside her relaxes. Then she spots the group of women on the bank – Kate, Sandra, Jazz and Hester already getting changed and chatting to one another – and a smile appears on her face as they wave at her warmly.

This time when they swim, they talk a bit more about their lives beyond the river, Kate sharing her struggles with early motherhood and Sandra reassuring her that everything she's been feeling is perfectly normal. 'I had the most awful postnatal depression after my second,' she announces breezily. 'Often thought about running away to go live by myself in a bothy in Scotland. But it got a lot better. You'll get there, sweetheart.'

Kate ducks her head underwater then and Phoebe wonders whether it is because she is suddenly possessed with the urge to look at the mud and rocks on the riverbed or maybe if it is to let tears merge with the river water. Either way, she bobs back to the surface seeming refreshed.

Jazz talks a bit more about the trials and tribulations of being a twenty-six-year-old back living with her parents and Hester updates them about her upcoming exams and how her application is coming along to study nursing at university the following year. As soon as she hears that Phoebe is a nurse, Hester's face lights up like a Christmas tree that's just been switched on and she bombards Phoebe with excited questions. To Phoebe's surprise, when she tells her she is a community mental health nurse, Hester's enthusiasm doesn't waver.

'Oh wow, that's awesome. I've been reading up about mental health nursing as part of my prep.'

'Have you? It's a field that can get overlooked. I've had

people tell me that what I do isn't "proper" nursing.'

'What a load of nonsense!' says Sandra. 'I've seen enough over the years to tell me that the mind is the most complex part of the human body. It's easy enough to set bones or take blood, but navigating the human mind ... that takes great skill. And courage, I'd rather imagine.'

'Well, those other things are tough too,' Phoebe replies, not wanting to undermine the work of anyone else in her field. But she's always secretly agreed with Sandra. It's one of the reasons she was so drawn to mental health nursing in the first place. The subtle complexities of the job, combined with a desire to help people through the toughest moments in their lives that came to her at a young age.

Her hand subconsciously lifts to her arm, where she traces the letters of the tattoo there. *This too shall pass.*

'My job is a bit different to being, say, a nurse in a cardiology or gastroenterology ward at a hospital. I administer all kinds of medication, but I do a lot of other things too that some people – old-fashioned people – don't think of when they think of nursing. For example, I've actually got an idea to run past you ...'

Phoebe had hoped they would like the idea, but the level of enthusiasm from the swimming group gives her a well-needed boost.

'What a great idea,' says Kate. They're back at the meadow now and help one another up the bank, which is slippier today from the rain that fell in the night. 'I'd love to help, if I can.'

'Me too,' says Jazz, wringing water from her hair.

'Count me in,' adds Sandra.

Hester nods her agreement too.

'Thanks, everyone,' Phoebe says as she rubs herself dry, enjoying the buzz from the cold water. There's a sound of quacking and feathers flapping as a pair of ducks descend on the river, ripples spreading out in their wake.

The women share tea and cake again, sitting down by the water and watching a few swimmers coming and going and a paddleboarder drifting by with a golden retriever perched on the front of the board. Phoebe takes it all in, thinking how long it has been since she let herself just *stop* like this.

She started the day stiff and hungover on her mattress on the floor, feeling like an idiot for everything that happened with Luca. But now she feels buoyed up by the swim and the support of her new friends. For the first time in a long time, she feels hopeful about the future. Maybe this new idea of hers can help her patients, but also maybe help her too.

She thinks ahead to her meeting with her boss Mel at the end of the day, nervous and excited to talk her through her plan and see if she can turn this idea that blossomed on the banks of the river into a reality.

CHAPTER 30

It's amazing what a difference a swim makes. The sun is shining and the village looks beautiful as Kate heads back towards home after her swim, spring flowers blooming in the hanging baskets and someone browsing the stacks of second-hand books in the repurposed telephone box.

She pauses for a moment, leaning against a wall and sending a selfie she took of herself by the river to her old Brockwell Lido friends.

Their replies come in quickly.

Jermaine: Wow, looks amazing!

Frank: You'll have to take us when we come to visit – because we promise we will come to visit soon. We're hopefully hiring a new member of staff so we'll actually be able to leave the bookshop sometimes!!

Hope: You l0ok so happy. Rosemary wOuLd be proud of yOu.

Kate looks at the photo again. She *does* look happy.

It's not just the swim and her new friends who have put her in a brighter mood. After opening up to Jay yesterday, she woke this morning feeling lighter. As she rolled over to check on Rosie, she didn't necessarily feel any differently towards her – she still looked like a very sweet little stranger – but the guilt about her feelings had lessened. Maybe Jay was right and those feelings will come in time. And maybe the fact she hasn't felt them yet doesn't mean she's a bad mother, just that she's falling in love in her own way, in her own time.

She continues on towards home, glancing in at the shops on the village high street. There's a little greengrocer with a striped awning that makes her think of Rosemary and her husband George, who Kate never got to meet but who she heard many stories about, including about the family fruit and veg shop he ran in Brixton. As she approaches the Cosy Corner Café, she lets herself glance inside the window. And as she does, she spots a collection of prams. Making a sudden decision, she pushes open the door of the café.

The group of women look up as she approaches. 'Kate?' says one of the women hesitantly.

They look the same as before, nursing coffees and babies and sporting messy buns and tired smiles. But this time, Kate feels different.

'Yes, that's me. Hi, Lexi. I spotted you all and thought I'd come and say hello.'

'It's nice to see you again. No Rosie today?'

Kate is touched that she remembered both her name and the name of her daughter.

'I'm having a baby-free morning today. Is it still OK if I join you, though?'

'Of course it is!' Lexi gestures at a free chair and the other women budge up to make room for her around the table. They smile at her warmly.

'I realise I was pretty rude the last time we met, to just leave like that and not come back. I thought I should come and explain. The truth is, I've been finding it really hard since Rosie was born.'

As soon as the words are out, all the others follow easily, as though saying the first bit has unstopped a cork and everything else just comes pouring out. The other mothers listen intently as Kate opens up and tells them everything. Mum buns bob up and down as the other women nod at her words. Occasionally, a baby's cry or babbling interrupts, but the women keep listening and Kate keeps going, sharing the troubles she has had with building a connection with Rosie, her doubts about herself as a mother, the frequent nightmares she's had about the birth and, most of all, the way she has been beating herself up for feeling all of these things.

'I just sometimes feel like I'm getting it all wrong. So, I think when I came to this group that first time, I found it all a bit overwhelming. You all seem to know what you're doing.'

Once she's finished, she feels exhausted but lighter too. She's ready to stand up and leave the women to it now she's said what she needed to say, but to her surprise, Lexi lets out a loud laugh.

'You think we know what we're doing?' She raises her

eyebrows and shakes her head, her messy blonde ponytail swishing. 'I haven't got a clue!'

One of the women beside her who Kate remembers as Mabel's mum bursts suddenly into tears. Holding her baby in one arm, she reaches for a paper napkin on the table with the other, wiping her face as she continues to bob her child up and down on her knee.

'I'm sorry,' she says between sobs. 'I just can't believe you've been feeling that way too. I thought it was just me. I know I should be feeling so happy, but there's so much I miss about my old life and I feel like I can't say that, because it's not that I don't want Mabel – I love her so much! – but sometimes I wish I could have even just one day of my old life again and not have any of this worry or responsibility.'

Kate can't quite believe what she's hearing. All this time, she thought this group wasn't for her.

'There's so much stuff like that, isn't there?' chips in the twins' mother, balancing one on each hip. 'Stuff you don't say about how hard this all is because you don't want anyone to judge you for it, or to think you're not grateful for what you have.'

'Why don't we say it all now?' Kate suggests, feeling a butter-fly spread its wings and flutter in her stomach. 'If you're happy to, that is?'

The women don't need encouraging. One by one, as they sip their cappuccinos and hold their children, the women share their stories – their true stories. The woman who has been getting therapy to deal with PTSD following a traumatic birth and still can't go back to the hospital where her son was born. The occasional fantasies about running away to a tiny cottage by the sea where absolutely no one could follow you. All the times that they have doubted themselves and their roles as mothers, feeling as though they are getting it all wrong.

Eventually, once the tears have stopped and hugs and smiles have been shared, Kate asks something that has been bothering her since she first met the group.

'One thing I didn't get to do last time I was here was learn all your names.'

As babies are bounced on knees and rocked in arms, Kate gets to know Lexi, Jess, Sophie and Olivia. Women who exist in their own right beyond their children, even if at times they might forget it. She learns that Lexi runs her own marketing business and Jess used to compete in triathlons and is just getting back into running, Sophie is a chemical engineer and Olivia went to the same university as Kate and her passion is roller skating.

And, most important of all, she realises that they have all been in, if not the exact same position as her, then something very similar. They have all struggled and done what they can to get by, which has often meant keeping the truth about their feelings hidden. They have all felt desperate at times, lonely, and afraid. But they are all still here, rocking and nursing their babies while also trying to maintain relationships with their partners and friends and return to work and maybe get back to exercising or perhaps contemplate an evening out one day soon, even if they will have to leave by nine because otherwise they might fall asleep in a pub corner. They're all exhausted but trying their best.

One by one, the babies start to get restless until a Mexican wave of crying spreads around the group and the women begin to gather their things to leave, but not before exchanging phone numbers. As Kate says goodbye to them all, she can't believe how close she suddenly feels to these women that she had been so nervous about seeing again. Last time, the conversation had felt at times as though they were competing to win the prize of best mother. But now Kate can see how much of it was just a front, a way of protecting themselves. And that these women aren't her competition. They're her teammates.

Just before she leaves the café, a thought enters Kate's mind and she pauses to ask a final question.

'Have any of you ever tried wild swimming?'

CHAPTER 31

The first half of the day passes by as normally as any day ever does for Phoebe: checking in with existing patients, getting to know new ones and, leant against her motorbike, typing up her notes between appointments. By mid-afternoon, she is tired, but satisfyingly so. She's making good progress on her appointment list and is looking forward to her meeting with Mel and to the thought of a weekend stretching ahead of her, even if she will have to lay low and avoid Luca after what happened.

But as she is about to head to the next appointment in her calendar, her phone rings – and as soon as she answers, she knows that something is very wrong.

'Ben? What is it?'

But she can't hear his words between his rapid, rasping breaths.

'Take a deep breath. It's OK.' She can't make out any words, just broken, painful sobs.

She isn't due to see him today. He'd been doing so much better. Yes, when she visited yesterday, he had seemed ever so slightly withdrawn compared to the exuberant energy of their previous meeting. But, overall, he seemed like a different person to the young man she had first met several months ago.

'Where are you?' she asks, her voice firm now.

Ben just about manages to get out the fact that he is at home. Phoebe glances at her watch. She can be there in fifteen minutes. Quicker than an ambulance.

'Are you hurt? Do you need to get to hospital?'

'No,' he manages. 'No, I'm OK. But can you come over? Please.'

'Of course,' she replies quickly. She'll send a message to Mel and get her to inform her later patients that things might need to be rearranged. But she'll get there. 'I'll be with you very soon, OK, Ben? I'll be there really soon.'

Her hands shake as she straddles her motorbike and revs the engine. It's times like these that she feels especially grateful for her bike. *I'll be there soon*, she tells herself as she zips down the country lanes, just like she told Ben. *I'll be there soon.*

When she arrives, she runs up to the front door of the little council house and knocks firmly on the door. The curtains are drawn.

'Ben? Ben?' she calls, through the letter box. 'Are you there?'

There's a painfully long pause, in which Phoebe can feel her heart pounding in her chest, her palms growing sweaty. She can't help but remember the times over the years when she has turned up to a home like this and knocked and knocked on the door but never received an answer.

Memories of her appointments with Ben flash through her mind. The two of them sitting in front of the telly, Ben telling Phoebe the names of all the Arsenal players and Phoebe trying her best to store them all in her mind so she could chat with him about them another time. How, when she brought him a pretzel that time when they'd only recently met, he insisted on sharing it with her. The happy grin on his face when he talked to her about his first session with the football club he'd joined and, later, when he'd told her about the interviews he had lined up.

He might still have his struggles, but his life was just starting to turn around.

She bangs on the door again.

She is just about to dial 999 when the door creaks open and she lets out a sigh of relief at the sight of Ben, gaunt and red-eyed but there.

'Oh, thank fucking God!' she says. She normally tries to monitor her language at work, but she can't help it.

Ben doesn't seem to notice. His expression is blank, as though barely registering that she's there.

'Can I come in?'

He doesn't say anything, but he opens the door a little wider before disappearing down the corridor. Phoebe closes the door and follows him. As she's heading to the living room, her phone buzzes in her pocket. There's a message from Mel saying that she's got it covered for the afternoon and to keep her updated about Ben. But there are two missed calls from her mum too. She'll call her back later.

In the living room, Ben is slumped on the sofa, his shoulders

215

bowed. His eyes are ringed with grey and she spots a flash of blood on his bottom lip. He always bites his lip when he's anxious; she noticed it the first time they met.

'I'm here now, Ben. Do you think you might be able to tell me what's going on?'

In the silence, Phoebe feels her phone ring in her pocket again. She tries her best to ignore it, focusing her attention on Ben.

'Has something happened?'

Her phone rings again.

Ben says nothing, sinking further down into the sofa cushions.

'How about a cup of tea first?' Phoebe asks. Ben nods very slightly. Phoebe leaps up, placing a hand gently on his arm as she passes. 'I'll be back in a minute, OK?'

In the tiny kitchen, she takes in the mess of unwashed dishes, then flicks on the kettle and quickly checks her phone. Three more missed calls from her mum. Glancing quickly through the hallway to check Ben is OK, she dials her mum's number.

'Mum, is everything OK? I'm at work and can't really talk right now …'

But then she realises that her mum is crying, sobs reaching her down the line. Her hands begin to shake as she grips the phone.

'Mum, what is it?'

Her mum goes as if to speak, but the only sound that comes out is a squeak and another sob. Phoebe can hear vague noises in the background but can't decipher what they are.

'Is it Dad? Is he OK?'

As the words leave her mouth, it strikes her that, even after all these years, she's lived her whole life terrified of receiving this call. But, to her relief, she suddenly makes out his muffled voice in the background.

'No, Dad's fine,' her mum replies. 'It's Mum. Your nan.'

The brief moment of relief is replaced by panic. 'What's happened?'

'She's had another fall.'

'Shit. Is she OK?'

'She slipped in the bathroom. She'd been in there a long time and I was starting to worry so knocked, but there was no reply. I got your dad to help me with the door and when we went in, there she was, lying on the ground in her dressing gown. She was unconscious.' Her mum's voice breaks again, another wave of sobs taking over.

'Where are you now?'

'We're at the hospital. They've taken her away for tests and we haven't been able to visit yet.'

'Is she going to be OK?'

'I don't know!' Her mum's voice breaks off again. 'I don't know ...'

Phoebe blinks back tears, thinking of all the times this week that she's said she'd speak to her nan. But she hasn't. Not once. And the last time she saw her in person was months ago. She kept telling herself that she was too busy, that she didn't have time, that she'd get down to Cornwall soon. But what if she's missed her chance?

The sound of the kettle boiling pulls her back into the room. She can't fall apart, not here. Not when she has someone else's crisis to deal with.

'Mum, I'm really sorry, but I've got to go. I'll call you back as soon as I can, though, OK? And call me again if there are any updates.'

There's a slight pause on the other end of the line and then her mother takes a faltering breath. 'OK.'

'I love you, Mum.'

She tries hard not to spill the tea as she carries two mugs through to the living room with shaking hands. Ben is still slumped on the sofa. Phoebe's mind races, picturing her parents finding her grandmother sprawled unconscious on the bathroom floor. But the expression on Ben's face means she has to push those thoughts away.

With all her strength, she tries to keep her voice level and steady as she says, 'I'm here now, Ben. Do you think you might be able to tell me what's going on?'

His dark eyes flick up towards hers and he sniffs loudly.

'They closed it. It's over.'

'They closed what?' Phoebe watches him closely. He's never exhibited any signs of psychosis before, but it's something she's always alert to. The word 'they' is an alarm bell. *They're watching me. They put something in my food. They told me to do it.*

'I heard a rumour yesterday. Something about cuts. I didn't want to believe it. But today they told us it's definite. It's being scrapped for good.'

'What's being scrapped?'

Ben looks up again, his eyes meeting hers. He looks so lost and suddenly much younger than nineteen.

'The football club. Today was the last session.'

To most people, the closure of a local football group might seem like a small thing. A shame, but not the end of the world. But Phoebe knows that this group has become Ben's world. She's seen the difference meeting up with other young people with mental health struggles has made to his confidence and mood. Before he started going to the sessions, he was barely leaving his flat. And now he has job interviews lined up. But with that support network so suddenly ripped from his life, his future suddenly seems precarious.

She's hit by an intense feeling of failure. It's her job to look after him. The closure of the football club might not be her fault, but it still feels as though she's let him down. Just like she's failed her nan by not being in touch. She recalls her mum's faltering voice on the phone just now and thinks she has probably let her down too.

'I'm so sorry. That must be so tough for you. I know how much your football sessions mean to you.'

Ben stares down at his mug of tea. She spots the red patches around the sides of his fingers where he's been chewing the skin there.

'I'm going to try to sort this for you. There must be something I can do.'

He looks up then, a glimmer of hope appearing in his eyes, which immediately makes her regret her words. She shouldn't make promises she can't keep. But what else is she supposed to do? She knows all too well what happened the last time he lost hope, is reminded of it every time her gaze falls on the scar on his left wrist.

'Really?' he says in a tentative voice. 'Please. I don't want to go back to how it was before.'

His words make her feel as though he is reaching out and clinging on to her to stay afloat. The trouble is, she suddenly isn't sure if she's strong enough to keep them both above water.

CHAPTER 32

Kate consults the small black notebook full of handwritten recipes as she stirs the pan and hums to herself, Rosie happily kicking her arms and legs in the sling. The notebook was a gift from Rosemary, but Kate hasn't used it in a long time. Either Jay has done the cooking because she's been too tired or they've resorted to ready meals or the one Chinese in the village. But after her conversation with him yesterday, she wanted to do something nice to show that she can look after him, just like he's been looking after her. Especially after he made space this morning for her to go down to the river again.

After her swim and then the impromptu meet-up with the Tired Mums Club, she arrived home feeling refreshed. When Rosie had spent the next hour cluster feeding, she let herself sink into the sofa and just enjoyed the feeling of her daughter in her arms rather than feeling frustrated. She sang to her, rotating through her limited repertoire of noughties classics.

Now that she's opened up to both Jay and the women who seemed like strangers at first but now feel like new friends, Kate itches to get real with other people in her life, as though honesty is a new addiction.

She pauses from stirring the pan and reaches for her phone, opening the WhatsApp group with her mum and sister.

Hey Mum, hey Erin. Hope you're both having good weeks. It feels a while since we last saw each other! I've got something to tell you – I've started wild swimming! Down by the river here in Farleigh-on-Avon. It's so beautiful and I've met some really nice women. I was wondering if I could tempt you both into the water with me? There's a café there, so we could get cake after. The weather looks nice over the weekend, so maybe Sunday afternoon?

Erin's reply comes in quickly.

That sounds great, sis. I haven't been swimming since last summer! Would be great to go with you xx

Kat smiles, reaching for the pepper grinder and adding a generous sprinkling into the pot where spring vegetables bubble away. She glances again at the recipe for 'Rosemary's favourite soup' and takes the fresh loaf she bought from the deli out of the bread bin, ready to serve alongside the soup with hearty slatherings of butter from the local dairy.

Her phone buzzes on the counter.

Mum: Sorry, girls, but I can't do this weekend. You have a great swim! Lots of love xx

Before Kate has time to process the fact her mum is brushing her off again, Jay is stepping into the kitchen and sniffing the air appreciatively.

'Wow, it smells amazing in here. You didn't have to do this.'

'I wanted to.'

They eat outside under the apple tree, Rosie lying in the Moses basket in the grass, looking up through the leaves and kicking her arms and legs. As they eat, Kate tells Jay about her morning swim and the experience with the Tired Mums Club and he talks about some upcoming shoots and what he has left to do in the studio. She'd gone in to visit him out there this afternoon with Rosie and had been blown away by the progress he'd made. The dusty old outbuilding has been transformed into a bright white space, with portraits of her and Rosie on the walls that he'd got her to pose for not long after Rosie was born. She had felt incredibly awkward but knew it meant a lot to him and he's a great photographer, so the photos are nice, even if she does look a little dead behind the eyes.

Rosie starts to cry and Kate reaches for her, bouncing her gently. As soon as she's in Kate's arms, she settles and a warmth spreads through Kate's body at the satisfaction of being able to comfort her.

'So, I've been meaning to tell you something … Emma is going wedding dress shopping in London tomorrow, and I'd like to go.'

Kate's conversation with Phoebe decided it for her. She realised she was at risk of letting her hurt feelings get in the way of being there for her friend. And that maybe they might be struggling with the shift in their friendship too.

'Leonie invited me and I wasn't going to go, but I think I should. I want to. I know it's quite last minute though …'

Jay shakes his head. 'It's OK, I think it's great that you want

223

to go. You'd regret it if you missed out. How about we all go together on the train? I can hang out nearby with Rosie in case she won't take the bottle and I need to bring her to you for a quick feed?'

'That would be amazing,' Kate replies, relieved. Because making the decision was only one step – next she had to work out the logistics of getting to London for the day when she has a three-month-old who often refuses a bottle. To think that before having Rosie she used to just *leave her house* without thinking. Sometimes she'd just grab her keys and a book and go and sit on her favourite bench in Brockwell Park and read, not even taking a bag with her. Now, getting out and about feels like a military operation.

'Oh shit,' Jay says suddenly. 'I just remembered. I've got a shoot tomorrow. It's been in the diary for ages. I'd completely forgotten about it.'

Kate holds Rosie a little tighter, feeling her nestle into her chest and glancing down at her sleepy, contented face. Looking at the expression of calm and ease on her daughter's face gives Kate a burst of courage.

'It's OK,' she replies. 'I'll take her with me.'

'Are you sure you'll be OK on your own?' Jay asks anxiously. 'That sounds like a lot, navigating a train and the Underground and everything with her ...'

Maybe it will be a lot. But then, the past few months have been a lot. And she's still here, isn't she? After everything she's been through, she reckons she can handle London's transport system.

'It will be fine. I did live in London for years. I'm not a tourist. I've got this.'

Once they've talked through the logistics for tomorrow, Kate passes Rosie over to Jay.

'Can you just take her for a second? I'm going to message Leonie to let her know I'm coming.'

Her reply comes in a few seconds later.

Leonie: Ahhh! I'm so pleased you're coming. Em will be too! xx

Kate: Thanks, can't wait to see you. Can you not tell Emma? I want it to be a surprise xx

Leonie: Great idea. She'll be so happy! Xx

Kate busies herself with plans for the next day, making a list of everything she needs to take with her for herself (not much) and Rosie (a lot). As she thinks about going to London for the first time since moving and having Rosie, and seeing her friends again, she switches between extreme excitement and extreme nerves. Because what if Leonie is wrong? What if, after their last conversation and the distance that's grown between them since, Emma isn't happy to see her at all?

CHAPTER 33

Phoebe isn't quite sure how she has makes it through the rest of the day. After the phone call from her mum, she just wants to jump on her motorbike and ride to Cornwall. But she has a job to do. She stays with Ben until he is calmer, updating his notes to let the rest of the team know to be on high alert. For the rest of the day, she listens to her patients and delivers their medication and types up her notes, trying to keep her mind on her work while sneaking glances at her phone to check for updates from her mum. She can't stop picturing her grandmother lying unconscious on the bathroom floor.

Normally, it's hard enough to maintain a smile in the face of tough moments with her patients. To keep her voice calm and steady as she bears witness to the challenges in their lives and, often, the trauma in their past. But this afternoon the stories of her patients and the sense of how much they need from her felt overwhelmingly heavy. It's too much.

And now she is tumbling into Mel's office at the clinic, her bag hanging from her shoulder and her red hair tangled from the motorbike ride, feeling as though she has been fed through a pulveriser; she just wants to crumple into a messy heap on the floor.

'Phoebe, it's good to see you,' says Mel from behind her desk stacked with paperwork, a pinboard with medical posters providing a backdrop. 'Come in and sit down.'

Phoebe tries her best to keep her expression neutral. This is the first meeting they've had in a long time and she needs it to go well. If her boss thinks she's having some sort of break-down, she's hardly likely to consider her for the promotion that Phoebe so desperately needs now that Max is gone and she's got the entire rent and bills to pay by herself. She's always prided herself on staying strong and holding it together at work. It's a requirement of the job – being resilient and pushing your own problems to the side to make space for the people who need you. The people you are paid to look after.

'How are things going, Phoebe?'

As soon as Mel asks the question, Phoebe bursts into tears.

'I-I'm s-sorry,' she says, wiping furiously at her face with her sleeve. But however hard she wipes her face, the tears keep on falling.

'You don't have to apologise, Phoebe,' Mel says, pushing a box of tissues across the table towards her. Phoebe takes one gratefully, blowing her nose loudly.

'This is so unprofessional. I'm *so* sorry.'

'Stop saying sorry!' Mel barks.

'But this is so bloody embarrassing. I'm stronger than this! I never cry at work!'

Another sob courses through her, making her shoulders shake.

'You're not a robot, Phoebe,' says Mel. 'You're only human. And I would say that being "only human" is one of your great strengths in your job. We're not so different from our patients, really, and that's important to remember.'

Mel passes her another tissue but looks completely unfazed. At least that's one good thing about having your breakdown in front of a mental health nurse, Phoebe supposes.

Once she has just about managed to pull it together, Mel leans forward slightly in her chair. 'Why don't you tell me what's been going on?'

And because there doesn't seem any other option but to tell the truth now that she has snot and tears dripping down her face, Phoebe tells Mel everything. About the break-up with Max and her feelings of failure about yet another relationship down the drain, plus the pressure it has put on her financially. She talks about Ben and Camilla, Maude and Tara and her worries for them and all her other patients too. How those worries have grown heavier and heavier recently, piling on top of her until she feels crushed at the bottom of the heap. She even tells her about the drinking, how it started as a way to unwind after a long day but has gradually become more than that. It used to be her way of dealing with her problems, but now it feels as though it's started to create its own problems. She keeps wondering if things with Luca would have gone differently last night if she'd stopped at the one glass of wine. Every time she thinks about the way he stepped backwards, her whole body cringes.

And then she tells Mel about her grandmother.

'I haven't seen her in too long,' she explains. 'I've been a completely shit granddaughter. What if I never get to see her again?'

The tears have at least stopped by now, leaving her face smudged with streaks of make-up.

'Oh, Phoebe. I wish you had said something sooner. You, of all people, should know that problems only get worse if you let them pile up without talking about them.'

'I know. Bit of a bloody hypocrite, aren't I?'

'We can often be the worst at taking our own advice. When we do jobs like we do, it can be easy to forget about looking after ourselves.'

'I don't think I've been very good at doing that.' If she's honest with herself, she isn't sure she's ever made space for it. She's known since she was young that this was the job she wanted to do and has always been motivated by a fierce drive. But in the midst of it all, she's lost her way. She's lost herself.

'You're definitely not the first person to sit down in that chair and tell me something like this. Why do you think I keep a box of tissues on my desk?'.

They share a laugh.

'I've been in your same position in the past too. It's not easy, looking after ourselves. But it's so important. It's the *most* important thing, in fact. So I want you to take next week off work. I'll sort out cover. Go and be with your family. Take some time. And when you get back, we'll talk about next steps, OK?'

Phoebe can't remember the last time she took a whole week off work. But she's too exhausted to refuse. 'OK. Thank you.'

'You're an excellent nurse, Phoebe. You are dedicated to your patients and have a knack for not just listening to them but really *hearing* them. You've always been incredibly organised and diligent too, which I've always admired but never expected because our jobs are so hectic. You can take a day or two to get your notes up to date and you don't have to reply to emails in the middle of the night – in fact, I'd really rather you didn't.'

'I just really care about this job. Even when it's really fucking hard, I do love what I do.'

'I know you do. And you are great at your job. But I think you need to look at the other areas in your life too.'

As Mel passes her a final tissue, it hits Phoebe that her boss might just be right.

CHAPTER 34

The bridal boutique is on a pretty little street in Islington full of vintage shops, homeware stores and the kind of sparsely stocked boutiques that smell like Diptyque candles and where it isn't certain exactly what they actually sell, but whatever it is, you want to buy it. Kate pushes the pram swiftly along the pavement, checking the address from Leonie on her phone.

Pulling into Paddington station with Rosie in tow, Kate had experienced a buzz of excitement. The guard helped her and the pram down off the train and then they were swept up into the crowds, the sound of buses and taxis filtering in from the street outside and pigeons flapping above them on the ornate rafters of the station.

It took her longer than she had expected to make her way to Islington. She'd had to make a quick detour to the station toilets to change Rosie's nappy and give her a feed before heading to the Underground.

As she looks up from her phone, she spots the shop she has been aiming for. The sign above the door is painted seashell pink and gold and, in the window, stands an ivory gown in flowing silk with a short train that ripples along the floor.

The door is locked, but a salesperson dressed in a chic navy jumpsuit and nude heels looks up from the counter and heads across to open it. Kate can glimpse Leonie and the rest of the group, minus Emma, sitting on a dusty pink velvet sofa at the back of the store sipping prosecco.

'Sorry I'm late.'

The shop assistant's professional smile droops as she spots the pram.

'Are you bringing that in?' She glances from the pram to the narrow doorway and back again.

'Unless you want me to leave my daughter out in the street?'

Rosie lets out a little grumble as if affronted at the thought.

'Of course, of course,' comes the quick response, a polished smile appearing on her face again as she unbolts the door, rattling it forcefully until it opens.

Together, the two of them just about manage to manoeuvre the pram up the steps and inside. The salesperson looks distinctly put out. *Try doing that across half of London*, Kate wants to say. But she smiles widely instead. 'Thank you so much, I really appreciate your help.'

There's laughter coming from the back of the room and as Kate approaches, everyone leaps up to greet her, but Leonie places a finger on her lips. 'Shh! We don't want to ruin the surprise,' she whispers, then turns to Kate and gives her a tight hug. 'She's just trying on the first dress. It's sooooo good to see you, Kate.'

A lump rises in her throat at the familiar smell of her friend's Calvin Klein perfume and the strength of the embrace. She gives a little wave to the other bridesmaids: there's Emma's sister, Clara, who seems to be taking the role of maid of honour extremely seriously, with a clipboard in hand and professional make-up, plus some old school friends and a cousin who Kate remembers meeting at various birthdays over the years. Emma's mum, Caren, is here too, her glass of prosecco nearly empty and her cheeks slightly flushed.

'Oooh! Pass her here!' Caren says as soon as she sees the pram.

Kate dressed Rosie in a puffy yellow dress for the occasion and everyone 'aww's as she hands her over to Caren, flashing matching yellow bloomers and very chubby little legs.

'She's just gorgeous!' Caren says, trying to keep her voice quiet. Seeing the way the women coo over her and watching as Rosie soaks it all up, batting her long lashes and making suitably adorable noises, something swells inside Kate's chest.

There's a sound of rustling and suddenly the curtain of the changing room is flung open to reveal Emma, absolutely radiant in a plunging white ballgown. Her mouth opens in shock. For a brief moment, Kate's stomach clenches with fear. It's so good to be back in London and to see Leonie, but maybe she should have told Emma she'd be coming, given her time to process her feelings rather than just showing up like this.

'Kate!' she cries, a look of unfiltered happiness spreading across her face. 'I'm so happy to see you!'

Kate is suddenly being folded up in a bundle of white taffeta and the fiercest of hugs. The knot in her stomach releases.

'I wouldn't have missed it,' she says into her friend's armpit, struggling to get her words out as all the air is squeezed out of her. 'I'm sorry for before.'

Emma steps back, holding Kate at arm's length. Then she glances over towards the rest of the group, spotting the pram. 'And Rosie too!'

'I hope it's OK that I brought her?'

'Of *course* it's OK. It's more than OK. Oh my God, look at her! She's such a little angel!'

Kate glances over to where Rosie is letting herself be passed around between the women, totally calm.

'Um, can we talk about you and this dress?' Kate says, returning her attention to her friend, who does a little twirl, the long train swishing along the floor. 'You look absolutely beautiful, Em.' Kate's eyes grow misty.

Caren is full-on sobbing and Clara passes her a tissue from her clutch bag; she's clearly come prepared.

'Yes, you look amazing, Em,' says Leonie, the other brides-maids echoing.

'I feel like a princess!' Emma says delightedly, her face giddy with happiness. 'But, obviously, a very empowered princess who doesn't need rescuing and does princessing part-time alongside her badass career.'

'Wow, that's quite a vibe,' laughs Leonie. 'But, seriously, babe. You're a knockout.'

Kate can't speak. She suddenly can't believe she nearly missed out on this moment, on seeing her friend so happy and being able to share in that glow as if Emma's joy is a campfire and they're all huddled around, soaking up the warmth.

'It's a bit long, though,' Emma says, swishing the skirt, her feet buried beneath the fabric.

'These are just samples!' chips in the hovering shop assistant. 'If you choose a dress with us, it will be precisely made to your measurements, with several fittings and rounds of alterations.'

'Ooh, fancy,' says Leonie, eyeing Kate and making her laugh.

'Very fancy,' agrees Emma, before turning her attention back to her reflection in the mirror. 'I'm not sure if it's *the* dress though.'

'It's only the first one you've tried on,' says Clara, consulting her clipboard. 'I'm going to give it a seven?'

'There are plenty more to try on!' trills the sales assistant, dashing to fetch a dress from the rails of silk and lace.

Emma's cousin pours Kate a glass of prosecco and she settles into the velvet cushions as Emma disappears back into the changing room to try on the next dress. Rosie is still being cuddled on the other end of the sofa, so Kate lets herself sink back and sip her prosecco, enjoying herself.

There are a lot of beautiful dresses. There's a minimalist white sheath dress that hugs Emma's body as tightly and lovingly as a best friend comforting you after a break-up and an oyster tulle confection covered in pearls, among many others. Each one is given a score, but none of them are deemed quite right. The longer they go on, the more determined the sales assistant seems, appearing with new dresses they hadn't spotted on the rails.

Finally, a loud squeal escapes from behind the curtain.

'Guys! This is it! This is the one! I love it so much!'

As the curtains part and Emma emerges, the group of women take a collective inhale. Even the sales assistant, who is hovering at the back of the group with another pile of dresses slung over her arm, audibly gasps.

'Oh, Emma. My darling, you look just perfect.' Caren's voice is soft with emotion.

Rosie, now back in Kate's arms and sitting on her lap so she can see, opens her eyes wide in wonder.

The dress is made from the faintest blush silk dotted with lace flowers. A tight bodice hugs Emma's frame perfectly before the fabric skims her hips and gathers in a shining pool at her feet. Tiny floaty sleeves hanging off the shoulder make her look like a Grecian goddess.

'And look, it has pockets!' Emma slips her hands inside them and twirls.

The women let out a collective 'Oooh!'

'It's perfect!' exclaims Leonie.

'You look like a film star.'

'The dress says princess, but the pockets say badass career woman.'

'I'm writing "this is the one!" on the clipboard! In capital letters!' says Clara, clapping her hands together.

Emma pauses in front of Kate and Rosie, her cheeks pink with delight.

'Kate, Rosie, what do you think?'

'I love it, Em. It's perfect. Rosie, how about you? Don't you think Auntie Emma looks beautiful?'

She looks down at her daughter and as she does, she notices

that a frown has appeared on Rosie's forehead. She opens her mouth and in one horrifying second, Kate recognises the expression on her daughter's face.

'No!' Kate cries, trying to stop what is about to happen. But she's too late.

Erin once told Kate that when her sons were babies they were able to projectile vomit a distance of up to three metres. Kate never believed her. Not until she watches her daughter open her mouth wide and empty the contents of her stomach directly onto her best friend's wedding dress.

There's a shocked silence as no one seems to know how to react.

'Oh Emma. I am so, so sorry …' Kate's eyes fill suddenly with hot tears. Maybe she shouldn't have come after all. She's ruined Emma's perfect dress and she's ruined the day too.

But then Emma tilts her head back and starts to laugh. And before long, the others are joining in too, Clara handing Kate a handful of tissues and Caren helping her wipe up both Rosie and the dress.

'At least she's still only breastfeeding,' says Caren as they dab at the material of the dress, while the sales assistant watches on in horror, mouth hanging open.

'I feel awful,' Kate says. 'I'll pay to get it dry-cleaned …' But Emma reaches out and squeezes her shoulder.

'Babe, I'm about to spend four grand on a dress. I think they can pay for dry cleaning.'

And suddenly everything is OK again.

CHAPTER 35

Phoebe grips her grandmother's hand tightly, trying to transmit everything she can't find the words to say out loud to her through the strength of the squeeze. Not that her nan would notice if she did manage to say everything she needs to say; her eyes are closed as she lies in the hospital bed looking incredibly small beneath the blanket. There are wires and tubes attached to her and every beep of the monitors makes Phoebe jump, terrified that it might be the sign that her grandmother is slipping away.

She hadn't trusted herself to do the long drive down to Cornwall on her motorbike, especially with the sun beginning to set and with her hands shaking and head spinning. She'd caught the train, stopping quickly by her flat to chuck some things in a bag. She isn't certain how long she'll stay for. Nothing feels certain right now, not with the doctors and nurses coming by regularly but with no new news. Her mum and dad are sitting in plastic chairs by the bedside, holding hands, their expressions solemn. Phoebe crouches by the bed because she wants to be as close as she can to her grandmother. With her spare hand, she gnaws at the edge of her fingernails, anxiety coursing through her body.

Phoebe's older brother, Seth, had been there when Phoebe arrived but had to get back to help his wife get their kids to bed so gave her a tight hug and asked them to keep him informed.

'I'm so sorry I couldn't get here earlier,' she says, her voice hoarse as she turns to face her mum. 'And I'm so sorry I never called back like I said I would. I feel awful.'

'That's OK, love,' her mum says faintly, her expression distant. 'I know how busy you are.'

'But I should never be too busy for you,' she says, her voice breaking. 'I'm a *terrible* granddaughter.'

'You're too hard on yourself, love. Your nan knows you love her, even if you haven't spoken in a while.'

But the guilt doesn't go away.

'It's getting late,' says her father, looking at this watch. 'I think we should all head home for the night.'

Phoebe can see her mum's hesitation.

'They'll phone us if there are any changes,' her dad says, softly but firmly. 'We could all do with some sleep.'

So, eventually, they kiss her nan goodbye and leave the hospital.

Phoebe ends up tumbling into her childhood bed, thinking she won't be able to sleep, but exhaustion quickly pulls her under.

It takes a moment to adjust to her surroundings when she

wakes the next morning, tuning in to the distant sound of the sea and looking up at the Hello Kitty posters on her old bedroom walls. The room has been turned into a home office, but her single bed remains, along with the posters on the far wall behind her dad's desk and bookshelves.

A light tapping on her door makes her sit up. The door opens and her father pokes his head inside. He looks surprisingly fresh-faced given the hour.

'Morning, Phoebs. Meet me downstairs in five minutes? We're going out.'

'To the hospital?' she asks, sitting up even straighter and scrabbling for her clothes. 'Has there been news?'

But to her surprise, he shakes his head. 'Not the hospital yet. You'll see. Five minutes.'

By the time she's downstairs in her jeans and an old T-shirt, her dad is waiting by the door, carrying two bags. He says nothing, simply leads her outside, chucks the bags in the boot of the car and opens the passenger door for her.

She's too sad and sleepy to protest, so climbs in, wishing they'd at least had time to make a coffee. As they set off, Phoebe leans her face against the cool glass, watching the fields flash past and letting the wind tangle her hair as it blows in from her dad's open window. He tunes in to Classic FM and hums quietly.

'How's Max?' he asks suddenly.

After everything that's happened, Phoebe doesn't have the energy to lie.

'Actually, we broke up. About a week or so ago. He moved out.'

Her father nods, eyes not veering from the road. 'Thank you for telling me.'

She frowns slightly. 'You don't sound surprised.'

Her father checks his mirror as he signals and turns off the main road and down a lane bordered by high, bushy hedge-rows. Songbirds dart out from the undergrowth as they pass.

'When your mum couldn't get hold of you after your nan's fall, she tried Max.'

'Ah.'

'She explained why she was calling. He was pretty surprised to hear from her. He explained that you two had broken up.'

'He didn't tell me. I haven't heard from him at all.' Even though he knew her grandmother was in the hospital? Even though he knew how much Phoebe adores her? She clenches her fists, digging her nails into her palm.

Without even looking at her, her father reaches one hand to her lap and quietly unclenches her hand, giving her fingers a little squeeze before returning his hand to the steering wheel.

'You're better off without him, love.'

'I'm sorry I didn't tell you.'

'That's OK. You would have done eventually.'

Why *hadn't* she told them as soon as he left?

'I think I was embarrassed.'

'You have nothing to be embarrassed about.'

'Even though I'm terrible at relationships?'

'You are not terrible at relationships. You just haven't met the right person yet.'

She knows her dad is one of the most biased people in the world, but it still feels good, his unwavering belief in her. As he turns left and the car slows, it hits her where they are heading. Another winding lane and then the car is pulling to a halt, tyres crunching on gravel.

'Dad, what are we doing here? We should get to the hospital.'

'We'll go in a bit. But first we need to do this. You need this. I can see it in your face and the way you haven't stopped chewing on your nails since you arrived.'

She looks down at her hands and the livid red that rims her bitten fingernails.

'I'm just worried about Nan. And the break-up has been shit.'

'It's not just that, though,' he says, shaking his head. 'I've noticed it for a while. You haven't been looking after yourself. You need a break. Come on.'

He opens the door and, once she's out too, he throws her one of the bags, slinging the other over his shoulders. Phoebe is hit by a blast of salty air and the sound of seagulls wheeling in the sky above them. Around them are a few other cars, but mostly the car park is empty. A sandy path leads towards the dunes, where marram grass waves in the brisk morning breeze.

'Shoes off, Phoebe Harrison.' He is already leaning to pull off his own deck shoes, so Phoebe does the same, knowing there's no point arguing with him.

As soon as she feels the sand between her bare toes, memories come rushing back of trips to the beach as a child. Running carefree on the sand, racing into the salty waves and swimming until her teeth chattered and her limbs ached.

He leads the way and Phoebe follows in silence. For a while,

242

they are surrounded by sand and grass and sheltered from the wind. And then they reach the summit of the dunes and the view opens up before them: a long stretch of sandy beach dotted with shells and seaweed and a wide, open sea, glinting in the morning light. There's something about the view that makes Phoebe feel as though her chest is opening.

'Pretty good, huh?' says her father, turning to catch her expression.

'Pretty good. It always has been.'

'You haven't been back in a while though.'

'No.'

'Come on, let's go down to our usual spot.'

They head for a section of sand that's far enough away from the car park to always be quiet, and where the steep slope of the dunes creates shelter from the sea wind. They drop their bags, her father sitting down and gesturing for her to join him. He scoots closer and wraps an arm around her shoulders. She leans her head against him, remembering all the times they sat like this when she was little, him providing a human wind-break when it was particularly wild on the beach, Phoebe on one side of him and Seth on the other.

But as she thinks of it, other memories come rushing into her mind too, recollections of days from her childhood that were very much not beach days.

'I remember coming here by myself one morning when I was recovering from my first depressive episode,' her father says suddenly, as if sensing the thoughts that have entered Phoebe's mind. 'We used to come here as a family a lot too, of course, but there was something about coming here early in the morning to watch the sea alone that I found very soothing. I still do it most days. I particularly like it on the wet and wild ones. More often than not, the weather will blow through before too long and the sun will come out.'

As her father speaks, Phoebe's fingers reach subconsciously to her arm, tracing the letters of her tattoo the way she so often does. *This too shall pass*. It's something her father used to repeat to himself on the tough days, something that helped him through when the clouds descended.

But Phoebe has never forgotten the times before he found the help he needed, back when his depression was just an unnamed darkness that would descend at random on their lives. It started happening when she was around six years old. One day, her dad just stopped getting out of bed and going to work.

'Your daddy smells funny,' a friend of hers said when she came over to play after school. Her father was sitting on the sofa in his dressing gown as he had been for several days. Phoebe wasn't sure of the last time he had showered and she quickly learnt not to invite her friends over.

She and Seth started referring to their dad as Normal Dad and Sad Dad. Normal Dad made pancakes at the weekend that he'd make a show of flipping extra high. Normal Dad took them to the beach and told them the different names of all the seabirds. Sad Dad would stare at the telly with a glazed expression on his face, barely noticing if they spoke or changed the channel.

One day, on one of the Sad Dad days, Phoebe came home from school to find a woman in a uniform sitting in the kitchen with her father. They were drinking tea together and talking. Nurse Lois became a regular fixture in their lives for a while and Phoebe wasn't sure how, but gradually her father grew brighter. He started shaving, returned to work part-time, started making pancakes again.

When Phoebe and Seth were a little older, her parents opened up about their dad's illness. They told them about the medication he now took, the therapy he'd received and the mental health nurses who had helped him get back on his feet.

'They saved my life,' her father said once, his eyes growing misty. And Phoebe never forgot it. She knew right then and there, at age eleven, what she wanted to do with her life. If someone could do that for her dad, then she wanted to do that for someone else. It would be her way of thanking the universe for the fact that the world still had her dad in it.

'Recently, when I've been coming down here, I've been thinking a lot about you,' her father continues. 'I've been worried about you, Phoebe. It's made me beyond proud the way you've chosen to spend your life and all that you do to help other people – people like me.' His voice wavers slightly, but he regains control. 'But you need a balance.'

'My boss said something similar yesterday.'

'Maybe she knows what she's talking about. And maybe so does your dad. You need places and moments where you can let go and unwind – preferably among good people. That's something that has helped me over the years.'

When Phoebe was a teenager her father decided to switch permanently to part-time hours, thanks to her mum getting a big promotion at work. At first, Phoebe could sense her dad was apprehensive about not being the breadwinner anymore, but her mum had talked him around. She loved her job and had always been able to compartmentalise, work not following her home the way it did for him. In his new-found free time, Phoebe's dad took on more of the household chores, always being the one to pick Phoebe and Seth up from their various clubs and cooking dinner for the family each night – an activity he seemed to find soothing.

And he took up a whole range of hobbies. At the time, she and Seth used to tease him about it, laughing at his new golfing gear and fishing waders. But, looking back, she can see that he was doing everything she advises her patients to do when they're struggling. He built networks for himself, finding friends he could chat to while playing golf, or sit in companionable silence with while they fished without ever really expecting to catch anything.

'I've actually started swimming at my local river,' she says. Just saying it brings to mind the peaceful green water and the people she has met there. A sense of calm immediately wraps around her.

Her dad's face spreads into a smile.

'You loved swimming so much when you were little.'

'Turns out I still love it.'

'Well, that's a relief ...' He leans back and fishes around in one of the bags, throwing a swimming costume at her and grabbing a pair of trunks for himself. 'That one's your mum's – hopefully it will fit. Come on, we're going in.'

'So that's what you had planned.'

'When I saw you at the hospital, you looked like you could do with a swim.'

Phoebe smiles to herself, remembering Sandra saying that to her the first time they met.

They get changed quickly and then race each other down to the water. Her dad reaches out for her hand and they run like that into the waves.

CHAPTER 36

'Do you have time for a coffee before your train?'

After the dress fitting, they all went for brunch at a nearby restaurant. The food was amazing and Rosie only cried a *little* bit, and Kate only flashed her nipple once at a passing waiter by mistake while doing a feed. All in all, it had been a success.

The group had disbanded then, Kate saying goodbye to Emma's friends and family and Rosie being passed around for final cuddles. Emma and Leonie insisted on accompanying Kate and Rosie back to the train station and helped her navigate the pram on and off the Tube. Now it's just the three of them plus Rosie, who is snoring in the pram after the excitement of the day.

Kate glances at the clock. 'I've got time.'

'Good. Because we're not ready to say goodbye to you just yet,' says Leonie.

'Let me push!' says Emma, taking the pram from Kate and

striding off towards Pret. Leonie links arms with her and squeezes her elbow. For a moment, it's as though nothing has changed.

Once they've got their coffees and are crowded around a little table with space for the pram, Kate takes a sip of her coffee. 'Sorry again about vomit-gate. I'm still mortified.'

Emma tosses her hair back and laughs. 'Vomit-gate! Seriously, don't worry about it. It's all good.'

'And I'm sorry I reacted so badly when you told me about the trip. I guess I just hate the thought of not being included in things. For ages, it's been the three of us. I don't want to get left behind.'

Emma and Leonie share a look. Leonie is the first to speak. 'But, Kate, that's exactly what we've been worried about too. Ever since you announced you were pregnant, we've been so happy for you – I mean, how could you not make the cutest baby ever? – but then you told us you were moving too ...'

'And we do get it,' chips in Emma. 'You wanted more space and to be close to your family. And Farleigh-on-Avon is *so* cute. But we're still here. And we miss you.'

'I miss you too,' she manages to get out. 'I think I haven't let myself acknowledge quite how much because I know that I was the one who chose all this. But it doesn't mean I don't miss you.'

'You are happy you moved, though? It was the right choice?'

Kate pictures her little cottage that might be a mess and not at all like the Pinterest board she made for herself when she moved but that is still hers, with its garden full of flowers and an apple tree that will make the perfect spot for a swing and

249

maybe a treehouse when Rosie is older. She thinks of the river bordered by reeds and bluebells.

'I'm getting there. But yes, I think it's where I need to be for this stage of my life. I loved my time in London, but I think now it was maybe just one chapter, not the whole story. But my life will always have you both in it. I don't want us to lose what we have.'

'Babe,' says Leonie, placing a hand over Kate's, 'you can't get rid of us just because you had a baby.'

'Yeah, it would take more than that.'

'Like my daughter ruining your wedding dress?'

They share a laugh. 'Seriously, chill, Kate. The dress is fine. *We're* fine.'

'How can we make sure you still feel included even if you're not here?' asks Leonie.

Kate thinks about it for a moment. 'I'd like to still be invited to things, even if I can't make them. I might have to say no to a lot of things for a while. But one day I'll be able to say yes again. And when that happens, I guess I just want to feel I can jump back in rather than feeling I'm on the outside of things.'

'We can do that.'

'And how about you two? What can I do to make you feel less like I'm leaving you behind?'

It breaks her heart to even think it.

'How about we try to have a regular video call once every couple of weeks?' suggests Emma. 'Even if we all end up being busy and can't make it, it would just be nice to at least try to have a regular catch-up.'

'I think that's a great idea.'

250

Kate's phone pings, telling her the platform number for her train. 'I better go.'

They squeeze each other tightly, and as Kate holds them for a final time before heading back to her new life in Somerset, she thinks about how much has changed but how much is still the same too. These women and how much she loves them ... That is never going to change.

CHAPTER 37

Phoebe and her father head back to the car park through the sand dunes, holding their shoes in their hands and with hair damp and salty from the sea. It had felt so good to swim together and then lie on the sand, warming up in the sun. At one point, Phoebe had glanced across at her father as he shielded his face from the sun with his hand, a smile spread across his face and his eyes half closed. And she'd thought how he didn't look like Sad Dad, or even Normal Dad. He looked like Happy Dad.

Then his phone rang and he reached for it quickly. 'Right,' he said, letting out a sigh. 'We'll meet you there.'

Phoebe's heart was hammering in her chest as he hung up and turned to her.

'Your nan is awake. Come on, let's go.'

*

Swimming is one thing, but Phoebe is not a runner. The last time she ran was probably as a kid when Seth chased her about with a toy tarantula, trying to scare her. But when they reach the hospital, she runs to her grandmother's ward, ignoring the looks from passing nurses and doctors. As she runs, she remembers why she doesn't do it, one arm held tightly over her chest because her bra absolutely does not offer enough support for this. But she doesn't care.

She arrives at the ward a sweaty mess. She spots her mum first, sitting by the bedside with tears rolling down her face. But she's smiling. Seth is there too, not in his suit like last time, but in his weekend gear of jeans and hoody. And then Phoebe sees her nan, propped up in bed and holding her mother's hands, her eyes open and a faint smile on her face too.

'Nan!'

Phoebe stumbles into the room, crouching down at the bedside and reaching for her grandmother's free hand. She lifts it up to her mouth and kisses it, relieved to feel how warm it is. Her face looks tired, but she is here.

'Are you OK? I've been so worried about you.'

Her nan goes to speak, but only a croak comes out. Phoebe's mum hands her a cup of water and she takes a sip, her hand shaking slightly.

'I was having the most lovely dream,' she says once she's finished, sounding more like herself now. 'George Clooney was in it …'

The tension breaks and everyone laughs. Phoebe glances at her mum, though, and sees the tiredness and worry on her face.

The sound of the curtain around the bed drawing open announces the arrival of a doctor. She smiles at them all and glances down at her notes.

'It's good to see you awake, Mrs Trelawney. Now, I'm going to do a few tests and checks – why don't you all go and get a cup of coffee? The machine stuff is pretty awful, I must admit, but there's a Costa on the ground floor.'

Phoebe catches her mum glancing nervously at her nan. She steps round to the other side of the bed and wraps an arm around her mum's shoulders. 'Come on, Mum. The doctor's got this.'

Her dad wraps an arm around her mum on the other side. She hesitates for a moment and then nods. 'OK. Coffee sounds good. See you soon, Mum.'

'We'll be back in a bit, Nan. Love you.'

'Love you too, pet.'

They find a table in the corner of the Costa with one armchair and two plastic seats. 'You take that one, Mum,' Phoebe says, leading her towards the comfier chair. She must be exhausted because she doesn't protest. Instead, she sinks down into it, letting out a long sigh. Then she bursts into tears.

'Oh, I'm sorry. This is ridiculous, she's awake now and seems like she's doing OK.'

'It's not ridiculous, Mum. It's been a really worrying time. You've had a lot on your plate.'

Her mum wipes her face, quickly composing herself again. 'I'm really glad you're here, sweetheart.' She reaches for Phoebe's hand.

'I'm glad I'm here too.'

254

As she squeezes her mother's hand and her mum squeezes back, Phoebe thinks about all the years she's been background-worrying about her father. Even though it's been a long time since his last bad depressive spell, the possibility of another one has always hovered there in Phoebe's mind. Maybe it's partly why she's always pushed herself so hard at work. Not just because she cares so deeply about her patients, but maybe, deep down, through some sense that if she dedicates her life to this it might repay the universe for making her dad better. But her mum, her lovely, sunny mum ... She maybe hasn't spent enough time thinking about how she's doing.

'I've got the week off work,' she says now. 'I can stay as long as you need me to. And after this, I want to get back to visit more often.'

'Oh, love, I know you have so much going on with work, though ... And with the break-up too, I'm sorry about that.'

'But I want to have time for my family too.' In spite of the awfulness of this trip, it's been strangely nice too. The morning swim with her dad, even being here in this random Costa ... She's missed moments with her family.

They don't say anything more, just sit drinking their coffees. Just being together. Sometimes that's enough.

'I should have a fall more often,' her nan says later that afternoon when the whole family is gathered around her bedside. The doctor has reassured them that she's doing well and should be able to go home in a couple of days. 'It's just so lovely to have you all here.'

'You say it like we're on holiday, Mum!'

'Oh, you know what I mean. I'm just so glad you're all here. And the doctor says I'm doing fine.'

'Thank goodness your hip wasn't broken, just bruised,' says Phoebe's dad.

'Just like my ego after you poor things had to find me bloody starkers like that on the bathroom floor.'

Phoebe can't help but laugh. She's always thought her dry sense of humour – and her language – comes from her nan. It's served her well in her job, when sometimes finding a way to laugh is the only way through.

A nurse pops in to check on her. 'We're just keeping an eye out for signs of concussion,' she explains. 'But we hope to be able to discharge you soon.'

'Oh, that's a shame. It's very comfortable here. Much better service than I get at home.' She winks up at Phoebe's mum, who rolls her eyes.

'Please ignore my mother. She lives with us and we will be taking *very* good care of her. We've already ordered grab rails for the bathroom.'

Phoebe's nan huffs. 'Those are for old people!'

'Or very youthful people who still manage to slip over in the bathroom and knock themselves unconscious,' teases Seth.

'OK, OK, I'll do as I'm told. But if I have to have a walking stick, can we at least please dress it up a bit? Some ribbons, bit of colour maybe? I've seen some oldies in here walking around with the most awful grey plastic monstrosities and I'm having none of that.'

'Mum!'

'It's OK, Nan,' says Phoebe. 'I can help with that. It will be fun.'

'Thanks, pet,' she says, giving her hand a little squeeze.

Phoebe squeezes back, already thinking about supplies she might get for the project. For a moment, thoughts of her life in Somerset come creeping back in. She wonders how Ben is doing and how her patients will manage next week when she's not at work. Mel has reassured her it will be fine, but she still worries.

And there's something else too: what will all this do to her chances of getting promoted? Mel was very kind and under-standing, but will she really think Phoebe is ready for even more responsibility? And if she doesn't, what does that mean for Phoebe's future and her chances of staying in her home in Farleigh-on-Avon? It hits her, too, that with everything that's been going on, she hasn't even started to tackle the issue of her flat being completely void of furniture. She's been meaning to see if she can find any freebies in local online groups, because there's no way she could afford to refurnish her whole flat, but hasn't had the time or energy. Her mind wanders to Luca then, reliving the moment when he pulled away from her and she felt like a huge idiot.

But then she forces herself to stop. None of that matters right now. Right now, she is here with her family. And for once, she is going to put thoughts of work and everything else aside and let herself be fully present.

CHAPTER 38

It's a good day when Kate gets to go for a swim. It's a great day when she gets to swim more than once. In the morning, she joins The Farleigh on Avon River Swimming, Bathing and Recreational Water-Based Activities Club, except today they are down one of their usual members. Phoebe isn't there. Kate assumes she must be busy with work, but she sends her a message anyway to check in. She's yet to receive a reply.

While Phoebe might not be there, some new swimmers join them. Kate's face lights up with excitement when she sees Lexi, Jess, Sophie and Olivia from the Tired Mums Club heading through the meadow carrying their swimming bags. She's even happier to see they have managed to make it here without their babies. They're a little nervous about getting in the water at first, but, in the end, Kate jumps in with them from the pontoon and as soon as they burst up from underwater, they are all laughing and smiling.

'God, I needed this!' cries Lexi.

The other women welcome the new members warmly. Jazz seems a little quieter than usual, but she explains it away as a headache and seems to brighten once they're in the water.

As they swim, they spot Bert the kingfisher again, much to their delight. It hits Kate that this is something that would never have happened back in London. As much as she loved her lido, there's something magical about being so close to nature here at the river. The bluebells are in full bloom now, their heads nodding in the slight breeze.

Afterwards, they share tea and cake from the Kingfisher. Kate finds it hard to look at Hamish without laughing after what Sandra told them last time and when it's Jazz's turn this time to be given his World's Best Lover mug.

'It's beautiful down here,' says Olivia. 'I can't believe I haven't been here before.'

The river feels new to Kate too and yet it has already worked its way into her heart.

She heads back home to a morning of nappies and nursing and singing to Rosie. But in the afternoon she makes her way back to the river again, Jay taking over with Rosie. As she waits for her sister beneath the willow trees, she thinks what a shame it is that their mum couldn't join them. It's beautiful here and it would be good for the three of them to spend some baby-free time together. But Kate can't begrudge her for having plans. She's put her life on hold these past few months, making herself available to help. It's natural that would come to an end and Kate feels able to face the prospect of having less help now. But she still misses her mum.

'Kate!' calls Erin, emerging through the gate and stepping her way down to the river through the long grass. She's dressed in a blue-and-white gingham dress with a matching bow tied in her ponytail and, not for the first time, Kate thinks how glamorous her older sister always manages to look. Kate is at least wearing trousers with an actual zip today.

They greet each other warmly and Kate realises it's the first time she's seen her sister one-on-one like this since Rosie was born. It wasn't exactly a common occurrence before then either, what with Erin's own two children and busy working life to juggle. These moments are likely to be rarer now that Kate is a mother too. But that makes them even more special.

'How was your trip to London yesterday? I saw Emma's photos on Instagram. It looked as if she had a great time.'

Kate had seen them too – tasteful crops of dresses so that you couldn't see the full design but just flashes of fabric, and one of all of them together in the bridal shop, taken by the sales assistant. As she 'liked' them and added a string of heart emojis in the comments, she thought how sad she would have been if she'd seen those photos but without her in them.

'Well …'

Kate tells her sister about vomit-gate and has to pause to allow Erin space to snort with laughter.

'I'm sorry. That must have been highly stressful. But that's also *hilarious*.'

'I thought I was going to die from embarrassment.'

'But you didn't.'

'No, I didn't. I'm pretty exhausted today, though. It was probably a bit mad, heading to London by myself with a newborn like that. But I so wanted to be there. And I think maybe I was trying to prove something to myself too. That I can still be fun now that I have a baby.'

Erin laughs again. 'God, I know that feeling. Do you know, when Ted was a baby, I convinced my friends to take me clubbing? I hadn't been clubbing in *years* before having him. But I got it into my head that it was what I desperately wanted to do.'

'You didn't tell me that,' laughs Kate. 'So how did it go?'

'Not well. I ended up having to pump in the grotty toilets when I thought my boobs were going to explode, and then going home at about ten.'

'Wow, a wild night then.'

Kate likes messy Erin. It makes her feel better about having no real clue what she's doing in her own life.

'Cut yourself some slack, sis,' Erin says. 'It's great that you made it yesterday. But your friends aren't going to forget about you just because you aren't able to go to every social event for a while. The good ones won't, anyway.'

Kate thinks back to her conversation with her friends yesterday.

'I think you're right.'

'I'm your big sister, I'm always right.'

'Mmm. What about the time you got that fringe?'

'Let's not talk about the fringe! So, are we going to swim, or what?'

They enter the water side by side. Erin gets a bit nervous for a minute about the thought of fish and mud, but then Kate reminds her she has given birth, twice.

'Oh yeah, you're right,' Erin replies before launching herself into the river.

As they swim, following the curve of the river bend beneath the canopy of trees, Erin catches Kate up on work and the boys and an upcoming holiday to Center Parcs.

'I never thought I'd be someone who would dream about a package holiday in huts in the woods, but then I went and everything was so *easy*. Bliss.'

Kate tells Erin more about the swimming club and her new friends. 'Oh, and I thought you should know that I swam this morning with women I met through the Tired Mums Club. Thanks for encouraging me to go.'

'That's great!'

They make their way back to the riverbank and get changed on the grass.

'Thanks for coming,' Kate says as she tries to wriggle back into her trousers. 'I've missed hanging out like this and ...' She takes a deep breath. 'Honestly, I've been finding things really hard since Rosie was born.'

Erin immediately stops reaching for her clothes and faces Kate, giving her all her attention.

'Oh, sis. Things will get easier soon. You've just got to get through the awful newborn bit.'

'What do you mean?' asks Kate, frowning. A breeze whips up, giving her goosebumps, and she wraps her damp towel tightly around her shoulders. 'You *loved* having newborns!'

When Kate thinks about her sister after both her sons were born, she pictures her looking totally blissed out, gazing down at them with such wonder. It's something that's come back to

262

her many times when she has held Rosie and felt many things – fear, anxiety, guilt – but not that lovestruck awe that Erin wore on her face when her sons were small. But Erin looks at Kate as though she's absolutely mad.

'Um, Kate, *no one* loves having a newborn. They're objectively awful. I mean, I adore my new niece and little babies are very cute, but they cry and feed all the time and can't talk to you to tell you what's wrong. My boys might be absolute animals, sometimes, but at least they can tell me with words when they're hungry.'

'But you seemed so chilled and happy when your boys were tiny!' exclaims Kate.

'Did I?' asks Erin, frowning. 'I think I was mostly medicated. And overwhelmed.'

They both pause for a moment, huddled beneath their towels on the side of the river. The sunshine of earlier has gone, clouds rolling across the sky and making the green of the trees look even greener, as if the world has been turned up to high contrast.

'I've been finding it pretty overwhelming too,' Kate finally admits to the older sister who she's always looked up to. 'And hard. Really hard.'

'That's because it *is* hard! Don't get me wrong, I adore my boys. I would literally chew off my own arm for them if I had to. Literally without a second's hesitation.' She mimes gnawing on her forearm, making Kate descend into giggles. Then Erin stops, more serious now. 'And now that they're a bit older ... They're so funny. But, my God, becoming a mother has been the single hardest thing I have ever done in my life. And I've run three marathons, started my own business and had a roommate at uni who used to knit in our communal living room using *human hair* that she'd *found on the ground*.'

'Oh God, I'd forgotten about her! I wonder what she's doing now?'

'The point is, becoming a mum is hard. Like, ridiculously hard. But there's all this pressure to be blissfully happy all the time. This idea that talking about the tough bits means you're a bad mum or don't love your kids is absolute bullshit.'

Erin's face is flushed, her usual composure replaced with a wild sort of energy. Kate gets the impression that these words have been stewing inside her sister for some time. She isn't sure quite what has released them. Maybe the calm setting of the riverbank has loosened something in her. Or maybe, until now, Kate hasn't opened up enough for Erin to feel she can do the same?

'Um, how have I had no idea up until right now that you felt this way? Why didn't you say anything back when Ted was born?'

Erin tilts her head for a second, looking thoughtful. Around them, the trees and reeds rustle and sway as the breeze grows stronger, the sky darkening even further.

'I suppose, after everything I went through with the IVF, I've always found it hard to complain. I wanted my babies so badly and went to such great lengths to have them that even now I find it hard to talk about the bits that aren't how I imagined. In case it makes me sound ungrateful.'

'Oh, Erin. No one would ever think that.'

'And no one would ever think badly of you for finding things hard too.'

Kate has spent so long feeling like she's so different from her sister because of this vision she had in her head of Erin as a mother. Nothing she has said has changed the fact that she still thinks Erin is a brilliant mum, but the vision is altered now, smudges and scratches making the picture less perfect. But maybe those things are what make her so great, actually.

'I think one of the hardest things is that I know this early bit is so fleeting,' Kate admits. 'I know there will come a day when Rosie is a grumpy teenager and I will probably ache to be able to hold her as a baby again. It makes me hate myself for not cherishing every moment, but I just can't.'

'Of course you can't.' Erin readjusts her towel, tucking it in at the front. 'Look, the truth is, not every moment is worth cherishing and I think people often forget that in their nostalgia. When they cry for hours on end? Or throw up on you? Or worse … But I do like to think about cherishing one moment from each day.'

'Hmm, I like that,' Kate replies, considering the idea.

To be expected to savour every second of every day feels like being at a party that never ends, when you're exhausted and want to just sit down but the music keeps playing and the lights keep flashing and you're expected to keep dancing. But one moment? That feels doable.

'Yeah, so, at the end of each day, I try to think about one moment that's made me really smile that day,' continues Erin. 'One thing I want to remember and hold onto. Even if it's been a shit day, I always find something. And it helps me keep

265

perspective on those tough days, to hold onto the good bits, even if they're only small.'

'What was it yesterday?'

A huge smile spreads across Erin's face.

'In the morning while I was getting their breakfast ready, Ted and Arlo "made" me a cup of tea. They'd put a teabag in my favourite mug and filled it up with cold water. They were so proud of themselves and so excited to have done something nice for me that I *drank it*. I didn't even care that it was disgusting. The day before, it was reading *We're Going on a Bear Hunt* with them before bed. And the day before that … That was when Arlo said "shit" for the first time and Mark and I couldn't stop laughing, even though we knew we should be telling him off. It was just too funny hearing it come out of his cute little mouth.'

Listening to Erin, it strikes Kate that none of the moments her sister describes are the moments she puts on Instagram or in their family WhatsApp group. Those are made up of posed photos where everyone is smiling and neatly dressed.

'It never stops being exhausting, sis, or overwhelming or difficult. I'm not going to sugar-coat things. But I wish I could express to you all the good stuff that you have ahead of you. You're in the trenches right now, but there is so much joy and laughter and absolutely fucking incredible stuff coming your way.'

'I hope so.'

'I *know* so.'

Kate pulls her T-shirt on over her still-damp skin and Erin does the same with her dress. Except now there's no swishing ponytail and matching bow, instead her hair hangs in wet knots on her shoulders just like Kate's does. They're both bare-faced, make-up washed away by the river. Kate thinks her sister looks beautiful.

'Hey,' says Erin, 'you know something I did really love when the boys were tiny? Baby swimming lessons. I started taking them both when they were around Rosie's age. Have you thought about signing Rosie up?'

Kate suddenly pictures the tiny pink swimsuit that her lido friends bought for Rosie when she was born but is still hanging unused in her room.

'I can't believe I hadn't thought of that.' Her mind races with the thought of being in the water with her daughter. It's something she thought about a lot when she was pregnant, but somehow, with everything that has happened since, it has slipped from her mind.

'I think you'd love it,' continues Erin. 'I found that time together really special.'

'That's a brilliant idea, thank you.'

'You'll get there, sis,' Erin says, and then she steps forward and takes Kate in her arms, squeezing her tightly. Their wet hair drips onto each other's shoulders. 'Do you know what my happy moment for today is?' Erin whispers into her ear.

'What?' Kate replies, not ready to let her sister go just yet.

'This one.'

CHAPTER 39

Suddenly, it begins to rain.

Raindrops hammer down onto the surface of the river and the roof of the Kingfisher Café and Book Barge. The lifeguard remains seated in her deckchair but reaches for a large golf umbrella and opens it above her head. Kate and Erin yelp, grabbing their things and dashing barefoot across the grass and towards the beach huts. They seek shelter inside an orange-and-white striped hut which is filled with kayaks. With the doors left open so they can see and hear the rain, they sit cross-legged on their towels, huddling close to one another for warmth.

'Listen to that!'

The sound is amazing as the shower becomes a torrential downpour, clattering against the wooden roof of the hut and dripping down through the trees to splash on the water. A family of ducks bob about happily, flapping their feathers.

There's one swimmer in the water, an older man with a thick grey beard, but the rain doesn't seem to bother him. In fact, he tilts his head to the sky and laughs.

'Wow, we got out at the right time,' says Erin.

As they watch the rain, something that's been bothering Kate rises to the surface.

'Do you think there's something going on with Mum?'

'What do you mean?'

'It's probably nothing, but I feel like she's been less active in our group chat recently. And I haven't seen her in a few days ...'

'Hmm, now I think about it, I haven't spoken to her properly in a bit either. But I'm sure she's just busy. Why don't we call her right now for a chat?'

Erin has her phone out before Kate can protest or wonder too hard why she even wants to protest. She loves her mum. But she can't shake the feeling that recently she's been asking too much of her. She doesn't want to become a burden.

Their mum answers after a few rings. It's a video call and she looks a little flustered at first, as though she's just woken from a nap, but quickly adjusts her face into a wide smile. 'Hello, girls! How nice to see you together. Are you in a shed?'

'Hi, Mum!' says Erin cheerily. 'We're down by the river, but it's pissing it down with rain so we're taking shelter. Look.'

She turns the camera round so their mum can see the view.

'Oh wow, it looks beautiful, even in the rain.'

'Everything OK there?' Kate asks once Erin has turned the camera round again.

'Oh yes, everything is fine,' she says brightly. 'Brian sends his love.' Kate thinks she can hear her stepdad pottering about in the background. 'So, tell me what's new with you both? How are my darling grandchildren?'

Erin gives updates about the boys and Kate tells her mum about her trip to London, her mum asking all the right questions and laughing in all the right places. It's a happy, chatty call, and Erin ends it with a satisfied smile on her face.

'See, she's fine!' she says after she's hung up.

'Yeah, you're probably right.' But Kate isn't so sure. Her mum asked lots of questions but shared very little from her own life. And it was clear from the call that she was at home. So why did she say she couldn't make the swim? Kate knows she's probably overthinking things, but the call has just added to her feeling that her mum might be avoiding her.

Her phone rings and she's a little surprised to see Phoebe's name on the screen.

'You take that,' says Erin, gathering her bags, slipping her shoes back on and standing up. 'I should get back to the boys. And the rain is easing up now.'

Kate looks outside and sees that her sister is right, the downpour having turned to a drizzle that blurs the river in a fine mist. Erin squeezes Kate's shoulder and kisses her on the cheek.

'Don't worry so much, sis. It's all going to be OK. Thanks for the swim, love you!' And then she's heading out into the rain, her towel draped over her head like a makeshift umbrella.

Kate manages to answer the phone just before it rings out.

'Hey, Phoebe, we missed you at the river this morning!'

'Hey, Kate. Thanks for your message checking in, I really

appreciated it. I just thought I'd give you a ring to tell you what's been going on …'

Kate listens as Phoebe tells her all about her grandmother's accident and Phoebe's trip to Cornwall.

'Oh my God, I'm so sorry, Phoebe. I'm glad to hear she's doing OK now. Are *you* OK though?'

Phoebe's voice wobbles a little as she replies. 'I've been better. These past couple of weeks have been …'

'Shit?' finishes Kate.

To her surprise, Phoebe laughs, a loud, deep cackle that makes Kate want to laugh too, it's so contagious.

'Yeah. Absolutely bloody shit.'

Phoebe tells Kate a bit more about her nan and about what happened with Luca.

'I'm sure things with Luca aren't as bad as you think they are,' she says once Phoebe has finished and let out a big sigh. 'And you don't need to worry about any of that right now. You just focus on being there with your family. And remember, you're not on your own when you get back, OK? I'm here for you and so are the members of the Farleigh-on-Avon River Swimming, Bathing and Recreational Water-Based Activities Club …'

She takes a huge, dramatic breath after finishing saying the long name, making them both laugh again.

'Thanks, Kate, I really appreciate that.'

'You don't need to thank me. You did the same for me. You helped me change my mind about going to London and I'm so glad I went.'

They chat a bit more, Kate filling Phoebe in on the London

trip. Phoebe nearly cries with laughter when she describes the incident with Rosie and the dress. Kate asks Phoebe to tell her more about her nan and listens to stories of them building sandcastles together on the beach when she was young and sharing favourite books with one another.

'I feel a lot better, thanks, Kate,' Phoebe affirms as they say goodbye. But even though Phoebe sounded much better at the end of their call, Kate thinks about all the things her new friend has been dealing with. Her break-up with Max, her work worries and now this ...

She creates a new WhatsApp group with all the swimming group except Phoebe.

Swimmer in distress! Hey, ladies, hope you don't mind the group message, but Phoebe has been having a bit of a rough time. I thought of something we could do to help, if you're up for it ...

Not long after she hits send, the replies come in.

Hester: **Count me in.**

Jazz: **Me too! x**

Sandra: **Ooh! I love a plan! The Farleigh-on-Avon River Swimming, Bathing and Recreational Water-Based Activities Club to the rescue!**

Jazz: **Oh God, we really do need to work on that name.**

Sandra: **Never mind the name, I was thinking of a uniform instead. I think we'd all look very fetching in capes ...**

As Kate gathers her things and readies herself to head home to Rosie and Jay, it hits her how far she has come over the past weeks. Things with Rosie might not be perfect, but she's let go of so much guilt and thinks she is moving forward at last, rather than feeling stuck at the beginning, back in that hospital bed consumed by fear. She's reconnected with her old friends and made new ones too, friends who have helped her get back on her feet. Now she wants to do the same for Phoebe. Because if motherhood has taught her anything so far, it's that when you're someone whose job it is to look after other people, it can be all too easy to forget to look after yourself.

CHAPTER 40

After a week in Cornwall, Phoebe feels ready to head back to Somerset. Her grandmother is back at home and doing well. And the sea air and several more swims with her dad have made Phoebe feel better too.

The day before she's due to leave, she receives an email from her boss, checking in and gently asking her if she might feel ready to return to work or if she needs more time off. Since arriving in Cornwall, Phoebe has had a lot of time to think. Usually, she'd use any spare moment to catch up on emails or check in with patients, but she's forced herself to hold back. Instead, she's spent the time considering whether she wants to go back to work or if it's time to contemplate a different career altogether. It's something she's thought about over the years when what she does feels too heavy. She's never acted on it because a good day always rolls around after the bad ones, but this week she has forced herself to consider the prospect more seriously.

However, every time she goes down that road, her mind pulls her down another path, back to a seed of an idea that was planted the very first time she visited the river and has been taking root ever since.

After reading Mel's email, she calls her.

'How's your nan doing?' is the first thing she asks and Phoebe suddenly feels grateful for having a boss who understands that she has a life outside of work – who encourages it, in fact.

'She's doing OK, thank you. And I'm doing much better too. I'm heading back to Somerset tomorrow.'

'I'm so pleased to hear it. And I don't want to put pressure on you, but how are you feeling about returning to work?'

Phoebe thinks of all her patients and how they have let her into their lives to share the tough days, but the better ones too. She pictures the feeling of satisfaction when she sees someone take a step forward. There's nothing like it.

'I'd like to come back,' she says decisively. 'But I'd like to shake things up a bit. My patients need more than I'm able to offer them. I can give them medication and time, but what they need too is community. A place to go where they can be among other people who share similar experiences, where they can chat, but also not chat too. Do something to help them take their minds to a different place.'

She remembers everything her father told her about the importance of his hobbies and the friends he's made in the process. And she thinks about the women she has met at the river who have so quickly made her feel as though she's part of something.

'I'd like to set up a mental health wild swimming group. I've started swimming at the river in Farleigh-on-Avon recently and it's so beautiful there and has an amazing sense of community. It got me thinking that if it's already helped me so much, then it could help my patients too. I know it sounds a bit out there, but I've done a lot of reading about the mental health benefits of cold-water swimming and time in nature and I think there could really be something to this. I think it could really help my patients.'

She speaks quickly so she can get it all out before changing her mind. She doesn't say that she thinks it could help her too, but it's there in her head. If she's going to continue doing this job, then something needs to change. And getting both herself and her patients into the water feels like a good first step.

'Yes.'

'Yes?' Phoebe realises that she'd been so focused on just putting her idea out there that she hadn't actually considered that her boss might say yes.

'Yes. I think it's a brilliant idea. This job isn't just about administering medication. You're right that the people we work with need community. We know how much loneliness affects all facets of health and something like this could be exactly what our patients need to help tackle the loneliness they face. This is exactly the kind of creative, proactive idea I love to see from my team. I'm going to adjust your schedule to make sure you have time to get this project off the ground. And when you're back, I think it's time we talk about next steps for you and your career. Well done, Phoebe.'

After they've made plans for next week and the first mental health wild swimming group meeting, they say goodbye and

Phoebe is left reeling. Well, shit. This is actually happening, then. For the first time since she received the phone call from her mum, excitement bubbles up inside of her. Mel is on board with her plan and it even sounds like her longed-for promotion might actually be on the cards. Next, she needs to convince her patients. She can already anticipate that this might be the tricky part.

'I promise I'll come back again soon,' she says to her grand-mother as she hugs her goodbye the next day. 'And I really mean it this time. I'm going to visit much more regularly from now on.'

'That's OK, dear, I know how busy you are.'

'But I want to,' Phoebe says, leaning forward to kiss her grandmother on the top of her soft white hair. She hugs her mum and brother tightly too.

Her dad drops her at the station and as they say goodbye, he gives her a tight hug.

'You take care of yourself, love.'

'I will,' she promises.

'Nothing makes me prouder than being a dad to you and Seth,' he says, his eyes growing teary. 'And that's not because of the jobs you do or the things you achieve, but because of who you are. You never forget that.'

As she settles in on the train, Phoebe sends a message to Kate telling her she's on her way home. Kate has been checking in with her all week and it's made Phoebe regret having let her other friendships fizzle out over the years. As the countryside rolls by outside the window, she scrolls back to one of her old WhatsApp groups. What if she were to send a message and resurrect the group? Her hands hover over her phone, thinking about what she might say. But it feels hard to know where to start. Would messaging out of the blue just be really fucking weird? Would they even want to hear from her after all this time?

She closes WhatsApp and instead lets herself open her email for the first time that week. And then she starts composing messages one by one to her patients, beginning with Ben.

Dear Ben,

I hope you're doing well. I'm sorry I've been away this week, but my colleague Mel tells me you are doing OK, if still understandably disappointed about the football group.

I have an idea to run past you. I've decided to start a new group myself. It's not football, I'm afraid. I might have learnt a lot from watching *Match of the Day* with you, but you are still very much the football expert, not me. This new group will bring together other people I work with, just like your football club did, but this time doing something that I love, that's helped me through a tough time. The first meet up of the Mental Health Wild Swimming Group will take place at Farleigh-on-Avon on Monday, at 10 a.m. Map attached. I'd love it if you'd consider giving it a go.

The countryside changes outside as the train crosses through Cornwall and up to Devon. Phoebe sends message after message about the new swimming group. So far, none of her patients have replied. But she keeps sending them anyway.

When Phoebe finally steps off the train at her stop, she nearly drops her bags in surprise, seeing not just one familiar face waiting for her, but four. Kate, Sandra, Jazz and Hester are gathered on the platform, waving at her and smiling. They are all dressed in boiler suits – Kate's yellow, Sandra's red, Jazz's pink and Hester's indigo denim.

'What are you guys doing here?' she asks after hugging them each in turn. 'And what are you wearing?! You look like a girl band.'

'Sandra was the one who suggested the outfits,' says Jazz. 'We weren't up for it at first. But then we chatted and worked out that we all own at least one boiler suit, so we thought, why the fuck not?'

'You look bloody ridiculous,' Phoebe laughs. 'But *awesome* too. I still don't totally get it, though.'

'We're superheroes. *Obviously*,' says Hester.

Jazz strikes a pose, hands on hips. 'Wild swimmers to the rescue!'

'Kate told us you'd been having a tough time,' explains Sandra, looping her arm over Phoebe's shoulder. She glances at Kate for confirmation, but she just shrugs her shoulders lightly. 'You spend your whole life looking after other people,' she continues, as if having a group of new friends turn up to rescue you in matching outfits is a totally normal thing to happen. 'It's our turn to do something for you.'

Phoebe blinks rapidly. She's already done enough bloody crying this week. But they're not making it easy for her ... She sniffs and tries to subtly wipe her face with her sleeve.

'This is only part one of the plan,' says Kate. 'Come on ...'

They travel back to Farleigh-on-Avon from the station, Kate driving, and when she pulls up onto the high street, the sight of Giuglia's makes Phoebe's palms grow clammy. She hasn't seen Luca since their almost-encounter in the deli, but she knows she can't put off running into him forever, not when they are neighbours and when he serves the best coffee in the village.

As she gets out of the car, she notices a pick-up truck parked on the pavement near the deli. To her surprise, Kate and the others head straight to the truck, Sandra jangling a set of keys in her hand.

'Is this your truck, Sandra?'

'What, do you think I don't look like a pick-up truck sort of person?' She puts her hands on her hips in mock outrage.

'I said the same thing,' says Jazz. 'I had her down as a Fiat 500 kind of woman myself.'

'A relic from my second marriage,' Sandra explains. 'It was one of his most treasured possessions. He ran off with one of my bridesmaids. I delight in driving the truck past their house every now and then, blaring feminist anthems. It's really quite useful too. It did the trick today perfectly. Right, shall we unload?'

'Unload?' asks Phoebe, and as she does, she looks properly at the contents of the truck. It is piled high with furniture. She

280

spots planks of wood that look like a bed frame piled on top of a pine table with its legs in the air. There's a mismatched array of dining chairs in different colours and, in the middle, an extremely bright orange sofa.

'I remember you telling me about your ex taking all the furniture from your flat when he left,' says Kate as Phoebe casts her eyes over it all, taking it in. 'Between us, we all had some bits and bobs we didn't need anymore. You don't have to keep it all forever if you hate it, but it might just help get you back on your feet?'

'The bed frame and dining table are from my parents' attic,' says Hester. 'They used to belong to my grandparents but have just been getting dusty up there since they passed away. I think they'd love to know they were being used.'

'The chairs are from all of us,' says Jazz. 'I hope you don't mind that they're not a matching set.'

'And the sofa is from me,' adds Sandra. 'I've been meaning to find a new home for it. I hope you don't mind the colour, I know it's not to everyone's taste ...'

The women are clearly waiting for her reaction, huddled around the pick-up truck in their matching boiler suits, all with equally eager expressions on their faces. But Phoebe can't find any words. She looks from the women to the truck and back again.

'I ... I love the colour. I love it all! This is one of the nicest things anyone's ever done for me.'

'Come on,' says Sandra, unlocking the truck. 'Let's get all this unloaded. Kate tells us you live above the deli?'

They start with the dining chairs. Jazz explains that she's

done her back in, so she guides them up the stairs as the others take a chair each.

'Lovely light in here,' Sandra comments as they set them down in the living room. 'It will be gorgeous when we're finished and once you've given the place a lick of paint. Only recently moved in, have you?'

'I've been here three years,' admits Phoebe. As she looks around, it strikes her how un-lived in the place looks, not just because of the lack of furniture but because of the plain walls and simple venetian blinds that were there when they moved in.

'Oh. Well, magnolia is a very practical choice. And some people do prefer to keep things simple ...'

'I don't,' replies Phoebe quickly, only really realising how true it is when she says the words out loud. 'I'd much prefer bright colours on the walls.' She pictures her parents' home, which is chaotic but colourful, the living room a sky blue and the kitchen filled with striped Cornishware crockery in multicoloured shades, the fridge covered in photographs. She glances down at her outfit of tight cropped trousers in a post-box red worn with a gingham shirt and her usual biker jacket over the top and it strikes her that the place where she lives has none of her personality visible in it. 'Max preferred things simple, and besides, we never seemed to find the time for decorating ...'

'Maybe we can head to the hardware store once the furniture is in?' Kate suggests. 'We can help you paint?'

'Ooh, I love painting,' says Jazz. 'I find it very soothing.'

'That would be amazing,' Phoebe replies, blown away yet again by their kindness.

As they head back downstairs for the next load of furniture, the door to Giuglia's swings open. Phoebe feels her stomach involuntarily tighten at the sight of Luca stepping out onto the street in his green apron, his mop of curls as messy as ever and a dab of something that looks like pesto smeared across one defined cheekbone. Through the window behind him, she can see that the deli is empty, apart from the same older gentleman with the Italian newspaper who Phoebe remembers seeing the first time she stepped inside the shop.

She meets Luca's eye and he raises a questioning eyebrow, but there's a faint smile on his mouth. Heat rises to her face.

'I know there was a bit of noise when I was getting the shop set up, but moving out? Am I really that bad a neighbour?'

His tone is teasing, as if he's forgotten the awkwardness of the last time they saw each other. But Phoebe hasn't forgotten. It's been *haunting* her, along with the frustration of knowing that she wouldn't have been so goddamn stupid if she hadn't been drinking. She hasn't touched alcohol since her conversation with Mel, even when her parents offered her wine at the table on her first night staying with them. After she refused, she noticed that the next day there were no wine glasses set out for any of them.

He puts his hands into his apron pockets and leans back against the door frame, that particularly mischievous curl falling down over one eyebrow. For the first time, Phoebe notices the dimple in his chin and the fact it looks exactly the size and shape of the pad of her little finger.

'I'm not going anywhere. Just, um, redecorating,' she explains, before adding reluctantly, 'bad break-up.'

'Ah.' He raises his eyebrows and nods. 'I know about those.'

It's her turn to raise an eyebrow now, but he offers no further explanation, just a steady smile.

'Just what we need!' declares Sandra, causing Phoebe to break eye contact with Luca and notice that the others are staring at him in varying degrees of subtlety. 'A big strong man.'

Luca's cheeks flush as red as Sandra's boiler suit.

'Um, isn't that a bit anti-feminist?' chips in Hester, scuffing the toes of her shoes into the ground.

'I was *joking*, dear,' replies Sandra, rolling her eyes and waving a hand carelessly. 'I know we are perfectly capable of moving the rest of the furniture by ourselves. But the fact we *could* do it by ourselves doesn't mean we *should* have to. We have nothing to prove here, ladies! And besides, given the gender pay gap, I think it's only fair to get men to do a bit extra to help out every now and then. After all, *we* are essentially working for free from January until March each year.'

'Yes, to that!' Jazz says with a cheer.

Sandra only somewhat undermines her speech by adding, 'Plus, look at those lovely arms, he looks highly suited to furniture-lifting.' She winks lasciviously and Phoebe tries her best not to follow her gaze to Luca's biceps.

Luca is practically squirming by now, his tanned neck blotched with crimson. Watching him wriggle uncomfortably makes Phoebe stifle a laugh. It makes her feel better, seeing him looking as uncomfortable as she feels to be seeing him again.

'Sure, I can help a neighbour out,' he says, flipping the shop sign to closed and leaving the one customer sitting contentedly with his newspaper, espresso and a biscotti. 'OK. I'm all yours.'

And Phoebe tries her best not to let her own face turn pink at his words.

CHAPTER 41

Phoebe hardly recognises her flat. The empty space is now filled with a dining table and a colourful mismatch of chairs and there's a big jug of tulips in the middle that Sandra insisted on buying as a house warming present.

'But I already told you, I've lived here for years.'

'I know. But that doesn't mean your home didn't need warming.'

In the middle of the living room is the tangerine sofa which goes perfectly with the bright yellow back wall that they painted with the help of Rosie, who Jay dropped off in the afternoon when she needed a feed. She was mostly very content in the sling on Kate's chest, holding a small paintbrush in one hand. When she grew grizzly, Phoebe could sense Kate starting to become anxious, but she was quickly passed around the group for cuddles and both of them soon calmed down.

Now, the early-evening sun slants in through the window, turning the yellow wall to a sun-kissed gold.

'It really does look great,' says Kate, cuddling Rosie, who is now fast asleep in her arms.

'Thank you,' Phoebe says with meaning. 'All of you, thank you so much. This place looks like a home now, thanks to you.'

She still isn't certain what her next chapter looks like and whether she will be able to stay living here, but for now, this place looks like home.

'Oh, by the way, my boss approved the mental health wild swimming group. The first meet-up is tomorrow. I'm not sure if anyone will come, though ...'

She still hasn't received replies from any of her patients.

'We can be there, if it would help?' suggests Kate, rocking Rosie back and forth gently. The others nod in agreement.

'Really? That would be great, if you don't mind. It would be nice to feel that there's a group there. So that even if just one patient turns up, they won't be on their own.'

'We'll be there.'

Once they're gone, Phoebe looks around the flat again, taking it all in appreciatively. As her eyes fall on her new orange sofa, an image flashes involuntarily into her mind of the muscles tautening across Luca's shoulders as he carried the front end up the stairs and Phoebe followed behind, trying to concentrate on her footing and not the sight in front of her. He headed back to the deli once everything was in and Phoebe has tried very hard all afternoon to not think about the fact that, as they've been painting and chatting up here, he's been working just below them.

Now that the place is looking so homely, she doesn't like the thought of there being awkwardness between her and her

287

downstairs neighbour. She doesn't want anything to encroach on her happy little oasis. She needs to bloody well pull her polka-dot socks up and clear the air. She'll explain that the mad moment the other week was down to a long day and too much wine and then they can move on.

She marches decisively down the stairs. As she does, the sound of Magic FM rises up from beneath her. When she pushes open the door to the deli, she stops in her tracks. A couple of the tables have been pushed to one side to create more space on the floor. In the middle of that space are Luca and the older gentleman who was there earlier. The pair of them are dancing, Van Morrison's 'Brown Eyed Girl' playing loudly through the speakers.

Luca is a surprisingly good dancer, twisting his hips and stepping his feet in perfect time to the music, his apron swinging slightly as he moves. The customer, however, is terrible. But he dances with such enthusiasm that you almost don't notice. Almost.

Phoebe pauses in the doorway for a moment, watching them as they dance, completely oblivious to her presence. But suddenly Luca looks up and spots her there. The older man looks up then too, stopping his dancing and letting out a loud puff of air.

'*Ciao!*' he says warmly.

'Er, sorry,' Luca mumbles. 'I hope the music didn't disturb you upstairs.' He turns down the volume.

'Ah, so you're the neighbour,' his dancing companion says, adjusting his trousers which have become rumpled from the dancing. '*Scusa!* I asked him to turn it up. That was my wife's favourite song.'

'Your wife?'

The man points to the sign at the back of the shop, where golden writing swirls across the wall. 'My Giuglia.'

He reaches into his shirt pocket and pulls out a handkerchief, dabbing at his eyes.

Luca looks up from beneath his dark curls, his eyes meeting hers. He smiles nervously, but there's a flicker of that expression she's seen a couple of times before, a slight darkening of his eyes as a shadow passes across them. They continue to stare at each other, neither one of them saying anything, although Phoebe wouldn't be surprised if he can hear her heart thumping.

'Anyway,' the old man says pointedly, 'I should go.' He picks up his paper from the counter and kisses Luca on both cheeks. '*Ciao, mio caro.*'

'Bye, Dad.'

He raises his paper to Phoebe as he leaves, giving her a little nod. And then it's just Phoebe and Luca alone in the deli, Luca standing still but shifting a few dishes and bowls of food about on the counter, not making eye contact with her.

'You can really dance,' Phoebe says, not knowing where else to start.

He looks up and she gets another jolt as their eyes meet.

'Ah. Well, I don't do it very often. My mum was the one who could really dance. I guess I inherited the gift from her. That and her hair.' He gestures at his wild curls.

'You got some of her best bits then,' she says without thinking.

They don't look away from one another and there's something about the way he looks at her that reminds her of *that* night. It's the same look that made her step towards him, tilting her face towards his. Surely she can't be imagining the energy that passes between them? But then she reminds herself of how he reacted then, the way he stepped back so suddenly, creating distance between them.

'No,' he says. 'Her best bit was her smile.'

Your smile is pretty great too, she wants to say but stops herself just in time.

'When did she pass away?'

He leans back against the counter where his mother's name runs along the wall behind him.

'A few months ago. Although she was ill for quite a while; it's why I moved back to this area, to be closer to my dad.'

'Where were you living before?'

'I was in Canary Wharf with my then-girlfriend. We both worked in the City. But when Mum got sick ... Well, it didn't really align with her vision of our future.'

Phoebe thinks back to when she mentioned her bad break-up to Luca earlier when they moved the furniture. *I know about those*, he'd said.

'I'm sorry, that's awful.'

He shrugs lightly. 'It was tough. All of it – the break-up, Mum's illness, eventually losing her ...' He drifts off, the pain so visible now in his face that Phoebe can't believe she hadn't spotted it before. She'd mistaken it for surliness or perhaps tiredness. And she calls herself a professional ... 'This place and the river have helped me through. I might not make it out to row as much as I'd like, but when I do, it's like everything else disappears for a bit.'

No wonder he didn't see or hear them in the water that first time they met. Phoebe had thought he was selfish, focused on recording his time on his fancy watch.

'And then, when I'm in here, I feel like I'm closer to her. Mum always dreamt of opening a place like this,' he continues, gesturing around him at the shelves stocked with Italian produce. 'We used to cook together all the time when I was little. After she died ... Well, I thought that if she never got the chance to make her dream a reality ...'

'Then you could,' she finishes for him.

He nods, silently blinking and biting his bottom lip, as though surprised by all the words that have just come tumbling out.

'You've done a great job. I'm sure she'd love it here.'

'Thank you.'

She takes the silence that follows as her chance.

'About the other night,' she begins, deciding that after everything he's just shared she has no excuses for not finding the courage to apologise about her drunken misstep, but before she can finish, he interrupts.

'Have you ever been rowing?'

The question throws her so much that she has no idea how to reply at first.

'Um ... I ... No.'

'Do you want to? With me?'

He looks directly at her now. Everything that she was going to say to him is still right there on her tongue, but his question has completely thrown her. Is he asking her on a date? And if he is, how does she feel about it? She told herself after Max that she wouldn't date. She's clearly terrible at it. And it's Luca, the man who nearly rowed her off the river when they first met. But after hearing him open up about his mum, the noisy neighbour and the man who nearly rowed into them on the river are gone. In their place is a man who uses cooking to remember his mum and rowing to forget.

So, even though things still feel uncertain between them, it doesn't take long for her to reply. 'Yes. I've always liked the idea of giving rowing a go.'

Which is about as true as her making out to her patient Ben that she has even the slightest interest in *Match of the Day*.

CHAPTER 42

Kate finds Jay in the garden studio.

'It's looking amazing in here,' she says as she steps through the door, Rosie asleep in the sling. He looks up from his computer, where he had been editing photos from his last shoot. The light might be dimming outside, but it still feels fresh and bright in here. He's added an armchair in the corner and Kate notices new photographs on the walls. She steps closer to look at them.

Alongside the posed images of Kate and Rosie that had been in here previously, there are some new ones too. Kate and Rosie fast asleep on the bed, Rosie lying on her back with arms splayed and Kate curled around her like a comma, a protective hand placed over her stomach. The room around them is a complete mess, dirty washing dumped in piles on the floor. But they look peaceful in the midst of it all. Another photo shows Kate sitting on the sofa nursing Rosie, the TV flickering in the background. There's a faraway look in her eyes that so captures how she feels in those moments, as though she is half here but half elsewhere too. And a final one of Kate holding Rosie out in front of her, beaming at her with her mouth wide open, her head flung back. She remembers the moment – she'd been singing 'Wonderwall' again. Rosie's face is violent red, her eyes scrunched up, but it somehow makes for a sweet and funny photograph, that contrast of emotions.

'These are beautiful. I didn't even notice you taking them.'

'I've been thinking about everything you said about how you were expecting all of this to be,' says Jay. 'And I think part of the problem is that people usually only share the best bits. It's something I'm guilty of as a photographer. But I was thinking about changing that.'

'Oh yes?' Kate replies, still lost in the images on the wall that so perfectly capture her experience over the past few months. She looks back at Jay and notices that his eyes are sparkling. The dark circles are still there, but there's an excited energy in him that she realises she hasn't seen for quite a while.

'Now that the studio is pretty much ready, I was thinking of doing my first portrait shoots. And I thought I could specialise in parent and baby photos. Not those posed ones you usually see …'

'Where the babies are arranged to look as if they're asleep on a bed of leaves?'

They both laugh, and Kate realises how much she has missed that special feeling of laughing together with the person she loves.

'Yeah, exactly. My photos would be the opposite of that.

Just real parents with their babies, showing up with whatever emotions they were feeling that day. Totally stripped back, just them showing it all. What do you think?'

He rubs his beard, glancing up at her from beneath his long-lashed eyes. Something inside her gives a little skip, reminding her of how it felt to fall in love with him at the lido all those years ago. She realises that over the past few months she's been so focused on Rosie and on her own emotions that she hasn't spent enough time just looking at her husband. Now she traces around his face with her eyes, taking in the familiar green eyes with the faint crinkles that have developed there, the strong line of his jaw, the scruffy beard flecked with gold and grey. His lips that she has kissed a thousand times before and not nearly enough.

'I think that sounds amazing.' She steps forward, holding onto his shoulders and lifting onto her tiptoes so that her lips can touch against his. And for the first time since Rosie was born, she doesn't pull away after a couple of seconds. She leans towards him, letting her mouth soften open. He's hesitant at first, as if the kiss has taken him by surprise, but then he quickly responds, matching her intensity and then increasing it. Goosebumps dart up the back of her neck.

He wraps his arms around her waist and takes a step forward, pulling her in. But they can only get so close with Rosie in the sling.

'I feel like there's something coming between us,' he says with a laugh. They both look down at Rosie and smile.

'Shall we put her to bed?' she says.

Once Rosie is settled in the Moses basket with the baby

monitor switched on, Kate takes Jay's hand and leads him back downstairs to the sofa. But instead of reaching for the TV remote to switch on something mindless before bed, Kate climbs into his lap. She wraps her arms around his neck and lets her fingers run through his strawberry blond hair, delighting in the way he shivers involuntarily at her touch.

'Mmm, that's nice.'

How long has it been since they last did something like this? Certainly not since Rosie, and in the final weeks of her pregnancy she hadn't felt like being touched either, her body hot and aching. Kate pauses to pull her hair out of its messy bun and then leans forward again, letting it fall around them so that she feels as though they're in a little cave for two.

'I've missed this so much,' he says softly, groaning as her fingers claw at his shoulders, enjoying the warmth and solid breadth of him that always makes her feel safe.

'I've missed *you* so much,' she replies.

They kiss some more, heat rising in her stomach and flowing all the way up to her cheeks. After a while, she pulls back ever so slightly.

'I'm not sure I'm ready for *that* yet …'

He kisses the tip of her nose, pushing her hair out of her face. 'That's OK, sweet. We don't have to do anything you don't want to. We don't have to do anything ever again and you know I'll still love you.'

'I didn't say I don't want to do *anything* …'

He lifts an eyebrow at her and flashes her a smile, the smile that's just for her.

'Then why don't you take off your clothes?'

Her heart hammers in her chest, but she does as she's told. But once she's naked, she finds herself wrapping her arms around her stomach, suddenly conscious of its softness and stretch marks. Ever since Rosie, her stomach feels the most tender and vulnerable part of her, not for the way it looks so much as for everything it has been through.

Very gently, Jay pulls her hands away, clasping them in his and locking eyes with her.

'You're so beautiful,' he says. And he guides her backwards against the sofa cushions, kissing his way down her chest. As he reaches her stomach, tears well in her eyes at the softness of his lips on the softest bit of her.

Hearing her sniff, his head snaps up. She looks down into his familiar eyes, spotting the flash of worry that has arrived there.

'Are you OK?'

She nods, a smile on her face even as the tears continue to fill her eyes.

'Yes. It feels good. Please, don't stop.' She leans forward to kiss him, getting his cheeks damp in the process. And then she lets herself sink back into the cushions and into the pleasure of his touch, letting everything go, letting herself think of absolutely nothing but this, nothing but him.

When she shudders in his arms, her hands clamped tightly in his, it feels like arriving home.

After the 4 a.m. feed, Kate can't get back to sleep. But for once, she doesn't mind. She glances at Rosie, milk drunk and snoring in her Moses basket, and then at Jay, who is curled up at

297

her side, one arm flung over her thigh. Careful not to disturb either of them, she reaches for her phone on the bedside table.

This time, instead of scrolling her way through reminders of her old life or the perfect depictions of motherhood that look nothing like her own experiences, she composes a post, selecting one of the candid photos of her and Rosie that she asked Jay to send her earlier after seeing them in his studio. And she begins to write.

This is me and my beautiful daughter. She is the cutest thing in the world. But I am not sure if I love her yet.

Everything I heard or read before having a baby made me think that the second she was born I'd be flooded with a love unlike anything I'd ever experienced. But that hasn't happened for us. For me, bonding isn't something that's happened immediately and without effort. It's taking time and work.

For ages, I've been terrified about anyone finding out my secret. What would people think? What if I'm the only person who's ever felt this way? But in not sharing my truth, I'm part of the problem too. If I don't speak with honesty, then I'm not doing justice to the one person who might read this and think – *that's me too*. I'm not doing justice to the me who spends far too long scrolling social media on the night feeds, trying to find a version of motherhood that looks like mine and wishing I could see a post like this that tells me I'm not alone.

I'm starting to think that everything I've felt or haven't felt doesn't make me a bad mother. It just makes me a mother. Messy, imperfect and sometimes terrified. But always trying my best. #UnfilteredMotherhood

Kate hits post, sending her words out into the world. Then she puts her phone back on the bedside table and falls asleep, sleeping deeper than she has in a long time.

While Kate joins in with her daughter's snores, on the bedside table, her phone begins to light up. As the sun begins to rise outside, Kate's phone glows with notification after notification after notification.

CHAPTER 43

What if no one shows up? It's the thought that rolls around in Phoebe's mind as she arrives at the river at 9.45 a.m. on Monday. It's a grey morning and she glances anxiously at the sky. She wants to show her patients the joys of wild swimming and if it chucks it down, then that might not be so easy. Ever since she mentioned the group to Mel and sent the invitations to her patients, she's been quietly panicking. It was one thing when the group was just an idea, but now it's actually real. What if it's a total failure? Mel has put her trust in her and she doesn't want to let her down, especially as, after a night in her newly homely flat, thoughts about the future and her finances are weighing on Phoebe's mind. She doesn't want to let her patients down either, especially after everything they've been through. She's seriously starting to freak out when she hears a familiar voice calling her name.

She turns to see the swimming group heading towards her

through the meadow, Kate leading the way with Rosie in the sling.

'I'm so glad to see you all!' she says, greeting them in turn.

'We're glad to be here,' replies Sandra.

'Wouldn't have missed it,' adds Jazz, Hester nodding beside her.

'I had study leave this morning,' she explains. 'I thought this could count as, like, work experience.'

'This is Rosie's first visit to the river,' says Kate. 'I think she likes it.'

Rosie looks around them with wide eyes, her arms and legs waving in the sling. It makes them all laugh and Phoebe finds herself relaxing a little.

The sound of someone clearing their throat causes Phoebe to turn around. Her face spreads into a relieved smile as she sees Ben standing somewhat awkwardly in the grass, a rucksack slung over his shoulder. Her eyebrows lift in surprise as she sees the diminutive figure of Maude beside him, the pair standing so close and seeming so comfortable in each other's presence that they look as though they could be grandmother and grandson.

'Ben! Maude! You came!'

It takes all her strength not to reach out and hug them both, but especially Ben. She's been worrying about him all week, terrified that the news about his football group had sent him back down a spiral. It had been so hard not to check in, and now, seeing him here in person, she feels something lift off her shoulders slightly.

'I found this one by the gate chatting to a hawthorn tree,'

he says, gesturing to Maude. 'I figured she was one of us mad ones.'

Phoebe never uses that word herself and remembers kicking off once when Max made an offhand comment when they were out with his friends about Phoebe and her 'mad patients'. She'd been seething, although he'd told her that she was overreacting. But the way Ben says it is different. He and Maude glance at each other and smile.

'He's a good shepherd, he is,' Maude says, patting his arm.

'Maude has been telling me filthy jokes.'

'Um, I hope it's OK that I'm here too?' comes a clipped voice and Phoebe turns to spot Arabella and Camilla heading towards them, Arabella picking her way through the grass in satin ballet pumps but her mother in more substantial Birkenstocks. Their arms are linked together and Arabella carries a large straw basket over her shoulder. Camilla looks around warily. But she's here.

'Of course it is, Arabella. It's great to see both of you.'

Phoebe meets Camilla's eye and sees the wariness in her expression, but the glimmer of something else behind it too. A new-found determination, perhaps? Or just the wonder of being out of the house at last. She turns to take in everything around her.

Phoebe makes the introductions and Maude blesses everyone with the sign of the cross, which they all accept gamely. Then Sandra begins pulling items of clothing over her head. 'I don't know about you all, but I'm ready for a swim.'

As everyone starts to undress, Phoebe glances towards the gate, hoping to see Tara pushing her way through. But there's no one else there, so she starts getting changed, trying not to feel disappointed.

'I hope you don't think I'm going to put trunks or one of them Speedos on,' Ben says gruffly. 'I'm going in like this.' He gestures at his outfit: an Arsenal football kit.

'That's fine. Whatever makes you feel comfortable.'

The others are ready now and Phoebe catches Ben glancing across at Camilla, her pale, lined skin spilling out of a chic navy high-waisted bikini, and then at Arabella, his face turning a violent purple at the sight of her athletic, tanned physique in a black one-piece with a low, scooping back.

'So, thank you all for being here,' Phoebe says once they're assembled on the riverbank, old swimmers and new standing side by side and barefoot. Kate is sitting this swim out but is stretched out happily on a blanket, tickling Rosie with a blade of grass. It feels good to have her new friend here, though, giving her the reassurance to continue. 'I really appreciate you giving this idea of mine a go. I know it can't have been easy to come.'

Ben shrugs. 'I wasn't going to. But then I realised I didn't have anything better to do.'

She knows there's more to it than that, though. That just getting out of bed, let alone out of the house and down here to a new place with new people, is something that for many people might seem small but for others is huge. She is about to say something, but it turns out she doesn't have to because Camilla is nodding along.

'I know that feeling. I thought I'd stay in bed forever after my Teddy died.'

They share a look of understanding and Phoebe catches

303

Ben's glance slipping to the scar on Camilla's wrist when he thinks no one is looking.

'I was the same after my first divorce,' says Sandra, surprising Phoebe. She's always so upbeat that it feels jarring to think of this other side of her, even though she knows better than anyone that everyone has that darker side in them somewhere.

Hester is nodding too. 'I feel that way sometimes when I think about my exams.'

Camilla smiles appreciatively. 'Thank you all, that really helps. When I got your email, Phoebe, I didn't think I'd come either. But then I realised I'm fed up with staying trapped inside my house. My husband wouldn't want that.' She glances around her, taking in the willow trees, the bluebells and the riverboat. 'I think he'd like it here,' she adds with a smile. Already, she seems more relaxed, as if being surrounded by nature is topping up her reserves, giving her strength.

Sandra shares a few tips, telling them all to breathe deeply and slowly once they're in the water.

'And if you start to feel anxious, just let me know, OK?' adds Phoebe. 'And there's a lifeguard on hand too.'

The lifeguard looks up and waves in their direction.

'Right, shall we get in then?'

'Abso-fucking-lutely!' cries Maude, before striding for the diving board and bombing in, causing an enormous splash.

'That's the spirit, Maude!' says Camilla, clapping her hands together, a sparkle appearing in her eyes.

Sandra and the others make their way in too and Phoebe follows, keeping the swear words inside this time as the cold water hits her.

'I'm not sure about this, Mum,' says Arabella, pausing on the bank.

'Neither am I,' says her mother. But she reaches out her hand. Phoebe watches as the women share a look, spotting the challenge in Camilla's eye that surfaced the first time they met.

Arabella hesitates and then takes her mother's hand. Together, the two women walk down into the river. A calm smile spreads immediately across Camilla's face, but Arabella's body is still tense, her shoulders up by her ears.

'Let go, darling,' Phoebe hears Camilla say softly. And Phoebe wonders whether the thing that persuaded Camilla to come here in the end wasn't actually a sense of claustrophobia in her home or even thoughts of her husband. Maybe it was this: the way she watches her daughter as she shakes her head, her body frozen with tension.

'I can't,' Arabella replies, her voice shaking. Phoebe thinks back to the first time she met Arabella, to her slick outfit and tight smile but the way she broke down as soon as Phoebe invited her to take off the mask for a moment.

'You need to, darling. Go on, sweetheart.'

And then Arabella takes a deep breath and lets herself fall backwards into the water, dunking underneath, her golden hair spreading out behind her. When she resurfaces, her eyelashes are dripping with what could be river water or tears but is probably a mix of both. Her pristine make-up is dripping down her face and her hair hangs in a tangled mess around her shoulders. But she is smiling, properly smiling this time.

Phoebe catches the way her mother looks at her, pride

plastered all over her face. The two women kick out into the middle of the river, joining the rest of the group.

As Phoebe turns to look back at the bank, she sees that Ben is still standing on the side.

'Are you OK?'

'I don't think I can do it.'

'It's all right. Just take your time.'

The lifeguard has spotted his hesitation too and chips in softly but reassuringly, 'It's OK, I'm right here watching. Make sure you take deep breaths.'

But Ben isn't taking deep breaths. In fact, they have become rapid and gasping. His whole body is shaking.

'I can't do it! I can't do anything. I'm useless.'

Phoebe watches from the water, suddenly wondering if this whole thing was a terrible idea. Maybe this was too much for him. Maybe it was too much for all of them.

Camilla, who is closest to the bank, strides towards him. She reaches out her hand and as she does, Ben's eyes fall again to the scar on her wrist.

'You are so much stronger than you think you are,' she says.

He hesitates and then takes a deep breath and reaches out his arm. Phoebe watches as Camilla's and Ben's gaze falls on the scar on Ben's own wrist. Their eyes meet.

Camilla continues to hold out her hand.

'*We* are so much stronger than we think we are,' she says softly. And then their hands connect and Camilla pulls Ben gently down into the water.

He puffs and splashes as he swims vigorously in circles. 'Bloody hell, you didn't say it was so cold!'

306

'It gets better quickly,' Phoebe says. 'You get used to it.'

He slows down, his breathing growing steadier. 'Oh yeah, you're right actually.'

'Try floating like this,' suggests Maude, lifting her head up slightly from where she is still lying on her back with her arms stretched wide. 'It's very relaxing.'

'Why don't we all give it a try?' suggests Phoebe.

One by one, they lift their feet off the river bed. Lying like this, the willow trees form a cocoon around them, a few patches of sky and cloud just visible between the leaves.

'Fill your lungs with air,' instructs the lifeguard from the bank. 'That will help you stay afloat. And remember to breathe slowly and deeply.'

Arabella lets out an audible sigh. Phoebe turns her head to glance over at the others. Maude and Ben are floating close to one another, both smiling. Maude kicks her toes slightly to create splashes that jump up onto Ben's feet and he does the same back. Arabella and Camilla are holding hands as they float. Phoebe lies back and swallows hard, warm despite the cold of the river.

'I think I've talked to you all before about mindfulness,' she says. 'But sometimes it can be difficult to achieve if you're just sitting at home or at work. Somewhere like this is a great place to try it out. If things feel overwhelming, it can really help to calm us to focus on the small sensations in our bodies.'

It's something she regularly encourages her patients to try, but for ages she hasn't had the time to be mindful herself and the last couple of weeks have shown her that it's time she tried taking her own advice.

'Focus on the feeling of the water lapping against your ears, the light filtering down through the trees. Listen to the sound of the birds and the rustling of the reeds. Now take a deep breath.'

There's the collective sound of them all inhaling.

'Notice how you're feeling. Be honest with yourself, don't feel you have to push anything away. And now just try to be still.'

A breeze rustles the grass and wildflowers in the meadow. Phoebe can hear Kate talking softly to Rosie on the bank and the distant sound of children playing down in the campsite, a radio play coming from inside Hamish's boat. Bees buzz and birds chirp softly in the trees. And the water holds them all afloat.

CHAPTER 44

Ben is the first to break the silence.

'Look, this is all really nice, but lying here like this is really making me need a piss.'

'I'm weeing right now!' declares Maude. Laughter ripples around the group.

'Maybe it's time to get out.' Phoebe rolls onto her front.

'I'd like to try that rope swing first,' comes a voice that Phoebe is very surprised to realise belongs to Arabella. She looks a little like a panda, with her eyeliner and mascara smeared around her eyes. But she looks about ten years younger too. 'Who's with me?'

They all line up to have a go, taking turns to grab hold of the swing, pushing themselves off and then letting go in mid-air, splashing down into the water.

'You have to do it too, Phoebe,' says Ben once he, Arabella, Maude and Camilla have all had a go, yelping and roaring in turn. 'You're the reason we're all here.'

'Oh, all right then. Here goes.'

She grabs hold of the swing and pushes herself firmly off the bank. As she whizzes into the air, her stomach lifts to her chest. There's a brief moment of sheer terror as she lets go and is suspended in the air before she crashes down into the water. Then she bobs up again, grinning.

All thoughts of professionalism go out the window as she cries, 'That was bloody fantastic!'

'Hurrah!' says Camilla.

'Um, hi,' comes a quiet voice. Everyone turns to the bank and there is Tara, arms wrapped around herself and biting her lip nervously. 'I'm late, I know.'

'Tara!' says Phoebe warmly. 'It's so good to see you and don't worry about that. I'm just so pleased you made it. Do you want to join us?'

'I'm not sure ...' She glances at the river and bites her lip harder.

'Well, we were just about to get out and have some tea and cake,' says Sandra. 'You could join for that bit instead?'

She pauses and then nods slowly. 'That sounds good.'

They all make their way out of the water, chatting as they get changed. Once Sandra is dressed, she takes Rosie so that Kate can go for a quick dip too and, after encouragement from the others, she enters the water from the rope swing.

'Look, Mama's in the river!' says Sandra, lifting Rosie's hand so it looks as though she is waving. Kate waves back, a huge smile on her face.

Once they are all dressed and mostly dry, they queue up outside the Kingfisher, towels draped over their shoulders.

'Hello, everyone,' says Hamish, today wearing a checked shirt and green waistcoat. 'Lovely day!'

Phoebe looks up at the sky. It is still grey and overcast. 'You're quite right, Hamish.'

He takes their orders and the others chat among themselves as he prepares them. The group has become all mixed up, so it isn't at all clear who is here for the mental health swimming group and who is part of the original morning swimming club. They're all just here for the river. And the cake. Obviously.

Phoebe notices that Maude is standing a little apart from the rest of the group, her eyes trained fixedly on the top of Hamish's riverboat.

'Are those beehives?' she says, her voice bursting with excitement.

Hamish glances up, following Maude's gaze, and Phoebe does the same. And there they are, the wooden hives sitting on the top of the riverboat's roof alongside the flowerpots. Yes! How had she not thought of it before?

'Ah yes, my little hives,' says Hamish. 'Although I must admit, I'm only a beginner. I haven't managed to gather much honey yet.'

'I could help you,' Maude says, practically jumping on the spot. 'I haven't done it for years, but I used to be pretty in tune with the bees.'

'Wow, that sounds brilliant, but only if you don't mind.'

'Mind? I'd fucking love to.'

The riverbank buzzes with conversation as stories are shared and new friendships are made. They spot Bert the kingfisher whizzing by and Sandra launches into a lilting rendition of 'Morning has Broken'.

'I'm glad I came,' says Tara as she says goodbye after a cup of tea and a generous slice of coffee and walnut cake.

'I'm so glad you did too,' replies Phoebe.

Arabella and Camilla are smiling and linking arms tightly by the time they head off too.

'Thank you for this,' says Arabella and her mother nods.

'Yes, thank you, Phoebe. Oh, and I've been meaning to tell you: I went running last week.'

'Really?!'

'Really, this time. I promise.'

'She really did,' chips in Arabella, giving her mother's arm a squeeze. 'I'm so proud of you, Mum.'

'And I'm proud of you too, darling. You've helped me so much these past months. I still have my dark days, but things feel …' She tilts her head to the sky, where a beam of sunlight is finally making its way through the clouds, ' … Brighter.'

'I'm so pleased to hear that, Camilla. And remember, I'm here for you on those dark days.'

Because Phoebe is experienced enough to know that one run and one wild swim isn't going to make her patients' problems go away. Mental health is far more complicated than that. But her job is to help her patients find tools to cope and today she feels as though she's offered them something new to add to their kits: a place and people to turn to when they need it. And it feels even sweeter that the thing she has shared with them is something that has helped her through her own dark patch.

'I hope you had a good time?' Phoebe asks Ben as he laces

312

up his trainers and pulls his rucksack onto his back.

He shrugs.

'It was all right.' But just as he is leaving, he turns over his shoulder. 'I might invite the football guys next time.'

As he walks away, Phoebe grins, full of hope at the thought of a next time.

CHAPTER 45

Kate's phone hasn't stopped buzzing since she shared her post. She's been flooded with messages from her friends, and as she walks back from the river with Rosie in the sling, she scrolls through them, trying her best not to get too emotional as she reads.

Emma: We're so proud of you, Kate! And Rosie is going to be too xx

Leonie: Well done for speaking your truth. We love you! Xx

Erin: Saw your post and wanted to say how proud I am of you, little sis. Xx

Frank: You're our hero, Kate! Love Frank, Jermaine and Sprout xx

Hope: I've SAid it Before and I'll say it agaIN. Rosemary would be so proud of you.

There are messages in the Tired Mums Club group that Lexi

added her to after their last swim, all the women cheering her on and thanking her for her honesty.

But as Kate scrolls through her phone, trying her best to keep up with replying to her friends, she isn't sure that she deserves their praise. Because the truth is that her reasons for opening up weren't entirely selfless.

This morning, she woke to a message from someone she went to school with but hasn't spoken to in years.

Hey Kate, I'm not sure if you remember me. When I saw your Instagram post about your experiences with your baby, I just had to get in touch. My son was born six months ago and these past six months have been the hardest six months of my life. Most of all because I have struggled to bond with my son. I've felt that there's something wrong with me, that when I look at him, I see a very cute little stranger but I have none of those gushy emotions that I thought I would feel. Reading your post made me feel so relieved. I had to get in touch to tell you that it's not just you. I understand exactly how you feel. I haven't told anyone else this, but seeing your post made me think that maybe I could. And that maybe it's going to be OK. Love, Lizzie xx

It's not the only message Kate has received like that. Throughout the day, she's been flooded with them, some from acquaintances and colleagues but a lot from strangers. Each message tells a unique story but holds the same message: *I understand. I see you. You're not on your own.*

For the first time in a long time, Kate feels truly hopeful for the future. She'd been so nervous about letting anyone see her vulnerability, but now she wishes she'd written her post ages ago.

As she crosses through the village, she lets herself think about all the things she is looking forward to. Rosie's first pair of wellies. Taking her to the beach. Their first Christmas as a family. And top of her list is her first swimming lesson this afternoon. She managed to book on to a class that takes place in the next town.

'Are you excited about going swimming later?' she says to Rosie as they turn onto their lane. 'I think you're going to love it.'

The cottage comes into view and she spots her mum's car parked on the drive.

Jay is making tea in the kitchen when Kate walks in and her mum looks up, a smile on her face. She's in one of her usually chic outfits, today a denim jumpsuit that makes Kate think about painting Phoebe's flat together with her new friends. Her bob is neat as ever, but Kate wonders if she looks a little tired and if her smile seems somewhat tight.

'Hello, darling. I brought a lasagne.' She gestures to the oven dish covered in foil that sits on the side.

'Thanks, Mum. That's really kind of you.'

'I'll leave you both to it,' says Jay. 'I've got work to do in the studio, but shout if you need anything.' Since Kate shared her Instagram post with his photo and tagged him in, he's been flooded with enquiries. Her friends from the Tired Mums Club have all booked portrait sessions with their babies and partners.

He kisses her as he passes and Kate lingers for a second, a hand rising involuntarily to his cheek. After last night, she woke feeling closer to him than she has in months. They brushed their teeth side by side and holding hands, and before she left to go to the river, they'd shared a long kiss, his arms tight and warm around her waist.

Once he's gone, a silence descends. Kate doesn't know how to bridge the distance that she feels has grown between her and her mum over recent weeks.

'I saw your Instagram post, darling.'

'Oh.' So that's why she's here.

'I just wanted to come and check on you.'

'Thanks, Mum. But I'm doing OK. People have been so supportive.'

'I saw that. What you said seems to have really connected with people – I scrolled through some of the comments and they're really lovely. I'm very proud of you.'

'Thank you, that means a lot, Mum.'

'And you will get there, I know you will,' she says now, putting down her tea so she can place a hand on Kate's arm. 'In your own time. I know you will utterly adore that little girl. Just like I adore my girls.'

Her eyes shine and she lets go of Kate's arm to quickly wipe her face before taking a sip of tea.

'I love you too, Mum. How are you doing, anyway? I feel like we haven't spoken too much recently. Is everything OK?'

317

'I …' Her mother opens her mouth but quickly closes it again. She takes another sip of tea and then the fixed smile returns to her face. 'I'm fine, sweetheart. Right, I've got to go now, actually, busy day. But I just wanted to come and check on you. Let's get something in the diary soon, though.' She kisses Rosie on the top of the head, then kisses Kate's cheek too. 'I'll just pop to the loo before I go.'

As her mum heads upstairs, Kate notices that she has left her phone behind on the counter. The screen lights up with a new message. She doesn't mean to look. But when she sees her stepfather's name, she can't help but glance over.

Brian: **Have you spoken to Kate? You know we'll have to tell them both eventually.**

When she hears her mum's footsteps on the stairs, she quickly turns her back on the phone and starts washing up in the sink, looking out at the garden.

'I'll leave you to it,' her mum says, slipping her phone into her pocket and grabbing her bag. 'Enjoy the lasagne. See you soon!'

There's so much that Kate wants to ask her mum. But she doesn't know how to even start the conversation without revealing that she invaded her privacy. So instead she hugs her and then watches from the doorway as she drives away, her mind spinning with the thought of what she might be hiding from her.

CHAPTER 46

Kate spends a long time weighing up whether or not to tell Erin about the message she saw on their mum's phone, but in the end decides she can't keep something like that from her sister.

Erin: **That does seem strange. Oh God, what if Mum and Brian are breaking up?**

The thought has entered Kate's mind too. As soon as her mum left, she went out to the studio to tell Jay about the message.

'Shit, I'm sorry. Whatever it is, though, I'm sure she'll tell you in her own time.'

She knows he's right, but it doesn't stop her thoughts from spiralling. But as she glances at her phone to type another message to her sister, she spots the time.

'We're going to be late for our swimming lesson,' she says to Rosie, who has just woken up from a nap in the sling, looking around with wide eyes.

As Kate drives them to the pool, her mind goes round and round in circles, thinking about her mum and stepdad and what the message she accidentally read might mean. As soon as she arrives at the pool, though, her attention is snapped back to the here and now by the smell of chlorine and the sound of splashing.

'Is this your first time?' one of the mums in the changing room asks as she wrestles her wriggly son into a pair of swimming trunks while trying to get changed herself.

'Yes, it is. I'm Kate and this is Rosie. I have no idea how she's going to find the water.'

'She might not like it at first, my Ivo didn't, but he loves it now.'

Kate pulls on her own swimsuit and then gets Rosie into hers. It looks even cuter on than it did hanging up in the nursery and she takes a photo to send to her family and her lido friends. Sadness invades for a second as she thinks about Rosemary and how much she wishes she could share the photo with her too. But she tries to console herself with the thought that part of Rosemary will always live on because it was Rosemary who taught Kate to love swimming and now it's Kate's turn to pass that on to her daughter. God, she hopes she doesn't hate it …

The water is as warm as a bath and stepping down into it makes Kate immediately relax. She starts with Rosie up on her shoulder and then very slowly crouches down so that they are both below the water level. At first, Rosie's eyes open wide at the surprising new sensations, a frown appearing on her face.

'It might take a while for her to get used to it, don't worry,' reassures the instructor. But the next second Rosie's face spreads into a wide, gummy smile. 'Or maybe not! She's clearly a water baby!'

Rosie moves her hands about in the water, opening and closing her mouth in pleasure. *That's my girl*, thinks Kate, beaming.

They sing some nursery rhymes and splash around in a circle in the small pool and even when water droplets fall onto Rosie's face, she doesn't seem to mind.

'Right,' says the instructor towards the end of the class, 'now is the time to take our babies underwater, but only if you feel comfortable. Kate, as it's the first time for you two you don't have to if you don't want to.'

Rosie seems very content, though, the smile from earlier barely having left her face.

'I think I'd like to have a go, if that's OK?'

'That's great! What I want you all to do is hold your baby in front of you at arm's length with them facing you, supporting them around the waist. We're then going to ask if they're ready, then together duck gently underwater, trying to keep eye contact if possible. If you've got goggles with you, do put them on so that you can see their reactions.'

Kate slips hers over her face and Rosie gives her a half-quizzical, half-amused look. Kate kisses her on her damp forehead.

The other women and their babies take it in turns to duck underwater until everyone has had a go and it's Kate and Rosie's turn.

'OK, then, are you ready?' asks the instructor.

Kate suddenly feels nervous, but she looks at her daughter

again and nods. She settles them both into the correct position, Rosie facing her, her eyes locked on Kate's.

'Are you ready, Rosie?' Kate asks. Rosie blinks back, her body relaxed, arms and legs floating calmly. Kate takes a deep breath and gently they both slip under the surface.

Instantly, everything grows quieter, the other women and babies feeling a long way away up there on the surface. Everything is calm and blue as Kate looks across at Rosie, feeling as though it's just the two of them in the whole world. Rosie opens her eyes wide, staring back. Her light red hair flows out from her head, her cheeks puffed slightly and a curious, inquisitive smile on her face.

As Kate looks at her daughter and her daughter looks back, for the first time since she was born, Kate doesn't see Jay in Rosie's face. She doesn't see a rather sweet but alien stranger either. Instead, she feels as though she is looking at herself. There she is, in her daughter's eyes, in her face, in her expression as she gazes back through the water at her.

There I am.

There you are.

When they pop back up just a few seconds later, Kate's face is damp with a mix of warm chlorine-scented water and hot salty tears. She lets the droplets merge into one another and drip into the pool, a huge smile growing on her face. Eyelashes dripping, hair plastered against her small head, Rosie smiles back.

'Well done, you both did great,' comes the voice of the instructor. But Kate barely hears her as she lifts Rosie up in the

322

air and then holds her close against her chest, feeling their two hearts beating against one another.

Once she has managed to get both herself and Rosie dressed and dry, she says goodbye to the other women. 'See you all next week!'

She's on a high as she heads back through the swimming pool reception towards the car park. But just as she is about to leave, her attention catches on a display by the door that she hadn't noticed before. Copies of the local free paper, the *Avon Times*, are stacked in a neat pile. She smiles as she remembers how she made her own start in journalism, working at the local paper in Brixton. Whenever she travels somewhere new, she loves finding and reading the local paper. It always gives you an immediate feel for the place and the community. She's been meaning to get a copy of the *Avon Times* since moving back to Somerset, but with everything else that's been going on, it has slipped her mind. The date on the copies shows that it's a brand-new edition, released just today.

She reaches for a copy, planning to put it into her rucksack to read when she gets home. But just as she's about to fold it up, the headline jumps out at her, making her stop still. In one second, she comes crashing down from her post-swim high, her whole body turning cold.

CHAPTER 47

Phoebe and Luca have made it to a stretch of river a little way downstream that Phoebe has never been to before. Here, the trees have fallen away and there are fields on either side of the banks, sheep grazing on one side and horses on the other. While the river swimming spot feels like a secluded little bubble, out here it feels open and light, the views stretching out for miles across a patchwork of English countryside.

She lets the oars drop from her hands and stretches her arms above her head.

'My hands are killing me already!'

'Yeah, I basically have permanent calluses on my palms from rowing,' Luca replies. 'It's worth it, though.'

Instead of taking her out on one of the tiny streamlined machines like the one Luca was rowing when they first met, they are in an old-fashioned wooden rowing boat painted bright red.

'Better for beginners,' he had said when they'd met at the riverside. 'And for snacks too,' he'd added, lifting up a bulging Giuglia's bag and placing it down inside the hull.

'Thank fuck for that,' she'd said. 'I'd been dreading getting into one of those tiny contraptions. And snacks are always a good choice.'

She has surprised herself by how much she has enjoyed the feeling of pulling the oars through the water, the satisfying tug as the paddle catches. And how much she has enjoyed Luca's company, even if the awkward kiss that they still haven't talked about hangs in the air between them. They've chatted as they've made their way along the river, Luca sharing more stories about his mum and Phoebe opening up about her father's struggles in a way she never did with Max. It wasn't that she was embarrassed about her dad's depression, just that she didn't want Max to see him any differently and she innately sensed that he would. But Luca listens without judgement. She talks about her work, too, and how it's consumed her life for the past few years.

'I get that,' he says, nodding. 'When I was getting the deli ready, it was all I could think about. And now it's open, it's not much better either. It's not just a job to me, it never will be.'

'Exactly,' Phoebe replies. 'My job isn't just a job either.' It's something Max never understood. How, even on the tough days, she would never be able to stop herself from caring deeply.

'I think it's all about balance, isn't it?' says Luca. 'Our jobs will always be important to us and there's nothing wrong with that. But other things have to be too. Things like this.'

He looks across at her, a dark curl falling in front of his face and his caramel eyes meeting hers. Does he mean the river, or something else?

A dragonfly comes to rest on the end of one of the oars and they both watch it for a moment before it darts off again. In the field beside them, a sheep lets out a loud bleat, but otherwise it's quiet.

'Oh, I nearly forgot about the snacks,' he says, twisting behind him, making the boat rock and Phoebe grab hold of the sides. He reaches inside the bag for a paper parcel that he opens to reveal crisp, golden scrolls of pastry lined up in rows, each bursting with a different-coloured filling.

She draws in a little breath.

'Your mum's cannoli.'

'I'd recommend the pistachio. That was always her favourite.'

He passes her one and she puts it in her mouth, the pastry snapping and crumbling and her tongue tingling with the sweet, creamy taste of pistachio and a bright burst of lemon.

Luca takes one too, his eyes closing. Phoebe watches a look of contentment spread across his face and something tugs inside her. 'They taste of my childhood,' he says and it feels like a precious kind of secret, getting to know this about him.

It makes her find the courage to at least try to clear the air, as she meant to yesterday.

'Look, Luca. About the other night. I'm really sorry for what happened. It had been a long day and I'd had too much to drink. It's something I'm working on.' She hasn't had a drink in over a week and while there were moments when she was

326

at her parents' place and worrying about her nan that she had craved the numbing warmth of a large gin and tonic, she hasn't missed the hangovers that she realises now had become a normal part of her existence. She thought everyone woke up each morning feeling like death. 'Anyway, I'm really sorry I launched on you like that when you clearly didn't want me to.'

Luca brushes the pastry crumbs from his fingertips and tilts his head, looking at her closely. There's a patch of icing sugar caught on his bottom lip.

'You think I didn't want to kiss you?'

The boat bobs slightly on the flowing river, a family of moorhens paddling serenely by. Phoebe focuses on watching them instead of the fact that her cheeks are probably co-ordinating perfectly with her hair right now.

'Well, you did step away from me. What else was I supposed to think?'

She might not have the most extensive experience with men, but someone physically recoiling from you feels like a pretty clear message.

'I wanted to kiss you, Phoebe. I've wanted to kiss you since the first time you stepped into the deli.'

She looks up at him now, meeting his eye again. He holds her gaze without looking away.

'Oh.'

'Yeah, oh. You were so annoyed at me that day. And you had every right to be,' he adds quickly. 'But, God, I couldn't believe how someone could look so annoyed but also so ... *vibrant* at the same time.'

'It's the hair, isn't it?' she says, gesturing to her bright red ponytail that perfectly matches the red lipstick she is wearing because there might be some people who wouldn't think to wear bright red lipstick when rowing down a river, but Phoebe is not one of those people.

'It's not just the hair,' he replies in a gruff voice. 'You're fucking luminous, Phoebe. Everything about you. Yeah, the outfits and the hair too. But it's also just *you*. That day you came into the deli like a whirlwind? Yeah, you were mad at me. But after you'd gone, I found myself feeling more alive than I'd been since Mum died. And the craziest thing is you don't even realise it – the fact you have this light inside of you that makes people want to be around you and open up to you. No wonder you're so great at your job. I've told you things I've never told anyone else and I've only known you, what, a couple of weeks? So, yeah, I wanted to kiss you.'

For once, she has absolutely no idea what to say.

'So then why did you pull away?' she eventually manages.

He winces slightly, brushing a hand through his curls.

'I knew you'd had … some wine to drink. I didn't know if you were kissing me because it was me or just because I was there.'

Sitting opposite her in the rowing boat, having just said what he's said, he looks vulnerable and exposed but OK with it too.

'It wasn't just because you were there,' she says quietly, looking up so that their eyes meet and the river and the fields around them disappear completely. 'I mean, I was glad you *were* there,' she adds with a wry smile. 'But it was because of the way you absolutely always have food somewhere on your face and when you talk about ingredients, it's like you're an extremely nerdy fan talking about an underrated album of your favourite band. Because you left me a care package on my doorstep even after I'd yelled at you. Because of how much you care about your business and how hard you've worked to make it a reality.'

There's more she could say too. The way he danced without inhibitions to his mum's favourite song in the middle of his deli with his dad. The way that one curl of hair always falls in front of his left eyebrow. The way that, ever since she found out he was her neighbour, it's been an absolute nightmare having to think about him right there in the space below hers.

It's his turn to appear lost for words. At the same moment, they both seem to decide they don't need to say anything at all as they each lean forward decisively, bridging the gap between them in the rowing boat. As they reach for one another, the boat rocks. And instead of finding herself falling forward into Luca's arms, Phoebe lets out a sharp scream as the boat tips and they capsize into the river.

Water rushes into her nose and mouth as she scrabbles about before bobbing up to the surface to see Luca opposite her, treading water and with his hair wet and bedraggled, making her think of an Old English sheepdog who has been caught in the rain.

'Shit,' says Luca, paddling with his arms, the upturned boat and oars floating beside them.

'The snacks!' cries Phoebe.

And then they both start to laugh.

Together, they push the boat over towards the bank where it is shallower and then plant their feet on the bottom. Phoebe's hair drips around her face and her sodden clothes cling to her. Luca's muscles are even more visible than usual through his soaking grey T-shirt and there's a strand of pondweed stuck to one shoulder. He strides through the water towards her.

'Come here,' he says, pushing strands of wet hair out of her face. He wraps his arms around her as they stand waist-deep in the river. 'This isn't exactly how I pictured it,' he says, revealing another little bit of himself that makes her shiver, and not just from the cold water. 'This date sucks, doesn't it?' He takes a step closer to her and she does the same, reaching her hands up and across his broad, solid back.

'It's the absolute worst,' she mumbles as their bodies press flush against one another and she tilts her face towards his and kisses him. This time, he doesn't pull away.

Phoebe's whole body tingles, and not just from the cold, as they drag the boat back up onto the riverbank and into the beach hut boat store, stacking the oars alongside. After the unexpected dip in the river, she's glad they thought to leave their phones and keys in here, tucked away under an upturned boat. As Phoebe reaches for her phone, she notices a whole string of messages in the swimming group's WhatsApp chat.

'Oh shit,' she says as she scrolls through, catching up on the frantic conversation she missed while she was on the water.

'It looks like something's going on outside,' Luca says, peering around the boathouse door. Her attention still half on her phone, they follow the rising sound of conversation back outside, where they spot a crowd gathered around the Kingfisher. The lifeguard is there, alongside a collection of swimmers, some of whom Phoebe recognises from previous dips. In the middle of them all is Hamish, handing out copies of the local newspaper.

Once they've joined the group, Luca reaches out for a copy, Phoebe catching snatches of the conversations happening around them.

'I can't believe it ...'

'It's just awful ...'

'What are we going to do?'

'To think we've been *swimming* in that ...'

Luca unfurls the newspaper and together they silently read the front page.

Sewage in the Avon

Locals told 'stay away from the river!'

A new water report conducted by the River Trust has revealed that levels of pollution in the stretch of river between Farleigh-on-Avon and Waterford are among the worst in the country.

Dangerously high levels of sewage have been detected in the river water, attributed to overflow from the local water treatment plant. Environmental laws state that overflow sewage is only allowed to be released into the river during storms or at other points when the drainage system is overwhelmed, but investigations by the *Avon Times* and the River Trust suggest that waste is being dumped in the river far more frequently.

The local environmental board has issued instructions to immediately cease water activities on this stretch of river due to the serious risk of ill health posed by the polluted water. This includes rowing, kayaking, paddleboarding and swimming.

The water will be tested again by Somerset Council in two
weeks and another statement will be issued then as to whether
it is safe to return to the river.

Once she's finished reading, Phoebe looks up and catches
Luca's eye. His expression looks just as horrified as she feels.

'Shit,' he repeats.

'Quite literally,' she replies.

He attempts a smile, but she can tell his heart isn't really in
it. Neither is hers. She suddenly wants nothing more than a
very hot shower and a gallon of mouthwash.

'I work here – how is this the first thing I'm hearing of this?'
she catches the lifeguard saying.

'And what about my business?' chips in Hamish, waving a
newspaper in the air. 'If people aren't going to come to the
river, then my business is over. "Here, have a cherry Bakewell
with a side of sewage." I don't think so. This is my livelihood.'

'Look!' someone says suddenly and Phoebe follows where
they are pointing to see two people in Somerset County
Council-branded T-shirts striding through the meadow, their
expressions grave, carrying a large bag.

'What do you think they're doing?' Luca asks. All Phoebe
can do is shake her head, watching them approach.

'Stand back, everyone,' one man says as they get nearer.
'Please stay away from the water.'

They reach into the bag and start pulling out equipment, the
crowd watching on as they begin to cordon off the entry point
to the river.

'What's going on?' asks the lifeguard.

One of the workers looks up, his eyes landing on the newspaper still held aloft in Hamish's hand.

'You've seen the papers. This water is severely contaminated. We're cordoning it off for everyone's safety.'

His colleague finishes attaching tape around a tree and heads off towards the diving board and pontoon to do the same there.

'Hey, that's my chair!' cries the lifeguard, rushing off as one of the workers drags her deckchair away to make way for the cordon.

Animated conversation continues around them, but Phoebe returns her attention to her phone. The WhatsApp group has gone wild ever since Kate shared a link to the news article earlier this afternoon, everyone expressing their disgust and shock.

But it always seems so idyllic, typed Jazz at 5.01 It feels so jarring to think of what's really been going on beneath the surface.

The latest string of messages are in response to one sent by Kate at 5.34.

Emergency meeting of the Farleigh-on-Avon River Swimming, Bathing and Recreational Water-Based Activities Club at mine tonight? 7 p.m., the Old Post Office. I've got wine. Bring snacks? Xxx

Everyone else has agreed that they'll be there. Phoebe checks the time: 6.45.

'I've got to go,' she says to Luca, putting her phone away and trying her best to keep her teeth from chattering in her soaking-wet clothes. God, she can't wait to get them off. Now she knows what's in the river, she can't stand the feel of the water on her skin. 'Actually . . .' she adds, glancing at Luca. Maybe she doesn't have to do this on her own. Maybe it doesn't matter if her past relationships have all failed. Because they weren't him. 'Why don't you come with me?'

CHAPTER 48

The Old Post Office is heaving. The regular swimming crew are here, plus Kate's new mum friends. Jay has been busy making cups of tea for everyone, Rosie in the sling, watching everything with fascination. When Phoebe and Luca arrive on the doorstep, still dripping wet, Kate sends them straight up to the bathroom, lending them clean towels and dry clothes from her and Jay's wardrobes.

Now they're all sitting in the small living room on an assortment of chairs and cushions. Jay stands by Kate's side with a hand placed on her shoulder. He might not be a swimmer, but he knows how much it means to her and how much the river has come to mean to her too.

Every time she glances again at the headline of the *Avon Times* which is spread out on the coffee table, she can't quite believe it. Not *their* river. She might only have been swimming there for a short space of time, but it's down on the riverbank and among these women that she has found herself again. She can't afford to lose that. Just the thought of going back to the dark place she has been in for so long makes her shiver. She can't let that happen, not for herself and not for Jay and Rosie either.

'Well, this is bloody awful,' says Sandra. She leans forward and reaches for a biscotti. Luca had briefly nipped down the lane to the deli for supplies. Kate likes him already. She wants to grill Phoebe about the date, but every time she looks at them and sees their damp hair, all she can think about is the river.

'I can't believe we've been swimming in, like, *sewage*,' says Hester.

'Or that the water company is able to get away with dumping literal crap into our river,' says Jazz.

'I fed my baby as soon as I got back from our first swim,' says Lexi, shuddering. 'I mean, I wiped myself with a wet wipe, but ...'

Kate glances at Rosie, thinking the same thing.

'So, no more swimming, then?' asks Phoebe.

'Or rowing,' adds Luca, looking just as dejected as everyone else.

'You don't know how much that river means to me,' says Sandra, her voice far quieter than usual.

'I know, we all love it there,' says Kate, passing her an understanding smile. But Sandra shakes her head.

'There's something I need to tell you. It's about my father.' She sniffs loudly. 'We were always so close. My mum died when I was young, you see, so, for most of my life, it was just me and Dad and my sister. He wasn't at all fazed by having two daughters – he did everything with us, playing with us, taking us swimming, learning how to do our hair. And when we grew up, he became an amazing grandfather too, so hands-on and involved.'

'He sounds great,' says Kate.

Sandra sniffs again.

'He was. And the river was his favourite place in the world.'

There's quiet as everyone takes in the meaning of Sandra's words.

'He passed away a year ago. He might have been eighty-five, but the truth is, I still miss him every day.'

'What was his name?' Kate asks quietly, already guessing the answer.

'Thank you for asking. His name was Bert.'

Kate blinks rapidly, a lump in her throat, and notices that the other women's eyes have grown shiny too.

'When I came here the week after Dad died, that's when I saw the kingfisher for the first time. It's not that I think my father has *actually* been reincarnated as a kingfisher – I'm not totally bonkers – but whenever I'm at the river, I feel him around me. "Morning Has Broken" was his favourite hymn. We sang it at his funeral and whenever I sing it, I think of him.'

'Oh, Sandra,' is all Kate can manage to say.

'I'm so sorry,' says Phoebe, reaching out a hand and squeezing Sandra's arm.

'I haven't told you everything either,' says Jazz suddenly. The others look in her direction and she takes a deep breath, brushing her curly blonde hair away from her face. 'I suffer from chronic pain. It's why I had to move back home. I was

337

struggling to cope with living on my own. I've spent the last few years going back and forth to a whole bunch of doctors, but they all end up telling me I'm mad, that the pain is in my head. But sometimes it's so bad I can't even get out of bed. Then I read an article about how cold water can help some people manage their chronic pain.'

'Has it helped?' asks Phoebe.

Jazz nods. 'I couldn't believe it, initially. The cold is always a shock at first – painful, almost – but once we get going, it always gets so much better. When I swim, it's like I'm not even aware of my body. That *never* happens. Something always, *always* hurts.'

Her normally bouncy voice shakes. Kate thinks back to the evening when they helped move all the furniture into Phoebe's flat and how Jazz held back, directing proceedings because she said she'd done her back in.

'Oh, honey, that's awful,' says Sandra, pulling the younger woman into a hug.

'I can't believe you've been dealing with so much,' says Kate. 'You poor thing.'

Sandra and Jazz part, but Kate notices that Sandra has taken hold of Jazz's hand and Jazz doesn't let go.

'Chronic pain is super common. But it has made life pretty … difficult. I watch my friends moving on with their lives, but I feel like I'm stuck. I'm still hopeful I might one day get some better help from doctors, but in the meantime, swimming is the one thing that helps. But I don't think I could manage driving to any swimming spots further afield. It would just be too much for me.'

338

'I think I'm going to fail my exams,' blurts out Hester suddenly, her already pink cheeks burning crimson. 'It's not that I'm stupid or anything. It's just … whenever I sit down in front of an exam paper, it's like my mind goes completely blank, like there's this bright light shining in my eyes and I can't see or think anything. But whenever I swim in the river … Well, I feel sort of OK afterwards. Like I can breathe again.'

There's a brief silence as they all sit with the weight of everyone's stories. Kate thinks about the first meet-up of the mental health swimming group too and of her mum friends who manage to carve out rare moments for themselves by the river. She thinks about her swim with Erin. And of all those mornings when she fled to the river and may only have paddled her toes but still found comfort and release on the water's edge among the reeds and the willows.

Then there are all the swimmers, kayakers and rowers who use the river who she has never even spoken to, but who all have their own reasons for choosing that particular stretch of river.

'So, what are we going to do about it then?' says Sandra, taking a deep breath, the usual vigour returning to her voice.

Kate can't help but smile. She glances at Jay and he nods at her, urging her onwards.

'Well, I *may* have been doing a bit of research this afternoon …'

She reaches under the papers on the table for her notebook. There are printouts poking from between the pages, sticky tabs marking out particularly useful pieces of information. Colour-coded, obviously.

'Just a little bit of research?' Jay says, raising an eyebrow. 'I've watched you this afternoon. You've been on an absolute mission. It's been pretty bloody impressive.'

Their eyes meet and they share a smile that speaks of all the years they have spent together. They've had their ups and downs, but he knows her. Over the past few months, she's felt as though she has lost herself, but throughout it all, he's been there, his faith in her never wavering.

'OK, maybe I have done a *lot* of research.'

And God, it had felt so good. Following the trail of information on and on, deeper and deeper … It always sent her into a sort of meditative state, giving her a buzz unlike anything else. Well, actually, *not* unlike anything else. When she is stuck into researching and writing a story, she feels the same way she does when she is swimming. As if everything else disappears.

'I think there might be a story here.'

The others look at each other, expressions shifting from anxious to intrigued, and maybe even hopeful.

'Go on?' urges Sandra. Jay nods at her too.

'Well, it seems that there's this whole underground thing happening where water companies and factories are illegally dumping into rivers, but there's nothing really being done about it. It's a lot bigger than just the River Avon. Very few rivers in the whole of the UK could be classed as clean or in any way ecologically sound. And it's not just sewage but pesticides and microplastics that are polluting the waterways too. The pollution isn't just bad for humans but awful for wildlife. The whole thing is one massive scandal. And I think the *Herald* could be interested in covering it. In fact, I know they are. I spoke to my boss just now.'

'Aren't you on maternity leave?' asks Jazz.

Her eyes find Jay's again.

'I am. But I think I'm ready to start easing myself back into work. Just a few hours a week at first. My colleagues Emma and Leonie are going to help me. We're going to cover the story together.'

When the idea came to her earlier, she'd felt initially hesitant. 'Maybe it's mad that I'm thinking about getting back to work when Rosie is so little,' she had said, glancing guiltily down at her daughter, who slept soundly in her arms. The moment they'd shared at the baby swimming class had been wonderful and Kate can already feel that connection that had been lacking start to grow, little by little. But while she's determined to do what's best by Rosie, she's starting to realise that doing what's best for her daughter might also mean doing what's best for *her*.

'It's not mad at all,' Jay had said. 'It's just you. And it's one of the reasons I love you. Having a baby hasn't changed the person you are. You're still Kate, a swimmer, a campaigner, a journalist. You're just a mother now too.'

'Jay's going to drop to part-time so he can help out more with Rosie,' Kate explains.

Ever since her social media post using his photographs, he has been inundated with bookings for his 'unfiltered' parent and baby photo shoots. It's given them the confidence to think he can scale back his hours. He's excited about the prospect of more time with Rosie and Kate already can't wait to get her teeth into a story again. And Emma and Leonie were beyond excited when she told them. The story will be something that brings them together again. Even if they will probably end up doing the bulk of things, Kate will still be involved.

It's a set-up that feels like it's going to work for her family, and for once, Kate is letting herself shake off the guilt of how she feels she *should* be doing things.

'That all sounds great,' says Phoebe. 'But what does it mean for our river swimming spot? None of us wants to stop swimming there. And my patients … They've only just fallen in love with the place. I hate the thought of what this could do to them.'

The mood falls sombre again.

'Oh yes, of course,' says Kate, flicking to another section in her notebook. 'I did research on that too and I think I have an idea …'

At that moment, her phone begins to ring on the coffee table. She glances down to see her stepfather's name on the screen. Her heart flips over inside her chest. When she calls home, she might hear her stepdad in the background, or her mum might put the call on speakerphone so he can chip in, but he never calls her by himself. Ever. Her thoughts return to the message she saw on her mum's phone that has slipped from her mind with everything else that's been going on.

'Sorry, everyone, I need to take this.'

She grabs the phone and disappears into the garden. The air smells of roses as she heads under the arbour and to the shade of the apple tree.

'Brian? Is everything OK?'

'Hi, Kate, sweetheart. Are you free right now? If you're not busy, it would be great if you could come over. Your mum and I have something to tell you. I've called your sister too and she's on her way.'

'Is everything OK?' Panic scratches at her voice.

Brian clears his throat.

'I think it might be best to talk in person. If you're free? I know you've got a lot going on, what with the little one …'

'No, no, it's OK. Of course I'll be there,' Kate replies, her heart hammering against her ribs. 'I'll be there soon.'

'Sorry, everyone, but I'm afraid I've got to go,' she says once she's back inside. They all look up at her in concern.

'Is everything OK?' asks Phoebe.

Kate feels dazed, the room spinning.

'Um, I'm not sure. I'm sorry to leave like this, but everything's in here …' She passes her notebook across to Phoebe, who takes it carefully as though holding something fragile.

'Got it,' she replies. 'We can take over from here, Kate. You go do what you need to do.'

'Yes, you've done so much already,' says Sandra. 'Let us help you now. We all want to, don't we?'

Everyone nods and chips in with their agreement and it warms her, despite the anxiety coursing through her body.

They say their goodbyes and Jay follows her out to the car, Kate catching him up on the call with Brian.

'Do you want me to come with you?'

'No, you stay here with Rosie. I think maybe it's best if it's just the four of us for now.'

'OK,' he says, kissing her on the forehead. 'But call if you need me and I'll be right there, OK?'

'I will,' she says, meaning it. She reaches for him, taking comfort in the feel of his lips on hers and then on the softness of Rosie's hair as she leans down to kiss the top of her head.

Then she's off, heading towards the family home and knowing that even though she isn't certain what is awaiting her when she gets there, life is surely about to change forever.

CHAPTER 49

Phoebe and Luca walk side by side back through the village later that evening. When he reaches for her hand, she lets him take it, feeling goosebumps dart their way up her arms despite the worries clouding her mind.

'Have you heard from Kate?' he asks as if reading her thoughts.

'No. I've messaged to see how she's doing but haven't heard anything yet.'

'I'm sure you'll hear from her soon,' he replies, squeezing her fingers.

'So, what do you think about Kate's plan?' After she'd left, they'd pored over her notes together, Jay helping them decipher bits where the handwriting grew particularly messy in Kate's haste to get it all down.

'I think it sounds good,' says Luca. 'I'd never heard of a "bathing water" before.'

'We have them on certain beaches down in Cornwall,' says Phoebe. 'It means the water quality gets regularly monitored and protected. I had no idea what was involved in the process of getting somewhere accredited as a bathing water though. It sounds like a lot of work.'

'Yeah, especially as this would be the first river in the country to have bathing water status. But everyone seemed keen to help. And I think I can get the rowers on board too. You'd be surprised how much water you accidentally swallow when you're rowing, from it splashing up off the oars. It's in all of our interests to clean up the river.'

'Exactly. And if we can clean the place up enough to get bathing water status, and prove how much the river means to everyone, then hopefully we can protect it for the future. I really don't want to lose that place.'

'I know you don't. Neither do I.'

It's still hard to think of their beautiful river as polluted. It doesn't *look* polluted. But Phoebe, of all people, knows that what goes on beneath the surface isn't always obvious just from a glance.

They reach the deli and pause for a moment to look in through the window, to where Luca's father is tucking into a sample of cheese and passing one across to a customer, talking animatedly to them. It's the deli's weekly cheese and wine night and the place is buzzing.

'I roped him in to help out so we could go out,' Luca explains.

'He looks as though he's enjoying himself far too much. You might be out of a job.'

346

'Maybe he could be my Saturday boy. I was thinking about expanding the workforce eventually if the business really takes off – as it seems to be doing. Take the pressure off, so I've got more time for myself. But is it unethical to hire your seventy-five-year-old father and pay him only in cheese?'

'I think cheese as reimbursement is frankly the answer to a happy workforce.'

They grin at each other.

'Hey, do you want to get something to eat?' he asks, but before Phoebe can answer, her attention is pulled down the street, to where a familiar voice is calling her name. She drops Luca's hand in surprise as she turns to follow the sound of the voice.

'Max?'

He is striding towards them, looking from Phoebe to Luca and back again. Phoebe instantly regrets having dropped Luca's hand, but as she reaches out for it again, she notices that he has stepped away from her.

'What are you doing here?'

'We need to talk, Phoebe,' Max says, doing his best to appear to ignore Luca.

Luca is hovering by the door to the deli and Phoebe glances inside at the lively atmosphere, wishing herself in there with Luca instead of out here, confronted with her ex-boyfriend. But before she can turn away, Max reaches out, placing a hand on her arm.

'It's over. I left her. It wasn't even a real thing anyway. I miss you.'

It all tumbles out in one breath and Phoebe is so startled

that she can't find any words. Looking at him, she realises for the first time quite how awful he looks. His face is gaunt, his eyes ringed with dark circles.

Luca clears his voice. 'Phoebe, do you want me to stay?'

Max's eyes meet hers and for a second she falls into them, pulled back by the memories of their life together. Jesus, it wasn't perfect. But they were together for three years. When she looks into Luca's eyes, she feels a spark of excitement and the thrill of getting to understand someone new. But Max's eyes are so known to her that it throws her for a moment.

'No, it's OK. I'll see you in a bit ...'

Phoebe turns just in time to catch the steely expression on his face as he silently turns and opens the deli door and then is gone. But it's too late then. Shit! What was she thinking? She wants to be in there with Luca, not out here with Max.

She finds her voice now, her expression hard. 'What, Max? What the fuck do you want?'

His face twists into a grimace, but suddenly she doesn't have any sympathy for his exhausted expression. He left her! He slept with someone else and took her bloody furniture!

'Can we go upstairs? I need to talk to you.'

'What if I don't want to talk to you?'

'Please, Phoebs.' He bobs up and down on the spot. 'Look, the truth is, I've been driving for ages and I'm dying for a piss. Please, just let me upstairs and I'll use the loo and then go.'

'OK, fine, but that's it.'

She follows him upstairs, lingering in the living room as he closes the bathroom door. She paces back and forth by the window.

The sound of the taps running and then the bathroom door opening causes her to spin around.

Max casts his eyes around the apartment, his gaze falling on the sofa.

'Wow. That's, um, bold.'

'It was a gift from a friend. I couldn't exactly be picky once you'd cleared the place out, could I?'

'Yes, yeah, of course.' He looks nervous now, resting a hand on the back of the sofa and seeming very interested in the fabric. 'I'm sorry about that. I was being a dick.'

'Why are you here, Max?'

He takes a deep breath, rubbing one hand along his jawline. 'I made a stupid mistake, Phoebs. I never cared about her. It wasn't even a thing. And I know that's not an excuse, I know I did a really shitty thing. But I was just feeling so lonely.'

His words hit her square in the chest. He looks smaller somehow and something inside her softens, anger releasing its grip.

'All those nights when I'd be at home on my own, waiting for you to come back. Or when you'd cancel a plan yet again ... I hated it. It made me feel that I didn't matter at all.'

'I know,' she says quietly, all the fight suddenly draining out of her. Yes, the way he left was bad. But she has to accept the part she played in ending their relationship too. It didn't break because of him. They broke it together. Or maybe it simply was never going to work to begin with.

'What you said in one of your messages when you left,' she says, perching on the edge of the bright orange sofa. 'Maybe you were right. You do deserve to be with someone who makes

349

you feel like they want to be with you. I clearly didn't do that and I'm sorry for that. But I also deserve to be with someone who understands how much my career means to me, who is proud of what I do rather than resenting it. And that will never be you, Max. We were never going to be right for each other. We can't make each other happy.'

When Max left, Phoebe thought it was proof that she couldn't make a relationship fit around her life, she'd just have to deal with being single forever. But now ...

Her thoughts turn immediately to the curly-haired man who smells like icing sugar and pesto, who she can sense moving about in the deli beneath the flat even if she can't see him. A man who understands the drive that sits at the very core of her being, spurring her on even when it's hard. Who doesn't want to rein her in or dull her shine. *You're fucking luminous*, he had told her. And when she's with him, she feels as if maybe she could be.

'I think you should probably go,' she says, but softly now.

Max hesitates for a moment and then nods. They share a brief awkward hug that she instantly regrets instigating.

'I'm sorry again about the furniture,' he says as he pauses for a second at the doorway. 'I think I'm going to stay with Mum and Dad for a bit, so I don't even need it. I'll bring it all back.'

But Phoebe shakes her head. 'Don't. I actually like my new things.' They make her think of her new friends and the new life that she is building for herself. A life where there's space for other things and other people to matter alongside her work.

'Even the sofa?' he asks, wrinkling his nose.

'Especially the sofa.'

When Phoebe's phone rings just after the door closes on Max, the sound makes her jump. Bloody hell. She just wants to get downstairs to Luca and to explain that Max is well and truly out of the picture. And just hope that he's still interested despite the way she dropped his hand when Max turned up on the scene.

But when she sees the name on her phone screen, she picks up immediately.

CHAPTER 50

'Is it true?' Ben asks as soon as Phoebe answers. 'Are we not allowed to swim in the river anymore?' His voice sounds tight and choked, as though he's trying very hard to not cry. 'I read something in the paper,' he adds. 'Saying the river is full of pollution. And the thing is, I don't even care. I can close my mouth. Have a shower after. I liked swimming there. I mean, it's not football. But still ... It made me feel good. It made me feel happy.'

He takes a couple of sharp inhales. She should have let him know the news herself. But, what with the date and then the emergency meeting, there hadn't been time.

'I know it's a shock. And disappointing, especially after what happened with the football club. Are you doing OK? I can come and see you if you're feeling especially low, or like hurting yourself?'

There's a sniff on the other end of the line, but when he

speaks again, his voice sounds a little bit steadier. 'No, it's OK. It's just so unfair.'

'It is. But I don't want this to be over either. I loved swimming with you all too and really want to be able to keep doing it.' As she says it, an idea comes to her. 'Actually, a group of us are getting together to try to do what we can to clean up the river and save our swimming spot. We will need plenty of volunteers to help. If you're interested?'

'You think we can do something about it?'

There's such a note of hope in his voice that it makes her hopeful too, renewing her determination.

'Yes, I do. It won't be easy, but then you know all about dealing with things that aren't easy, don't you?'

'You really think *I* can help?'

Phoebe thinks about all the ways life has knocked this young man back, never giving him the confidence to feel he could amount to much. But Phoebe has always seen the potential for joy in him, the way he lights up when he talks about Arsenal football club or how he chatted so animatedly with Maude and the others when he was down by the river. She believes in him and his capacity to take charge of his own life, regardless of all the stones that have been thrown at him. If she didn't, she would have quit her job a long time ago.

'Yes, I do.'

'OK. You just tell me what you need me to do, Nurse Harrison,' he says firmly – and once she is off the phone, she contacts the other members of the Mental Health Wild Swimming Group to let them know the news.

'That's OK,' says Maude. 'I was more interested in the bees

353

anyway. Hamish says I can keep visiting to help out.'

But the others seem just as concerned as Ben.

'I know I didn't actually swim with you all,' says Tara. 'But I hoped that next time I might.'

The fact that Tara, who hadn't left her house in months up until that point, has been thinking about a 'next time' breaks Phoebe's heart but strengthens her resolve all at once.

After doing her best to reassure both Tara and Camilla, who also tells her how much the visit to the river helped both her and Amanda, Phoebe types an email to Mel, updating her on everything that has happened.

All of this news means that my new mental health wild swimming group has been temporarily suspended. I hope to get it started again eventually, but at the moment it's uncertain. However, myself and a group of other swimmers have decided to launch a campaign to clean up the river and protect it for future generations. And I was hoping to get my patients involved, if they're interested.

I know it's not the same sort of group I initially planned, but I thought that volunteering might still bring our patients a sense of community and belonging. It's these things – feeling connected and feeling part of something – that I've seen make the biggest difference to the people I've worked with over the years. Isn't that what we all crave? I certainly know it's something I'm trying to make more time for in my own life.

Anyway, I know this will probably impact on our conversations about a promotion, as my scheme to start the river swimming club has been far from a success. In fact, you could say it's been a complete failure.

I understand if that is the case. The most important thing is to feel like I'm doing my bit to help a place and people I care about.

As she hits send, she hears the sound of 'Brown Eyed Girl' drifting up from the deli below. A smile appears on her face as she recalls the sight of Luca and his father dancing together to the same song. So many other images of Luca come rushing into her mind. Him rearranging the displays with such attention and care. How it felt to have his knee brushing against hers as they rowed together down the river, Phoebe struggling to concentrate because of the warmth of his skin against hers. And his face when Max called her name on the street and they pulled apart from where they'd been standing, just centimetres away from one another.

She gets up quickly, her body suddenly rushing with a bubbling kind of energy. She doesn't know what the future holds for herself, her career, the river or her patients. But she knows that the sight of Luca's flour-smeared face and wild curls makes her feel happy. And that even though her job is about helping other people find their version of happiness, she deserves to find hers too.

She rushes out of the flat, shutting the door quickly behind her. When she makes it downstairs to the deli, she pushes open the door firmly, making the bell jingle loudly. But instead of Luca, she sees his father, who looks up from behind the counter where he'd been mopping and dancing along to the song, his eyes misty but a warm smile on his face.

'*Ciao*, Phoebe,' he says, resting the mop against the counter. 'I was just closing up. A successful night, I'd say.'

'Hi there. Is Luca around?'

He shakes his head. 'He headed out a little while ago. Said he needed some air. He seemed upset.' He raises an eyebrow and Phoebe wonders whether he saw the two of them in the street together and how much Luca has told him about her.

There were things that she and Max had needed to say to one another, but she still wishes that she hadn't let go of Luca's hand. And now Luca isn't here. But she thinks she might now where he could be.

'Thanks anyway,' she calls back to his father as she heads for the door again. As she pushes it open, she catches a glimpse of him shaking his head, smiling to himself.

She attempts to break into a run as she heads out of the village and towards the fields, but several years of no exercise and a carb-heavy diet mean that the run quickly becomes a jog and not long after that, a fast walk. In the vision she has of this moment in her mind, she would be running towards Luca, red hair flying behind her in the breeze, but she will have to settle for a speedy walk towards her future instead.

Even knowing what she knows about the state of the water, it still gives her a pang to see a sign that has been tied to the gate into the meadow which reads, *Do NOT enter the water. Danger of serious illness. No rowing, no kayaking, no paddleboarding, no swimming, until further notice.* It's equally jarring to see the meadow so empty as she ducks under the hawthorn tree and steps down towards the riverside.

It's a golden summer's evening, so the meadow should be filled with groups picnicking and having barbecues, teenagers jumping in from the rope swing and people floating about in the water. But the place is empty, the hatch on the Kingfisher closed and access to the river cut off by yellow tape and more warning signs.

Then she spots the figure sitting on the pontoon, legs dangling down over the river. Phoebe makes her way slowly through the buttercups and wildflowers.

At the sound of her approach, Luca spins around, his face a mix of emotions as he spots her coming towards him. He turns back to watching the river flowing by as she ducks under the tape and lowers herself down until she is sitting next to him on the pontoon. She can feel the heat from his body but makes sure she leaves just a centimetre of space between them so their bodies aren't actually touching. He is leaning back against his hands and she does the same.

'Hey. I hope I'm not disturbing you.'

'That's OK. I was just thinking about my mum. She used to come swimming here.'

'You never told me that,' Phoebe says with surprise.

'I'm still getting used to talking about her in the past tense.'

She reaches out for his hand, wrapping her fingers through his.

'I'm so sorry, Luca, about your mum and everything you've been dealing with.'

There were so many times when Phoebe was younger when she was forced to consider what it might be like to live life without her dad in it. In the really tough moments, when she could see just how painful it was for her dad simply to be alive, it felt almost inevitable that one day she would lose him. But he got through it. *They* got through it. Seeing Luca's pain reminds her of her promise to herself to hold her family more tightly from now on. Her life might still be here in Somerset and not down with them all in Cornwall, but she needs to make space for them, not just for the odd rushed phone conversation but for proper quality time together. For swimming in the sea with her dad, watching their favourite cooking shows with her nan and having proper catch-ups with her mum over cups of tea in the kitchen.

'Thank you. Mostly I've just been trying to look after Dad. They'd been together since they were teenagers, so it's been huge for him, losing her. I just want to do what I can to help him through this.'

That curl of hair, now so familiar, falls over his left eyebrow. Phoebe shuffles slightly, the space between them shrinking to just millimetres.

'That's great, and he's really lucky to have you. But you lost your mum. You're allowed to need help too.'

He leans forward, resting his elbows on his knees and his chin in his hands, his attention down on the water.

'I guess you're right. It's taken me a while to accept that. A friend sent me a link to a local grief support group. I wasn't thinking of going, but maybe . . .' He trails off, his eyes fixed on the water that flows beneath them. Butterflies zip about in the air, and insects land on the water every now and then, causing the tiniest of ripples before moving off again. It still looks beautiful here, even with everything they now know about the place.

'I think that sounds like a great idea.' She gives him a sideways glance, taking in his shifting, thoughtful expression. 'You might inspire me to get help with my drinking. I haven't had a drink in a while, but still, maybe I could do with talking to someone about why I turn to it when I'm stressed. Jesus, a mental health nurse who uses alcohol as a coping mechanism ... Alcohol is literally a depressant. I, of all people, should know that.'

'Your job comes with a lot of pressure,' he says. 'I wouldn't be surprised if there are lots of other people in your profession who do the same or similar.'

Phoebe wonders for the first time if it's true. So much of her work is done alone, out and about in the community with her patients. She doesn't spend much time with other nurses, other than her boss, Mel, who, come to think of it, does always look exhausted. It sparks something in Phoebe's mind. But she pushes it away to turn so she is fully facing Luca.

'I'm sorry about earlier. I shouldn't have left like that. Things with my ex are very, very much over.'

'And this?'

He gestures between them.

She takes a steadying breath.

'I like to think it's just getting started?'

As they reach for one another, the trees above them dip their branches down into the water, making it feel as though it's just the two of them in the world, as if this place is theirs and all its problems have for a moment disappeared.

CHAPTER 51

'Kate. It's good to see you.' Brian looks exhausted as he opens the front door, but he manages a smile for Kate that makes her reach out and pull him into a tight hug. All the way here, she's been thinking about what it would mean if her mum and stepfather really are separating. Brian has been in her life for nearly twenty years, a quiet man who has never taken up much space and always steps back to allow the three of them to be the Mathews Girls, even after all these years. But the idea of life without him still feels strange and wrong, like trying to picture a house without doors and windows.

He lets himself be hugged back and Kate takes an inhale of his bookish smell and lets her fingers feel the familiar scratch of one of the wool jumpers that he always wears, despite it being the start of summer. He might be quiet, but he has always been there, a reliable, solid presence in her life.

'Your mum and sister are through here,' he says, leading her through to the living room, where she sees her mum and sister seated side by side on the sofa. Her mum's hair is pulled back in a clip and her face is free of make-up for once.

Erin looks just as confused and anxious as Kate feels and as she looks up, they share a questioning look with one another. Kate feels a rush of love and gratitude for her sister, knowing that whatever is about to happen, she won't be facing it alone.

Kate joins them on the sofa, her mum in the middle, while Brian busies himself pouring everyone cups of tea.

'Hello, darling,' Miriam says softly. 'It's good to see you.'

'You too, Mum. But is everything OK?'

'Yes, Mum, what's going on?' asks Erin.

Kate glances at Brian, trying to get a sense of what's happening from his face, but his expression is unreadable as he focuses on pouring from the teapot and carefully stirring in the milk. She looks quickly around the room too, trying to find any signs that her suspicions about their relationship might be right. But his books are still on the shelves alongside her mother's and there is no suitcase in the hallway like she remembers from when her father left when she was very small.

As Brian hands round the mugs of tea, Kate notices that his hands are shaking.

'Go on, love,' he says, looking up at Miriam. His voice cracks slightly and in the splinter it hits Kate that maybe she has been very wrong about all of this. 'You need to tell them.'

Their mother takes a faltering breath.

'Brian's right. I need to tell you something.' Her voice trembles and she glances at Brian, who has sat down in the armchair facing them all.

He gives a little nod. She returns the nod and then turns back to Kate and Erin.

'A couple of weeks ago, I found a lump.'

Without saying anything, both Kate and Erin reach out for their mother's hands.

The words repeat themselves in Kate's mind, over and over. *A lump. A lump.* It doesn't feel quite real. She doesn't want it to be real. But the sofa is firm beneath her, the sound of the clock on the wall making it impossible to imagine this is all some hallucination and she is not sitting here with her family, hearing something she hoped she would never have to hear.

Erin is the first to speak.

'A couple of weeks ago? Mum, why didn't you say anything?'

Kate squeezes her mum's hand tightly, thinking she might possibly never let go.

'I didn't want to worry you. You both have so much going on, especially with Rosie being so little ...'

The events of the past few weeks come back to Kate in a flash. The way her mum fell quiet on their WhatsApp chat and stopped coming by to visit so much ... At the time, Kate thought it was because her mum was putting in boundaries because Kate had been demanding too much of her time. How could she have been so focused on her own problems that it didn't even enter her mind that her mum might be dealing with something so huge?

'Oh Mum. I hate the thought that you've been dealing with this on your own.'

Her mum glances across the coffee table then. 'Well, I haven't been on my own. Brian has been so supportive. He told me I should tell you both, but I didn't want to burden you. I'm sorry if it's made me seem distant. I just worried that if I saw you or we chatted too much, then it all might come spilling out and I didn't want to put you both through that.'

Across the table, Kate meets her stepdad's eye and sees the stress and worry that's written all over his face. His eyes glisten behind his round glasses. He's holding a cup of tea in his hand but not drinking from it.

'You could never be a burden,' Kate says. 'You're our mum.'

'Yes,' adds Erin, 'just because we've got stuff going on in our own lives doesn't mean we don't have space for you.'

'Thank you, darlings,' their mum says in a trembling voice.

'So, what comes next?' asks ever-practical Erin. Kate can hear right through her steady, optimistic voice, though. She might be nine years older than Kate, but Kate can hear the frightened little girl hiding behind her sister's calm tone.

'Well, I went in for a biopsy last week.'

Kate tries not to wince, hating the thought of her mother going through that on her own. But, of course, as her mum said, she wouldn't have been on her own. Kate flashes her stepdad a glance and tries to transmit all her love and gratitude to him for being unwaveringly there for her mum. Even if he's usually the quietest person in the room, he's the kind of person who will nonetheless be there by your side, no matter how frightening the situation.

'The doctors have asked me to come back in next week so they can tell me the results.'

'We'll be there,' Erin says instantly. 'Won't we, Kate?'

'Of course. I'm sorry you felt you couldn't tell us, but I'm

364

so glad you have now. You have always, always been there for us, Mum ...' Kate thinks about the fish pie her mum left in the fridge for her when she was in labour. All the times she's taken Rosie so that Kate can squeeze in a nap. And everything that came before that. The silly articles her mum would read that Kate used to write for an imaginary paper when she was a child. How she supported her through those tough years in London when she struggled to find her place in the world. The love and kindness she gave her after Rosemary died ... Tears fill her eyes as she thinks of all the ways her mum has shown up for her and all the ways she vows to show up for her mum from now on. 'Let us be there for you too.'

Her mum lets out a deep breath, nodding silently. Kate and Erin wrap their arms around her and their mother's shoulders relax as she finally lets herself lean on them.

Kate looks up, spotting her stepfather watching them from his armchair on the other side of the room, tears dripping down his face. She shuffles up along the sofa, patting the cushions beside her. Because they might always be the Mathews Girls, but he is part of their family too. And, right now, as they contemplate what might lie ahead of them, it at least brings her some comfort to know that they will be facing it together. Her mum isn't alone and neither is she.

'There's room for you too. Come on, Dad.'

CHAPTER 52

FIFTEEN MONTHS LATER

Chairs are set up in a circle, a table at the back of the room spread out with hot drinks and biscuits. The room is already starting to get busy, a few people chatting, but most standing apart, scrolling through their phones and doing their best not to make eye contact with one another.

Phoebe pours herself what looks like a potentially terrible Americano and catches the eye of the woman next to her who had been eyeing up the coffee urn too. She's a woman around Phoebe's age. Phoebe hasn't met her before but recognises the grey circles under her eyes, the bitten nails and the air of general exhaustion.

'It might not be as bad as it looks,' Phoebe says, gesturing to the coffee.

The woman raises an eyebrow. 'It could be worse.'

'Hmm, that's true.' She takes a sip. 'Oh yes, definitely worse.' The woman laughs and Phoebe abandons the coffee on the table. 'Probably best not to risk it.'

'No, I might go for a tea instead myself.' They smile at one another for a moment. 'I'm feeling a bit nervous, actually,' the woman says, fidgeting with her bag with one hand as she stirs her tea with the other. 'I haven't been to anything like this before, have you?'

'I have. Don't worry, everyone else is most likely feeling just as nervous as you are. You're in good company.' Phoebe glances at the clock. 'Right, we should probably get started. I'm Phoebe, by the way. I'll be leading the session.'

She gives the woman a reassuring smile and heads to the front of the room, everyone beginning to take their seats. The group is a real mix of people, in a rainbow of colourful scrubs as well as the smart suits of consultants and the more casual attire of a couple of community nurses. Everyone sits down on the plastic chairs, shuffling about in an attempt to get comfortable and glancing around at one another before turning their attention to Phoebe.

As eyes fall on her, she's aware for a moment that she might not be what everyone was expecting, with her bright red hair and covering of tattoos, including a new line drawing on her left wrist of a sprig of Rosemary, in honour of her goddaughter. But she also knows that none of that matters.

She stands up tall, pushing her shoulders back while maintaining a warm and approachable smile.

'Welcome, everyone, I'm Phoebe. Or Nurse Harrison a lot of the time, but in here with you all, I'm just Phoebe. Some of you might be feeling a bit nervous ...' Here, she catches the eye of the woman she'd been chatting to and smiles. They share a look of understanding. 'Maybe you chose to come here yourself or perhaps you were encouraged, or maybe even forced, to attend by a colleague. Maybe you would rather be anywhere else.'

There's a nervous flutter of laughter.

'You might be mentally flicking through your to-do list, ready to get on to the next thing and checking the clock to count how many minutes until you can get out of here.'

More quiet laughter and a few pink cheeks. One of the consultants makes a show of removing his phone from his lap and putting it in his pocket and the people either side of him do the same. Phoebe nods at them.

'For this next hour, I want you to try not to think about all the responsibilities waiting for you outside but to focus on yourselves and the other people in this room. Just for one hour. I reckon you all deserve that. We *all* deserve that.'

Phoebe pulls over a chair and joins the group in the gap in the circle, completing the loop. She takes a breath. She has done these sessions many times, chatting with doctors and nurses and health assistants all across Somerset. It's part of her slightly altered job role and the promotion she received last year, much to her surprise. She thought she had made a mess of everything, given what happened with the river swimming group that had to close before it barely got started. But Mel had seen things differently.

'Obstacles will always arise. Our patients know that better than everyone. But it's how you deal with them.'

Phoebe still has patients, but her caseload has become lighter, allowing her time to do things like this where she acts not just as a nurse but as an advocate for her peers.

But however experienced she might be at delivering sessions like these, this bit is always tricky. It's getting easier though. Each time, it gets easier.

'I want to tell you a bit about where I was just over a year ago.' She can sense the others in the room leaning closer slightly, their attention now fully focused on her. 'I have been a community mental health nurse for ten years. I love my job. I love having the privilege of helping people through their toughest moments, of looking after their overall health – both physical and mental – and I love the sense of satisfaction when you see someone you've worked with flourish. But it's not always easy. Actually, it's *never* easy. I don't think anyone goes into healthcare looking for an easy job.'

Another rumble of quiet laughter.

'I cared so much about my job, as I'm sure that everyone here in this room does too.' A murmur of agreement. 'But somewhere along the way, I stopped caring for myself. I stopped eating properly. I stopped sleeping. I was drinking too much. I felt exhausted, wrung out, overwhelmed. My social life suffered, friends falling away as I cancelled yet more plans. My family became used to only hearing from me very occasionally and to me always sounding low when we did talk. Most of all, I felt helpless. I knew I couldn't continue as I was, feeling so burnt out and stretched to breaking point. But I didn't know how to stop, either. I still cared about what I did so much and didn't want to let anyone down.'

Phoebe pauses, letting her breathing steady itself as she remembers what it felt like to be in that dark place. She glances around the room. By now, the group is transfixed. Some are nodding, others are simply watching her intently. She catches the eye again of the woman she spoke to earlier and notices that her eyes are glistening, emotion flickering.

'I think it's hard to ask for help when you're used to being the one helping others. But we need it too, sometimes. I eventually told my manager how I was feeling and she was so understanding. She'd been there before in the past too, something I think that we often forget when we're feeling particularly low. It can feel like you're alone in that feeling, but you're not. We worked together to set boundaries so that I could continue doing a job I love but without it completely taking over my life. I started looking after myself. Making time for a social life. Eating proper food instead of hastily grabbed ready meals.'

A private smile appears on her face as she thinks about all the food. Jesus, the food. The fresh tomatoes and mozzarella tossed in the most perfect of olive oils. Slow-roasted lamb on a Sunday. Crisp and sweet cannoli that she has even had a go at making herself a few times. Pasta. A lot of pasta. She recalls the pizza she ate on a recent holiday to Italy, pizza that tasted nothing like any pizza she had ever eaten before and, in fact, changed her understanding of the word pizza.

'These are all things that I now know that I deserve to do just for myself, because I'm a human being and deserve to take care of myself. But I also think that establishing a better balance in my life has helped me to be better at my job too. I need to be emotionally resilient for my patients, the one who turns up with a smile when they need it the most. But it was getting harder and harder to do that.'

She can feel the energy in the room now, the shift as people go from reluctant and hesitant to being right there with her. It always happens and it's one of the things she loves about these sessions. People might go into them thinking it's not for them, but as she paints a picture that looks a lot like their own, she can feel them joining her.

It's not that her life is perfect now. No one's life is. She still has days at work where someone's story breaks her heart, moments where it's hard to feel patient or hopeful or strong. But she has ways now of stopping those feelings from pulling her under. And she has people to turn to when she's feeling that way.

'When I think about the issue of burnout, something that I'm sure many of you have either dealt with in the past or are maybe going through right now ...' Some looks of recognition, a couple of nods. 'When I think about finding a cure for our burnout, I don't just think about self-care. Yes, self-care is important. Finding things that help you switch off and making time for those things. Treating yourself how you would a patient – with kindness and attention ...'

She thinks about the books on her bookshelves that she now makes the time to actually read, even if it's just half an hour before bed. The moments she enjoys just sitting on her bright orange sofa in her little flat overlooking the village, drinking a cup of tea and letting herself be without jumping straight to all the things she should be doing. Cheese and wine nights in the deli with friends.

'But it's not just about looking after yourself. It's about

caring for one another too. Because we're not alone in having these struggles and we shouldn't feel alone in solving them either. That's what this group is.'

She looks around at each of them now in turn.

'It's a place where we can hold space for each other. Share our experiences and listen to one another. Come up with some solutions as to how we might change things to help ourselves but also the other people we work with to feel more supported. So, who would like to start?'

The attendees linger behind at the end of the session, chatting in small groups or pairs. Unlike when they arrived, no one is standing alone or looking at a phone. There's a buzzing atmosphere as people chat and grab a quick extra cup of tea before heading back to their jobs. A cluster of four nurses are engaged in a group hug, squeezing each other tightly. Phoebe is pretty certain they had never met before this afternoon.

'Thank you so much for today,' says the woman Phoebe spoke with at the beginning. Throughout the course of the session, she learnt that the woman's name is Syreeta and she's an intensive care nurse who has also been helping her parents care for her elderly grandmother. She shared how hard she's been finding it to not let her personal life encroach on her work and vice versa. 'I feel better just having said some of that stuff out loud. And I think I'm going to take up your advice about getting back to the gym. It feels like a luxury when I'm so busy, but it always makes me feel so much better.'

'I think that sounds a great idea. And I run these sessions every month, so do come back next time.'

'I will.'

Once the woman has thanked her again and said goodbye, Phoebe glances down at her phone. There are new messages in the WhatsApp groups with her old friends from university and her colleagues from her time working in the local hospital. Last year, she decided to finally reach out and try to reconnect and they'd all seemed delighted to hear from her, apologising for also dropping out of touch. Now they have regular meet-ups in the local pub, where they offload about work but also just eat chips and pie and chat about nonsense too.

There's a notification in her family group chat and she clicks on it to see a photograph from her mum, showing her, her father and her nan having a picnic on the beach. They are all smiling, the sun in their faces and their hair whipped about by the wind.

Can't wait to see you and Luca next week, writes her mum. **Lots of love from us all xx.**

Phoebe sends a string of heart and beach emojis in reply and is about to put her phone away and grab her things when a message comes in from Kate.

Hope your session went well. The ceremony will start at 4. I'm so glad you can make it. See you there. xx

Over the past year, Kate has become one of Phoebe's closest friends and she'll always be grateful that their lives were brought together. Kate has had a tough year, but Phoebe has tried her best to be there for her, just as Kate has been there for Phoebe on the days when her patients experience inevitable setbacks or the weight of a new person's crisis feels hard to carry on her own.

Of course I'll be there, she writes in reply. **See you soon**
xxx

As everyone begins to filter out of the room, Phoebe grabs her bag and black jacket. The old Phoebe would most likely stay behind to catch up on some paperwork and make a start on tomorrow's to-do list. But she has other people who need her now, people she has let herself rely on too.

She walks purposefully to the door. Phoebe Harrison has somewhere to be.

CHAPTER 53

Kate loads a tub of sausage rolls and pork pies into the shopping trolley, which is already piled high with a selection of crisps, biscuits, scones and punnets of strawberries. She wasn't quite sure what to buy for the occasion. In the past, she probably would have felt the need to make everything herself and for it all to be perfect, but now she opts for things that are easy and faff-free instead. Nobody is likely to really care about the food anyway. Today is about being together.

It feels strange to navigate a supermarket without a toddler sitting in the front, shouting instructions like the somewhat drunken captain of a ship.

'No!' 'Apple!' 'Ba ba ba BA!'

But they agreed it would be easier for Kate to do this bit on her own.

She glances briefly at the time on her phone, the background photo of Jay and Rosie on Rosie's first birthday six months ago making her pause and smile. Rosie is wearing a glittery crown that she refused to put on at first but then wouldn't take off for a whole week. In the photo, Jay and Rosie are facing each other, Rosie held in Jay's arms and their hands on each other's faces, Rosie's little podgy fingers spread across Jay's cheeks. Their mouths are open wide. They had been practising their lion roars. Kate had joined in the moment after she'd snapped the picture, the three of them roaring like a family of lions and then collapsing into giggles.

The photo brings back memories of the whole day. Erin had baked the most beautiful cake decorated with sea creatures and Rosie's eyes widened as she'd had her first taste of icing and proceeded to have her little mind blown. Jay's parents came down for the weekend and ran around in the garden, letting themselves be chased by their granddaughter. Kate's mum had sat on a blanket beneath the apple tree and watched and Kate knew that she wanted to join in too but was feeling too tired. It had been one of her bad days. Brian had hovered nearby until Rosie had insisted that Grandpa give her a tiger ride and then he was on his hands and knees in the grass with a squealing little girl on his back, Miriam watching and smiling, tears glistening in her eyes. Kate had joined her mum, silently squeezing her hand. Neither of them had to describe the bittersweetness of the moment, happiness and sadness sitting side by side as they soaked up every precious second.

Thinking of her mum, a lump swells in Kate's throat, tears pricking her eyes. She takes a moment to open her photos app and flick to an image that Jay captured last year of her mother and Brian together. They're both half laughing, half crying, holding hands tightly, a pot of tea on the table next to them. It's a photo that feels painful to look at sometimes, but she thinks it's one of Jay's most beautiful photos.

It's made her so proud to think how his career has taken off this year. He's now branched out from the parent and baby photos that launched his business to photograph all sorts of different relationships, but the element that has remained is the way he captures both the pain and joy of real, unfiltered human emotions. His photos of Kate and Rosie still regularly feature on Kate's own social media, and through sharing her own unfiltered version of motherhood, she's interacted with countless other mothers who have shared their stories too, making her feel less alone. It's felt like having a tribe walking alongside her. And, God, there have been moments recently when she's needed that tribe.

But she needs to get going soon. Remembering that she needs cream for the strawberries, Kate spins the trolley around swiftly, heading back in the other direction, glad for a task to distract her from her emotions. When she finds the section she is looking for, she grabs a few pots of clotted cream, then adds another couple for good measure. She has no idea how many people are going to turn up. Anyone who wants to be there is welcome, but you never know with these things.

Just as she's about to turn and head towards the tills, she spots a woman standing dead still in front of the shelves of milk. Her eyes are trained on the lined-up cartons of milk, but she isn't moving. She's barely even blinking. She is dressed in a baggy shirt and a pair of stained tracksuit bottoms. In the front of her trolley, squished up into a car seat, is a tiny and very pink-faced baby.

As Kate watches the woman, it's as though the past year and a bit disappears. She is right back there beside this woman, standing in the aisle of a supermarket with her brand-new daughter, feeling as though she might melt from exhaustion and crack in half from terror.

So much might have changed about Kate's life since those days, but it is still so easy to access everything she felt back then. The bone-aching tiredness. The brain fog. The constant state of bewilderment. It's like recalling a familiar meal. She can almost taste it, all the flavours of that very particular period of time. Back then, she thought life would always taste like that.

Tentatively, Kate steps towards the woman.

'Hey, are you all right?'

The woman's head snaps around as though she's been jolted awake. 'Oh! Sorry. I was just choosing which milk to get. But I must have zoned out, I guess.'

'How old is he?' Kate asks softly, gesturing into the trolley.

The woman follows her gaze. 'Two months.'

Kate makes a point of turning her attention away from the baby and towards the woman pushing the trolley. 'How are you feeling?'

'Tired,' the woman replies.

Kate smiles. 'I'm not surprised. I remember that early bit so vividly. It's really tough.'

'It's ...' The woman falters, her face wearing the expression of utter shell shock that Kate recalls so well. She blinks, a strand of unbrushed hair coming loose from her bun and falling in front of her face. 'It's … a lot.'

The baby lets out a little gurgle and the woman's eyes dart towards the car seat, a look of panic appearing on her face. But the baby settles, eyelids closing again.

Kate nods. 'It *is* a lot. When I had my daughter, I felt like a bomb had gone off in my life. Like I'd exploded into a million pieces and wasn't sure I'd ever be able to even find those pieces of myself again, let alone put them back together.'

'And did you?'

She tilts her head, thinking about everything that has happened over the past year and a bit. 'Yes, I did. But they got put back together in a different order.'

When she thinks about the person she was before having Rosie, the elements of that Kate are still there inside her now. But she is different too. Her daughter has forever changed her, in that way that certain people or places or moments do. She likes the version of herself that has Rosie's fingerprints all over her heart.

She still isn't really sure she knows what she's doing. But she's accepted that she probably never will and that's OK. It doesn't make her a bad mother. It makes her human.

'It's hard to imagine things getting better when they are so tiny and can't even smile at you. I hope you've got a good support network to help you through this really hard bit. There's strength in asking for help. And, believe me, you have so much good coming your way.' As she says it, she remembers a conversation with her sister from just over a year ago when Erin told her the same thing and she hadn't quite believed her, but it had given her hope. And then she came to see it for herself. 'Things get so much better. They get so, so good.'

Kate's mind races with a slideshow of small moments. The expression Rosie pulled when she tried grapefruit for the first time. Her first pair of shoes. Her dragging a book over from the bookshelf and throwing it in Kate's lap, climbing in after and settling herself with a satisfied sigh, her little socked feet crossed at the ankles. Their weekly swimming sessions that have become the highlight of Kate's week. The smell of Calpol on Rosie's breath as she slept in Kate's arms when she had a particularly bad cold and Kate hadn't wanted to be anywhere else in the whole world but there, holding her daughter. The fact that even though everyone *still* tells Kate that Rosie looks exactly like Jay, when it came to Rosie's first word, it wasn't *Daddy* but *Mama*. The word that has become her favourite in the entire English language when said with the voice of her little red-haired, chubby-cheeked girl. Mama. Mama. Mama.

Each time she hears it, she feels it directly in her heart.

The past year has been the hardest year of Kate's life. And yet, among all the sadness, there has been Rosie. Pulling her out from her darkness with her infectious joy, with small moments of happiness that are so much sweeter for being so unexpected.

The woman in the supermarket stares back with a dazed expression.

'Sorry, I'll leave you to it, but just know you're doing great.'

Kate smiles and then turns away, leaving the woman and her new baby to contemplate the milk selection and Kate's words. Maybe what she said won't land in the way that the words of a kind stranger once landed with her. But perhaps it will.

CHAPTER 54

As Kate steps into the meadow, she has to fight back tears as she sees how many people are gathered on the grass.

The August sun beats down on the river, bees and butterflies drifting lazily in the hot air. There's music coming from the Kingfisher and her heart catches as she recognises 'What a Wonderful World' – her mum's favourite song.

'Kate, let us help you with those bags,' comes a voice and then her old friend, Frank, is stepping away from the huddle of her London friends and taking the bags out of her hands, his husband, Jermaine, helping and their dog, Sprout, leaping about at their feet.

'Thank you so much for coming,' she says, hugging them all in turn. It takes a while: they each squeeze her very tightly and are not quick in letting go.

'You know we wouldn't have missed it,' says Emma, nursing her five-month pregnant bump.

'Yeah, we wanted to be here to support you,' adds Leonie, kissing her on the cheek.

Hope and her daughter, Jamila, and granddaughter, Aiesha, are here too.

'We brought these,' says Hope, handing Kate a tight bouquet of dahlias. 'But it looks like you've got a whole flower garden here.' She gestures to the meadow and the colourful riot of wildflowers.

'They're beautiful, thank you,' she says, her voice choked at their thoughtfulness.

Although her London friends have all individually been to visit over the course of the past year and Kate has seen them in London when she's been there for work, it's the first time they've all been together like this in a long time. It feels surreal to see them here in the middle of a Somerset field instead of in London, as though her two worlds have finally collided.

Kate spots her family down by the water. Jay is holding Rosie on his shoulders and talking to Brian. Erin and Mark are working together to wrangle their boys, who are dashing about in the grass. Hope catches Kate looking in their direction.

'You go be with them,' she urges, giving her hand a warm squeeze. 'We'll catch up properly later.'

'And we'll set this food up,' Frank adds, 'don't you worry.' Jermaine is already reaching into the bags and pulling things out onto one of the fold-up picnic tables. There are other tables that are already laden with food: cakes she recognises from the Kingfisher and large bowls of salads from Giuglia's. Everyone has chipped in to help share the load and make today special.

'OK,' she nods, hearing her daughter's voice and feeling the sudden urge to hold her close. 'Thank you. And thank you again for being here. It means a lot.'

As she makes her way down to the water, she says a brief hello to people, thanking them for being there. She spots her mum friends from the Tired Mums Club and those made at her weekly swimming lessons with Rosie, feeling touched that they made the effort to be here. They have been such a support over the past year and she now can't imagine her life without them.

Jay looks up as she approaches.

'Look who it is,' he says to Rosie.

'Mama!'

Kate scoops her daughter into her arms, resting her on her hip. 'Hello, darling.'

'Mama!' repeats Rosie, clapping her hands together.

Kate kisses Jay, grateful as ever to have him by her side on a day like this.

With Rosie still nestled snugly at her side, Kate hugs her sister, brother-in-law and stepdad in turn, giving Brian an extra little squeeze. They've grown closer over the past year. He's needed them and it has helped with Kate's own pain to be able to focus on looking after him.

'Hey, Kate, do you think we've got time before the ceremony?' Erin gestures towards the water.

Kate checks the time. Maybe she should be focusing on what's to come and the speech she shortly has to make, but, suddenly, a swim feels like exactly what she needs. And she suddenly recalls that their mum suggested they do this – a swim before the ceremony. Because a swim is always a good idea.

While Kate and Erin get changed, Jay pulls Rosie's sundress over her head. Beneath is a sunshine yellow swimsuit that matches Kate's. He zips her into a little wetsuit decorated in flamingos.

'Cute,' says Erin.

They head down the meadow to where the river is shallower and the bank slopes gently, creating an easy spot to access the water. Ever since the water was declared clean enough to swim in, Kate has been coming here every day. She even swam all the way through the winter. Even on the days when she really, really doesn't feel like swimming, it always makes her feel better. So the days when she doesn't want to swim are the days when she knows she really *needs* to swim.

Erin strides into the water and pushes off in a confident breaststroke, Brian, Mark and the boys waving to her from the bank. Kate steps in next, planting her feet firmly in the gritty riverbed.

'Are you ready for her?'

Kate nods up at Jay, reaching out for her daughter, who stretches towards her too. Carefully, Kate pulls Rosie close and then slowly crouches down until the water reaches her. Rosie giggles, splashing her hands on the surface of the river.

'Mama! Swim!' says Rosie, kicking her legs behind her and circling her arms. 'Rosie! Swim!'

Holding her daughter in her arms as the river flows around them, Kate thinks about everything she has been through over the past eighteen months. The words of 'What A Wonderful World' float in the air around her, making her eyes sting and her heart ache. Because the world doesn't always seem

384

wonderful. Sometimes it seems awful. But over the past couple of years, as well as the very worst moments, there have been wonderful ones too. Often when she has least expected them. A friend managing to make her laugh even when she didn't think she could. Jay kissing her forehead and letting her know that she is loved. The sun peeking out from behind a cloud and shining down on a river. And this girl. No matter what else happens, and no matter how hard their beginning may have been, the world will always feel wonderful because of this girl.

'Yes, that's right, darling. Mama swim. Rosie swim.'

'And Granny wants to swim too!' comes a voice from across the meadow.

Kate turns at the sound, a smile spreading across her face. Her mum strides through the grass, a bag slung over her shoulder and a wide-brimmed sun hat flopping on her head.

'Hi, Mum, the water's lovely!' calls Erin, waving.

'Granny!' cries Rosie, splashing eagerly.

'That's right, darling. It's Granny.' Kate tries not to let her voice shake too much. It still catches her when she thinks how close Rosie came to growing up without her grandmother. But she's here, thinner than before since the final round of chemo, but regaining her strength day by day. And she's going to be OK. Kate still can't quite believe that her mum is going to be OK. They found out the good news just last week that the treatments did their job and she is now cancer-free. Every time Kate thinks about it, she doesn't know whether to cry or cheer.

Miriam hugs Jay, Mark and the boys and gives Brian a lingering kiss.

'Eww! Granny, Grandpa, yuck!' cries Ted, shielding his eyes. But Kate's parents don't seem to care.

'Sorry I'm late, darlings. My yoga class overran. But I came prepared!' She whips off her yoga top to reveal a blue swimsuit. Then she steps down into the water, Brian standing on the bank and offering her his hand for support. 'Ahh! This is wonderful as always,' she says with a smile as she sinks into the water, a happy, peaceful expression spreading across her face. Swimming in the cold water was one of the things that helped when she was dealing with the nausea from the chemo. The three of them started doing it regularly and haven't stopped. Sometimes, their swims are less swims and more dips, just bobbing about in the water and chatting. With cake at the Kingfisher afterwards, of course. Because, as Kate's old friend Rosemary always said, a swim isn't a swim without cake.

Erin kicks over towards them until they are all standing in the shallows of the river, Kate's mum in the middle, Erin on one side and Kate and Rosie on the other.

'My girls,' her mum says, wrapping an arm around the three of them.

And who knows what will come next in the winding rivers of their lives? But right now, right here in this place and with these people, Kate's world is wonderful.

CHAPTER 55

Phoebe can't quite believe how many people came. The meadow is buzzing – quite literally, in the case of the beehives on the top of Hamish's riverboat. She spots Maude and Hamish as soon as she steps through the gate. They are clearly making the most of the gathering and have lined up pots of their honey on a pop-up table outside the Kingfisher.

'This thing is heavy!' says Sandra from behind her and Phoebe turns, readjusting the weight of the roll of fabric in her own hands. She is carrying the front, with Hester in the middle and Sandra at the back. Jazz is in front of them, holding open the gate.

'Not long now, we're nearly there!'

They shuffle their way through, various groups looking up and waving as they approach.

'Hey, Phoebe!' calls Ben from down by the pontoon, where he is gathered with his girlfriend, Rachel, met through his job at the local sports shop, and a group of his football mates. They're smiling and laughing and Phoebe experiences a rush of happiness and pride. Ben's journey hasn't been without its potholes, but to see him here, surrounded by people, is a stark reminder of how far he has come since Phoebe first met him. His beloved football club never reopened, but after months of mourning its loss, he decided to set one up himself.

Over by the Kingfisher, she spots Camilla browsing for books with the women Phoebe recognises as her running group friends. They've come along to the wild swimming group a few times, often having jogged there through the fields.

Phoebe searches around for Arabella and eventually sees her on the river, floating in a large inflatable ring shaped like a flamingo, sunglasses on and head leant back, her fingers trailing in the water. She looks like a completely different person to the woman Phoebe first met over a year ago. She was never Phoebe's patient and yet her transformation has been just as dramatic as her mother's.

The one person she can't see here is Tara. She messaged this morning to say she wouldn't be able to make it. She's having one of her bad days and the thought of leaving the house just felt like too much. Phoebe replied straight away to say they'd miss her but not to worry. She'll be round to visit tomorrow and they can have a good chat. Phoebe isn't giving up on her, just like she won't give up on all her other patients who are having more bad days than good right now. Her job will always have its dark and heavy parts. But, over the years, she's discovered what a privilege it is to be there with people in their very worst moments. And to try, little by little, to help them find their own version of happiness. Whether that means swimming in a river or making honey or kicking about a ball with a bunch of friends.

'Hey, let me help,' says Luca, spotting them and stepping away from the groaning table of food and running a hand through his messy hair, making Phoebe's heart squeeze a little.

Kate spots them approaching too and strides over, a towel slung over her shoulders and her hair damp.

'Hi, guys!'

'Sorry we're late, we had to wait a while to collect the banner. But I think it looks bloody great!'

They line up on the edge of the river with the fabric rolled up in their hands.

'On the count of three,' calls Phoebe, her friends nodding in agreement. 'One, two, three!'

They let the fabric go and the banner releases, revealing images of kingfishers and otters, kayaks and a riverboat. Dotted about are pictures of swimmers, floating and drifting down the river. In the middle are the words, 'Welcome to Farleigh-on-Avon, an official bathing water.'

From the *Avon Times*:

Local river swimming spot becomes designated 'bathing water'

Yesterday, locals came together to celebrate the designation of Farleigh-on-Avon as an official bathing water, the first riverside location in the country to gain this status. Bathing

389

status marks the river out as an official swimming spot and will ensure that the water quality is monitored and protected in the future.

Just over a year ago, this stretch of river was condemned due to high levels of pollution, but thanks to tireless local campaigning, the health of the river has been rejuvenated.

Last year, the *Avon Times* reported on high levels of sewage in the local river. A subsequent investigation, conducted jointly between the *Avon Times* and the national newspaper the *Herald*, found that the local water treatment facility in nearby Waterford had been illegally dumping sewage into the river for years. But on the back of the investigation, and a media campaign led by journalist Kate Mathews-Chapman, stricter sanctions have now been put into place, with the water company also facing a hefty fine and the CEO, Douglas Rainford, stepping down from his position.

The campaign to secure bathing status was led by the Farleigh-on-Avon River Swimming, Bathing and Recreational Water-Based Activities Club (FoARSBRWAC) and the Farleigh-on-Avon Mental Health Swimming Group. As well as putting pressure on the local water company to change their practices, they managed to persuade local farms to move to pesticide-free farming methods, thereby reducing run-off of chemicals into the river. And a group of young people created the River Clean-Up initiative, where, on the first Saturday of every month, locals pick litter from the river, either on the riverbanks or via kayak or paddleboard.

Hester Samuels, 18, who started the project and is a Farleigh-on-Avon native, soon to be heading to the University of Bristol to study nursing, said, 'It's easy to feel like you don't have any control over things like this, but you do. Last weekend when we did the River Clean-Up, I collected three bin bags of litter. That stuff would still be floating about there now, endangering wildlife, if we hadn't got out there.'

In a recent water test conducted by the River Trust, the water quality in the stretch of the Avon between Farleigh-on-Avon and Waterford was found to be 'excellent'.

Wildlife at the river is thriving, according to the River Trust survey. Several locals have cited spottings of a new family of otters that have chosen to make this stretch of the river their home.

To mark the appointment of bathing status, yesterday local swimmers came together at Farleigh-on-Avon for a picnic and group swim.

In a speech to those gathered by the river, campaigner Kate Mathews-Chapman said, 'It's wonderful to be able to celebrate the hard work of so many people and the success in turning the state of this river around. This river has been a lifeline to so many, offering a place to escape and a community to turn to. But it was our turn to protect the wildlife and ecosystem that we share this place with. I'm so pleased that we have managed to save the river that saved us.'

AUTHOR'S NOTE

I never thought I would write a follow-up to my first book, *The Lido*. When I finished that novel, I thought that Kate's story was finished. And then, in the five years that followed, I went through some huge changes in my own life – leaving London for Somerset, getting married and becoming a mother – and I realised that actually Kate's ending in *The Lido* was only just the beginning.

Returning to the world of the book that launched my career has been nerve-wracking but also a joy. Thank you, from the bottom of my heart, for reading it.

I hope you ended this novel with a smile on your face. But I am aware that alongside the laughter and splashing in this novel, there are also some heavy themes (because I try to reflect life in my writing and my experience of life is that light always comes with shade). If you are affected by any of the harder themes in the book, I'm including the following resources for support. Remember, you are not on your own.

Mental health support

Samaritans, 116 123, 24-hour phone line, samaritans.org

SHOUT – Support line
Text 'FRONTLINE' to 85258, giveusashout.org

Hub of Hope, hubofhope.org

The Mind Infoline (0300 123 3393) provides information about mental health problems, where to get help near you, treatment options and advocacy services.

Mind's Side by Side online community is a place where you can talk to other people about your experiences. It's a safe space where people with experience of a mental health problem can listen, share and be heard.

NHS mental health helpline for 24-hour advice and support

Mental health support for new parents

PANDAS Foundation, offering support to those affected by perinatal mental ill health, free helpline 0808 1961 776, pandasfoundation.org.uk

Tommy's, helpline 0800 014 7800, tommys.org

Cancer support

Macmillan Cancer Support, macmillan.org.uk

ACKNOWLEDGEMENTS

As this book is a follow-up to my first book *The Lido*, I would like to start by thanking everyone who supported that book and who in doing so changed my life. Thank you to my kind and supportive agent Robert Caskie, who took a chance on me. To all the reviewers, booksellers, librarians and readers who championed that book (and my subsequent ones): a huge, enormous THANK YOU.

Thank you to the entire team at Orion, in particular Rhea Kurien, Sahil Javed, Ellie Nightingale, Ellen Turner and Virginia Woolstencroft. Thank you also to Sarah Benton for your input on the early version of the manuscript.

This book was inspired in large part by my own experiences of becoming a mother and finding the first bit overwhelming, to say the least. Thank you to the friends who checked in and kept checking in. Thank you to my NCT pals who responded to late-night worried WhatsApp messages. Thank you to my mum for filling the fridge with fish pie and driving us to and from the hospital and to my lovely in-laws for always leaving the house tidier than when you arrive. Our boy adores his grandparents and we appreciate you all so much. Thank you to my sister, Alex, and to my son's wonderful godfather, 'Cool'. Sally, I wish you could have read this book (and all the books still stuck inside my head), but I will always feel grateful for all the ways you supported and inspired me.

A big thank you to Frome Birth Talk. Some of the wisdom from the counselling sessions I received in the early weeks of my son's life has made its way into this book, in the hope that it might help other parents as much as it helped me. Jane, what you told me about love being a verb transformed the way I thought about myself as a mother. I hope you don't mind Jay borrowing the sentiment.

Thank you to everyone who reached out to me on social media when I shared some of my struggles during that period of early motherhood. The kindness and honesty that I received really made a difference. And to anyone who might still be struggling with adapting to becoming a new parent: I hope this book makes you realise you are not alone. Talk to people. Seek out support. And I'll repeat the words of the characters in this book: you have so much joy coming your way. It gets so good.

Thank you to Alex Cotton for talking to me about life as a community mental health nurse. And a big thank you to Dr

Emma Wadey Ph.D RNMH for all your support and guidance in making sure Phoebe's part of this story rings true to the experience of working as a mental health professional. I found it fascinating to hear about this vital and often overlooked role and have huge admiration for all who work in this field.

Thank you to The Write Place for providing a quiet place to write away from the piles of washing at home, and to Louise Dean and The Novelry for the sense of community and constant source of inspiration. To the writers I coach: your courage in turning up again and again to the page despite the many demands of your busy lives inspires me to do the same.

Last, but certainly not least, thank you to my little family. Bruno, it's been such a joy to watch you become a father and Robin and I are so lucky to have you. And to Robin, thank you for everything you have taught me so far and for the sunshine you bring to our lives. My world really is a wonderful place with you in it.

CREDITS

Libby Page and Orion Fiction would like to thank everyone at Orion who worked on the publication of *The Lifeline* in the UK.

Editorial
Rhea Kurien
Snigdha Koirala

Audio
Paul Stark
Louise Richardson

Copyeditor
Kati Nicholl

Proofreader
Jade Craddock

Editorial Management
Charlie Panayiotou
Jane Hughes
Bartley Shaw

Contracts
Dan Herron
Ellie Bowker

Design
Charlotte Abrams-Simpson

Finance
Jasdip Nandra
Sue Baker

Production
Ameenah Khan

Marketing
Ellie Nightingale

Publicity
Ellen Turner

Sales
Catherine Worsley
Esther Waters
Victoria Laws
Toluwalope Ayo-Ajala
Rachael Hum
Frances Doyle
Georgina Cutler

Operations
Jo Jacobs

IF YOU ENJOYED *THE LIFELINE*, GO BACK TO WHERE IT ALL BEGAN WITH *THE LIDO* . . .

THE SUNDAY TIMES TOP TEN BESTSELLER

Meet Rosemary, 86, and Kate, 26. Dreamers, campaigners, outdoor swimmers.

Rosemary has lived in Brixton all her life, but everything she knows is changing. Only the local lido, where she swims every day, remains a constant reminder of the past and her beloved husband George.

Kate has just moved to London and feels adrift in the city. She's on the bottom rung of her career as a local journalist and is determined to make something of it.

So when the lido is threatened with closure, Kate knows this story could be her chance to shine. But for Rosemary, it could be the end of everything. Together, they are determined to make a stand, and to prove that the pool is more than just a place to swim – it is the heart of the community.

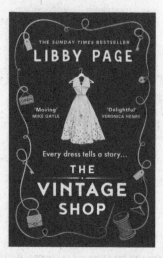

ONE DRESS. THREE WOMEN. A LIFETIME OF SECRETS.

Among the cobbled streets of Frome in Somerset, **Lou** is about to start something new. After losing her mother, she knows it's time to take a chance and open her own vintage clothes shop.

In upstate New York, **Donna** receives some news about her family which throws everything she thought she knew into question. The only clue she has to unlock her past is a picture of a yellow dress.

Maggy is in her seventies, newly divorced and all alone in an empty house. Visiting the little vintage shop in Frome, with its rows of beautiful dresses, brings back cherished memories she'd long put aside.

For these three women, only by uncovering the secrets of the yellow dress can they unlock their next chapter…

LORNA'S WORLD IS SMALL BUT SAFE.

She loves her daughter and the two of them are all that matter.
But after nearly twenty years, she and Ella are suddenly leaving
London for the Isle of Kip, the tiny remote Scottish island where
Lorna grew up.

ALICE'S WORLD IS TINY BUT FULL.

She loves the community on Kip and how her yoga classes draw
women across the tiny island together. Now Lorna's arrival might
help their family finally mend itself – even if forgiveness means
returning to the past . . .

CAN COMING HOME MEAN STARTING AGAIN?

WELCOME TO THE CAFÉ THAT NEVER SLEEPS …

Day and night, Stella's Café opens its doors to the lonely and the lost, the morning people and the night owls. It's a place where everyone is always welcome, where life can wait at the door.

Meet Hannah and Mona: best friends, waitresses, dreamers. They love working at Stella's – the different people they meet, the small kindnesses exchanged. But is it time to step outside and make their own way in life?

Come inside and spend twenty-four hours at Stella's Café, where one day might just be enough to change your life . . .